The Jewelry Case

By Catherine McGreevy

About the author:
Catherine McGreevy lives in Northern California with her family. A former newspaper reporter and teacher, she loves to travel, read, and is a historical enthusiast. You can follow her at:

https://www.facebook.com/cathy.mcgreevy.9
http://www.twitter.com/catherinemcgreevy
https://cathymcgreevy.wordpress.com

ISBN 9781495425073

The Jewelry Case

By Catherine McGreevy

The Jewelry Case

Prologue

Vienna, 1895

The Nightingale of Warsaw stood alone while the notes of her final aria dissipated into the air. Silence hung for a moment, like an ocean wave before it crashes on the shore, then the audience exploded into deafening cheers.

As the performer curtseyed, her serene face hid the fact that her heart was pounding under the red satin bodice of her gown—not because of the crowd's response, which she was used to, but because tonight *he* was there. Somewhere in the box seats above the blinding gaslights, the count sat with the others, set apart from the others by his height and virile good looks as well as the sash and medals that proclaimed his rank.

She remembered when he had knocked at her dressing room door an hour earlier, holding a small ebony box instead of the usual bouquet of flowers. Staring at him for a moment, she stepped back to let him in. "You came!"

He smiled down at her. "I always come when I can get away."

"But you said your family—"

He shrugged. "Never mind. Here. I want you to have this."

Ruth took the ebony box he held out, and gasped when she opened it.

He chuckled at the look on her face. "Those rubies will look far better on you than on my horse-faced Aunt Ludmilla. Stop staring, darling, and put them on. After all, they're meant to be worn."

"But Grigori....!"

Without waiting for her objection, he pressed the ruby ring onto her finger, the matching tiara onto her dark curls and fastened the heavy necklace against the smooth skin of her throat before nudging her toward the door. "I've a feeling you'll sing your finest tonight in these, my dear. Afterward..."

She turned back to give him a last kiss. "Yes, my love. Afterward."

Chapter One

The diesel truck came from nowhere.

One moment, Paisley was watching her husband's angry face as he gunned the Porsche down the Autobahn. The next, he veered to pass another car, and she looked back at the road just as a fourteen-wheeler filled the windshield. Her scream rose above the deafening sound of twisting metal and breaking glass.

She woke from darkness to blinding light and searing pain.

"Frau Perleman? Frau Perleman, can you hear me?"

Her eyes tried to focus on the concerned features of a woman in a doctor's white lab coat. "Frau Perleman? You've been in a terrible accident. You've come through all right, but unfortunately your husband is dead."

Paisley had learned enough German to sing operas like *The Magic Flute* and *Fidelio*, but it took a moment for the doctor's meaning to percolate through. "Jonathan? Dead?" She tried to say more, but only a croak emerged from her throat. Her hand clutched her neck and found it encased in something thick and soft. Bandages.

A nurse bent over to speak in the doctor's ear, and the latter switched to fluent but accented English. "I know it is hard to deal with so much bad news after an injury, *Frau*, but I believe it is not good to hold back information from patients. You have a right to know the rest."

There was more? What else could possibly matter if Jonathan was dead?

The doctor's voice continued. "A piece of glass pierced your throat and damaged your vocal cords. They may heal, but it will be a while before we know how much of your voice will return. With luck you should be released from the hospital within two or three weeks."

It was too much to grasp. First Jonathan, then her ability to sing … maybe even to speak. The only things in her life that gave it meaning. Paisley closed her eyes as the doctor described the titanium rod implanted in her injured leg and the multitude of lesser injuries to her aching body. None of that mattered. All that mattered was nothing would ever be the same.

A month later, Paisley sat in her financial advisor's Manhattan office listening to yet more bad news.

"How can there be no money in our bank account?" The ugly croak that emerged from her mouth was that of a stranger. It still made her cringe. "My husband was a premier opera conductor who performed all over the world. We were hardly paupers."

Barry Foster nudged a spreadsheet toward her. "I'm sorry, Ms. Perleman, but you and your husband were living beyond your means. If you don't believe me, look at this."

Hesitatingly, Paisley took the paper. The jumble of numbers skittered around meaninglessly, but Barry's words were clear enough. Whatever money Jonathan and she had earned was gone.

He pulled out more documents and spread them across the table. "Fortunately, as you can see, insurance covered Jonathan's funeral expenses and most of your medical bills. Selling the stocks will pay down the other debts. That leaves enough to live on until you can work again. If, that is, you live frugally."

Although Barry had been too tactful to mention it, Paisley knew the accident could not have come at a worse time. Only a week before, she had been offered the part of Mimi in the Metropolitan Opera's upcoming production of *La Bohème*, a prize that could have sent her rising career into the stratosphere. Now, someone else would take the role.

Worse, what if she could never sing again? Performing in opera was all she had ever wanted to do.

If only Jonathan were here. A decade older than Paisley, he had always taken care of her career and everything else. Now,

Paisley was coming to realize that had been a mistake. Not only had her late husband mismanaged their funds, but now, at only age twenty-five, she felt unprepared to handle life on her own.

Paisley chided herself for the lapse into self-pity. At least she was alive. Jonathan wasn't as lucky.

Summoning the spirit of the headstrong heroine Tosca, a role she'd dreamed of playing someday, Paisley brushed aside the spreadsheet. "This is ridiculous. I thought we were paying you to manage our financial affairs."

Barry Foster's mouth compressed, and Paisley knew she wasn't being fair. Over the past few years he'd sent several tersely worded letters warning them to stop spending money on designer clothes, travel, and the luxurious rooms in Paris and Milan, affordable to only a handful of the biggest opera stars. But she and Jonathan had been too busy enjoying life to listen.

He took back the spreadsheet. "Actually, there is one other asset. That old house in Northern California. It must be worth something."

Paisley's forehead creased. "What house?"

"Don't tell me you've forgotten." Barry peered at her over the rims of his glasses. "When Jonathan's great-aunt died last year, she left all her possessions to you, from her house to her safety deposit box."

Paisley thought for a moment. "Oh, you mean Auntie Esther. I only met her once, at our wedding, but I quite liked her. I'd forgotten she passed away."

"Then perhaps you don't remember the letter I sent you at the time, although it made enough of an impression that both you and your husband came to my office to discuss it."

Her brain felt like a computer with a failing hard-drive, whirring without bringing up any information. The doctors had warned her that her recollections would be spotty at first, along with the strange dreams that disturbed her sleep. Then, without warning, the memory popped into Paisley's head.

Jonathan had been peevish when he learned his elderly, never-married great-aunt had passed over him in her will. "You must have made quite an impression on the old bat at our wedding." He held the lawyer's letter between two fingers while staring at her accusingly. "What did you say to butter her up?"

Paisley was equally mystified. Auntie Esther was Jonathan's only living relative except for a female cousin back east somewhere. A tiny, withered woman with hair as black as Jonathan's and intense dark eyes, she'd been pushing ninety years old.

When meeting the old woman, Paisley had had the strange feeling of looking in a mirror seventy years into the future. The two were nearly the same height, allowing for shrinkage on the part of the older woman, and they both had jet-black hair, although Aunt Esther's had been assisted by a bottle and fluffed out by curlers, while Paisley's glossy ringlets were natural.

Aunt Esther peered closely at her for several long moments. "You look just like that photograph in People Magazine article. The one I saw at the beauty parlor."

Paisley wondered which article Esther meant. Since winning the National Opera Association competition, Paisley had been interviewed numerous times by newspapers, magazines, and television reporters. Opera had become more popular lately, with the emergence of attractive singers like Josh Groban, Charlotte Church and Jackie Evancho.

"In the magazine, you said you planned to start an opera company for inner-city children." Aunt Esther was still studying her.

"Oh, that," Paisley said with a guilty start. She recalled telling the reporter about a youthful ambition to create a group in Chicago patterned after the children's choir of Harlem. After marrying, though, Jonathan had advised her to focus on her own budding career. "I'm afraid I haven't done that yet but I still hope to work with children someday. I believe music can enrich young people's lives and cure all sorts of social ills." The words sounded trite and stilted, but she meant every syllable. Music had changed her own life, hadn't it?

"'Cure social ills?' Yes, that's the phrase you used in the article." Esther pursed her lips. "Odd. I never expected my nephew would end up marrying a girl like you. You hardly seem his type at all."

Paisley was taken aback by the blunt comment, but privately she agreed. Sophisticated, worldly, and handsome, Jonathan had dated some of the world's most beautiful models and actresses. She, on the other hand, was the offspring of an alcoholic car salesman who couldn't keep a job and had dragged his small family around the country looking for work.

Although the old woman's words could easily have been meant as an insult—*My nephew could have had any one he wanted, so why would he want to marry someone like you?*— somehow Paisley was sure Esther was complimenting her. Impulsively, she reached out and squeezed Jonathan's great-aunt's feather-boned hand. "Thank you."

Esther looked pleased. "I wasn't sure before ... but I am now. Please take this. I want you to keep it." She pressed something into Paisley's palm.

Paisley looked down at a square of fine yellowed linen that had once been white, with intricate hand-made lace edging. It smelled faintly of rose perfume. "What a lovely handkerchief! Did you make it yourself?"

"Long ago, when I was about your age. Not many people these days know how to make this kind of lace. 'Tatting,' we called it. Maybe this will do as the 'something old' brides are supposed to wear." Jonathan's great aunt ran her eyes over Paisley's sleek wedding gown. "The Perlemans aren't a particularly close family, my dear, nor are we believers in tradition, but perhaps this gift will remind you that you're not alone."

"Thank you." Paisley thought the statement odd. Alone? What did the old woman mean?

Auntie Esther nudged her toward the reception line. "Go on, dear, you've wasted enough time on an old lady like me. Your husband is waiting for you to finish your performance."

Paisley turned back, more puzzled than before, but the crowd of milling guests had already swallowed up Aunt Esther's tiny form.

In Barry Foster's glass-and-teak office, Paisley rubbed the raw scar running up and down her throat, a new habit, while contemplating the financial spreadsheet lying on the desk. Perhaps Aunt Esther had bequeathed the house to her because of that odd connection they had felt during that short conversation at the wedding. Although the two had never met in person afterward, Paisley had added the old woman to her Christmas card list.

Jonathan had glanced over her shoulder while she addressed the envelope and snorted. "You're not sending Aunt Esther a *Christmas* card, are you? She's Jewish, remember? Why not send her a holiday ham while you're at it?"

"The card is generic." Paisley sealed the envelope. Jonathan rarely mentioned his heritage, and sometimes Paisley forgot that his family was Jewish. It evidently wasn't important to him, anyway. "I doubt she'd be offended by 'Season's Greetings' and a picture of penguins wearing ice skates. Besides, I like your great aunt. This is my way of keeping in touch."

"Well, don't hold your breath waiting for a response. She never cared much for me, or the rest of the family for that matter."

He sank into his armchair and opened the score for Carmen. His next appearance would be at La Scala, an achievement he had worked his whole life to attain. At the age of thirty-four he was finally about to achieve that goal, and was as nervous as a cat perched atop a saguaro cactus.

Two weeks later, Paisley waved a greeting card from Auntie Esther in Jonathan's face. The card featured three tabby kittens wearing Santa hats. "Ha! I told you she wouldn't be offended."

Three years later, however, Paisley's annual Christmas card was returned unopened, and shortly after, their lawyer notified them that Auntie Esther had passed away, leaving Paisley the house.

"The house?" Jonathan demanded as they sat side by side facing the financial advisor. "Wasn't there anything else? Some…" He paused. "Well, some jewelry, for instance? There's a story in my family that Esther might have owned some valuables of that sort."

The lawyer clucked his tongue at his forgetfulness, and pulled a small package from his desk drawer, which he handed to Paisley. "Mrs. Perleman did leave you this."

With an exclamation, Jonathan snatched the package from hers hand. When he tore it open, a small cameo pin fell onto the desk with a musical tinkle.

"How lovely!" Paisley exclaimed, picking up the blue-and-white brooch and examining it with admiration. "I'll think of her whenever I wear it."

Jonathan's face turned beet red and he hunched his shoulders. "So that's all? I should have known she'd have the last laugh."

"What do you mean?" Paisley pinned the cameo to her lapel, wondering at her husband's mood.

He scraped his chair back and got to his feet. "I mean that you now own a worthless piece of costume jewelry and a run-down house in the sticks. And I got nothing. After all these years…." To the attorney, he snarled, "Why waste our time asking us to come to your office? You could have sent the trinket by mail."

"My apologies." The other man stiffly stood as well. "But since you were in New York to conduct the Philharmonic this weekend, I thought—"

"Never mind." Jonathan brushed the explanation away and took Paisley by the elbow, escorting her out of the room so fast that she had to trot to keep up.

Paisley was genuinely sorry that Auntie Esther had passed away, but life was too busy to grieve long for an old woman she had not known very well and who, by all accounts, had lived a long and happy life. Caught up in an ever-increasing whirl of travel and international performances, Paisley had put the experience behind her, forgetting the inherited house until today.

Now she realized Barry was waiting with for her answer. "What do I intend to do with Esther's place? Sell it, I guess." She massaged the rough scar on her neck. "It sounds like I'll need the money."

Barry nodded approvingly. "A real-estate agent from River Bend has already asked me for permission to put it on the market." He flicked a business card across the desk, and she picked it up. "His name's Ray Henderson. Says he has a potential buyer."

"All right. Go ahead and tell Mr. Henderson.... " Paisley's voice faded when she glimpsed a snapshot that had spilled out of the file folder. The photograph showed a small house that had clearly seen better times. A steeply pitched roof was visible behind an enormous oak tree guarding the front door, a perfect tree for climbing. If she were a little girl, Paisley wouldn't have been able to resist scampering up its strong, spreading limbs. The small house behind it must once have been charming, but now it looked somewhat forlorn, surrounded by flourishing weeds and overgrown flowerbeds.

Barry picked up the photo and handed it over. "Take a closer look if you like."

"Thank you," she said automatically. At the touch of the photograph a strange emotion flashed through her, so powerfully that for a moment she forgot where she was. The sensation was one of familiarity, like hearing a piece of music and feeling as if she had heard it before.

So this was the old Perleman family home? The one her husband had grown up in, before his parents retired to Florida and Esther had moved back in. The house Esther had bequeathed her more than a year ago. Why had she never troubled to visit the place? Jonathan had once told her something intriguing about it, and now she tried to remember what it was. Some old family legend, something they had laughed about together. That, of course, had been before Esther's death, before her husband's black moods had grown worse and they had started growing apart.

"As you can see," Barry said, "the place has deteriorated. It must be nearly a century old, and it's been vacant since her death last year. You're lucky anyone's interested."

Paisley stared at the photograph. The impression of familiarity lingered like a fragrance. "Go ahead and put it on the market," she said slowly, "but I'd like to take a look at it before it sells. I'm going to have to sell the lease on my Manhattan flat, so I might even stay there a while. Maybe until my singing voice comes back."

If my voice comes back. She tried not to listen to the niggling thought in the back of her mind.

Barry cleared his throat. "Do you have any idea where River Bend is located?"

"I believe Jonathan said it's in Northern California, about halfway between San Francisco and Sacramento."

"Forty miles from both cities, in the middle of nothing but vineyards. Suffice it to say, the town is hardly New York or Paris." Barry leaned back and crossed an ankle across a knee. "It's so secluded and quiet that you'll have trouble finding a decent place to shop."

"Secluded? Quiet?" She pounced on the words. "It sounds perfect. And you just told me I have no money for that sort of shopping anyway."

"Very well, you might as well visit it, then." Barry scooped the papers back into the file. He fixed her with an intent look from under his eyebrows, and a look of sympathy crossed his features. "Just remember, Ms. Perleman, you can't crawl into a hole and hide from your troubles."

She nodded without listening. Something about the little white house was pulling her like a fish on a line. Jonathan would have jeered at her for flying clear across the country for no reason, but Jonathan was not here to stop her. "I haven't decided yet what I'll do," she said, standing up. "Maybe I'll stay there for a while, maybe I won't. But I've got to start somewhere. Why not there?"

Chapter Two

Paisley swung her legs out of the real estate agent's shiny black SUV and planted her high-heeled shoes in a patch of weeds. Perspiring in the late-afternoon California sun, she put her hands on her hips and stared in dismay at the house in the photograph.

The structure was smaller than it had appeared in the picture, overwhelmed by an ancient oak tree that towered over the porch and huge bank of roses blooming next to the sagging porch. Unconsciously she touched the lace handkerchief in her jacket pocket. So this had been Auntie Esther's house? Hard to believe it was now *hers*. It was hardly a comfortable cottage where she could hide away until recovering from the accident. The place barely looked habitable.

When Paisley gazed at the structure, however, a familiar sensation swept over her, the same one she'd felt while studying at the photograph in Barry Foster's Manhattan office. A feeling of welcome, of homecoming. It was as tangible as someone sweeping her into waiting arms.

The real estate agent sauntered up behind her, drinking from an oversized coffee mug bearing a anchor and eagle logo. Everything about him was oversized. As hulking as his shiny black SUV, Ray Henderson had picked her up from the Sacramento airport, playing country music loudly and talking non-stop all the way to River Bend.

"Just like I emailed you, ma'am," he boomed. "Hardly worth flying all the way from New York. I coulda sold the place without you bothering your little head about it."

Paisley hardly heard him, still trying to figure out why the sight of the structure affected her so strongly. All her life she'd lived in a series of interchangeable hotel rooms or rented apartments, first as the child of an itinerant father, then as Jonathan's wife. A psychologist might have suggested that the impression of homecoming was because subconsciously, Paisley wished for a permanent home of her own.

She knew better. Paisley loved traveling around the world, experiencing foreign cities and a varying lifestyle. The only homemaking art she enjoyed was baking, which she rarely had a chance to do any more.

Ray drained his mug and returned it to the SUV. When he returned, she thought his wide shoulders, thick neck, and buzz haircut made him look like a former football player—or, as the emblem on the mug implied, a former Marine. Certainly, his physique looked more like someone selling memberships at the local gym than this fragile Victorian house which had seen better days.

He jingled the keys. "When the old lady went into the convalescent home last year, they turned off the utilities. There's been vandalism since then, too. See that broken window on the right? Like I said, ma'am, would have been a lot simpler to accept your neighbor's offer. I coulda faxed you the paperwork, easy."

Paisley nodded. Despite the broken window and neglected air, the structure was appealing. Delicate tracery lined the eaves of the porch, and casement windows peeped out of untrimmed bushes like a shy girl hiding from visitors. A branch of the enormous oak she remembered from the photograph b,kocurved protectively over the front porch. The place must have been a suitable setting for Jonathan's great-aunt: old-fashioned, charming, and private.

Of course, Ray was right. The thick growth of ivy failed to hide the missing bricks in the chimney, and some of the roof tiles were cracked. But the structure was not likely to fall down this week, nor the next. Maybe….

Ray stroked his chin with stubby fingers, flashing a watch that was either a real Rolex or a good knock-off. Selling real estate in California, even in a rural area like this, must be profitable.

"Any particular reason you decided to fly out?" he asked. "We don't get a lot of outsiders around here. Too far away from all the tourist places."

"No particular reason." Paisley started toward the front door of the little white house, wishing he weren't so friendly. She didn't feel like conversation, and not just because of the jarring sound of her ugly new voice.

Ray didn't take her hint. "I'm a local boy myself, just like your husband was." He followed close behind. "Jonathan must have told some interesting stories about this old place, huh?"

Paisley fought down growing annoyance. She wanted to bathe in the warm feeling emanating from the house, the sense of welcome that grew ever stronger. "Just that as a child Aunt Esther lived in this house with her aunt, uncle, and cousins. Eventually Jonathan's parents inherited the place, and he grew up here as well. You probably know more about it than I do."

Ray shrugged. "Not really. I just know Steve's doing you a favor, offering to take this piece of junk off your hands."

"Steve?" Her mind went blank, as it did so often these days.

"Steve Lopez. Your neighbor. The guy who wants to buy the place." From the overly-patient expression on his face, Paisley realized Ray must have mentioned the name before. "He's looking to expand his vineyard, remember? That's why he wants the land."

Belatedly she remembered riding past a road sign in front of the property next door, purple grapes and green vines artistically forming the words, "Lopez Winery." Her mind was unreliable lately. The hospital shrink had said it was due to trauma and that the symptoms would likely decrease over time. She hoped so.

Tilting her head back, Paisley squinted at the house's roof. Despite the peeling paint and broken window, the structure appeared sturdy enough, but what did she know? She was a singer, not a building inspector.

Had been a singer. Her hand rose to the scar along her throat. For a moment she was back in the Porsche at the very instant

Jonathan swung out to pass the lumbering truck, his face turned toward her, eyes blazing, mouth open to say something hurtful. Her scream filled her ears as the oncoming truck hurtled toward them.

Realizing Ray was watching her, Paisley dropped her hand, hoping he hadn't seen the flash of memory had shaken her. "The house looks in better shape than it might have been, being vacant so long."

"What about what you can't see? Termites, roof leaks...." Ray's voice drifted off ominously. "Lucky for you, Steve's had his eye on the property for a long time. Not the house—that's obviously worthless. No one else is likely to want the place, even if it was fixed up. It's too far from town, too isolated for a family, and this area doesn't attract enough tourists to run a successful bed and breakfast."

Despite the flashy Rolex, Ray didn't appear to be much of a salesman. Paisley hoped he hadn't pointed out all those detractions to prospective customers. Perversely, his comments made her feel even more determined to stay. Newfound freedom from commitments meant her visit could stretch to a couple of weeks, even a few months. The prospect was surprisingly appealing. Maybe being separated from her New York friends and colleagues while coming to terms with her new circumstances was just what she needed.

Paisley met the burly real estate agent's eyes. "I've decided not to sell. Not immediately, anyway. I'm going to stay for a while. Maybe throughout the summer."

She saw a muscle twitch in his cheek, but Ray controlled his disappointment well. "Sure, ma'am. Whatever you want. Although over the phone, your financial advisor did give the impression—."

"You just said the house can be fixed up, didn't you?"

"Yeah, sure, for a price. But, er … wasn't money a bit of an issue?"

Paisley's eyebrows flew up, and her cheeks grew warm. Had Barry Foster spilled her personal information to this agent? If so it was a serious breach of ethics.

There was no point letting the real estate agent know how serious her financial situation really was. Without thinking she quipped, "Don't worry, I can always sell the family jewels, if need be."

Ray's eyes widened. Embarrassed, she realized that the words might come across as a *double entendre*. Her blush deepened. "I didn't mean it that way. I only meant.... "

What *had* she meant, exactly? Paisley recalled Jonathan's mention of jewelry in the lawyer's office, around the time of Esther's death. And now that she thought of it, he'd said something else once, long before, in passing. Something about emeralds or sapphires that had once belonged to his family. She strained to remember the details, but gave up. It had not seemed important at the time.

"It's just a saying," Paisley said quickly as Ray grinned. "It just means I'll do whatever it takes to get the house in shape. This place has too much character to knock it down. When I accept a buyer, it must be someone who will cherish it. The house is beautiful under all that peeling paint. A diamond in the rough."

Ray looked back at the house and an odd, fleeting expression crossed his face. "Diamond in the rough, eh? I guess so. Forget what I said, ma'am. Take all the time you need. All summer, if you want. Why not?" He repeated to himself, "Family jewels," and chuckled. Without warning he launched into song, an unexpected rich, smooth baritone: "Some women are dri-i-ipping in diamonds, some women are dri-i-i-pping with pearls...."

Paisley stared, as surprised by his sudden about-face as by his singing. The notes from the Broadway musical *Annie* echoed incongruously in the rural setting. No one in the world could have looked or sounded less like the greedy orphanage director, Miss Hannigan.

Ray glanced at her and turned red. A hand went up and twitched his tie with embarrassment. "Sorry, ma'am," he muttered. "My ex used to drag me to musicals at the Mondavi Center over in Davis. Some of the songs got stuck in my head."

Paisley smiled at the thought of Ray Henderson fidgeting through musicals at the behest of an insistent wife. Her guess was that he'd have preferred watching a football game or monster truck rally. "You must have been in the military," she commented. "No one else outside the South says 'sir' and 'ma'am.' And I saw the logo on your cup. Marines?"

"Yes, ma'am." Ray looked pleased that she'd noticed. "Home from Afghanistan two years, now." He used his electronic key to open the lock-box on the door. "How 'bout we take a look-see inside?"

A stuffy but not unpleasant scent, dried rose petals in a gift shop, met them. The dirt-streaked windows afforded a view of the lowest branches of the enormous oak tree, complete with hanging hummingbird feeder. Paisley smiled to herself at the prospect of feathered visitors. Esther must have enjoyed the tiny, jewel-like birds.

Turning, Paisley saw an old Steinway baby grand piano, black surface softened by a layer of dust. She pictured Jonathan as a child running his small hands over the ivory keys while learning to play, and emotional pain shot through her again. Pushing back the keyboard cover, she experimentally plunked a few keys. It was badly out of tune, but that was no problem. Tuning pianos was one of the skills she'd learned at the conservatory in Omaha, after winning the scholarship her senior year in high school.

Buying such an expensive piano must have been a stretch for Jonathan's middle-class family. Paisley gazed around at the room's modest furnishings. But Jonathan had told her how important music had been to his family, stemming back to Poland, the land of his ancestors. Jonathan never talked much about his family, though, and Paisley had been too caught up in her own exciting new life to ask more questions.

While Ray waited, she investigated a hi-fi console standing along one wall. Mid-century modern furniture was popular these days. The piece might bring a hundred dollars or so at a vintage store. In fact, maybe selling some of the other outdated furnishings would bring in some much-needed cash. It would be worthwhile to go through the house and take an inventory.

Just then, her gaze fell on a bookcase crammed with LP albums, and she forgot everything else.

Ray folded his arms across his barrel chest. "Gotta be a few hundred records there. Jonathan's parents left those behind when they moved, just before the old lady came back. Nobody listens to records anymore."

"Vinyl is getting popular again," Paisley corrected him. "Some of these could be worth a few dollars."

"We got a couple of antique stores downtown might sell them for you."

She nodded and kneeled to sift through the bottom row of records, thrilling at the sight and feel of them. There were easily enough to stock a small shop by themselves. Pulling out a cover at random, Paisley ran a finger across the image of the sloe-eyed, black-haired diva. "Look, Maria Callas! Did you know she never actually played Carmen on stage, although she was famous for singing the role on records?"

"No kidding." Ray glanced at his gold watch, but Paisley refused to be hurried. She moved on to an extensive stack of CDs arranged in alphabetical order on an upper shelf. Esther Perleman had obviously upgraded to newer technology after moving into the house. It was nice to see that even an eighty-year-old woman could adapt. Esther's taste also ran to classical music.

"Look! Here's one of Jonathan's first albums." Paisley held up one. The photographer had caught her late husband in the middle of conducting a concert. The lean face glittered with sweat, and straight black hair fell in tousled strands across his high, pale forehead. She'd always loved how distinguished Jonathan looked in white tie and tails, how gracefully his long-fingered hand wielded the baton. The CD had been nominated for a Grammy, and she remembered how disappointed he was not to have won.

"How about you?" Ray asked, showing a sign of interest. "I heard you met Jonathan because you were an opera singer. Made any CDs of your own?"

She wistfully ran a finger across the plastic case and returned it to the stack. "I'm featured on a couple of cast albums from the Met, and you can probably find a few of my solo performances on YouTube. But this coming fall...." Paisley pushed herself to her feet. "Never mind. Show me the rest of the house."

The kitchen was even more dated than the living room, boasting an antique harvest-gold refrigerator, peeling laminate cupboards, and a chipped-enamel gas stove. When she tested the faucet, a stream of brown water spurted into the sink, turning clear after a few moments. "At least there's water. I thought you said the utilities had been turned off?"

Ray tried a light switch and fluorescent tubes flickered on. "Waddaya know. The electricity musta been left on auto pay."

Paisley checked the cramped pantry, its doors painted mint-green, filled with canned goods, boxes of breakfast cereal, and a well-used cookbook, post-it notes marking Esther's favorite recipes. The cereal may need to be thrown out, but she could live on the cans of soup and chili for several days.

She pulled out a drawer by the sink and found it full of boxes of candles, matches, an emergency radio, and spare batteries. Esther apparently believed in being prepared. Maybe the electricity wasn't so reliable after all.

The glass sliding kitchen door opened to a patio, where she spotted a hand-painted china pet-food bowl.

"The Perleman family always had a cat." Ray followed the direction of her eyes. "Long as anyone can remember. Esther had one too, as you see."

"Do you know what happened to Esther's pet?" Although Paisley was not a cat lover, she hated to think of any creature suffering from neglect.

"A neighbor might have taken it in, or maybe it went feral. Or got eaten by coyotes. There's still a few wild animals around here, out in the country. If you step this way, ma'am, I believe there's a powder room down the hall."

"The powder room" had luridly pink floral wallpaper, dating from the 1970s, and was situated near a set of creaky stairs that led to three small upstairs bedrooms. A fourth door opened into a spacious bathroom with an enamel claw-tooth tub.

For a moment, the cracked tiles and the old-fashioned wallpaper faded away. Paisley envisioned herself soaking in bubbles, surrounded by scented candles, hair piled atop her head. Then she looked up and saw brown stains on the ceiling. Ray was right. The roof leaked.

The old stairs creaked under Ray's weight as he came upstairs. His voice floated upward. "So what do you think? Still plan to stay?"

"A cold shower or two won't hurt me, and if it rains, I'll put buckets under the roof leaks."

Ray fished out one of his business cards from a little metal case, jotted down a phone number on the back, and handed it to her. "It's your decision. If you do stay, you might call my buddy, Bruce Harris, to fix the place up for you. You can't trust just any contractor these days."

Before going, he couldn't resist one more test of her resolve. "Are you sure you want me to leave you here without transportation? We're a mile out of town."

"I'll be fine for tonight. Thanks."

"All right, ma'am. But if you really intend to stay here alone, be sure to shut the windows and lock the doors. We're semi-rural out here, but that doesn't mean there's no crime." He flashed square white teeth.

By the time the real estate agent's car rolled away, her head ached and her bad leg was throbbing. She still had to call the bank and see what, if anything, was in the bank account Esther had left her. A few taps on her cellphone, a few minutes on hold, and a male teller's voice informed her the account was all but empty. "As for the safety deposit box, you are welcome to come check it out," the voice said. "Our hours are nine-thirty to five o'clock, Monday through Friday."

Paisley glanced at the time. Five minutes to five o'clock. The safety deposit box would have to wait until after the weekend.

"Thank you." Resignedly putting the phone back into her purse, she went into the kitchen, opened a can of tuna, and dumped it in the cat bowl on the back step. The poor animal probably had disappeared for good, either gone feral, or starved to death, or hit by a car. But just in case....

What had prompted Ray Henderson to sing that snatch from *Annie*? she wondered, returning to the living room and sinking into the couch to rest her aching leg. What made him think of Miss Hannigan, singing about her dream of unearned luxury? Perhaps Ray had been prompted by Paisley's unthinking use of the word "jewels." She fingered the cameo brooch thoughtfully.

Jewels. Once, long ago, Jonathan had said something about jewels. Now it occurred to her he'd also mentioned some connection with the house he'd grown up in. What was it?

Outside the front window, beyond the trees and tall weeds, she spotted another, larger Queen Anne-style house in the distance. That must be her neighbor Steve's Lopez's home. In front stood the hand-painted sign she had passed earlier, bearing the vineyard's name. Paisley wondered how much Mr. Lopez was prepared to pay for her land. According to the real estate agent, her neighbor appeared to want it badly. Maybe it would be worth entertaining her neighbor's offer after all. She could pay off the last of her debts, and return to New York.

An odd sensation rushed through her, as if a pair of ghostly hands were restraining her. An unheard voice seemed to whisper in her ear, "No! You belong here."

Paisley shivered, and she almost glanced over her shoulder to see who was speaking. What had the hospital shrink told her, right before scribbling out the prescription for the little blue sleeping pills? "Don't worry about the dreams, they'll lessen eventually."

But until now, the dreams had only come at night. Right now, she was wide awake.

With effort, she shook off the strange feeling. It would be good for her to be here in the country, Paisley told herself firmly. There would be peace. Plenty of long walks, fresh air, sunshine ... and nothing to remind her of her lost career, of the role that would now go to someone else.

And maybe, although she was afraid to say the words, perhaps her voice would come back. The doctors hadn't ruled it out entirely, after all. A glimmer of hope rose inside her.

She stood restlessly and went to the window, looking out past the branches of the oak tree and the hummingbird feeder. Behind them, the two-lane country road wound away like a faded ribbon. The whoosh of an occasional car sounded muted from this distance, like wind in the trees. For the first time in a long time, longer than she could remember, Paisley was completely alone. No grim-faced doctors, no busy nurses, no hovering friends, concerned agents or publicists calling to ask how her recovery was going.

And no husband. *Jonathan.*

Paisley wrenched her thoughts away. She leaned her head against floral-patterned cushions, submitting to the pain like a patient allowing a nurse to sink a syringe into his arm.

It seemed odd that, except for the piano, the only sign of Jonathan was a framed high-school portrait amidst a cluster of family photos arranged on the hallway wall. He had left River Bend after graduating, and a few years later, when Jonathan's parents retired and moved to Florida, Great Aunt Esther moved back into the house. Her presence seemed to have erased the traces of the house's previous occupants.

The tight muscles in Paisley's neck and shoulders gradually relaxed. For the first time since her marriage three years ago, the future was entirely up to her, she thought drowsily. The thought was oddly liberating. In the silence of the house, her breathing slowed, and her body slumped on the sofa.

Sleep came, and with it, a new dream, different than the others.

Chapter Three

Paisley found herself onstage in an unfamiliar opera house wearing a long, full-skirted wine-colored gown. She had performed in period costumes dozens of times, and was used to tight corsets like this one that held her spine unnaturally erect and whittled her waist to nothing. Something felt different this time, but she could not describe what it was.

In the dark, the audience rustled impatiently. As always, their presence gave Paisley a prickle of excitement mingled with fear, yet that did not explain the strange feeling either.

Then it occurred to her. Somehow, she was not *herself*. Inexplicably, it felt was as if she were inhabiting someone else's body, that of another young woman her own age and height. Paisley felt the weight of the other woman's abundant dark hair coiled on top of her own head, hairpins jabbing painfully into her scalp. Who was this person, who was somehow simultaneously her and yet *not* her?

In the pit below, the orchestra began to play. Instinctively, Paisley opened her mouth and began to sing, although she'd never heard the song before. The voice that poured out of their shared throat was lighter than her own, a lyric soprano that she couldn't help admiring with curious detachment. The song was in a language Paisley did not know, but she sang the unfamiliar words fluently. As the aria rose to a glorious conclusion, the audience surged to its feet in one mass, applauding thunderously.

Curtseying, Paisley noticed flickering lights along the front of the stage, contained in small glass cylinders. *Gaslight?* Looking up, she saw the men in the front row wore silk ascots and embroidered waistcoats, as well as white kid gloves. As she stared in disbelief, the scene faded.

***

Paisley found herself lying on the couch, wearing her own rumpled clothes. The scarlet designer jacket was still flung across the back, and her purse lay on the coffee table. Sunshine streamed through the dust-smeared windowpanes, proof she had not been asleep more than an hour or so. She laughed with relief. Of course it was another dream, like those that had disturbed her sleep since the accident. Yet this one had felt so *real*.

Heart beating rapidly, she pushed damp strands of dark hair out of her eyes, trying to recapture the fading images. She could almost hear the unfamiliar melody still vibrating in the air. Her brain knew it was a dream, but Paisley could not shake the disturbing sensation the dream was not just some invention of her subconscious. It had felt like living a real experience. Something that had actually happened somewhere. *Some when.*

Except that was impossible, of course.

Shaken by the vividness of the experience, Paisley reached for her purse and groped inside for the translucent amber-colored plastic vial. She unscrewed the cap, poured a few pills into her palm, and stared at them. It had been several hours since she'd taken a painkiller, and they had never before caused her to hallucinate. Tilting the pills back into the vial, she returned it to her purse. What had triggered the experience? Something Ray Henderson had said? A forgotten memory of something Jonathan had told her?

Shrugging, she took her small flight bag upstairs to unpack. Although the dream had been powerful, there was no reason to allow it to disturb her. Paisley shook out her change of clothes and arranged her toiletries in the upstairs bathroom.

A rumble in her stomach reminded her it had been a long time since lunch on the airplane. She scratched together a meal from the canned food she had seen in the pantry: Dinty Moore stew and canned peaches. Making a face, she vowed to go into town tomorrow morning and load up on as many staples as she could reasonably carry back.

Typing a "to do" list into her phone, Paisley added a visit to a car rental agency. Ray was right that she needed her own transportation if she was going to stay for more than a day or two. The small town was not likely to have buses or taxis, or, possibly, Uber and Lyft.

Last, she typed in "handyman." It was possible to do without satellite TV, or even a microwave, but hot water was a necessity. When Paisley told Ray Hendersonm she didn't mind cold showers, she hadn't been entirely truthful.

Washing the dishes by hand in cold water, in silence interrupted only by a bird's twitter outside the window, Paisley sighed, thinking what it would take to make the house habitable. Maybe coming here *had* been a mistake. Yet somehow she could not bring herself to regret it. Outside the window, bright roses bloomed among the weeds, and the quiet did not feel oppressive, but rather peaceful.

Even the dream, odd as it was, had been pleasant. She'd felt more than just a physical connection with the girl in the dream. The experience had been much like meeting Esther that first time: an instant sense of liking, of *understanding*. Paisley had never felt the sensation with anyone else, not even her most intimate friends or colleagues. It made her curious to know if the woman in her dream was a real person, and if so, who.

Leaving the dishes to dry, she dug in her purse for the business card Ray had given. After a few layers of recorded voices, a receptionist finally answered the phone. "You need repairs to an old house a mile outside River Bend, Miss? Hey, I think I know the one you're talking about!" The cheerful young female voice made Paisley pictured an eighteen-year-old with hot-pink streaks in her hair and a Tinkerbell tattoo on her shoulder. "That pretty little white place on Highway 30, just past where the river curves around? Big oak tree in front?"

"That's the one."

"I thought so. Not many houses that side of River Bend. It's mostly farms and vineyards over there. Hang on, please."

Classical music filled Paisley's ear: *The Hall of the Mountain King*, by Grieg. At least the contractor, Bruce Harris, had good musical taste. Or someone on his office staff did. She doubted the melody was the receptionist's choice.

The young woman's voice returned, crestfallen. "Gosh, sorry, lady, but it looks like we're all booked up. The earliest we can take you is in four weeks."

"Four weeks!" How could there be that much work in such a small town?

"I'm really sorry," the girl repeated. "But there's a nice motel in town you could stay at."

Paisley removed her cell phone from her ear and stared at it. Ray had also suggested she stay in a motel. Did everyone in this area own stock in the local Motel 6?

She put the phone back to her ear. "That's not acceptable." Despite its raspy sound, her voice was firm. "The only reason I came to California was to stay in this house." Otherwise, she would be in New York right now, going to dinner with sympathetic friends and attending ballets at the Lincoln Center. Thinking of a possible summer's worth of cold showers, Paisley wondered again if she had been foolish to reject Ray and Barry's excellent advice. It might not be too late to change her mind.

"Sorry," the receptionist told her. "I can't promise anything, but maybe someone will cancel before then."

Thanking her, Paisley hung up and sat staring at the phone, massaging the rough scar on her neck. No way would she sit around until Bruce Harris shoehorned her into his busy schedule. Nor was she going to knuckle under and retreat to the local Motel 6, or whatever other lodgings River Bend had to offer. She clicked on her cell phone again. Unfortuately *Yelp* didn't turn up any other nearby contractors.

Rummaging around the house, she found an old Yellow Pages in a closet, which showed one other home repairman within an hour's drive. The simple listing consisted only of the contractor's name, followed only by a license number and a local phone number. It contrasted with the half-page advertisement for Bruce Harris's services. Paisley told herself at least this guy was probably less busy. And hopefully cheaper.

No one answered the first five rings, but just before the phone went to voice mail, a sleepy voice yawned into the receiver. "Yeah? Who's this?"

Paisley had obviously dialed a wrong number, but something kept her from hanging up. "I'm sorry to bother you. I was trying to reach Marvin McMullin Construction."

Curiosity crept into the male voice, now sounding slightly more alert. Paisley wasn't sure if the curiosity was because of her markedly gravelly voice, or something else. "McMullin Construction? Um, yeah, that's right. This is McMullin Construction. What do you want?"

Whoever the guy was on the other end of the line, it sounded like he was still in bed although it was nearly four o'clock in the afternoon. What kind of construction company was this? Paisley wondered. No wonder Ray Henderson had referred her to the competition. Nevertheless, she briefly explained what she had in mind.

"The Perleman place, huh? Exactly what kind of repairs were you thinking of?"

Her initial picture of a paunchy guy scratching an unshaven jaw evaporated as she realized the male voice was younger than she had first thought, now it was no longer gruff with sleep. Someone in his mid-to –late twenties, maybe.

Paisley remembered Ray's warning about calling just any random contractor. Still, there was no choice. She couldn't live in the house in its current condition, and the repairs would just be basic ones. "Some roof tiles need to be replaced, and the water heater doesn't work." Paisley eyed the peeling wallpaper. "Maybe some cosmetic improvements, too, if it doesn't cost too much extra."

"I'll have to take a look at the place before I can give you a quote." The voice sounded brisker, more professional.

"What's the earliest you can come? I'm hoping to start as soon as possible."

"Well, I guess I can squeeze you in, ah ..." A pause, as if he were consulting a calendar. "...How about tomorrow morning?"

A hot bath might be available sooner than Paisley had expected. Relief surged through her. A contractor who was willing to work on Saturday! "Perfect. I'll see you tomorrow, Marvin."

"'Ian,'" the voice corrected her abruptly. "Marvin McMullin was my father." The line went dead.

Ian McMullin hadn't asked for her address. Apparently everyone around here knew where the Perleman's house was located. River Bend was a small town, after all. For better or worse, Paisley had committed herself to staying here until the repairs were finished.

She yawned. New York City was three hours ahead of California time, and jet lag had caught up with her. She went upstairs and pulled on the silky short nightgown she'd packed, just in case. Without touching the sleeping pills in her purse, she fell asleep at once.

This time, the dream was even more vivid.

Instead of performing onstage, she was wearing a ball gown and waltzing with a handsome bearded man at the Russian Czar's Winter Palace. Rubies sparkled at her throat, falling as pendants from a collar of pearls. Matching earrings dangled from her ears, and a tiara glittered in her upswept dark hair.

The music ended, and her partner led her away from the dance floor. The string quartet began the delicate strains of a Polonaise against the low rumble of conversations around them as they passed by the wall of mirrors and left the palace. Outside, the silence was so complete she could hear the sound of her slippers on the marble steps as, arm in arm, they made their way toward a waiting coach.

It was winter, and she shivered a little. The count—somehow she knew his name was Grigori—bent over and kissed her gloved hand, before helping her into the coach.

"It is cold, but don't worry. I will make you warm," he said, smiling.

Paisley/Ruth looked up into his eyes. A wave of love, of trust, filled her entire body, so much so that she trembled.

"I know you will always take care of me, dearest. I love you."

"And I love you." His arm came around her and pulled her closer. "What do you think of my gift? You look lovely in those rubies. They are perfect with your coloring."

"They are too costly, Grigori. Your parents are right, you mustn't be so extravagant."

His hand went to her earlobe and lifted one of the earrings. "Nothing is too good for you." He bent to kiss her.

When Paisley's eyes opened, it took her longer than before to remember where she was … and *who* she was. Despite its vividness, the dream had not disturbed her this time, nor the fact that she had somehow blended into that other young woman who so eerily resembled her. The sensation had been *familiar*. It was as if she'd been returning to a time and place she belonged. What disconcerted her was being pulled back to the present. To reality.

Her hand reached for her throat, half-expecting to touch the pearl and ruby necklace. When her fingers felt nothing but the rough edges of her scar, a profound sense of loss stabbed through her. How odd, that the dream seemed more real than the rumpled bed she was lying in, or the tousled hair spilling around her shoulders.

Why was she so sure the dream had taken place at a Czar's reception? Or that her handsomenescort was a Russian count named Grigori? She knew nothing about Russia, had no interest in it. Certainly, she'd never visited there. And yet somehow Paisley was as certain of the accuracy of the surroundings as if she had actually walked through the palace's halls.

Paisley closed her eyes, teasing details of the dream from her consciousness. Again she saw the Russian Czar greeting his long line of guests, his sandy side whiskers and stylish Van Dyke beard. A red satin sash crossed his chest, which bore an array of medals. If she Googled Russian Czars, Paisley suspected she'd find a picture of one on the Internet that looked just like the man in her dream.

What about the other man in her dream, her escort? Had he been real too, the tall, broad-shouldered, dark-haired count who had led her to the carriage and helped her in, who'd pulled her close and pressed his warm lips to hers?

Paisley became aware of a distant pounding downstairs. Groggily she realized that the noise must have been what had awakened her. Was it an earthquake? Gradually it occurred to her that the pounding sounded more like a fist striking wood than a shaking house. Someone must have been banging at the front door for several minutes.

Fumbling for her cell phone, she checked the time. Barely seven o'clock in the morning. Grumbling under her breath, Paisley kicked off the sheet and pushed her curls out of her face. She splashed cold water on her cheeks and scowled into the bathroom mirror at the dark circles under her eyes.

The hammering downstairs didn't stop. Instead, it redoubled, and small bits of brittle, curling wallpaper fluttered to the floor. She sprinted downstairs just as the knocking's pattern resolved itself into the rhythm of "Shave and a Haircut." Just before "two bits," she yanked it open, and a man's fist nearly connected with her nose.

Yelping, she fell back as startled light-gray eyes stared down at her. They were set in a narrow face with high cheekbones and a wide mouth, which hung open in an almost comical expression of surprise. His jeans were faded nearly to white, and the untucked flannel shirt had one collar point sticking up. She almost reached out and pulled the collar down but restrained herself.

The young man's shock of tousled hair looked dusty, but on second thought, she decided that might have been his natural hair color. A wide leather tool belt hung low around his hips like a gun belt, reminding Paisley of a character in an old western movie. He held a clipboard.

"You must be Ian McMullin," she said.

The handyman's eyes went to the scar at the side of her throat, but he had enough manners not to mention it. "And you must be Paisley Perleman. I thought you weren't home." Today, his voice did not sound at all slurred or sleepy.

Self-consciously she pulled a lock of hair over her neck, and wished she'd changed out of her skimpy nightgown. "If you thought I wasn't home, why did you keep knocking?"

"Because you'd told me you'd be here."

Instead of trying to make sense of the contradictory statements, she stood back to allow him in. He stopped in the center of the room and looked around, his eyes taking in the designer red jacket slung across the back of the 1970-s era gold-and-brown couch, the expensive leather handbag lying on the scuffed coffee table with the bottle of pills spilling out of it.

Paisley grew annoyed. Who showed up at such an insanely early hour? It wasn't even eight o'clock. She should have tidied up a bit more last night, because the stranger appeared to be noticing too much. Paisley consoled herself that he was just here to do a job, get paid, and leave. It didn't matter what his impressions were.

"Do you realize what time it is?" Irritation lent an edge to her already rough voice. "I thought you'd be sleeping in late."

"Why would you think that?" He blinked at her.

"You were asleep when I called you yesterday afternoon. I assumed—"

A look of comprehension dawned on his features. "I don't usually party all night and sleep all day, if that's what you were thinking. You caught me in the middle of a nap, but that's not a habit. Morning is my favorite time of day. By the way, I've already found your first problem." He gestured toward the front door. "The doorbell doesn't work. That's why I had to knock so hard to wake *you* up."

She bit her tongue while he wandered around inspecting the rest of the room, making notes on the clipboard. He missed nothing: the fraying carpet by the kitchen, the broken pane in the living room, the water-stained ceiling upstairs. Finally he turned. "What were the other improvements you were thinking of?"

"Just enough to make it habitable for the summer." She cleared her throat. "I'm on a tight budget."

His eyes flicked to the jacket, but he didn't mention it. "Most people would have just bulldozed the place. If you're looking for a place to stay for the summer, you'd probably be more comfortable in a motel. Cheaper, too."

That was what Ray had said, and the other handyman's receptionist. But that odd sensation returned, tangible as a gentle hand on her shoulder. She *couldn't* allow bulldozers to knock over this charming house. That is, it would be charming again after the repairs were finished. Some buyer, some day, would thank her for preserving the historical structure.

"I don't care. I want to save the house."

To her surprise, Ian nodded approvingly. "Good for you." He stepped over a scattering of mouse droppings. "It's a nice example of a Queen Anne, and there aren't too many of them left around here. The basic structure looks sound, too. Are the services on?"

"No hot water, but there's electricity." She flipped the light switch, and the overhead light went on.

"The bills must be on auto-pay." He echoed Ray's earlier guess. "I'll go look at the water heater. Want to come along? Or, er, would you rather get dressed?"

Paisley looked down and her face grew hot. She'd forgotten she was still wearing her short nightgown. "Go ahead. I'll join you in a minute." She backed toward the staircase.

He was already strolling toward the kitchen, with that sense of purpose that marked all his movements. "Do you know if the circuit breakers are back here?"

"No idea. Feel free to look around."

When Paisley came back downstairs dressed in a cotton top, skirt, and sandals, Ian was standing in the hallway staring at the framed photographs and running a hand through his dust-colored hair, which stood on end like that of a scientist experimenting with electricity. Paisley couldn't imagine why he appeared fascinated by the Perleman's family portraits. She'd given them little more than a glance herself. Except for a few pictures of Jonathan as a child, most were of ancestors she'd never met.

"Hey, you've got to see this." Ian turned and beckoned her over.

"What is it?"

"Something struck me as strange when I first saw you," he said bluntly. "I didn't realize what it was until I saw this."

Paisley studied the picture Ian pointed at. It was a faded black-and-white photo of a married middle-aged couple which, based on their old-fashioned clothing and hairstyles, appeared to have been taken in the early 1920s. The husband wore curled mustaches, a pince nez, and a rounded cellophane collar. Next to him stood a slender dark-haired woman with sad eyes, her hand resting lightly on his shoulder. "So, what is it?"

Ian stared down at her. "You don't see it?"

"See what?"

He gave her a long, considering look, then shoved his hands deep into the pockets of his jeans. His lids slid half-closed over his eyes. "Never mind. Come outside. I have to show you something you won't be happy about." He led her out the kitchen door and pointed at the eaves, directly above the empty china cat bowl.

Paisley looked upward with a feeling of dread. "Termites?"

"Unfortunately. And that looks like the source of the leak over there."

She suppressed a groan. Roofs were notoriously expensive to replace. "Can you just patch the part where the water gets through?"

"Won't know for sure until I get up there. The good news is your water heater's fine. I relit the pilot light, and you should have hot water in a couple of hours."

Ian jotted something else on the clipboard, and she stood on tiptoes to look over his shoulder, close enough to notice the scent of fresh-smelling soap. The penciled list was disconcertingly long. She crossed her fingers behind her back, for luck. "How much will all that cost?"

"Depends on what you decide to have done." He chewed the end of his pencil, then added one more item. "I'll write you up an estimate when I get back ho …back to the office, and give you a call with the total." A smile lit up his light-gray eyes, and she wondered why she had thought of him as homely. He reminded her a little of the actor John Krasinski. They had the same quirky attractiveness. "Don't look so worried, I won't overcharge you. Number Two always tries harder, remember?"

"Number Two? How do you know you weren't the first place I called?"

"Was I?"

"Well...."

He nodded, unoffended. "You're lucky that Bruce Harris was too busy to take you on. That swindler would have sucked your wallet dry, and half his repairs wouldn't have held up anyway."

"How did you know…?" she began, before giving up. Small-town grapevines were apparently still effective. Or maybe Ian had just applied common sense, since it was logical that she'd call the only major contractor in River Bend first.

Ian held up his notepad. "I'll call you later with the estimate."

She followed him to the rusty green pickup parked in the gravel driveway, curiosity overcoming her. "Before you go, why did you point out that old photograph in the hallway to me? What was so strange about it?"

Ian raised his eyebrows at her. "That was a portrait of Jonathan's great-grandmother, Ruth Klaczko, and her husband, Jakub Perleman. You're the spitting image of her."

"I don't think she looked like me at all."

"No?" Looking thoughtful, he ducked into the cab of the pickup, slamming the door. "Guess I was wrong, then." Gravel stung her shins as the pick-up drove away.

Chapter Four

Paisley watched the old pickup grow smaller in the distance while her head teemed with questions. Was the photo really of Jonathan's famous ancestor he'd once mentioned, the Polish opera singer? And did Paisley really look like ... what was her name again? Ruth Klaczko? ... if that's really who the woman was? True, they were both petite with wavy black hair and dark eyes. But those similarities were superficial.

Returning to the hallway, Paisley took the framed photograph off the wall and inspected it more closely, staring into the strangely haunting eyes of the pretty, slender woman. This time, she realized that the face did look familiar—not because it resembled *her*, but because it resembled the woman in her dreams.

Looking for more clues, Paisley turned it over and saw, penciled on the back of the frame in shaky handwriting which she recognized from Esther's holiday postcards: "Ruth Klaczko Perleman."

Paisley stared at the name for a moment, heart beating faster, before hanging the photograph back on the wall. So Ian was right. The woman was the Polish opera singer. Score one for him. How had he known? He must have done handywork in this house before. Esther, lonely and old, might understandably have mentioned the famous ancestor who'd once been the toast of Eastern Europe. Yes, that must be how Ian knew the identity of the woman in the photograph.

That left unanswered a more disturbing question. How had Paisley visualized what Ruth Klaczko looked like in those vivid dreams? Before she'd even seen the photograph, much less known the woman's identity?

Ruth Klaczko stared enigmatically from the dark frame, at least twenty years older than she'd appeared in Paisley's dreams. Her graying hair was bobbed in the fashion of the mid-1920 and she wore a dark, long-sleeved frock with a simple lace collar and a brooch at the throat. Her eyes met Paisley's under thick, sharply pitched eyebrows, like Jonathan's. Paisley thought the woman looked more like a middle-class housewife than the glamorous former opera singer of her dreams, although there was still charm about the pointed chin, round cheeks, and large, expressive eyes. In her prime, the singer must have been considered a beauty.

Paisley's eyes fell on the cameo brooch pinned to the woman's lapel, and she gasped. Paisley had no doubt it was the same one that lay in her jewelry box, along with her other possessions, in a friend's guest bedroom in Manhattan.

It was another unsettling coincidence, but not necessarily a significant one. After all, Esther had told her the brooch was an old family heirloom. It made sense that it had once belonged to Ruth Klaczko. No doubt the piece was the source of those rumors about jewelry Jonathan had mentioned.

Paisley's stomach growled, reminding her that it had been a long time since lunch yesterday. There was only so long that she could rely on Esther's supply of canned food. Soon, she'd have to walk to town to shop for groceries. It might as well be today.

She threw away two boxes of stale cereal and heated a can of soup on the old electric range for breakfast. While eating, Paisley's thoughts turned to the tall young man who had come to fix her house. From the sound of his voice on the telephone yesterday, she'd expected an incompetent boor with a stained shirt and a beer belly. Instead, this morning she'd met an alert and intelligent young man. His brashness and know-it-all air annoyed her slightly, true, but those qualities were overshadowed by another, which she found hard to identify until, unbidden, a word popped into her head. *Integrity.*

An old-fashioned word, used more in her grandparents' time than her own. But something about Ian McMullin made her instinctively trust him.

Trust didn't come easily to Paisley. Not only had her childhood been a string of broken promises, but the newspapers carried stories every day about gullible widows signing over their life's savings to charming young con men. Auntie Esther might even have been one of those women. Paisley reminded herself that she didn't know Ian McMullin at all. Even Jonathan had turned out to have a side she had never known, and hadn't she trusted him?

Paisley glanced at the clock. The shops in River Bend wouldn't open until ten. She might as well clean up a little first. It appeared that no one had cleaned the house since Esther had gone into the retirement home a year ago. Besides, maybe more items would turn up that were worth selling at that antique store the real estate agent had mentioned.

Paisley rolled up her sleeves and put the Maria Callas record on the old hi-fi to play while she worked. She was thrilled to find the old equipment still worked. To the soaring vocals of *Carmen*, she found Lysol, rags, and a bucket under the sink. As she swept and vacuumed, Paisley couldn't help remembering the day she had fallen in love with opera.

It was sixth grade. As usual on school field trips, Paisley sat alone in the front of a yellow school bus because she didn't know the other kids very well. The cool kids sat at the back of the bus, joking and singing campfire songs she'd never heard before. She knew they were the cool kids because of their self-confidence, and the way they loudly joked back and forth.

She'd chosen a seat directly behind the field trip driver because he wouldn't ask embarrassing questions like "Where are you from?" or, worse, tease her because she was wearing the wrong clothes or didn't know the same slang terms. Glumly she watched Washington D.C. go by, a gray city in the fog.

Later, when she walked up the wide steps of the Kennedy Center, trailing behind the others, one of the chaperone moms hung back with her, perhaps out of pity.

"Have you ever been to an opera before?" The mom's blond hair was tied back in a ponytail and she wore fashionable, expensive clothes, like all the other moms.

Paisley lowered her eyes and shook her head.

"It may seem strange at first, but everyone should be exposed to culture." The woman quickened her steps and raised her voice. "Brad! Jessica! Cut it out and stay with the group!

"Exposed to culture?" It sounded like getting inoculated to smallpox. All Paisley knew about opera was that overweight ladies stood around a stage wearing funny-looking Viking outfits and yellow braids, and broke wine glasses from singing too shrilly. She mentally shrugged. Anything beat suffering through another day of school. She could always daydream through the matinee.

Paisley followed the rest of the class through glass doors and into a world of thick, soft carpets and glittering chandeliers, cut off from the ugly gray world outside. Despite throngs of people crowding the lobby, the space felt hushed, as if something important and wonderful was about to happen.

The sensation deepened when she stepped into the auditorium, even more lavishly beautiful than the lobby. Soon the lights lowered, and the space filled with music different from what blared on the radio in her parents' car. It was solemn, stately, beautiful in a way that vibrated to her bones and made her heart beat quicker. Tears sprung to her eyes but Paisley she didn't know why, except something about the music expressed raw emotion in a way that she had never experienced before.

Some of the other kids down the row were whispering or tittering. A chaperone hushed them. Paisley hardly noticed because the heavy velvet curtain was rising now, and people moved onto the stage wearing gorgeous clothes of silks and velvets like those of another era. Instead of speaking to each other, like ordinary people, they *sang*.

Whenever she was alone, Paisley sang too. She didn't do it when others were around, but she'd always felt that pouring out her feelings in music made it easier to bear loneliness or disappointment. The songs she sang, however, were nothing like the ones she heard now, soaring, dignified, and full of passion.

Rapt, Paisley watched and listened until it was over. The drama onstage reminded her in a way of her parent's fights and reconciliations, the tears, the promises…but somehow, instead of frightening her and making her want to hide under her covers, the emotions made her feel more alert and alive than ever before. The rising melodies, the booming bass of the villainous father, trying to ruin his son's happiness by forbidding him to be with the woman he loved. The tragic (name), singing a beautiful aria with the last of her strength, then dying in her lover's arms….

When it was over, Paisley felt as if every one of her emotions had been wrung out. And the music! The melodies floated in her head. She couldn't wait until she got home, before her mother returned from work, so she could sing in private, try to recreate what she had just heard. Maybe, even though she knew they couldn't afford it, she could talk her mom into singing lessons….

If the answer was 'no'—well, she was old enough to babysit. She'd save every penny to study music however possible. Because Paisley now knew she wanted to be one of those beautiful ladies onstage, in a world of enchantment, where the real world's problems faded far, far away.

To the strains of Carmen, grown-up Paisey tidied the living room, kitchen, and bedroom, before returning the ancient vacuum cleaner to the closet and heading for a much-needed bath in the clawfoot tub. Thanks to Ian's turning on the pilot light, a steaming waterfall burst out of the tap. She soaped her legs and arms until they were shiny and pink. If only the other problems with the house would be as easily solved.

Soaking blissfully among the bubbles, Paisley thought of the tasks Ian promised to take on: replacing the bad roof tiles, filling in the crack in the front steps, slapping on a new coat of paint. Maybe the project would give her a sense of purpose that had been lacking since the accident. When the place sold, she might even make a profit. Some people made a living fixing up old houses. She'd seen some of the shows on TV.

Paisley's mouth curved upward. What if Auntie Esther's spirit had coaxed her into coming to River Bend, knowing she needed what the house had to offer? If so, Paisley doubted she would want her to turn around and sell the house right away.

Submerged up to her neck in deliciously hot water, Paisley allowed her mind to drift. Then she sat upright, almost banging her knee on the tub faucet. Hot water. Utility bills. Presumably the funds for the auto-paid gas and electric bills came from Esther's bank account. There may not be much left in it, but it was worth checking out.

Drying off with a slightly musty towel she found folded in the linen closet, Paisley said another silent prayer of gratitude to her kind, generous fairy godmother, Auntie Esther.

The sun shone boldly in the Northern California sky as Paisley limped past her neighbor's vineyard toward the town of River Bend, half a mile down the road. A black-and-white cow in an adjacent field raised its head to watch her pass by, before lowering it again. Bees buzzed lazily among the yellow and white wildflowers, whose fresh scent filled the air.

A large hill rose from the river from which the town undoubtedly got its name. At the top, Paisley stopped to catch her breath. The scene that stretched out before her looked like Main Street at Disneyland, its two-story 19th-century buildings painted pale yellow and light blue, with crisp white trim. Baskets hanging from the green-painted light poles overflowed with red, pink, and white geraniums, and hand-painted signs above store entrances bore names like "Grab Bag" and "Grannie's Attic."

Unlike Disneyland, however, this town was real. The ornate iron posts were not for decoration: a century ago, horses had been tethered there. The wrought-iron street lamps had once been lit by gas. Paisley looked around, blinking. Why hadn't Barry told her the town was so quaint? Perhaps he didn't know. Likely, he had never traveled west of the Mississippi River.

She noticed a large black banner featuring a pair of crossed cutlasses advertising an upcoming local theater production. *The Pirates of Penzance.* She loved Gilbert and Sullivan operettas— who didn't? She'd been in a few such productions herself as a youngster.

One of the stores bore the name, "Chapter Two." On the sidewalk under the sign sat a plump, bespectacled woman with orange hair, reading a paperback and apparently enjoying the sunshine. On the other side of the entrance stood a bright-red wheelbarrow crammed with out-of-print books and former bestsellers. Scribbled in black marker on a scrap of paper scotch-taped to the front were the words, "Half Off!"

Paisley could never pass up a book store. She crossed the street and was happily rummaging through the wheelbarrow when a large trade paperback with a sepia cover caught her eye: *Prominent Residents of Solano County, Northern California.* She flipped through its pages, wondering if it mentioned the Perleman family. Jonathan was one of the region's most successful citizens, after all, and his family had lived here for several generations.

"Hi, there. Find something interesting?"

Paisley looked up to see the shopkeeper smiling at her. The woman wore a baggy sweater appliquéd with bright sunflowers, which covered generous curves. Her inexpertly trimmed hair had a rag-tag look matching that of the used books. A pair of enormous plastic-framed glasses slipped down her short nose.

"My husband grew up here," Paisley explained, holding up the book. "Do you know if this contains any information about River Bend?"

The red-haired woman glanced at it. "I'm not sure. There's more in the back of the store, if you're interested in local history. Got a whole shelf of books on gold mines, haunted houses, speakeasies...." The proprietor jerked her thumb toward the back of the shop. "Feel free to take a look."

Paisley wished she could spend all afternoon in the bookshop, but she still had to buy groceries. "How much is this one?"

"Just two bucks, hon. Everything's half off today."

Normally, Paisley would have bridled at being called 'hon.' Barely five feet four inches in her highest heels, weighing a hundred and five pounds, she was sensitive about being treated as younger than she actually was. Still, there was no taking offense at the other woman's friendly, open gaze. "May I pick it up after I do my other errands?"

"Sure." The woman took the volume, got up and found some Post-its, and slapped one on the cover. Then she paused, pen in hand. "What's your name, hon?"

"Paisley. Paisley Perleman."

The shopkeeper scribbled on the note. Then her head swiveled. Her eyes opened wide, revealing hazel irises behind the lenses of her glasses. "Did you say Perleman?"

"That's right." To prevent any more questions Paisley started to walk away. Then, remembering, she turned back. "By the way, is there a bank nearby? And what about a car rental agency?"

"The only bank in town is closed today. As for a car rental place, I'm sorry, hon, but you'd have to go all the way to Davis to find one."

Paisley's heart sank. Then she remembered Ray Henderson's glossy black Chevy Tahoe. Maybe the real estate agent would give her a ride to a larger town where she could rent her own transportation. Her bad leg was throbbing from the short walk to town. "Thank you. And where's the nearest grocery store?"

"Keep on down the street. It's right across from the high school." The shopkeeper pointed.

As Paisley thanked her and walked away, she was conscious of the woman's curious gaze. She'd imagined River Bend might be a good place to hide away while body and spirit healed. In a small town like this, though, everything she did was bound to be noticed and discussed—the last thing Paisley wanted.

Lugging a heavy bag of groceries, Paisley returned to the used-bookshop, puffing. The red-haired proprietor looked up from the same paperback she had been reading earlier, pushed up her glasses, and smiled. "Ready to pick up that book now?"

"Yes, thanks," Paisley said, setting down the bag on the counter and pushing back a lock of damp hair from her forehead.

As she paid, the woman commented, "I couldn't help noticing you looking at that banner across the street when you came by before."

"It's hard to miss. I saw Jolly Roger flags plastered all over town."

The woman eyed her. "Interested in seeing the show? Curtain goes up in eight weeks, and the play's sure to be a crowd-pleaser."

"I might check it out if I'm still in River Bend." Paisley crossed her fingers behind her back. She probably would be gone by then, and even if she wasn't, she'd likely be doing something else. She was not in the mood for off-key singing and low-budget production values. It would be too strong a reminder of the world-class production of *La Bohème* that she would never appear in.

The woman looked pleased. "Oh, I hope you're here long enough to come. How long do you plan to stay?"

Paisley hesitated. It wasn't as if the shopkeeper was a reporter for *The National Enquirer* ... even if that rag were interested in the doings of an opera singer whose career was over before it fully launched. "I'm not sure, exactly." Until she recovered or ran out of money, whichever came first.

The shopkeeper set down her paperback. "You said your name is Paisley Perleman. You must be Jonathan's widow, aren't you? I'm so sorry, my dear." Her slightly protruding hazel eyes, enlarged by the lenses, looked sympathetic. "I ought to introduce myself." She thrust out a large, chapped hand. "I'm Shirley Zacarias. I'll admit right up front that I had a huge crush on Jonathan back in high school. All that dark, lean intensity….Needless to say, he never knew I existed."

Paisley shook the offered hand and picked up her groceries. She didn't want to talk about young girls with crushes on Jonathan. It brought back too many painful memories.

"Stay and rest a while." Shirley heaved herself out of her seat. "You're limping, poor thing. Here, let me get you a chair."

"Thank you, but…."

Shirley had already found another metal folding chair and set it up next to hers on the sidewalk. "Sit here. I'll get some fresh lemonade from the fridge. It'll be good for your throat."

Paisley touched her scar, embarrassed that the woman had noticed her raspy voiced, but obey. Shirley disappeared into the shop, emerging a couple of minutes carrying a pitcher clinking with ice cubes.

"It's nice having someone to talk to. Sometimes it gets lonely sitting here by myself." Shirley plopped back into her seat. "There are days when I wonder why I bother opening the store."

Paisley sipped at the cold glass of lemonade. The beverage did soothe her throat, and it felt good to rest her bad leg.

Shirley watched approvingly. "The lemons came off my brother's tree. We've all been wondering what was going to happen to the Perlemans' place since Esther passed away. So sad, seeing it stay vacant, deteriorating day after day. Those old houses have so much character, and there aren't many of them left."

Paisley felt a pang of guilt. It was her fault the house had been neglected for so long. Perhaps she should have appointed a caretaker or rented it, but life had been so busy that she'd completely forgotten that she owned the place.

Shirley didn't seem to notice Paisley's reaction. "So what do you plan to do with it now?"

The question was a reasonable one, but Paisley didn't know the answer. So many decisions to make. Just thinking of them made her head ache.

"We'll see." She changed the subject. "Are you involved with the *Pirates of Penzance*? It seems you know a lot about the production."

Shirley leapt to the bait. "Involved? This year I'm running the whole darned thing! Esther used to do most of the work, while I just lent a hand. She started the community theater when she moved back here fifteen years ago or so. Recruited a group of local actors and even directed the plays herself. After she died, I couldn't bear to see it all disappear, so I sort of took over. It won't be the same without her, though."

"It must be a lot of work." Paisley knew how much time and effort went into pulling off any theatrical production.

Shirley nodded vigorously. "It's way more challenging than I expected, but the play will come together in the end. Esther said they always do. Come see a rehearsal, why don't you? That way if you leave River Bend before opening night, you'll at least get an idea of what it's like."

"I might," said Paisley politely. She drained her lemonade. "Thanks for the drink."

As she began to cross the street, Shirley called out. "Drop by again next time you're in town. I'd like to pick your brains about that house of yours. I'm a member of the historical society, and I've heard some interesting stories about that place."

Paisley waved and hurried away. She planned to spend the next few weeks wallowing in self-pity and hiding from the world, but that goal appeared to be growing more and more remote.

The bag of groceries grew heavier with each step. A car swooshed at full speed down the hill by the bend in the river, and when Paisley hopped to the side of the road to avoid being hit, pain stabbed her weak leg.

A large "Do Not Trespass" sign was nailed to a post by the pasture next to her house. Rubbing her calf, she considered it thoughtfully. The shortcut would save several minutes of walking and, besides, it wasn't as if she would harm anything. The cow was grazing peacefully in the far corner, and no one was around to see.

Paisley slipped through the barbed wire and had nearly reached the other side of the field when she noticed the cow ambling in her direction. The animal was bigger than she had realized. So were its horns. And it was picking up its pace.

When the animal began to trot toward her, she gave up any attempt at dignity and broke into a sprint in spite of her weak leg. It gave out under her, and the grocery bag flew out of her grasp, scattering several cans of soup, a jar of mayonnaise, and a plastic bag of fruit. It was too late: the animal was looming over her, its flanks solid as the sides of a warship. Curling into a fetal position, she waited helplessly for the sharp horns to carve into her side.

"Lizzie! Get out of there! Shoo!"

A dirt clod bounced off the cow's massive flank, and the beast bellowed in protest.

"Hey, are you all right?" a male teen-age voice asked from somewhere above.

Paisley opened a cautious eye. The cow was gone, and a not-too-clean hand was reaching down to offer help. She allowed its possessor to haul her to her unsteady feet. A youth about seventeen years old looked down at her from a face crowned by a thatch of midnight-black hair. He wore jeans and checkered Vans sneakers. Although she had never seen the boy before, something struck her as vaguely familiar, and she found herself staring at him.

His eyes narrowed under thick dark eyebrows. "You okay? Don't worry. Lizzie's not going to hurt you."

The cow was plodding away. At a distance, it paused to crop the grass again.

Paisley looked down at her left leg, still bearing the long red scar from the implanted titanium rod. Beads of blood welled out of a network of fresh scratches, and suddenly everything seemed very far away. *Blood all over the dashboard. Broken glass everywhere. And next to her, Jonathan's limp body, slumped over the steering wheel....*

"Hey, Miss! You'd better lean on me. You don't look so good." The teenager grabbed her arm, and she gratefully clung to him. "Come on, we've got some Band-Aids in the house."

When she could stand on her own, the boy released her and bent to scoop the scattered groceries back into the bag. "You weren't scared of Miss Lizzie, were you?" he asked as they started toward the large Queen Anne house near her own, smaller one. He glanced at her from the corner of his eye, and there was a hint of humor in his voice.

"Lizz—oh, the cow? Of course not. I was just—"

"—Worried about trespassing?"

The boy's tone was bland, but she felt herself blush. "Sorry. I saw the sign, but I thought it wouldn't matter, just this once."

"It's okay. You can cross any time you want, as long as you don't mind confronting Lizzie again. I might not be here next time." Although his face was deadpan, humor glinted in the dark-brown eyes.

"Thanks for rescuing me." She stuck out her hand. "My name's Paisley Perleman. If that house is the one you live in, then we're neighbors. I own the smaller one next door."

His smile disappeared as if she had suddenly transformed into a monster with three heads and slobbering jowls. After a moment she lowered her hand. *What had she said wrong?*

"You're a Perleman?" he said slowly. "I thought you were a weekend tourist. Sometimes someone drives past the sign and thinks our winery is open for visits."

"I'm related to the family by marriage," she told him. For some reason, her voice sounded apologetic. "The last owner of the house, Esther Perleman, was my late husband's great-aunt. And what is your name?"

"Kevin Jackson." His footsteps quickened, and Paisley had to hurry to keep up, puzzled at his change of mood. "I live with my step-dad, Steve Lopez. He owns the house next to yours."

The painted boards of the large house's porch were spotless, and the windows sparkled like freshly washed dinner glasses. Either Steve Lopez was a neat freak or he employed a superb cleaning woman, she thought. Two cars were parked side-by-side in the long driveway: a red pick-up truck and a gleaming low-slung black Audi R8 that looked like something Jonathan would have driven. The sleek sports car seemed out of place in the semi-rural setting, and she eyed it curiously.

The teenager opened the front door for her, and she preceded him into what had once been a traditional parlor, now a man cave with a slouchy distressed-leather sofa, a full-sized pool table where a formal dining table once stood, and an enormous flat-screen television hanging over the fireplace.

A pair of abstract paintings covered two of the other walls, slashing streaks of red and orange, while a long-handled metal object leaned against a corner like an equally abstract piece of sculpture. It must be a farm tool of some type, she thought, or maybe an implement for a hobby. While she was trying to identify the strange contraption, the boy called upstairs, "Hey, Steve! We have a visitor."

"Who is it?"

Paisley turned toward a slim man strolling downstairs dressed in a black button-up shirt and black slacks. He stopped with apparent surprise when he saw her, and she had an impression of high cheekbones, a narrow nose, a down-curving mouth.

"This lady fell down crossing the pasture." Kevin gestured at the thin line of blood trickling down Paisley's calf, under her skirt.

She stuck out a hand to hide her embarrassment. "Hello, I'm Paisley Perleman, your neighbor."

A hard hand engulfed hers briefly, and she had the impression of banked strength behind it. "Jonathan's widow. Yes, I heard you were in town." Her neighbor inspected her, but it was impossible to decipher his expression. "Get the Band-Aids, Kevin."

Kevin disappeared like a gopher into a hole. Steve gestured for her to sit on the couch. "My friend Ray Henderson told me you might be flying out here to see the house, but he didn't mention you were going to stay."

"I didn't expect to. It was supposed to be a brief visit, but ... well ... on impulse I decided to spend the summer there."

"Welcome to River Bend. I hope you won't sue me for getting hurt on my property."

Paisley glanced at him sharply, unsure if he were joking. "It's just a scratch. And I was trespassing, after all."

"*That* was definitely no scratch." His eyes shifted to the three-inch scar, not far from the grass stains and freshly brimming scratches.

She fervently wished she had not worn a skirt today. Kevin reappeared, bearing a box of Band-Aids, and vanished again. Moments later, she heard loud, discordant rock music blaring upstairs.

"Sorry about that noise," Steve said, a crease appearing between his eyebrows. A look of displeasure appeared in his hazel eyes. "I've asked my step-son to confine his guitar-playing to the garage, but he doesn't listen."

"That's Kevin playing? I thought it was the radio."

Steve grimaced. "His skill has improved a bit over the last few months, since he came to live here. He's spent all summer holed up practicing."

"Kevin just moved here?" For some reason, the fact surprised Paisley. "I hope I'm not being too personal, but did you and his mother marry recently?"

Fortunately, he did not seem offended. "No, I moved back to River Bend after Rachel and I divorced a few years ago. I met her in New Jersey, where I was living at the time. Kevin is her child from a previous relationship." As if sensing more explanation was needed, he added, "Unfortunately, she died of cancer last year. We hadn't been in touch in some time, but because his grandmother was too old to care for him, I agreed to take him in."

"That was nice of you."

Steve shrugged off the compliment. "It was the least I could do. Poor kid's been through a lot. First losing his mother, then having to leave his friends to live in this small, rural town … well, it hasn't been easy for him. It hasn't been an easy transition for me, either, for that matter." He gestured at her bandaged leg, as if eager to change the subject. "Better?"

"Yes, thank you." She rose with him. "I heard you want to buy my property."

"And I heard you turned down my offer. Any chance you'll change your mind?"

"I don't know yet." That wasn't exactly true. She had to put the place on the market eventually, and Steve was the most likely buyer, but she didn't want to think about it. Maybe she could talk him into saving the house, even if he used the rest of the property for his grapevines.

"Why aren't you selling right away? Ray thought you intended to look around and leave right after."

She wanted to snap that Ray had a big mouth. "I don't know that either. If I like it here, I may decide to stay for the summer."

"Then I hope you like it here," Steve said, but she had the impression he was just being polite.

"Thanks for the first aid." She picked up her grocery bag. "I promise to be more careful next time."

"Cows can be dangerous. I don't know why I keep the darned thing. A nod to the ranch my father ran here when I was a kid, I guess, before I planted the vineyard."

When Steve put his hand on the knob to open the door, he startled her with another observation. "By the way, I heard you hired Ian McMullin to come out and work on the old house."

She raised her eyebrows. Who could have told him? Ray again? Bruce Harris's young receptionist? "That's right. So?"

"The guy's competent enough, I guess. It's just...." He broke off, shrugging, causing an interesting ripple of muscles under his tight-fitting black shirt. "None of my business. Forget I brought it up. Would you like a lift home?"

"No, thanks. It's an easy walk." In the back of her mind, she mulled over his implied criticism of Ian. What did Steve mean by "competent enough, I guess?"

"Are you sure?" Steve insisted. "In your condition...."

At first she thought he was referring to her scratched knee. Belatedly she realized he meant her limp, and her face grew warm again. She was growing tired of being reminded of her infirmity. "No thanks. I'll be fine."

"All right. But if you need a ride some time, let me know. It's not easy getting around without transportation, and after all, we're neighbors."

Paisley tried to remember if she had mentioned that she didn't have a car. For the second time that day, she realized she would have to get used to the small town way of life, where everybody knew everyone else's business, no matter how trivial.

As she started down the steps, he stopped her a final time. "Now that we've met, why don't you come over for dinner some time? It'll give us a chance to know each other a bit better, seeing as we're going to be living next door to each other. I make pretty decent enchiladas. An old Mexican recipe of my grandmother's."

He favored her with a sudden blindingly white smile, and Paisley thought Ray had been right about her neighbor being a lady-killer. For some reason, he had suddenly chosen to turn his charm on her full blast. She wasn't about to complain. Nevertheless, she hesitated. Being alone with a strange man wasn't something she was ready for.

He seemed to sense her reaction. "Kevin will be here."

She felt her face relax into an answering smile. "Okay, then." An hour in the company of a great-looking neighbor? Why not? She could almost forgive him for noticing her limp.

"Enchiladas it is," he said, still smiling. "You'll be busy settling in the next few days, so how about Sunday? In the meantime, if you need anything, give me a call." He produced a business card from his breast pocket and handed it to her. It was the same design as the sign by the road, grape leaves weaving the name of his vineyard. "A woman living alone in the middle of nowhere.... You never know what could happen."

"Thanks," she said, slipping the card into her purse. With her free hand, she managed to pull out a slip of paper and awkwardly jotted down her own cell phone number. "And here's mine. Maybe I can help you out sometime as well. You never know."

Steve gravely accepted the slip of paper, and they shook hands like professionals in an office.

On the way home, she tried to walk steadily, bemused by the fact that she had come looking for peaceful isolation and yet, on her first day, she had received two social invitations: one from the bookshop keeper, Shirley, and one from her Heathcliff-lookalike neighbor, Steve Lopez. Maybe it was just as well. Keeping busy would keep her from dwelling on uncomfortable questions like how she was going to pay those mounting bills, and—her mind shrank from the thought—whether she would ever sing again.

When Paisley arrived back at the little white house under the towering oak tree, she collapsed onto the front-porch swing, too tired to go another step. Just then her purse began playing the Toreador song from *Carmen*, and she fished out her cell phone. The name on the screen brightened her spirits.

"Nigel!" she squealed into the receiver.

An English accent poured into her ear, smooth as oil. "Hullo, Paisley dearest. How's my favorite former student? I was starting to think you were avoiding me. You haven't returned any of my calls."

"I'm sorry. I did get your messages, but...."

"I know, love, I know. You've been laid up in hospital. I've heard the whole, tragic story. Did you get the roses? The entire faculty chipped in, but I picked them out myself. Those dark-red ones are your favorites, aren't they? The scent is absolutely divine."

Suddenly there was a lump in her throat. "Yes, I got the roses. And yes, they were beautiful."

Nigel's voice grew serious. "So sorry about Jonathan. Such a shock to all of us."

She swallowed. "Yes. It's been ... difficult."

"The Internet stories said you'd lost that lovely voice of yours. Could the fates be so cruel? Please tell me, darling, is the condition expected to be, ah, permanent?"

She tucked up her feet under her legs on the swing, detecting the undernote of concern in Nigel's tone that matched her own fear. He had good reason to be concerned, for he knew exactly what she faced. Nigel's own career as a celebrated tenor in Europe had been cut short ten years earlier when an operation to remove a node from his throat went awry. He had found his way to the conservatory in Omaha, where he had built up a respected music program, hand-selecting his own students, one of whom was Paisley. She owed him everything: he was the one who had arranged for her try-out at the Met, and he had taken a great interest in her career, even after Jonathan swooped in and carried her away.

"I don't know if the loss of my voice is permanent," she admitted, realizing Nigel was patiently waiting for her answer. "The doctors.... " She paused again. "They think it might be psychosomatic. That happens sometimes, apparently, after a shock."

There was a moment of silence on the other end while her former instructor absorbed this. "Whatever happens, darling," he said at last, "I want you to know I would be happy to offer you a position at the conservatory. One needn't be able to sing to teach, you know."

She felt a sudden rush of sympathy and gratitude. "I know. I do appreciate the offer, Nigel."

"…But?"

"You know I've never wanted to teach. I've only ever wanted to perform."

He chuckled, and she could picture him running his free hand through his prematurely thinning blond hair. "You were born to be onstage, Paisley, my dear. But I thought that under the circumstances...."

She closed her eyes, remembering the cliché: "Those who can, do; those who can't, teach." And, as another cliché pointed out, beggars couldn't be choosers. Was she destined to end up like Nigel, a former singer forced to stand by and watch others go on to glory? Paisley imagined her peers regarding her with pity and whispering "...Was up for 'Mimi' at the Met … A car accident. Such a sad story...."

No. She wasn't *that* desperate, not yet.

She thanked Nigel again, and after a short friendly conversation about mutual acquaintances, said good-bye and rang off.

Silence closed in on her as she stood up and faced the little house Aunt Esther had left her, the refuge to which she had fled in hope of a miracle. The structure looked very ordinary in the shadows cast by the huge oak tree that dwarfed it, with the painted clapboard sides and small porch, and white gingerbread on the eaves like decorative frosting on a wedding cake. A worn, tattered wedding cake. It was the kind of house that ought to be cared for, cherished, that should have kids running around the yard and a tire swing hanging from the big oak tree near the front door, the tree she had noticed in the photograph that seemed so perfect for climbing. It was the kind of house, she thought, where one wouldn't think twice about borrowing a cup of sugar from the next-door neighbor.

That would be Steve Lopez. In many ways, he reminded her of Jonathan: darkly handsome, smooth, a shade mysterious. Hardly the type of man Paisley would think of borrowing a cup of sugar from. Although if she asked for one, she suspected Steve would give her more than just sugar.

The corners of Paisley's mouth twitched at the thought of a flirtation with Steve. Just because the last thing she wanted right now was a man in her life didn't mean that she needed to give up on all of them forever. Maybe later, when she was ready. When she'd forgotten Jonathan's betrayal. When the healing was over. For the first time, that eventuality felt possible.

Something else niggled at the back of her brain, however: Kevin's negative reaction when he had found out she was related to the Perlemans. Why? He couldn't even have known Aunt Esther. From what Steven had said, the boy hadn't moved to River Bend until after the old lady's death.

As she walked inside to start preparing a light supper with her newly acquired groceries, Paisley wondered what elderly Aunt Esther had made of her handsome neighbor with the vineyard and flashy cars. Had she stood peering out the living room curtains as Steve Lopez brought over a parade of lady friends in his fancy car, to his bachelor home with its cozy leather couch and striking modern art? Had Esther been shocked, or amused? Remembering the lively sparkle in the old woman's eyes, Paisley thought it was probably the latter.

She washed the lettuce, chopped up the tomatoes, and threw together a tossed salad, a welcome change from Spaghettios and canned chili. While setting the table for one, a sense of loneliness rushed through her and she took the plate into the living room where she sank into the couch in front of the TV.

Paying no attention to the reality show that was airing, she thought again of the house's previous occupant. Esther Perleman had lost her parents, brothers and sisters in the Holocaust, but as a child, she managed to escape to America, never returning to Europe. Paisley compared that with how she had handled her own recent tragedy; the guilt, the self-pity, the pills. Yet Esther had not allowed a far greater burden to prevent her from living a happy and productive life.

Hmmm, Paisley thought. Perhaps there was a lesson to be learned there.

Of course, the question remained what she should do once the last of the money ran out. Maybe Paisley would have to accept Nigel's generous offer after all. But like Scarlett O'Hara, that indomitable heroine of *Gone With the Wind,* had said, tomorrow was another day.

Halfway through *Jeopardy!* Paisley heard the Toreador song go off again. She checked her phone and found that Ian had texted the appraisal for the house repairs. The amount was surprisingly reasonable, but still she hesitated. This was her last chance to back out. Everyone had advised her to sell the place, and surely they were right: the wise course of action was to get as much money as possible out of it, instead of sinking her rapidly vanishing savings into fixing it up.

From the corner of her eye, she saw a flash of gray outside the window. Esther's cat, no doubt. Somehow, the sight confirmed her decision. The cat had stayed. So would she.

She texted Ian her response.

The squeal of Ian's pickup truck awoke her early the next morning, followed by a clatter and banging that sounded like people unloading heavy equipment. Yawning, she descended to find Ian and three strangers in front of the house, removing a table saw from the back of his pickup and uncoiling long electric cables. They wore virtually identical faded jeans, old T-shirts, and tool belts, but that was where the resemblance ended. One was a handsome, dark-haired man with Native American features, one was a short woman with close-cropped hair, and one was a thin, sandy-haired man with the beginnings of a straggling beard.

Ian looked up as she approached. "Oh, hi. I thought we'd start right away," he said. "You don't mind, do you?" Paisley noted that his hair had lost its dusty, tousled look and was damply combed into bangs over his forehead. He had shaved, possibly with a dull straight razor. His jaw looked raw. He gestured toward his co-workers. "This is my team, Quinn, Alix, and Rusty. They're going to help me gut the upstairs bathroom today. Got to take care of mold first, it's a health issue."

"Okay, fine," she said, shuddering a little at the thought of mold infiltrating the house. "I'll leave you guys to it."

She went back to sleep and, around noon, wandered to the kitchen to make herself lunch while idly planning the rest of her day: perhaps a short walk in the woods behind the house, another nap before dinner, and lots of reading, curled up on the old sofa with Esther's records playing on the hi-fi in the background. There was a whole bookshelf of paperback mysteries in the living room.

Eating her turkey sandwich, she watched through the kitchen window as Ian walked around overseeing the work as it progressed, and working alongside the others. His co-workers accepted his directions with nods, jokes, or friendly high-fives. Everything seemed to be progressing smoothly and efficiently. Why should the fact surprise her?

With a jolt, Paisley realized that it was something Steve Lopez had said. What was it? Nothing specific, just a vague innuendo about Ian's competence. From what she could tell, though, Ian certainly seemed to know what he was doing. Of course, she could be wrong. No one could be more ignorant about home repairs than she was.

Her hopes for a peaceful day were shattered by the ringing of hammers and whirring of saws, and by afternoon she developed a pounding headache. Even turning up Wagner's *Ride of the Valkyries* did not drown out the din. Perhaps this was as good a time as any to go back to town and finish the errands she had not been able to accomplish yesterday, she decided.

This time, as Paisley passed the field next door, she made sure to give it a wide berth. Puffing up the long, steep hill, she saw a black sports car pull up from behind her.

"Hey there! Going to town?" Steve Lopez looked fresh and cool in a spotless white shirt, his tanned arm propped against the open window frame.

Paisley pushed a strand of sweaty hair out of her eyes. "Hi." She didn't bother to answer his question, since her destination was obvious. Eyeing the Audi R8, she thought the vineyard must be doing well for Steve to be able to afford such a flashy model.

"Still no wheels, huh?" Steve's tone was that of a Californian who wasn't used to seeing someone actually *walk* somewhere. "This isn't New York, you know," he said, confirming her impression. "No public transportation around here."

"I guess that explains why I couldn't find the subway stop."

Without smiling at her feeble attempt at a joke, he leaned over and pushed open the passenger door. "You shouldn't overdo it in this heat, not with that bad leg. Hop in."

She hesitated. She had been taught not to get in the car with strangers. But then, Paisley reminded herself, Steve Lopez wasn't a stranger. After all, she had already visited his house and had even accepted an invitation to dinner. Besides, her leg was throbbing again.

"I've been meaning to ask what brought you to River Bend," Steve said as she settled into the soft leather seat with a sigh of comfort. He glanced at her dusty sandals, but she couldn't tell if it was from sympathy or out of concern for the car's immaculate carpeting. "This doesn't seem the kind of town that would attract a woman of your background."

"Impulse, I guess. I wanted to check out my inheritance."

His eyes remained focused on the road, but his dark eyebrows shot up. "Inheritance? Oh, you mean Esther's place. I can understand why you wanted to see it. A person doesn't inherit a house every day."

She didn't answer right away, for it *wasn't* the house alone that had brought her. That sharp flash of recognition while looking at the photograph had come from something else. Something centered in the house, perhaps, but which had nothing to do with paint or floorboards. But Paisley could hardly explain that to Steve, not when she didn't fully understand it herself.

"I'm not sure what I mean." Her tone indicated that she didn't want to talk about it anymore, and to Paisley's relief, Steve did not follow up with any more questions.

Perversely, his silence made her begin speaking again after a few moments. "To be honest, I don't understand why Esther left the house to me," she admitted. "I mean, I'm not even related to her."

"You were married to Jonathan," he pointed out. "That makes you a Perleman, doesn't it?"

"But that's the odd thing." Paisley turned toward Steve, noting in the back of her mind that he looked well dressed for a wine-grower, or whatever the fancy term was for the profession. *Vintner*, was that it? She doubted that the crisp, button-up shirt he wore open at the throat and which fit his shoulders perfectly came off the rack at Wal-mart or Sears. It reminded her of the ones

Jonathan used to buy at Nordstrom's, and the slim watch on his wrist looked like real gold. "Esther didn't leave anything at all in her will to Jonathan, just to me. And I didn't even know her that well!"

"I understand why that seems odd." His mouth relaxed into the charming smile she remembered from yesterday. "But it's not that surprising if you knew the family. They had a long-running feud with Esther stemming back to when she was a girl."

Paisley studied him with curiosity. "Oh? How do you know that?"

"I grew up next door, remember? Jonathan and I used to play together when we were kids, and my parents knew his parents. There are no secrets in a small town."

His words echoed what Shirley had told her, not long ago.

"It still seems strange to me," she mused, as they reached the top of the hill. "Esther seemed too nice to carry a grudge like that. Shouldn't she have made more effort to find another blood relative to leave it to, even a distant one?"

He gave her a quick look. "It's to your credit to think that way. But blood is not always thicker than water, apparently." He pulled the car to a stop. "I'll drop you off here if that's okay. It's just a short walk to Main Street."

She opened the door. "Thanks for the lift. You're a lifesaver."

"No problem." He touched his forehead in a salute and drove off.

As Paisley watched the Audi recede into the distance, she kicked herself for talking about personal matters with a virtual stranger. What did Steve care whom Esther had left the house to? At least, she thought, he had been too polite to show boredom.

Remembering their upcoming dinner together, she found to her surprise that she was looking forward to it. Perhaps it wasn't too early to build a social life again. It would do her good to climb out of the rut of isolation and depression into which she had sunk after the accident.

Chapter Five

It was a sunny Friday afternoon, and clusters of patrons filled the outside tables of the café with its cheerful blue-and-yellow striped awning. Paisley walked across the street to the used book store facing the cafe. The little bell on the door jingled, and the red-haired shopkeeper turned to Paisley with a wide smile, pushing her thick plastic-rimmed glasses up her snub nose.

"Hi, there!" Shirley greeted Paisley brightly. "I hear you hired Marvin McMullin's kid to fix up Esther's house."

Paisley could not hide her surprise that Shirley had heard the news so quickly. "How did you know?"

Shirley's grin grew wider. She leaned her elbows on the counter in the manner of someone readying for a nice, long, chat. "Haven't you learned yet that there's no privacy around here? I'm itching to know how you got Ian to take on the job. Last time he popped into my store, he claimed me he would be working on his college thesis all summer."

Paisley was stunned. "You mean Ian's a college student? I thought he was a handyman."

"Ian worked for his dad's local contracting company until being accepted into a prestigious architectural program at Berkeley a few years ago. He always said his passion was to design buildings, not make them himself."

"I called him from Esther's old yellow pages," Paisley said, frowning. "McMullin Construction."

"That should have been a clue, honey. McMullin Construction hasn't existed since Ian's dad passed away three years ago."

No wonder Ian had seemed confused when her first phone call woke him up. Why hadn't he just told her the truth? Why had he shown up the next morning with a clipboard, as if he was used to taking on such jobs every day?

Shirley pushed her glasses up her broad nose. "He probably needed the money. College gets more expensive every year, even for kids with a scholarship. But don't worry, sweetie, Ian knows what he's doing." She glanced at her Timex wristwatch. "Let me treat you to lunch, hon. I have lots of questions for you, although you don't have to answer all of them, of course."

Paisley looked down at the black-and-white squares of the linoleum floor, sorting through a mixture of emotions. It was upsetting to learn Ian had kept a secret from her, even if it was a trivial one. Nor was she sure she wanted to sit through lunch with Shirley. Paisley had already spilled enough personal information to Steve. She'd learned to sound forthcoming in press interviews while keeping her private affairs, well, private, but she suspected Shirley would be harder to foist off.

On the other hand, the prospect was tempting. Having grown up with Jonathan, Shirley probably knew aspects of him that Paisley didn't. And, in an odd way, the red-haired shopkeeper's frankness was refreshing. The hospital shrink had said it would be therapeutic to talk about the past.

Throwing caution to the winds, she took a deep breath. "Sure. Let's go eat."

"Great." Shirley disappeared, reappearing moments later carrying a purse, orange lipstick freshly applied to her lips and a green, red, and yellow knitted cap crammed over her bright hair. Escorting Paisley to a beat-up Volvo parked behind the building, she reminded her passenger to fasten the seat-belt, not that Paisley needed warning. These days she never got into a car without always, always, buckling up.

"Fred's Fish Shack is halfway between here and Calistoga." Shirley gunned the ancient motor. "A thirty-minute drive, but worth it. Even if you don't like fish, I promise you'll like it at Fred's."

Paisley had been looking forward to trying the pretty café across the street, but she nodded meekly.

They had to wait in a long line to place their orders, but once they were seated on barstools at the counter, a young server brought them a tray full of delicious-smelling food. The cod turned out to be flaky and flavorful, the rolls yeasty and warm from the oven.

As Paisley expected, their talk turned to her life with Jonathan, their travels, celebrities she had met, and her career as an opera singer. Paisley found herself answering freely. There was something unexpectedly reassuring about Shirley's plain, open face and blunt questions. Journalists saw Paisley as a story to sell magazines. Shirley, by contrast, treated her like a real person.

"You said you knew about the house's history," Paisley said, when the conversation turned to the Perlemans. She broke apart a roll and buttered it. "Has it always belonged to the family?"

"No, they moved in a couple of decades after it was built in the 1880s. They say it was constructed by the same guy who built the house next door."

"Steve Lopez' house?"

"Have you noticed the similarity? Same windows, same decorative tower. All the land used to be part of a huge rancho, back when California was part of Mexico. The two properties didn't get split up until Borys and Henka Perleman emigrated from Poland around 1900. They bought their parcel from Steve's great-grandparents, the original *Californios*." Shirley paused. "Must be fun, puttering around an old house like that. Find anything interesting? Antiques or old family heirlooms or anything?"

Paisley thought about the jewelry Jonathan had mentioned. Did Shirley know about it? "Someone put sheets over the furniture and emptied the fridge when Esther moved out," she said evasively, fingering her water glass, "but otherwise it looks pretty much as it must have when she lived there. She has a nice record collection."

Shirley looked disappointed. "That's it, huh?"

Paisley didn't want to talk about how Ian thought he saw a strange resemblance between her and Esther's ancestor, Ruth Klaczko. Nor did she want to bring up the unsettling dreams that first day in the house.

"Nothing other than the ordinary things you'd expect," she lied. "Nothing that sheds any light on the history of the house. Although...." Paisley wrinkled her forehead. "If the family lived there so long, you'd think there would be more documents, photo albums, and things of that sort lying around. All I've seen is a few old pictures on the wall."

"Esther wasn't sentimental. And she wasn't overly fond of her family members." Shirley finished off her fish and beckoned the server over to order chocolate lava cake for dessert, asking for two spoons." Turning back to Paisley, she continued, "Esther offered me a box of old books when Jonathan's parents moved out, mostly Ellery Queen and other pulp writers that weren't to her taste. I was hoping you might have found some more stuff in the attic I could sell. I pay cash, as long as it's marketable."

Paisley considered. "Esther did have a lot of paperbacks. Mostly romantic suspense, mysteries, and that sort of thing. Can you use them?"

Shirley perked up. "Kindle and Amazon will put me out of business eventually, but there are still people who prefer to cuddle up with a good, old-fashioned book. Bring me what you've got and I'll make an offer. Or, if you prefer, I'll come by. I'd love to see the inside of Esther's house again."

"'Again?'"

Shirley chuckled. "Honey, I've been in that old house a hundred times. When I was a kid, I used to play under that big oak tree with Jonathan until his grandma came out and chased us away. It was a great place to play Tarzan and Jane, or pirates, or astronauts."

"Did you know Esther well?" Paisley asked. "Outside of working together on the community theater plays, I mean."

"Sure. I used to go over to her house to play cards every month with a group from the historical society. Esther would tell hilarious stories about teaching high school in Sacramento, and serve us Polish sausages, sauerkraut, and homemade lemonade." Shirley smacked her lips reminiscently, her eyes shining behind the lenses of her glasses. "We'd stay up until two in the morning, having a grand old time."

"Esther was a teacher?"

"Yup, she taught at McClatchy High, I think it was. They have some kind of magnet program there. She came back here some twenty years ago, after Jonathan's parents moved to Florida."

"What subject did she teach?"

"History. Losing her family in the Holocaust must have given her a certain perspective on world events, don't you think?" Shirley grew uncharacteristically sober. "Esther encouraged teenagers to make a difference in life, and some took on the challenge. Her students became doctors, ambassadors, and politicians—*good* ones. Once Esther returned, she made it a project to turn River Bend into a better place to live, too. Those pretty flower baskets hanging from the lamp poles? Her idea. The new senior center?" Shirley shrugged. "She ran fundraisers until they could afford to buy the old Moose hall and fix it up."

"What about the community theater? How did Esther start that?"

Shirley settled more comfortably in her seat. "The school district said they didn't have funds to continue the high school drama program, so Esther brought her numerous friends to the board meeting. She bullied the members until they granted use of the high school auditorium, as long as she raised money for the program. Sure enough, she pulled together a group of volunteers to run it, including me. No one thought it was possible, but Esther managed it."

"I wonder why Jonathan never told me about it," Paisley mused. "If both he and his great-aunt had an interest in theater, it's even stranger that...." She broke off.

Shirley prompted, her hazel eyes bright with curiosity. "That what?"

It was the question that had puzzled her from the beginning. "That she left the house to me, not to Jonathan. He was her nephew, after all, the closest living relative she had, except a long-lost cousin back east."

Shirley eyed her shrewdly. "You mean you really don't know? Come on, you were married to the guy."

Paisley blushed. She was well aware of Jonathan's flaws. They had fought over them often enough: his stubbornness, his insistence on doing things his own way. And, then, of course, that last, awful argument in the hotel room.... Paisley's fingernails dug painfully into her palms.

"Look." Shirley rested her jowels on her hand, plump elbow braced on the counter. "We all admired Jonathan's talent, but the truth is, when he left he didn't leave behind many friends. Most of his family were pretty much the same. Cold and aloof, selfish. All except Esther. She must have been a throwback to the European branch of the family."

Paisley remained silent, and Shirley cocked a sparse eyebrow. "You're not contradicting me. It was no secret Esther wasn't a big fan of her own relatives here in River Bend. In fact, when Jonathan surprised everyone by marrying you...." She stopped, gulped down a too-big bite of chocolate cake, and began coughing.

Paisley was dying to hear what her companion had been about to say. Fighting down her curiosity, she waited until Shirley caught her breath.

Shirley drained her glass of water and looked over the top of her thick-framed glasses at Paisley. "What the heck, I'll tell you. We were at rehearsal ... that year it was *The Music Man* ... and during one of the cast breaks, Esther told me, *a propos* of nothing, 'You know, Shirley, I feel sorry for that lovely young girl that Jonathan just married. She's not at all what I expected.' Those were her exact words." Shirley's eyes twinkled behind her glasses. "You must have made quite an impression on her. That, you see, is why she left you the house."

"I still don't understand," Paisley murmured.

"Oh come on, honey. You put on an act of being tough, like so many girls these days, and yet you agreed to have lunch when it would have been easy to brush me off. How many famous opera stars would do that? Here you are, showing interest in the life of an even older woman you hardly knew, Esther Perleman. To me, that spells *mensch,* as Esther would put it. That was a quality lacking in most of the American side of her family."

Paisley grimaced. Once, maybe, Shirley's description might have fit, before she'd met Jonathan and learned one had to fight to get what one wanted. "Thanks," she muttered.

"Kindness isn't exactly in vogue these days. Maybe it's a good thing you've developed that protective shell. Not everyone can be trusted. Even in River Bend."

Paisley looked at her new friend's suddenly serious round face. The somber warning sounded out of place in this restaurant decorated with fishing nets and filled with chattering day-trippers carrying cell phones and wearing baseball caps. "Don't worry. I can take care of myself."

Shirley's face wreathed itself in its usual cheerful smile. "Good. Hey, if you don't have any plans this afternoon, drop by the rehearsal for *Pirates of Penzance.* You might get a kick out of it. Three o'clock in the high school auditorium. Nathan's mom is bringing donuts."

"What about your bookstore?"

Shirley shrugged. "I'll hang up a 'gone-fishing' sign. One of the perks of living in a small town."

Paisley tried to think of a polite way to refuse. Attending a noisy rehearsal with a bunch of high school kids didn't interest her, but she had already admitted having no plans for the afternoon. "Okay," she said reluctantly. What could it hurt?

Not until later did she realize that phrase sounded like famous last words.

Instead of going home before rehearsal, Paisley used Shirley's old desktop computer to browse the Internet. On Wikipedia, she read about Ruth Perleman's brief singing career as "The Nightingale of Warsaw," but there was no picture with the text. The account merely listed the roles for which the singer had been known, mostly obscure German operas, along with her birth and death dates. Nothing more. Nothing to prove her dreams were anything more than that—dreams.

She logged out while Shirley rang up purchases for a pair of tourists. In the bookcase, Paisley saw another copy of *True Stories of Northern California*, reminding her of the one sitting on her nightstand at home, unread. The awkward prose and blurry photographs had not been able to compete with the old paperback mysteries in Auntie Esther's downstairs bookcase.

She took it down and flipped through its pages. After detailed histories of Napa, Calistoga, and Sonoma came a short chapter one about River Bend. Settling on a metal folding chair in the back of the store, she read highlights of the town's history from the the original Spanish land grant to a regional championship by the local high-school wrestling team. The only reference to the Perleman family was a grainy snapshot of Jonathan at age seventeen accepting a national high-school orchestra award, looking skinny and impossibly young.

Upon closer examination, Paisley was rewarded by a footnote mentioning Auntie Esther's house. The text informed her that the house was acquired from its builder by Esther's uncle, Borys Perleman, who immigrated from Warsaw with his wife, Henka, in

1914. Venturing west to California as a peddler, he had settled in River Bend and opened a dry goods store. The home was "a particularly good example of the Queen Anne style, similar to a larger house constructed by the same builder on the adjacent lot."

That was all.

Disappointed, Paisley returned the book to the shelf and wandered outside. Shirley, still chatting with the tourists, waved good-bye. As she passed the senior center, Paisley heard a bingo caller's clarion voice drift through the open window. The two white-haired men she'd met before were still at their chess game on the sidewalk outside, looking as if they hadn't budged.

The tall one with red suspenders sensed her presence first. He looked up and winked at her. "Well, hello there! Pull up a chair, young lady, and I'll show you how an expert plays this game."

Paisley obliged with a smile. Soon she was fast friends with Hugo Smith and Walter Conti and was even talked into playing a game with the winner, which she lost with humiliating speed. With more finesse than Shirley, the men pried out the same information about her background and plans for the summer. In turn they reminisced about her late husband when he was young, and his increasingly evident musical prodigy. Both claimed to be the first to predict his success.

"Talented family," Walter stated, nodding his white-bearded head for emphasis. "All of 'em were musical, but everyone knew Jonathan would make it big. I gave him his first job, you know, before I sold the gas station and retired." He chuckled. "Truth is, he wasn't much good at it. Always studying music scores under the counter and ignoring the customers. Had to let him go after a couple of weeks, but by then he'd already got news of his scholarship to Julliard so he didn't care."

"Jonathan was the biggest thing to ever come out of River Bend," Hugo agreed, hooking his thumbs under his suspenders. "Even now, we sometimes get visitors from as far away as San Francisco wanting to see where the maestro grew up. Then they stop for apple pie at Rosie's Diner, gas up their cars, and maybe stop at a coupla antique stores. We don't get as many tourists as Calistoga or Napa, 'course, but any extra traffic helps."

"People come to see where Jonathan grew up?" repeated Paisley, touched by the news. Jonathan had never shown much interest in his home town. She suspected he hadn't known or cared how the local residents followed his career, nor the pride they took in his success. Now she wished she'd insisted he visit River Bend once in a while.

"Now, looky here," Hugo said sternly, looking at Walter over the top of his spectacles. "No sense reminding this young lady of her loss. I apologize for my friend's thoughtlessness, Mrs. Perleman. I know this must be a hard time for you."

She shook her head. "Call me Paisley. And it's okay. I'm fine." Oddly, it was true. She could now think of Jonathan without a stab of mixed grief and anger. Perhaps she was starting to heal. "Tell me about his Great-aunt Esther," she said to change the subject. "Did you know her well?"

"'Course we did." Hugo settled back in his seat, his expression softening. "Everyone around here did. Not just because it's a small town, either. Esther liked to join things. She was always in the middle of everything, putting in her two cents and getting things done. The little lady was a pint-size dynamo." He chuckled, and Paisley wondered with a jolt of surprise if Hugo and Esther might have enjoyed a flirtation while she was still been alive. Why not?

"Did she come to the senior center often?" She tried to picture Esther playing chess or bingo.

Walter shook his white head. "Nope. She didn't have time to hang out with 'old' folks. If she ever dropped by it was to serve lunch, organize activities, or try to get everyone to buy tickets to that play she put on every year. Most of us would go, to support her and because it was a hecka lot of fun."

Hecka? Paisley blinked at the odd phrase, then remembered Jonathan had used it once or twice when he forgot himself. Maybe a Northern California regionalism?

"The kids always seemed to get a kick out of it, too." Hugo pushed his golf hat back to reveal a high pink forehead. "Not a lot to do in a town like this, as you can imagine. The theater kept 'em out of trouble. She kept the plays going until her first stroke a year and a half ago. That's when she went to live at the senior home, up on route 70."

Paisley had forgotten that Esther had ended her days in a full-care institution. The thought dampened her mood.

Walter noticed. "Don't worry, it's a nice place, as far as those kind of facilities go, and it wasn't as if she didn't have friends up there." He looked over at Hugo, scratching his ear. "Why, Georgiana's been up at Sunny Acres for a couple of years now, hasn't she?"

Hugo nodded, his head bobbing up and down on his long neck as if on a spring. "Talked to her just last Thursday. It was her birthday. Ninety-one years old and doesn't look a day over seventy. Still pretty as a peach."

Walter swung his head back in Paisley's direction. "Georgiana was a good friend of Esther's. If you have any questions about your husband's great-aunt, she's the one to ask."

"I will." Glancing at her watch, Paisley got to her feet. "Sorry to run, but if I miss rehearsal, Shirley will be disappointed."

"Come back and see us some time." Walter winked. "Maybe you'll have better luck winning at chess."

The men half-stood, legs creaking, and lifted their golf caps as she left. Wishing she hadn't agreed to go to the rehearsal, Paisley turned her steps toward River Bend High School, visible three blocks away.

Pushing through unlocked double doors, Paisley was struck by a blend of smells reminiscent of her own high-school years: sweaty locker rooms, greasy remnants of cafeteria food, industrial-

strength cleaning solutions, dusty textbooks, and Old Spice
cologne. The ringing sound of her footsteps walking down the
empty, recently waxed corridor brought back a mix of memories
as well. Back then her love of opera, ignited during that never-
forgotten field trip, hadn't exactly branded her as "cool." Music
and drama teachers had been supportive, but not until she started
winning competitions at the conservatory had she gained
confidence and pride in her soprano voice, so unexpectedly
powerful pouring from her small frame.

The school auditorium was easy to find: she merely followed
the loud, high-pitched chatter that spilled out into the hall. A hand-
scrawled sign had been taped to the door on lined notebook paper:
"Stay Out - Rehearsal!!!!" Ignoring it, she took a deep breath and
pushed through.

A group of teenage girls in tank tops and shorts sat on the
stage, all long hair and long limbs, swinging tanned legs, chatting,
and texting on sequined cell phones. Boys sporting that year's
fashion in haircuts clustered like ants around an almost empty
oversized box of donuts. Considerably raising the average age in
the room was a tall gray-haired woman with a crepey throat,
playing arpeggios on a battered piano despite the pandemonium
around her. Several other adults ran around, frantically trying to
wrangle order from the chaos. One of them was Shirley.

A few moments later, she hustled up to Paisley, panting. "Bad
news," she said. "I just got a call from our music director. She's
having contractions."

It took a moment for Paisley to understand. "She's pregnant?"

Shirley nodded, her plump face showing lines of stress. "The
baby's not due for three months, so the doctor has ordered
complete bed rest. I hate to ask this, Paisley, but would you mind
filling in for her for today? I mean, you do have the right
background, after all."

Paisley shrank back. It was one thing to watch rehearsal as a
detached observer. Being an active participant was something else

altogether. She opened her mouth to tell Shirley this, but all that came out was "Uh...."

"Thanks, Paisley." Shirley shoved a sheaf of music into her arms. "We're doing a full-cast rehearsal of the Finale of Act I today. Normally I wouldn't dream of asking you to do this, but since it's an emergency.... You do know the songs for *The Pirates of Penzance*, don't you?"

"I'm familiar with the music, but...."

"I knew I could count on you." Shirley was gone. A gaggle of teenagers drifted toward Paisley, looking at her expectantly. She stared back at them, feeling panicked. She hadn't been around so many high school students since ... well, since high school.

"I ... uh... hello, everybody."

"So what do you want us to do?" A pretty blond drummed her fingernails impatiently on the edge of the stage while waiting for an answer. Paisley recognized her as the server she had seen at the café on Main Street, although the girl looked different with her hair around her shoulders, wearing denim shorts and a bright-pink T-shirt. The elderly piano player waited, knobby fingers curved expectantly over the keyboard.

"I guess we'll run through the first ensemble piece. Here, please pass out these scores." Paisley unloaded the stack on the blond and rubbed her sweaty palms on her jeans, trying not to look nervous. Jonathan had been the conductor, not her. But Shirley was right: Paisley was no novice in this setting. Reminding herself of this, she raised her voice and put steel in it.

"All right, everyone. Onto the stage." She would get back at Shirley later for putting her on the spot like this. Fortunately she had once starred in a production in Ohio shortly before meeting Jonathan, and loved the play.

The cast straggled onto the stage, and Paisley quickly realized the absent musical director had not worked on blocking yet. Or if so, everyone had forgotten their positions. She spent the next ten minutes shuffling cast members around on the stage until the arrangement of characters worked smoothly. Then she realized the Pirate King was missing.

Someone eventually found Nathan in the lighting booth. He was playing a game on his phone, feet propped on the equipment, the empty the box of donuts next to him. The boy took his mark with bad grace, wiping powdered sugar from the corner of his sulky mouth. Despite his lacking charm or stage presence, he had a decent voice and could hit the right notes most of the time—no doubt why Shirley had cast him as the Pirate King.

At Paisley's nod, the piano player struck up the melody, and the students faltered through *Oh Men of Dark and Dismal Fate*. The lead actors, of course, were the best singers. The pretty blond server from the café, Chloe, had the part of Mabel. That girl had potential, Paisley thought, tapping her foot in time to the music as the company launched into the next song. With some one-on-one time, she could pull a decent performance out of Chloe and the others.

Except, of course, Paisley reminded herself firmly, she was only helping out today.

Then, of course, there were the hopeless ones, a few kids in the chorus who couldn't carry a tune in the proverbial bucket. One couldn't kick them out, of course: for a production like this, as many warm bodies as possible were needed to fill the stage. Paisley admired Shirley for scraping together a respectable-sized cast from such a tiny town. The feat was nothing short of miraculous.

As the rehearsal continued, she noted each of the students' strengths and weaknesses and thought how the less talented singers could be used to comic effect. That tall gawky kid with the wispy brown beard and awkward gait, for example, might make a perfect head policeman. His amusing awkwardness, put to good purpose, could bring the house down....

She spent the next few hours like a drill sergeant, running the performers through vocal exercises, making them repeat the trouble spots over and over, and separating them into sections to practice their parts together. Finally she brought the company back together to try it again. Her increasingly raspy voice was too weak to bark directions, but someone found her a microphone, and sipping frequently from a bottle of water, she managed to get through the afternoon.

Before she realized it, rehearsal was over.

"'Bye, Mrs. P," one of the boys said, the tall one with the wispy beard, as he picked up his backpack and strolled toward the exit. "See you around, huh?"

"Bye," she said automatically. "And please, call me Paisley."

As the rest of the students trickled away in small groups, singing snatches of the songs they had been rehearsing and giggling, she found that she hoped the play would turn out well. Really, the actors only needed some tweaking: a suggestion here, a correction there. The potential was clearly present. She felt like a master painter who couldn't resist picking up the paintbrush and correcting a line on the canvas.

Hopefully the pregnant musical director would be able to return. If not, Paisley prayed that Shirley would find someone skillful to fill the slot. After all their hard work, these kids deserved a chance to pull off a decent production. Heck, maybe she'd even attend opening night to cheer them on. It would be interesting to see if any of her ideas helped, such as that suggestion she'd made for the first scene, where the girls came out single file twirling their parasols. She'd thought of a couple of casting changes as well.

Shirley reappeared, bearing an armload of costumes. "Sorry," she said, panting. "I swear, I wasn't planning on dragging you into this. I did hope that you might volunteer to give us a few pointers, but when Marcie didn't turn up, I panicked. I don't know a lick about music."

"It's okay. I enjoyed it." The fact surprised Paisley. She took another swig from her water bottle and opened her mouth to tell Shirley about her casting ideas, but Shirley rushed on.

"Gee, that's really good to hear, because Marcie just called back. She said the doctor wants her to stay in bed until the baby's born."

Paisley stiffened, guessing what was coming next.

Shirley's brown eyes were pleading behind her glasses. "Look, I know you're new in town and you don't have any obligation to help out. But you did a fantastic job today. The kids really seem to like you. Is there any way you can fill in tomorrow, as well? Just until I can find someone else to take over. I swear, I'll do anything."

Paisley wanted to say "No." Instead, what came out was, "Um, I'll think about it. Can I give you a call later?"

"Sure. You're the best." Shirley looked relieved. "No pressure, I'll understand if you say 'no.' Say, can I give you a lift home? I know you came on foot, and with that limp and all, it's the least I can do. No luck finding a car yet, huh?"

Paisley thought about the scare she'd had crossing the field yesterday and her scraped knee throbbed again. She really didn't feel like walking home again, especially with night coming on. And Shirley was right about her limp. She was supposed to be taking it easy.

"Thanks," she said. "But I can't keep bumming rides off you every time I come to town. I haven't found any suitable cars on Craigslist. Do you know anyone around here who has one they want get rid of?"

"You poor thing, I promised to help and I completely forgot! I'll ask around. I give you my word.

As Shirley drove Paisley home, they chatted about the play, the weather, and politics. Shirley was much more interested in the latter than Paisley, who didn't follow any national news, and merely mumbled "uh huh, uh huh," to everything her companion said. When Paisley mentioned her ideas for the casting changes, however, Shirley listened with interest.

"You're right about the Major General," she said. "The boy I put in the part doesn't look older than twelve, even in makeup, and he doesn't really want to do it. But no one else can say the patter fast enough. Maybe...."

They discussed the casting problems until they arrived at the little white house sheltered under the big protective oak. Once again, Paisley felt the surge of homecoming leap inside her chest.

Shirley waved as Paisley opened the passenger door. "Thanks again, hon. Let me know what you decide, okay? And I'll ask around about a car."

Silence settled around Paisley like a comforter as she watched Shirley's Volvo disappear down the dark road. The quiet was so heavy that she could hear the cooing of birds in the oak tree overhead, the whisper of a breeze rustling through the long grass. She felt relaxed, calm, peaceful ... even happy.

When she set a foot on the first step of the porch, a tall figure peeled itself from where it had been sitting in the rocker and loomed over her, causing her to gasp and grope in her purse for a can of mace..

Then the moon glinted off a thatch of sandy hair and she practically shrieked her relief. "Ian! What are you doing here?"

"I didn't expect you to be out this late." Standing with fists on his hips, he looked and sounded like an outraged father waiting up for a teen-age daughter.

"Why are you still here?" Paisley countered. "Aren't you and your crew finished for the day?" Belatedly, she realized there was something different about him. It was in the tone of his voice, and in the air of excitement that hung about him like the subtle scent of his aftershave. *Aftershave?*

"What is it?" she asked, pausing at the door with the key in her hand. "Did something happen? Is everything all right?"

"I found something today when we took down the wall between the bathroom and the second bedroom."

Her heart nearly flew through her chest as he thrust out a battered cardboard container somewhat larger than a shoebox. It was covered with a thick layer of dust and sealed with yellowed cellophane tape.

"This was hidden between the framing," Ian told her. "As you can see, somebody must have placed it in there a long time ago. I thought you might be interested."

"You haven't opened it?"

"It's yours, isn't it? That's why I waited for you."

Her fingers closed convulsively over the box. The story Jonathan had told her about Esther and the lost jewels... could it have been true after all?

"But where—?" she began.

"Come on, I'll show you."

Still clutching the box, she followed him up to the smallest bedroom, the one with the sharply slanting ceiling and the view of the oak tree outside the window. His crew had started to pull down an interior wall to get to the mold, Ian explained, when they saw the box hidden behind the plaster. "A long time ago someone cut a hole in the wall, and later it was wallpapered over. Interesting, huh?" His breath warmed the nape of her neck as she bent to examine the opening in the wall. "Just like that TV show, *If These Walls Could Talk*. Alix wanted to open the box right away, but I said no, it belongs to you." He added, "I wonder what's in it?"

She did not react to the hint. Her nails left small dents in the sides of the box. If the story was real ... her heart beat faster. No more money concerns. No more bill collectors, no need to take on a job at the conservatory. Funny how money could make all problems go away, she thought. Paisley had never been more aware of the fact than in that moment.

Ian was waiting. "Well?" he prodded. "Aren't you going to open it?"

Not with you watching, she thought. She forced a weak smile, the best she could manage. "I'd rather do it alone, if you don't mind."

A disappointed expression flitted across his features. He straightened, a complicated procedure reminding her of a camel rising, all long legs and joints. "Oh. I see. Okay, fine."

He's hurt, she thought. *He waited to share his discovery with me, and now I've hurt his feelings.* The realization made her feel guilty. But not guilty enough to let him stay and watch. The contents of the box were hers, and hers alone. She had no desire to share the discovery with anyone, especially a young architecture student whom she barely knew, and who had lied to her about his contracting business — or lack thereof.

"I'm sorry," she said, touching his arm in an effort to reassure him and leaving a smear of gray dust on his skin. He must have showered and changed after finishing work, probably the same time he'd put on the after-shave. "Thank you for keeping the box safe. I'll tell you what's inside tomorrow. I promise."

"Sure," he said flatly. "Okay, gotta go. Hot date tonight." He nodded an abrupt good-bye and headed downstairs. She watched through the window while he strode toward his truck, the long form quickly swallowed up in the shadows.

A hot date? That explained the aftershave, she thought, standing on the porch and watching the pickup's tail lights fade into the distance. Paisley wondered mildly who the girl was, and if he was going to stop at home long enough to change again. Or maybe his girlfriend liked rumpled T-shirts and jeans with the knees worn out. Maybe they were going to an evening monster truck rally, or something.

Then she remembered her conversation with Shirley over lunch. No, Ian wouldn't be going to a monster truck rally. An architecture student was likely to have more intellectual hobbies. Maybe he and his date were going to an anti-war demonstration in

San Francisco, or a foreign movie in Berkeley, or a raw-food restaurant in Oakland.

Remembering she was still holding the cardboard box, she hurried to the kitchen, set it on the table, and got out a sharp knife. Her hand trembled slightly, and she had to wait a moment before slicing through the crumbling tape. Lifting off the lid, she stood, staring down at its contents.

Chapter Six

Paisley's heart sank. No jewels. Nothing but an old doll with a cracked china head and soiled clothes, a child's tea set, a molding bird's nest, and a folded letter. The treasure was nothing but a cache of sentimental keepsakes, valueless to anyone but the person who had put them there.

Shoving aside her disappointment, she picked up the doll and examined it. The stuffing in the cloth body was coming out, and the lace on the once-pink dress was torn and filthy, as if someone had dragged it through a ditch. The porcelain head smiled coquettishly up at her. She turned the doll over, wondering idly how old it was. Seventy-five years? A hundred? She had seen something like it on Antiques Roadshow once, but that one had been in far better condition. This one might fetch twenty bucks. If that much.

The letter raised her interest. The light-blue paper, thin as tissue, was folded over like an envelope. Carefully she opened it and experienced her second stab of disappointment. The tiny, precise handwriting was in a foreign language she didn't recognize. Even some of the letters were unfamiliar.

She put the envelope back in the box, and didn't bother to take out the china tea set. Like the doll, it was cracked and obviously worthless.

Setting the box on a shelf in her bedroom closet, Paisley rested her forehead against the door jamb, trying to overcome her disappointment, made keener by an even more unpleasant sensation of guilt. She was uncomfortably aware that she had been unfair to Ian. He had gone to the trouble to save the box for her, although he had obviously been as curious as she was.

Why hadn't he opened it? She suspected most workmen might not have hesitated to look inside. Had there been valuables inside, Ian could have kept them, and she would never have known about the discovery. Some might not even have been honest enough to report the find. But he had not looked. He had not kept it. The old, fragile tape remained intact, the thick layer of dust a testament to his honesty.

A voice inside whispered she should have allowed Ian to share the excitement of opening the box with her. It would have cost her nothing. Her refusal seemed selfish. Maybe that's what greed did to a person, she thought with a sudden pang of self-loathing. She had hoped Ruth's jewels were inside the box, and she had wanted to hoard the discovery to herself. To think Shirley had called her a *mensch*!

Tomorrow, she thought. Tomorrow she would show Ian the box's contents. That would salve her conscience, and redeem her in his eyes. She did not ask herself why it should matter what he thought of her.

The next day, however, Paisley's resolve to show Ian what she had found in the old box wavered. In last night's burst of sentimentality she'd forgotten that Ian was working under false pretenses. Weren't there legal ramifications for working without a license? All the renovations might have to be torn down, and she had neither the time nor the money to start over.

But when she looked around at the repairs that had taken place, they appeared to her untrained eye to have been done beautifully. No, she decided, there was no reason to report him to whomever one was supposed to report such things to.

From her vantage on the front porch, she watched Ian walk up the path, his helpers behind him. As a means of atonement for her rudeness, she had arisen early and made blueberry muffins using a recipe she had found in the old cookbook from the pantry, and the house smelled heavenly.

Ian saw the basket of golden-topped muffins waiting on the side table just outside the front door, and his face brightened. "Hey, these look homemade!" He bent over and sniffed. "I wouldn't have thought you were the type to bake."

"I can't imagine why you would assume that," she said, not sure whether to be offended. "I love to cook and bake, when I have time."

It was true. She wasn't much of a homebody, but she had always found baking relaxing, although there had been little time for it these past few years. Eating out was more convenient when one lived on the road, and she hadn't realized until now that she enjoyed having her own kitchen.

"I can't take full credit for these," Paisley added. "The recipe was Esther's. I found her personal cookbook while cleaning the kitchen. Here, everybody, have one." She passed the basket around to Ian's crew, who had gathered hopefully around, filling the cramped porch.

After Quinn, Rusty, and Alix gobbled up several muffins each and finally went off to finish their work, she pulled up a rocking chair for Ian and nudged the basket closer to his elbow, while she sat in the porch swing. "Have another one, there's plenty more," she encouraged. "So, what are you working on today?"

He eyed her while devouring the muffin, as if wondering what motive lay behind her sudden affability. "We're finishing the bathroom and putting up drywall in the bedroom, over the wall we tore up yesterday. I brought some paint samples, so you can pick out the color. Maybe yellow in the bedroom, like it was before. And light blue would look nice with those black-and-white tiles in the bathroom; that would be historically accurate, too. Or you could try a patterned wallpaper. Tomorrow, we'll be patching the roof. After that, all that's left is...."

She listened, nodding from time to time. When Ian finished the last crumb and started to unfold his legs to get up, she stopped him by laying a hand on his arm. "Wait a minute. I have something to show you."

Paisley brought the unsealed box outside and gave it to him, like a cat presenting a gift of a mouse. He looked at it, then at her. "I should have shown you this last night," she admitted, hanging her head. "After all, it was your discovery. Go ahead, look inside, but I hope you're not disappointed. It just seems to be some old junk."

"It's okay, you didn't have to—wow!" He reached into the box and lifted out the letter. "What do you mean, 'junk?' Look at this!"

She shrugged. "I did. It's just an old letter to Esther."

"Just an old letter?" he repeated, incredulous. "Is that all you think it is?"

Paisley peered over his shoulder. "Why? Is it something important?"

He turned it over to inspect the back. "Esther would have just arrived from Poland when this was written. It must be from one of her family members there." He squinted at a faint postmark on one of the envelopes. "Hard to make out, but it looks like it says 1930-something. Is that an eight or a nine?"

She stepped in closer to see, detecting lingering hints of the cologne he'd worn last night. "A nine, I think. You're right. Do you think this letter might be from Esther's parents?"

"Or from her grandparents, or one of her aunts and uncles." He looked at her critically. "You mean you haven't opened it yet? You've had it since last night."

"Like I said, I couldn't read it."

His eyes widened. "Aren't you even curious?"

She drew back and heard her tone grow defensive. "What does it matter, anyway? Everything happened so long ago. And why are you so interested, anyway?"

"Because I was Esther's friend, and her death was a loss to our whole town. She brought it to life. Everyone around here liked her, as far as I know."

Paisley remembered Ian's familiarity with the photograph of Ruth Klaczko in the hallway. "I'll bet you used to come over here and chat with her, just like Shirley used to do. And those two men at the senior center. Was everybody Esther's buddy?"

"Just about." Ian's eyes lit reminiscently. "She was a heck of a woman. Hardly ever talked about her childhood, but it was obvious she'd been through a lot. She was a survivor, even if she never actually spent time in a concentration camp."

"You're too young to have been one of her students. She had already retired by the time she moved to River Bend."

Ian leaned back in his chair, his long legs sprawled out. "I used to walk by here on my way home from school every day. Esther used to sit on the porch, right where you are now. She'd call me over, stuff me with muffins. Just like these. She'd ask about my day, listen to my self-pitying complaints, and give me advice. She's the one who insisted I apply to Berkeley. Helped me find a scholarship, too, or I couldn't have afforded it."

"How nice." Paisley's eyes misted over. She had come to think of Auntie Esther as her own personal good fairy, but it sounded as if Esther had played a similar role for others also.

"Take a closer look at this." Ian held out the faded aerogramme. "This is your history, now. Who knows? Maybe you'll learn something interesting."

Shrugging, she bent her head over the letter. "All I can understand is the signature: *Adelajda Perleman*." The name looked strange, but it was definitely legible. She looked up. "So you're right. This must be a letter from one of Esther's relatives. But that doesn't help much, since I don't speak Polish any more than you do." She stopped. "Or do you?"

For all she knew, Ian McMullin might be able to speak seven languages fluently and juggle flaming batons while riding a unicycle. She was learning new things about him all the time. But he shook his head.

"Then how can we get it translated?" she wondered. Ian's curiosity was contagious.

"There are Internet translation programs, but even better, I know someone who can do it for us," Ian said, holding out his hand for the letter. "Do you mind?"

She was oddly hesitant to give it up. But there was something solid and reliable about him, in spite of, or perhaps because of, his slow speech and lanky physique. His eyes gazed guilelessly into hers. For the first time, she noticed that they were rather attractive light-gray eyes, intelligent and frank, fringed by long lashes several shades darker than his hair. A long-dormant sensation stirred inside her, surprising her.

"Okay." She handed over the envelope. "But I want it back."

"Don't worry." He put the letter in his shirt pocket and patted it reassuringly, then leveraged himself to his feet, smiling down at her.

Suddenly it seemed clear why Ian had taken on the job of repairing the house. Not just for the money, although surely that was part of it. He must see the work as a way of paying his respects to Esther. That explained his ridiculously low fee.

Feeling a rush of warmth toward him, she returned the lid to the box, and a puff of dust rose into the air. "Thanks again for telling me about this. If you find anything else interesting, let me know, okay? And I promise to share the next reveal with you."

Ian's head came up. "'Anything else'? Just how many long-lost boxes are you expecting to be hidden away in these walls, anyway?"

She tried hard to look innocent. "I just mean that if you happen to stumble across anything else that seems unusual or odd or—" Paisley snapped her mouth shut.

A hearty voice boomed out behind them, making her jump: "Well, well, look what the cat dragged in. Hello, Ian. I didn't expect to find you here."

Engrossed in their conversation, neither of them had seen or heard the black Chevy Tahoe pull up behind them. She wondered if Ray had heard their conversation through the open car window.

Ray extricated his bulky frame from the driver's seat and sauntered toward the porch, grinning. She hid the box behind her. Not that it mattered, she told herself. The contents were perfectly innocent. But for some reason, she wanted to keep their findings private.

"So Ian's doing your repairs, eh?" Ray said to Paisley. "What happened to my old buddy, Bruce Harris?"

"His calender was full."

"You shoulda told me. I coulda got you in." He glanced at Ian. "Remember, Mrs. Perleman, you get what you pay for."

Ian looked as if a cat had just dropped a lizard tail at his feet. "What brings you here?" he asked.

"Well, Ian, I heard you'd taken on the job and thought I'd better come out and take a look-see. Contractors can get in a lot of trouble working without a license, you know."

Ian's prominent ears turned red, but his voice did not change. "What makes you think I don't have a license?"

"Just a guess. Didn't you once say you'd rather put a gun to your head than go into your dad's line of business?"

"I don't see how that's any of your business."

Ray's smile broadened. "What a nice guy, helping out the pretty little lady."

"So why are you here, Ray?" Paisley asked.

Ray turned toward her. His broad good-old-boy smile returned. "Like I said, I heard you were going ahead with fixing up the house," he said. "Looks like it's coming along all right, as far as I can tell without a full-on inspection."

For a moment, she wondered if Ian had, in fact, pulled all the necessary permits, and if he had, indeed, kept his license up-to-date. The work looked solid enough to her, but the truth was, she had no way of knowing.

"Still thinking of selling when you're through?" Ray asked her.

"You know I am," she said. "I never intended to stay here permanently."

"I got a couple more nibbles from prospective buyers. Come by the office some time, and we'll go over things. Set a price, put up another sign, get the place listed on the MLS."

"I'm not ready yet."

"Remember, it takes time to sell a house. Opportunities don't come along that often, out here." Ray didn't add, "in the sticks," but the implication was clear.

"Thanks."

Ray touched the brim of an imaginary hat, nodded pleasantly at Ian, whose face was still red with anger, and got back in his big black SUV.

After the car disappeared around the curve in the road, she turned on Ian. "Which reminds me," Paisley said accusingly. "Why didn't you tell me?"

He stared down at her, his face blank. "Tell you what?"

"That you're not a real contractor."

"I *am* a real contractor. I worked for my dad every summer after I turned fourteen, and my license doesn't expire for another two months." He pulled a beat-up leather wallet out of his back pocket and waved a card at her. "Look. Everything I've done on your house is legal. I pulled permits and everything."

She wasn't finished. "I still don't understand. When I telephoned that first day, why didn't you say your father's business no longer existed?"

"You sounded desperate to get the job done. Just because I'm studying architecture now doesn't mean I can't still pick up a hammer and a saw. I knew I could do the work better than Bruce Harris for a fraction of what he'd charge. On a crazy impulse I thought I'd do you a favor."

"How did you know that I called Bruce Harris first?"

"That real estate agent of yours, Ray Henderson, always feeds his customers to Harris. The rivalry between him and my dad goes way back. I'll admit it gave me a little satisfaction to snatch you out of the shark's mouth. Besides," he added, ears reddening, "I can use extra money. My scholarship only covers tuition, and architecture textbooks are expensive." He paused to take a deep breath. "Besides, this place has good memories for me. If I could scrape together the money, I'd buy it from you myself."

She frowned. "Hmmm. That's interesting. Steve told me the house was only worth tearing down."

"Steve? Steve Lopez?"

"Do you know him?"

"This is a small town." Ian sounded grim. "Everybody knows everybody. Yeah, I know Steve. Reserved type. Likes the finer things in life. You and he must get along real well."

She thought about telling him that Steve had invited her to dinner, and discarded the idea. It was none of Ian's business anyway.

"He didn't sound too happy to hear you were working on my house," she admitted. "I can understand the professional rivalry between Ray Henderson and your dad, but what does Steve have against you?"

Ian shrugged. "I don't know. He's a few years older than me, so I never knew him that well. Steve moved back east after high school and didn't come back until inheriting his father's property. I know he wants your land too, but I don't see that it's his business what you do with it."

"Nor do I." Paisley passed up the opportunity to remind Ian that it wasn't his business either. She picked up the dusty box and headed toward the kitchen.

He took the hint and started toward the back of the house. "As for that letter, I'll take it to my friend," he said over his shoulder. "I'll let you know what it says later, okay?"

"Thanks," she called back, turning on the kitchen faucet to rinse the grit off her hands. She thought that Ian was like one of those genealogy enthusiasts one read about, fascinated by anything from the past.

Thanks to Ian, Paisley was curious what that old letter said too. She was no historian, but she knew that a lot happened in Europe in 1939, little of it good.

Living in this old house surrounded by Esther's possessions, it was impossible not to feel connected to the old woman's past. No doubt that was the reason for those disturbingly real dreams Paisley had experienced about Esther's ancestress, Ruth Klaczko. Both Esther and Ruth had been involved in theater, Esther as a supporter, not a performer. According to Shirley, Esther had dedicated her last years to launching the community theater, and had been active in it until her death.

Paisley dried her hands and looked at her cell phone, poking out of her purse on the kitchen table. Impulsively, she reached for it and found the phone number of the red-haired book store owner.

Shirley answered on the second ring. "Paisley! I was hoping to hear from you!"

"Just called to tell you I'll attend rehearsal this afternoon after all." Paisley hesitated, then took the plunge. "And yes, I'll be happy to continue on as musical director. That is, if you still want me." *Was she crazy?* she thought. What impulse had made her volunteer, when she had been so determined not to? Blame it on Esther's interfering ghost, pressing her into actions she had no intention of doing.

Shirley nearly fell all over herself thanking her, and Paisley hung up on gushing expressions of gratitude.

She tucked her cell phone back in her purse, shaking her head. She'd come to River Bend expecting to withdraw from the world and feel sorry for herself. Instead, she had committed herself to several weeks of hard work and stress. What had she gotten herself into?

The walk to town felt longer that afternoon, and this time Steve did not appear in his shining black Audi to give her a lift. While Paisley limped, sweating, up the long incline of the river bend, she wondered once again why she'd agreed to help with the play when she could have spent the summer lounging in the hammock in the cool, shady backyard. She had better things to do with her time than helping a bunch of adolescents pull together a third-rate show on a shoestring budget. Like ... like....

Like listening to the headache-inducing ring of hammers and electric saws from Ian and his crew. Maybe it was just as well that she had an excuse to get out of the house.

Opening the door to the high-school auditorium, she walked into a deafening babble of voices, bodies rushing from one place to another, heavy pieces of scenery being shifted by jeans-clad volunteers onstage. From her visit yesterday, she recognized most of the young actors who were gathered in clusters about the room. Several waved at her, and she smiled back. Theater kids were a friendly bunch. Not like the moody ones you saw on the news or

TV reality shows. Like her troubled young neighbor, Kevin. Her smile faltered, remembering the boy's hunched-over shoulders and dark expression when his stepfather addressed him curtly. How quickly he disappeared into his room. The loud, discordant music that emerged, like a scream of anguish.

She was too busy to worry about Kevin, though. This time, she got the actors into order with a little less difficulty and soon had them practicing their parts. The tall kid with the wispy beard grinned ear to ear when he learned he would play the lead policeman, and she didn't have the heart to tell him it was because his off-tune singing and loose-limbed gait would increase the comic effect. He'd be happy enough when the audience roared at his antics on opening night.

Shirley came up, looking, if anything, more harried than yesterday. Her short red hair stood on end, as if she'd been pulling at it.

"I can't wait until this darned thing is over," she muttered, contradicting her earlier assurances about how fun it would be to work on the play. "The Pirate King didn't even bother to show up today."

"The Pirate King?" Paisley said blankly.

"Nathan Greenblatt. You know, the chunky kid who ate all the donuts? His mom just called and told us he had a soccer tournament today. Naturally, he forgot to tell us about it." She shook her head. "Esther always said never to cast a kid who does sport: their loyalty to the game always comes first."

Paisley nodded sympathetically. "You should have the cast sign a contract promising they won't get involved in any competing activities. That would help."

Shirley's head came up, and her round eyes blinked behind her glasses. "Hey, that's a good idea. I'll remember that. But what do I do now?"

"Fire him."

"Fire him?"

Paisley nodded. "Replace him. You can't run a professional production if you can't rely on your star. He wasn't that good anyway."

"I know, but he was the best I had. Who do I replace him with?" Shirley's voice rose to a wail.

"You know your cast better than I do. Who has a decent voice and is a ham?"

Shirley looked around the room vaguely. "Caleb can sing, but I need him in the part of Frederic. He's the only tenor who can reach the high notes." She wrung her hands. "We were already short on males. For some reason, it always seems to be girls who sign on for this kind of thing."

Paisley sighed. Shirley meant well, but it was obvious she had little experience running a show. Esther must have done the major lifting, strange as it seemed for a woman of nearly ninety years.

"Why not have some girl pirates, too?" she suggested. "After all, the character of Ruth in the play is a female pirate, isn't she?" She remembered that by coincidence Jonathan's ancestor, the famous singer, was named Ruth, too. "Penelope Cruz played a pirate in one of the *Pirates of the Caribbean* movies," she added. "And there were women pirates in real life."

"Hmmm." Shirley looked thoughtful. "Sure, why not?"

"Another thing," Paisley went on. "Have you thought of recruiting adults for some lead roles? You've billed this as a community theater, but it looks more like youth theater, since so far the cast is all kids."

"We've had a few adults participate over the years, but most of them have moved away, or don't want to do it anymore." Shirley considered. "You're right. There's got to be some untapped talent around here."

Paisley cleared her throat. "What about that real estate agent, Ray Henderson?"

"Ray?" Shirley's hazel eyes popped. "He's the last guy I can envision on stage."

"It's not quite as ridiculous as it sounds. I actually heard him sing a few lines of a Broadway musical." Paisley didn't say which one, Ray might kill her for telling. "It wasn't bad. He can carry a tune."

Shirley drummed her bitten fingernails on the back of one of the auditorium seats. "Then go ahead and ask him. Now that I think of it, he'd make a great Major General, wouldn't he? He's already got the military bearing, and can't you just see him in a handle-bar mustache and mutton-chop sideburns?" She chuckled. "It would be an improvement on that awful buzz-cut."

Paisley laughed. "I'll turn up the charm and hope for the best. But that still leaves us without a Pirate King. Is there anyone else in River Bend who can sing?"

Shirley turned up her palms. "No other adults that I know of. And every kid who wants to be is already involved. We sent out flyers the last week of school."

"What about that new kid that moved here earlier this summer?" Chloe, the pretty blond girl, the one who played Mabel, was listening.

"New kid?" Paisley asked, turning her head. "Do you mean Kevin Avery? Tall, thin, dark hair?"

"Yeah, that's him. He's kinda shy, but he has an *a-mazing* voice." The girl tossed her mass of shining fair hair over her bare shoulder. "I heard him at open-mic night down at Starbucks."

"Starbucks has open-mic night?"

"This one does, and they're putting one on tonight. Maybe he'll be there. You really should check it out, if you're looking for another singer." Chloe wandered off to join her friends. Paisley stared after her.

Kevin could sing? Well, that shouldn't be so surprising. He played the guitar, after all, so he must be at least somewhat musical. And as Shirley pointed out, the play needed bodies to fill the stage. If by some stroke of luck it were true that her handsome young neighbor could carry a tune ... and *if* she could persuade him to take the role.

She and Shirley spent a few minutes with their heads together, discussing other possible replacements for the Pirate King. After rehearsal, Paisley was sipping from her water bottle to soothe her raspy throat when the blond girl approached again.

"Hey, um, Mrs. Perleman?" Chloe was twirling a strand of hair around her finger self-consciously. Her entourage of friends had already disappeared.

"What is it, Chloe?" Paisley asked, impatient to leave.

"I was wondering if you, um, offered singing lessons? I've got that big solo at the beginning of the play, but I'm having trouble with the high notes. Since you're a professional opera singer and all, I thought you might have some tips. My mom will pay whatever your going rate is."

Paisley was unsure how to respond. The final remnants of her free time threatened to slip from her grasp. Then she remembered her empty bank account. A letter had arrived just yesterday from one of her creditors, forwarded by Barry Foster. And although Ian was doing the repairs on the house for cheap, he certainly wasn't doing it for free.

"Sure," she said, feigning enthusiasm. "Have your mother give me a call, and we'll arrange a time."

"Great!" Chloe's face lit up. "A couple of my friends are interested too. Would it be okay if they sign up?"

Paisley saw the last of her long, lazy evenings evaporate. Count your blessings, she told herself sternly. This would put food on the table ... and delay the inevitability of accepting the teaching position offered by her old conservatory mentor, Nigel.

Before the auditorium cleared, several other students asked for her telephone number, and Paisley made a mental note to print up business cards. Without realizing it, she had started a home business giving voice lessons. Maybe that wasn't such a bad idea. It might bring in enough to keep her from worrying so much about her finances. She couldn't stay unemployed forever.

She could post a sign in the house's front window, she thought, smiling to herself: "Perleman Academy of Music." She could print up flyers and put them on the windshields of the cars in the parking lot tomorrow.

Her smile disappeared. During the final break, she mentioned her idea to Shirley, who was enthusiastic. "Great! Drop in at the chamber of commerce and they'll give you tips on starting a business. The folks around here would be willing to pay top dollar for someone like you to teach their kids."

"Really?" Paisley thought again of her debts. It would be nice to get everything paid off, finally, and be free of that gnawing anxiety. "How much do you think I should charge for singing lessons in a town this size?"

Shirley named a sum that made Paisley's eyes grow wide. "You're kidding! That much?"

"Why not? You're a big name. Besides, you should see how much parents around here plunk down every month for national tutoring companies like Kumon or Mathnasium. Don't worry, you won't get rich off teaching singing to the little darlings, but it could be a decent living."

"Do you really think it would work?" Paisley asked slowly. Somehow this seemed less of an acknowledgment of failure than going back to teach at the conservatory. For one thing, she wouldn't have to deal with Nigel's pity or commiseration. Besides, she told herself, it would just be for the summer; she could quit any time she wanted.

"Sure. I live off selling books, and my bookstore ain't exactly Amazon.com." Shirley grimaced. "Besides, you'll be teaching out of your house, so you won't have overhead. If I remember, there's a pretty decent Steinway in that living room. You probably need some source of income, unless Jonathan left you independently wealthy."

Paisley shook her head slightly. If only.

Shirley's eyes widened. "He didn't? The louse." She paused with what was, for her, a moment of delicacy. "I haven't asked your plans before, hon, because it's none of my business...."

Paisley managed a wan smile.

"...But what else were you planning to do if your voice doesn't come back?"

Paisley tried not to wince at the thought. "I thought I might have to go back to the conservatory where I trained. It's in Omaha." She added, "A friend has been encouraging me to take a teaching position there."

Shirley saw the expression on her friend's face. "Or you can go into business for yourself here," she said gently. "At least think about it."

At the end of rehearsal, Shirley came over, holding a colorful patchwork handbag which looked like a bargain she'd snagged at an arts and crafts fair. She surveyed Paisley. "Hey, want a ride home? You look pretty beat."

Paisley forced her eyes open. "Actually, I was thinking of going to Starbucks, to check out that open-mic night that Chloe mentioned. And I don't want to keep taking advantage of you, just because I still don't have a car."

"My goodness, I'm the one who's been taking advantage of *you*! You came to River Bend to recuperate, and here I am working you like a draft horse. Hey, I forgot to tell you, I did think of someone who might be able to sell you a car cheap. You'll never guess who it is: that nice guy who's working on your house."

Paisley looked blank. "Ian McMullin?"

"Yeah, him. I just remembered that he's been storing an old VW bug in his garage since he started driving his father's truck. Don't know if it still runs, but you should ask him about it."

"Thanks, I will." Paisley wondered why Ian hadn't brought it up himself. But then, she'd never thought to tell him about her search for a car. Somehow, with all the other things they talked about, the subject never came up. Maybe Ian assumed she walked everywhere by choice. Or maybe he was just oblivious.

As the two women walked outside, Shirley eyed Paisley consideringly. "That little Volkswagen will be quite a comedown for someone who's used to private jets and limos. Punch me if I'm being too personal, but why is someone like you looking for a used car, anyway? Why not pick out something nice, like that pretty Audi that belongs to your neighbor, Steve Lopez?"

"Jonathan and I hardly lived on the level of private jets and Ferraris." Paisley rolled her eyes. "I don't know where people get this idea that all musicians are wealthy and famous. I wish it were true."

"Oh yeah?" Shirley sounded skeptical. "That's interesting, because I have a copy of *Time* magazine with Jonathan's picture on the cover. And those look like gold cuff links he was wearing."

"Jonathan was successful as far as conductors go," Paisley admitted. She remembered that magazine cover. Jonathan was proud of it, even framed a copy. "But few people outside the opera world would recognize me. Besides," she added dryly, "fame and money are not the same thing."

"Uh huh." Shirley did not look convinced. She turned on the engine of her battered Volvo and pulled into the road.

"Really, I'm not a diva," Paisley said after they had driven in silence for a while. For some reason, it was important to her that Shirley realize this. She considered the woman a friend, and she didn't have many of those, not close ones, anyway. Her itinerant lifestyle hadn't allowed for it. "I don't have expensive tastes. And I *like* this town. I didn't expect to, really, at first, but it's growing on me. The people are friendly, and it's so ... so ... peaceful."

"So boring, you mean," Shirley snorted. But she looked pleased. River Bend was, after all, her home. When the red-haired shopkeeper pulled up to the curb in front of Starbucks where the open-mic night was to be held, Paisley stepped out.

"Don't forget," Shirley called. "No rehearsal tomorrow! Good luck getting that Kevin kid to join the play," she added. "I hope he's as good a singer as Chloe claims. And hey, if you ever get bored, call me. We can go shopping or something, huh?"

Paisley waved goodbye before pushing open the glass door of the coffee shop. Her heart beat a little faster, with hope and a bit of anxiety. This could be an answer to the play's problems, or it could be a waste of her time. She had no idea what to expect.

Chapter Seven

The sun was setting as Paisley walked inside the coffeeshop, curious to find out if her young neighbor had a decent singing voice. Her expectations were low. She didn't even know if Kevin would be performing tonight. She only hoped that Chloe, the young blond actress, was right, and that he might be there.

The space was crowded with teenagers sipping iced lattes and gossiping, and the rush of air conditioning, chatter, and coffee aroma assaulted her senses. In the far back, someone had set up a microphone and a stool, creating a small makeshift stage.

Paisley felt like a dowager as she squeezed past fresh-faced sixteen- and seventeen-year-olds in torn jeans and T-shirts sporting logos of popular rock bands. Several customers recognized her and waved. She returned their greetings.

For the next hour she listened to amateur singers of varying quality, applauding politely after each song while waiting for Kevin to appear. A feeling of longing rushed through her. How she missed performing; missed her voice!

She finally gave up and edged toward the door, when a commotion started and she turned to look. A familiar thatch of spiky dark hair and pair of slouching shoulders moved through the crowd. Kevin was threading his way to the improvised stage. He adjusted his guitar strings, and, when the audience settled down, strummed a few tentative notes. Then he launched into a song she'd heard a few times on the radio, but which she could not identify.

His voice was unexpectedly rich and deep coming from such a thin frame. Its slight husky rasp suited the tone of the song, and she found herself tapping her foot along with the rest of the crowd. Chloe was right, she thought. The kid could sing.

When Kevin finished, he looked up at the audience. He wore his usual jeans and black-and-white checkered Vans sneakers, and the two silver hoops through his lower lip glinted in the spotlight. His coffee-brown eyes looked startled and a bit suspicious, as if he didn't expect the applause and whistles from the audience. He ducked his head and plucked out the opening notes of another song, one she had never heard before.

When the last note ended, Paisley didn't move to congratulate him. She slipped out of the coffee shop, feeling pleased. She had found her Pirate King.

Plenty of time to tell him tomorrow, she thought, without the horde of teenage girls shoving each other to be closer to the stage. Now she just had to work on recruiting the Major General.

At 10 o'clock sharp Wednesday morning, Paisley stopped in front of the town's only realty office, a tiny storefront a few doors down from Shirley Zacarias's used bookstore. Through tinted plate-glass windows plastered with snapshots of local homes for sale, she saw Ray leaning against a metal desk, holding a heavy white ceramic coffee mug while he chatted with a co-worker. When the door chime jangled, his thick eyebrows shot up.

"Mrs. Perleman! Have you finally decided to put the house up for sale?" He strode forward to pump her hand with his free hand before escorting her to his desk, which was piled high with flyers and documents, and set down his mug on a clear spot.

Several framed photographs hung on the wall behind his desk. One featured a large dog, some muscular tan-and-brown breed with heavy jowls, and another a slightly younger, thinner Ray wearing desert camouflage and brandishing a rifle, surrounded by fellow soldiers. A memento from his time in Afghanistan, no doubt.

"Your dog?" She nodded at the first photo.

A shadow crossed his heavy features. "Buzz died a couple of years ago. I haven't found the right one to replace him."

"I've heard how it is with a pet," she said, thinking about Esther's elusive cat. Cats were supposed to be unsentimental, but perhaps the gray ball of fluff missed its previous owner. "As for the house, no, I'm still not ready to put it on the market. I came to talk to you about a topic that may surprise you."

"Oh?" He gestured her to a seat looking slightly wary, and steepled his large fingers. "Well, ma'am, what can I help you with?"

"It's about the play I'm helping out with, *The Pirates of Penzance*. I'm sure you've heard of it, there are posters are all over town."

He leaned back in his seat, chuckling. "So that's it. No thanks, I already bought a half-page in the program."

"I'm not here to sell ads," she corrected him. "We need someone to play the role of the Major General. You'd be perfect for the part."

For a moment she thought perhaps he hadn't heard her. Then, Ray rolled back his chair a few inches. "Let me get this straight. You want me to perform in *The Pirates of Penzance*? As an actor?"

"I heard you sing," she reminded him, annoyed at the note of incredulity in his tone. "Just a snatch, but it was enough. Besides, the role is comedic, so you don't need professional training."

He folded his arms across his barrel chest, and his mouth set in a thin line. "Absolutely not."

Paisley had expected this. "Just think what it could do for your business." She gestured around the cramped office. "The publicity you'd get would be much greater than an ad in the back of the program. The local newspaper will provide coverage, and they'll probably mention what you do for a living." Surely there was a local paper? But of course there was. There always was in towns like this, she told herself confidently, even if its content consisted mainly of classified ads or public notices. "I've been working with the cast every day, and trust me, it is going to be a production you'll be proud to be in."

At that, Ray sat up straighter, and his stubborn look altered. The blond woman at the other desk was busy talking on the telephone, presumably with a client, and they had a moment of privacy.

"I bet Shirley would give you that half-page ad for free if you are in the cast," Paisley added impulsively. She wasn't sure what her friend's reaction would be: the budget for the community theater was tight. But that bridge could be crossed later.

"Hmmm." The rumble came from his chest. Not an answer, but a long way from "Absolutely not."

"Let Shirley know," she said, rising. "She's just two doors down."

Being a professional performer, Paisley knew how to make an effective exit. The little bell jingled like a good-luck charm as she let herself out, drowning out the sound of the blond woman's chatter on the telephone.

Walking home in the beautiful Northern California sunshine after lingering in several of the quaint shops on Main Street, Paisley pulled out her cell and called Steve Lopez to ask how she could get in touch with his stepson.

"Kevin usually doesn't come home until six o'clock for dinner." Steve's pleasant voice sounded concerned. "Why? Is he in some sort of trouble?"

She was surprised by her neighbor's quick assumption something was wrong. "No, not at all. I have something to ask him. A favor, you could say." She wasn't sure how Steve would react to her request, and besides, she felt she ought to ask Kevin if he were interested in participating in the play before dragging his stepdad into it. "Do you have any idea where I might find him?"

"No, but I'll give you his cell phone number. You know how teenagers are," Steve added critically. "Like feral cats. Always wandering around, impossible to tie down."

"Except at six o'clock, for dinner," she said, displeased by the note of criticism. Kevin seemed like a nice kid in spite of his piercings and mercurial temperament.

Steve chuckled. "Touché. Speaking of dinner, don't forget you promised to come over Sunday for homemade enchiladas."

With everything else going on, she'd forgotten the invitation. To make up for it, she put extra enthusiasm into her tongue-in-cheek response. "Dinner to be served at six o'clock, I presume?"

His laugh sounded unforced, and she thought he was starting to loosen up around her. "Of course."

"See you Sunday." Next she dialed Kevin's cell phone and left a brief voicemail without revealing the object of her call. She wanted a chance to sell him on the idea of being in the play. That was a task best performed in person.

Last, she opened the day's mail, a stack of hospital and credit card bills forwarded from New York. She contemplated them in dismay, wondering how in the world she would pay them off. Should she consider bankruptcy? She could sell the house to pay down the bills, but with every day that passed the prospect of giving it up grew more painful. Strange, but she had grown to love the old place.

Thank goodness Ian had agreed to let her pay for the renovations in installments, she thought, rubbing her temples. The income from providing singing lessons would help, once she got her fledgling music school off the ground and started collecting tuition.

Then she remembered that she had not yet checked Esther's safety deposit box. Might it contain something that would help? It certainly wouldn't hurt to look.

"Why, yes," the bank teller said after checking Paisley's identification. "Follow me to the back, please."

The bank was old and quaint, like all of River Bend's downtown buildings, with a false front trimmed in cream and forest-green. It looked like something out of the Gold Rush days. The teller led her to a vault off the small lobby, lined with rows of metal safety security boxes. He stepped on a step stool and reached up to insert a small key in one of the upper boxes, while Paisley watched, palms tingling with anticipation.

Carefully he pulled out the long box and set it on a wooden table in the middle of the room. "Here you go," he said, bowing slightly, although he looked barely out of high school himself, with a freshly scrubbed face above a perfectly ironed blue uniform shirt and conservatively striped tie. "Take all the time you need, Miss."

He left, discreetly closing the door behind him.

Paisley stared at the box while imagining what Esther might have left inside. Stacks of stocks and bonds? Or perhaps a glittering array of ruby, pearl, and diamond jewelry, like those she had worn in that vivid dream?

Heart beating faster, she reached out and opened the box. Her breath came out in a rush of disappointment. All that lay in the container was a passport whose gold letters had worn off with use, and a green diary with a broken clasp, the sort children wrote in.

Just like the dusty cardboard box Ian had found in the second bedroom, she thought dejectedly. Nothing valuable. She contemplated the two objects for a moment, then reached in and took out the diary. It fitted perfectly in the palm of her hand. The gilt clasp was tarnished, and the faded cloth cover was ripped at the corners.

In spite of herself, Paisley's interest began to grow again as she contemplated the small volume. In its own way, the diary was a sort of treasure: a chance to get to know Esther better. Who knew? This discovery may be even more revealing than the blue aerogramme Ian had been so excited about. Not everything important had to be of monetary value, did it?

She gently touched the worn cover before opening the yellowed pages. The rounded penmanship was that of a young schoolgirl; it hardly resembled the spidery handwriting of Esther's later years.

Sifting through the pages, Paisley noted that the entries began in the early 1940s. Esther must have been about ten years old by then. The writing seemed remarkably fluent for a girl who had only lived in the United States less than a year, and it was dotted with frequent exclamation points.

"Georgiana gave me a kitten for my birthday! So pretty! Gray is my favorite color!"

Paisley wondered if the cat was an ancestor of the one that still haunted the premises. Then, something struck her. Georgiana. Hadn't she heard that name before, recently? The memory eluded her, however, and shrugging, she tucked the small green diary in her purse to finish reading later.

At that point, the young bank teller returned to ask if she needed any help, so she only glanced briefly inside the passport. Although Esther was an old woman by the time the photograph was taken, it somehow managed to capture the sparkle in the dark eyes. When she rifled through its pages she found stamps for England, France, Mexico, Egypt, Israel, and Italy. The sight gave her an unexpected thrill of pleasure. How nice to find more evidence that Jonathan's great-aunt, whose childhood had started with such trauma, had gone on to live a full rich life.

There was no stamp for Poland, she noticed. Perhaps that country had held too many painful memories. According to Jonathan, none of their European loved ones had survived the war. They were all gone: grandparents, uncles, cousins ... even kindly Aunt Adeladja.Tears stung Paisley's eyes as she returned the empty safety deposit box to the clerk.

Had Ian's Polish-speaking friend translated the old aerogramme yet? she wondered, leaving the bank. What did that letter reveal about Esther's flight to America? Did it reveal how such a young child managed to stay a step ahead of the Nazis who would eventually destroy her family? Paisley found herself desperately wanting to know.

*   *   *

Anxious to learn the answers to her questions and bothered by Kevin's failure to return her phone call, Paisley had trouble focusing on rehearsal that afternoon. The Pirate King understudy flubbed the lines yet again, looking anxious to return to the chorus and hang out with his friends. Well, the play would just have to make do with a weak Pirate King if necessary, she decided from her seat in the center of the front row.

During breaks, she resisted with difficulty the lure of the diary in her purse. Plenty of time for that at home, later. She used the time to leave several more telephone messages for Kevin.

She considered following up with Ray Henderson as well, but instinct told her that nagging wouldn't help. More likely, it would only cause him to dig in his thick-soled tasseled loafers. Maybe if she sent a plate of brownies to his office with a nice note ... and promised a free, *full*-page ad for his real estate office in the program....

Neither bribe turned out to be necessary. Paisley returned from taking a short break to find Ray standing in front of the stage, looking self-conscious in his ill-fitting gold jacket. He held a script awkwardly in his hand, while Shirley danced attention on him, chattering brightly, thick glasses slipping down the bridge of her snub nose.

Paisley managed to catch her friend's eye and telegraphed a fist pump. What had changed Ray's mind: flattery, or the prospect of publicity for his business? It didn't matter. He was in. Now if only they could snag Kevin.

Shirley came over while the play's cowardly policemen practiced their big number *Tarantara* onstage, where they did their comic best to avoid setting off to capture the pirates. The actors bumped into each other and tripped over their feet as much by accident as for humorous effect.

"I was right," Shirley whispered into Paisley's ear. "You're magic."

"Pure luck. Ray brings a certain authenticity to the role, don't you think?" Paisley smiled as the former marine swaggered amidst the younger actors as if born to the stage.

"Authentic? Sure, except he doesn't have kids, let alone ten daughters like the Major General! I heard Ray wasn't even in the Marines that long, in spite of that military bearing, and all those 'Yes, ma'ams.'" Shirley frowned. "I'm not sure why."

"Was he injured? Washed out?"

"Dunno. Ray talks about his service all the time, but now that I think about it, the details are sort of vague. Maybe he was involved in something top secret, or maybe he just doesn't want to remember what he's seen." Shirley shrugged. "I'm just glad he's in the play. An older actor gives the production more *gravitas*, if that's the right word for a light operetta. Want a ride home?"

Paisley turned down the offer, although she soon regretted her show of independence. The weather was beautiful most of the time, but it had rained early that morning, and she had to skirt puddles in the unpaved side of the road. By the time she got home, the sun was setting and long purple shadows stretched across the deep yard.

Her stomach was rumbling when she fumbled the key into the lock of the side door leading directly into the kitchen. Too tired to cook, she heated up a can of vegetable soup and carried the bowl toward the living room, intending to eat dinner on the couch while listening to one of Esther's old opera records. Something light and humorous to lift her mood. *Die Fledermaus,* perhaps.

Under the arch that separated parlor and dining room, she came to a sudden halt. The hot soup almost splashed over the side of the bowl.

The living room had been in immaculate condition when she left that morning. Now the gold brocade sofa cushions were askew, and the books were no longer neatly lined up in the bookcases. The front door, the one she had not come through when returning home, was slightly ajar.

With unsteady hands, Paisley set the bowl on the coffee table and went through the rest of the house, searching for more signs of the break-in. It might have been her imagination, but every room showed some slight evidence of being disarranged. In her bedroom, the edges of the bedspread hung crookedly, and her shoes in the closet were jumbled instead of lined up neatly. In the bathroom, a towel had slipped to the floor, and the trash can was on the wrong side of the sink. She hurried back to the kitchen, and found the toaster was pushed farther back from the sink than usual.

The hairs at the back of her neck stood up, and fear chilled her blood. Sour bile rose in her stomach, and she stumbled into the powder room. Weak and frightened, she clung to the porcelain sink while terrifying thoughts swirled in her head. She hadn't even considered until now the possibility that the intruder was still there. Frozen, she waited, listening for any noise other than the sound of her own breathing. Nothing was audible but a faint ringing in her ears, the twitter of a bird outside, and the hum of the refrigerator. At a distance, a car swished by on the road that led to and from River Bend.

As her heart began to beat slower, she wondered why the burglar had not caused greater destruction. He must have been searching the house, but why hadn't he left a bigger mess? Cushions on the floor, her clothes in a heap, the dresser drawers gaping open? It appeared whoever it was had tried to inexpertly cover his tracks. Not a professional, then, but someone who hoped she wouldn't notice that he had been there.

That should have been a relief, but it wasn't. The burglar, whoever it was, must have waited until Ian and his crew had gone home for the day. That meant he knew her schedule. The thought made her feel even more vulnerable. She threw the cold soup away, appetite gone.

Nothing seemed to be missing, fortunately. Her own clothes and personal possessions seemed to be intact.

Then she remembered that the house had been broken into before she moved in. Hadn't Ray pointed out the smashed window that Ian had replaced? Both could have been random acts, but she could not help thinking about the jewels. The thought was crazy, since no one even knew if they existed. But what other motive could the intruder have? She owned nothing of value, just the few clothes she had brought with her, and Esther's old furnishings. Of course, the burglars might believe otherwise. In this small town, rumors might be circulating. Celebrities, even minor ones, were usually thought of as rich.

She shuddered at the thought of unknown persons invading her space, running their hands through her underwear and makeup. Until now, she'd thought of the little frame house as place of refuge, of safety. Somehow, that made the violation even worse.

*   *   *

A few minutes after her phone call, a black-and-white police car pulled in front of the house and a stocky policeman leisurely got out and strolled up to the door. Standing on the porch, he pulled out a notebook and asked if anything was missing.

"No," Paisley said, then stopped. Could the burglar have found something hidden in the house that she'd missed? She couldn't possibly know.

The policeman waited patiently, pencil poised over his notepad. "Er ... nothing that I know of," Paisley said. There was no reason to report that some jewelry might be missing from behind a secret panel or under a loose board, with no proof that such jewelry even existed.

"Anybody or anything hurt?"

"No," she admitted.

Officer Smith snapped his gum.

Paisley had the impression that the importance of the report had sunk below the level of an unpaid parking ticket or rescuing a kitten from a tree.

He finished the report, then advised Paisley that it was doubtful the miscreants would be found. Before leaving, he warned her to be sure to lock her doors and windows in the future.

"You did lock your doors when you went out this afternoon, didn't you?" he asked.

Paisley was forced to admit that she wasn't sure. The question made her feel she was somehow at fault for the break-in. "I didn't double-check," she said defensively. "Besides, I had a work crew here most of the day."

"Everybody thinks it's safe in the country, ma'am. Well, it isn't. Big city problems happen everywhere. You name it. Burglary, assault, meth ... we've got it all, just like Sacramento or San Jose. Might want to invest in a deadbolt and a house alarm, just in case the fellow comes back."

"Thank you, officer," Paisley said, gulping. She hadn't considered the possibility that whoever it was might return. When the black and white police car pulled away a few minutes later, she realized the officer hadn't dusted for fingerprints or even checked the premises for whatever it was that police checked premises for. A dropped business card engraved with the burglar's name? At any rate, she suspected the report would be filed away at the station, and nothing would be done to follow up. Maybe a deadbolt was in order.

Despite her exhaustion, she tried to straighten the house up so there would be no reminders of the break-in tomorrow. Before settling down, however, she found a crowbar the working crew had left behind and set it next to her bed. During the night she got up several times to check that the locks and the windows were securely fastened.

As Paisley tossed and turned, she remembered that she had not called Steve about the incident, although he'd asked her to telephone at the least sign of trouble. Tomorrow, she thought. First thing in the morning. As un-modern as it sounded, it was reassuring to have a big, strong neighbor who was willing to protect her.

Chapter Eight

The morning after the burglary, before Paisley could call Steve about the break-in, Ian arrived at the house, even earlier than usual. He looked freshly showered and chipper in a clean T-shirt and jeans, but when she opened the door, his cheerful whistle faded away. "What happened?"

"Why do you assume anything happened?" Her voice sounded like it had gravel in it. Her hair was disheveled and the mirror had revealed dark circles were under her eyes. "Maybe I was drinking last night and have a hangover."

He dismissed her words. "Fat chance. You don't drink."

She blinked. "How do you know?

"Shirley told me. The grapevine in River Bend works fine, if you'll pardon the pun. I probably know more about you than you think." His gaze moved past her into the house, and his eyes widened. "Hey, what happened?"

Paisley followed his gaze. While cleaning up, she had missed a few things. A couple of Esther's paperback novels lay on the floor behind the couch, and a lampshade hung slightly askew.

She stepped back to allow Ian in. "I had an anonymous visitor yesterday."

"He doesn't seem to have been very well behaved." Ian crossed the room and inspected the back of the TV, where a raw gash lay across the freshly painted wall. The intruder must have shoved it carelessly.

"The police think it was a burglar," she said, trailing him during his inspection. "Someone looking to support a drug habit or something. It could have been a lot worse."

"Did they take anything?"

She shoved aside the image of jewels that flitted across her mind. "No, They didn't. Not that there's anything of value in the house worth taking."

Ian gave a sudden yelp and bounded up the stairs. Banging and heavy footsteps came from overhead, before he descended a few minutes later, shaking his head. "I left my father's tools up there, but thank goodness that's not what they were looking for." He looked at her. "Okay, Paisley. Time to put your cards on the table."

"What do you mean?"

He let out a long breath and ran a hand through his hair, leaving it tousled. "You seem to be a fairly intelligent person, and I don't consider myself a total idiot, either. Maybe we should trust each other."

"I still have no idea what you're talking about."

"Then I'll start. Unlike the cops, I don't think your burglar was a random drug addict looking for a stash of cash under your mattress. I know you're not here just for rest and relaxation, Paisley, or to share your talents with the River Bend Community Theater." He stopped, holding her eyes. "I know what your burglars were looking for, and I think you can too. The Perleman's lost jewels."

Paisley's gasped. "You said yourself they don't exist."

"*You* believe they do, though. Apparently, so does someone else."

"You're wrong. They're probably nothing but a rumor, someone's imagination run amok."

"Then why did you come to River Bend?"

"You said it yourself. I needed a place to recuperate after the accident. Esther had left me the house, so it made sense to spend the summer here."

"Sure. *And* to find out if those rumors about hidden rubies were true. Come on, it's the only explanation. Otherwise, you'd be recuperating somewhere swankier, like the Riviera or Malibu. Those places are more your league, aren't they?"

She opened her mouth to tell him such places were out of her budget these days. That, in reality, they always had been. But he didn't give her a chance.

"My first clue was when you got so excited about that old box in the wall, yet showed no interest in the letter it held," Ian said. "I'm no Sherlock Holmes, but it was obvious you were hoping to find something else. I'd heard the old stories about Esther's jewels, and it made sense that you had too."

She sat down heavily. "I thought that story was a heavily guarded family secret."

"I hate to disappoint you, Paisley, but if those jewels existed, they'd have been found long ago. Jonathan's great-grandmother spent her whole life looking for them."

"Aunt Henka never found Esther's treasure box, either. But it was there, hidden inside the wall, until you took down the paneling."

Paisley realized that there could be other explanations for the box's undisturbed appearance. Maybe the jewelry had been in the box, and Esther's Aunt Henka—or someone else—removed the jewelry and returned the box to its original hiding place long ago.

She considered the idea for a moment, then shook her head. If Aunt Henka had found the jewels, it was unlikely the woman would have kept the discovery a secret, especially from her own family members. No, Aunt Henka would have announced it triumphantly.

"So how *did* you hear about the jewels?" Paisley asked. "Jonathan said only his family was aware of the story."

"That's odd, because the whole community suspected Aunt Henka was looking for something valuable, since she was out digging in the yard all the time. Esther told me the whole story when I was seventeen. I told you that she used to invite me into this house after school. She'd pour a pot of hot chocolate, serve blueberry muffins, and sit down for a chat."

"About the jewels?" Paisley raised her eyebrows.

He chuckled. "Mostly she discussed history, politics, and literature. In spite of our age difference, Esther never talked down to me. I considered her a friend. But yes, eventually our conversations got around to the subject of jewels. She told me they'd never existed, and she always had a good hearty laugh at people who made fools of themselves over colored bits of rock. Probably, Esther was thinking of Aunt Henka."

Paisley was silent. She'd thought the jewels were her personal secret. To find out that Ian knew … more, even, than she did … was an almost physical blow. Perhaps she shouldn't be surprised. Even Shirley had been familiar with the tale. As was, apparently, someone else. Someone who rifled through her home this afternoon looking for them.

A loud meow, followed by the outraged caw of a raven, interrupted them. For a moment, they listened to the cat chasing the bird outside the front door.

"I'd like to know what Esther told you," Paisley said when the racket quieted. Either the raven had made its escape, or the cat had dragged away its next meal. The thought made her shudder. "She was probably the only one who knew the truth."

Ian shrugged. "She said that during her entire life people had spied on her, hoping she would lead them to the cache. 'Do I look like a duchess?' Esther asked me, and threw up her bare hands. 'See? No rings, not even from a box of Cracker Jacks.' And then she laughed even harder."

Paisley smiled, imagining Esther's raspy chuckle.

Ian's face grew serious. "There is no treasure, Paisley. I hope that doesn't disappoint you. If you thought there would be a pot of gold at the end of the rainbow, you're wrong."

"Why should I be disappointed? I didn't really expect to find a hidden stash of jewels any more than I expect to win the lottery." Except for, deep inside, maybe she had.

Paisley glanced around the disarranged room and shivered slightly. "But it looks like someone else did. Hopefully, now they've given up looking for them." She stood, wiping her hands on her skirt. "So long as you're in here, would you like some breakfast?"

"Any muffins left over from yesterday?" Ian perked up.

"Your crew gobbled them all up. How about scrambled eggs and toast instead?" She led the way into the kitchen, listening to his footsteps follow her down the hall.

While the eggs bubbled in a frying pan, she heated some milk in another pot for hot chocolate, and then poured it into two ceramic cups.

Ian stretched out his long legs at the table as she cooked, hands clasped behind his head. He seemed in no hurry to start the repairs. Wearing clean clothes and neatly shaved, he actually looked like the aspiring architect he was. Ian really wasn't bad looking after all, she thought.

It occurred to her she hadn't seen Rusty, Quinn, or Alix yet. His crew must be running late.

Setting two plates on the table, she looked at him. "Why a burglary now? The house has been vacant for nearly a year. They could have come in then." She thought of the broken window Ray had pointed out when she arrived, the one Ian had recently replaced.

"Finding that box may have reignited their interest. Whoever 'they' are." Ian dug into his breakfast with relish, buttering his toast thickly and throwing back a glass of orange juice in a single swallow. "You're lucky they didn't tear down any more walls. After breakfast I'll install new locks on all your doors. Deadbolts."

"That's what the policeman who took the report suggested. But nobody knew about that hidden box except us." She paused, a fork of scrambled eggs suspended in midair. "And Rusty, Quinn, and Alix. They saw it."

He caught her meaning. "I can assure you they have nothing to do with the break-in." His gray eyes met hers across the table. "My endorsement may not mean much to you, but I'd trust them with my life. None of them are capable of breaking into someone else's home."

She shuddered. "You have no idea how horrible it was, Ian. Just the thought of someone going through my things…. Ugh." Then her eyes widened. "Whoever broke in must be someone who has heard the old story. Why don't we make a list of everyone who has knowledge of it?"

He swallowed a mouthful of eggs. "I have no idea who does and who doesn't. Most of the old timers probably are familiar with the story. That wouldn't narrow down the list of suspects much."

Paisley slumped in her chair, disappointed.

Ian relented. "I suppose it wouldn't hurt to try to come up with a list of suspects based on motive and opportunity. What about Ray Henderson, to start with?"

"Ray?" Her eyebrows shot up. "You only say that because you don't like him."

Ian reached for another piece of toast. "Maybe I'm prejudiced, but didn't he try to prevent you from coming to River Bend by pressuring you to sell Esther's house sight unseen? Then when you came anyway, he tried to get you to leave."

"Any real estate agent chasing a commission would encourage me to sell," she pointed out. "And he was right: there was no need for me to come all the way to California for that. Besides, we have no reason to think Ray knew about the…." She broke off.

He turned abruptly. "What?"

She gulped. "I just remembered I *did* mention jewels to him in an off-hand way, trying to be funny. He picked up on it, making a joke that was slightly off-color and had absolutely nothing to do with what we're talking about."

"Still." He held up a finger. "It looks like we have suspect number one."

"But Ray had a key to the house. He had no need to break in."

"What about suspect number two?" He held up another finger. "Steve Lopez."

Her eyes widened. "Steve? Ian. Why him?"

He set down his fork, the plate scraped clean. "Your neighbor likes expensive things. Look at his clothes, at that flashy car he drives. The winery has been losing money ever since he inherited the land from his dad. He's been pouring funds into it like pouring a bottle of Two-Buck Chuck down a wino's gullet."

"That's silly." Paisley thought of Steve gallantly struggling to be a good stepfather to a troubled teenager. "So what if he wears nice clothes? That doesn't mean—"

"And your neighbor is perfectly situated to spy your comings and goings. I wouldn't be surprised if he had a telescope strategically placed, facing your windows."

She started putting the dirty dishes into the sink, fighting back laughter at the absurd image. "Don't you realize Steve could searched my house multiple times while it was vacant? He had no more need to break in than Ray did." A thought made her turn around. "Maybe you think he believed I already had the jewels and brought them to River Bend only to leave them lying on my dresser. But that's ridiculous. Our theory is that the gems were hidden on these premises seventy-five years ago and remain unfound."

Ian stubbornly folded his arms across his chest. "Steve might believe you did bring those jewels with you. After all, he doesn't know what we know."

"We haven't any idea what he knows." She filled the sink with soapy water. "If having heard the legend of the Perlemans' heirloom jewels makes someone a suspect, you should be at the top of that list." Leaving the dishes soaking, she went in the living room, and sank into the sofa. Oddly, being around Ian had helped her forget her fear after discovering the burglary. Their absurd conversation made her feel like cracking jokes instead of locking herself into a closet to hide.

He followed, sitting casually to her. Paisley liked the warmth of his body next to hers, the fact that he didn't seem in awe of her fame or career success. In companionable silence they sat watching motes dance in the sunlight of the cozy room.

"So," she said after a while, feeling relaxed and sleepy and fighting a desire to rest her head on his shoulder. "What about the last suspect I brought up? What might *his* motives be?"

He thought for a minute and chuckled. "Oh, you mean me?"

She turned and looked at him. "It's true, Ian. You knew the story of the jewels, and I've given you free run of this house. Who knows what you've been up to all day while I'm away?" Her lips quivered at the thought of Ian sneaking inside with a black skier's hat pulled over his face. He'd probably trip over a rug be caught red-handed, like those goofy crooks in the movie *Home Alone.*

Somehow his arm found its way around her shoulder, perhaps to erase the last of her nerves. "As you just pointed out, if I were searching for something I wouldn't need to break in. And do you remember what happened when I actually did find something?"

She nodded. "You handed over the sealed box without even trying to open it. There was no way to tamper with that old tape without my detecting it." Paisley had never really considered Ian a possibility. Maybe it was that Jimmy Stewart-style integrity that radiated from him. Or maybe it was something else that kept her from suspecting him, which she still wasn't ready to admit, even to herself.

Looking around at the disarranged books and crooked lampshade, evidence that an intruder had recently stood in this very room, she shuddered again and Ian's arm tightened around her shoulder.

"Think," he said. "Have you done anything, said anything, that would make someone think you had run across proof the jewels existed? Besides Ray, I mean."

While Paisley considered, she let her head settle on his shoulder. "I may have said something to Shirley, but that's all. I've hardly gone around town chattering to everyone. My intention was to keep the jewels a secret until I was able to find...." Breaking off, she sat up straight, her face growing hot.

Ian chuckled. "So you really *do* believe in them. Why does locating those jewels matter so much to you, Paisley? Surely Jonathan left you financially well enough off that you don't need to sell a few baubles to get by." He didn't appear to notice that she did not respond. "Besides, even if the jewels did exist, they'd belong to you anyway. After all, you're Esther's only heir. There's no need to be secretive—"

This time he was the one who broke off, and the light-gray eyes narrowed. "Let's back up a little. Are you broke?"

Her chin rose. "None of my checks to you have bounced, have they?"

The hesitation had been enough. His lips pursed in a silent whistle. "I knew you'd been living simply and you asked to spread out the payments. But I assumed...." He stared at her as if seeing her for the first time and his brows came down. "So this treasure hunt isn't just some hare-brained hobby after all. Did Jonathan gamble? Put all his income in bad investments? Surely he didn't leave you high and dry financially, not with his flourishing career."

Paisley drew herself up. "I told you the truth. I didn't come to River Bend for the jewelry." She hesitated. "Not really. Anyway, my finances are none of your business. As long as I pay for your work, that's all you need be concerned about."

He picked up the implication immediately.

"Back to an employer/employee relationship now, are we?" The brows lowered until they met above the bridge of his nose, and he stood jerkily. "Believe it or not, I don't need your measly paychecks. I've only been charging you the cost of the materials. Berkeley provided me a free-ride scholarship and my paid position as a teaching assistant more than covers my expenses. But you're right. It's none of my business."

He stomped toward the door.

Caught off guard by his reaction, Paisley wondered if she had been looking for some excuse to push him back. Was she uncomfortable with the fact that their relationship seemed to be rapidly moving past that of employer and employee? As a graduate student, he must be nearly her age—at least in his mid-twenties.

Without analyzing things further, she hurried after him. "Sorry, Ian. I was out of line." Paisley caught his arm to stop him just as he reached the steps. Then her brow furrowed as she belatedly wondered why his work crew was absent. "Where are Alix, Quinn, and Rusty?"

When he turned toward her, the flush of anger was leaving his cheeks. "It's Saturday, remember? We don't work weekends."

In the excitement of the burglary, she had lost track of what day it was. "Oh. Why are *you* here, then?"

"I came to give you this but forgot." He pulled from his pocket two neatly folded pieces of paper. The top one was the blue aerogramme. Paper-clipped to it was a crisp, new sheet of college-ruled binder paper, the kind used by students, covered with slanted handwriting in English.

"You got Aunt Adelajda's letter to Esther translated!" Paisley grabbed the papers, forgetting their brief argument.

Ian watched her unfold the pages. "My friend specializes in eastern-European dialects. This translation is better than what you could get online."

"Oh, have you read it?"

He gave her an exasperated glare. Of course. Go ahead and see what it says."

Remembered how she'd selfishly saved the box to open by herself, Paisley couldn't blame him for sneaking a peak. She sat on the porch swing and devoured the letter's contents before looking up, disappointed. "It doesn't reveal much, does it?"

He joined her on the swing. Now that they'd cleared the air, she was glad for his presence. It made her feel more secure.

"It's pretty much what I expected." He gestured toward the letter. "Aunt Adelajda wrote to reassure her young niece about their safety. Not a word about jewels," he added.

Paisley re-read the passage, sensing the fear concealed under Esther's aunt's carefully selected words.

"Don't worry about us, my little darling. Please do not let the stories in the newspapers frighten you. We had dinner at Babka's yesterday—her golabki were as delicious as ever. Our pleasure was only diminished by the absence of our own dear little Esther. Take care not to lose the special coat Babka+ sewed for you, my sweet girl, and remember to be good for Auntie Henka and Uncle Borys. Do not forget how kind they are to take you in."

"How stupid," Paisley said soberly, "that we've been sitting here worrying about what young Esther might have done with a bunch of hypothetical jewels, when something much more profound was going on in her life. Did she know she'd never see her family again?"

"Esther wasn't entirely alone," he reminded her. "She had Aunt Henka and her American relatives."

"Yes." Paisley looked down at the letter through stinging eyes. Blinking away the tears, she held the aerogramme closer and reread one of the sentences.

"What is it?" Ian asked.

"Listen." Paisley read aloud: "'Take care not to lose the special coat that Babka sewed for you.'"

"*Babka* is Polish for 'grandmother. Naturally the grandma would make Esther was warm before sending her on a long trip in the middle of winter."

She stared up at him, eyes wide. "What if it's a clue that the jewels really did exist after all?"

He shook his head. "Remember, Esther told me they didn't."

"Maybe she didn't want anyone to know—even you. The diary makes it clear young Esther disliked Aunt Henka from the beginning. What if she didn't turn the jewels over to her mean American relatives? It would serve them right. The coat might be proof, but it must be long gone by now. I didn't see any child's clothing while going through the house. There are other ways, though. A photograph of Ruth wearing the jewelry..."

Ian looked thoughtful. "Or a reference in an old newspaper or biography. If you are right, something like that might exist. Ruth used to be famous in Eastern Europe, and not all the old photos and documents were destroyed during the Holocaust."

Paisley told him, "I've already searched the internet for that sort of thing, but all I found was a brief bio on Wikipedia that didn't refer to any jewels. There are no scrapbooks or family histories in the house, either, just those family photos in the hallway.

Ian ran a hand through his hair, leaving it standing on end. "Maybe I can dig up something. I'm driving back to Berkeley to hang out with some college friends. They have a great historical library there, that might have stuff that isn't posted on the Internet." He stood and paused. "Want to come along?"

For a moment she was tempted to accept the unexpected invitation. But she had looked forward to relaxing by herself. Thanks to Shirley and the community theater, she'd had precious little time to do that. And there was that dinner at Steve Lopez's house tomorrow.

"No thanks, I'll pass. Before I forget, though, a friend of mine mentioned you might have a car you'd be willing to sell. Is that true?"

He thought for a second. "You must be referring to that old VW beetle that's been sitting in the garage since I graduated from high school. It ran okay the last time I took it out." Ian grinned. "Somehow I never pictured a gorgeous opera star driving my old high school ride. Don't worry, I'll sell it cheap. We paupers have to stick together."

She reluctantly grinned.

"I'll drop the car off tomorrow, when I get back," he promised, looking at his watch. "I'd better get going if I want to get there before the library closes."

Paisley felt oddly reluctant to let him go. After last night's burglary, there was something reassuring about having a man present. The frightening incident had reminded her all too vividly of the downside of living alone.

"Thank you for getting the aerogramme translated," she said, walking with him to the parked pickup truck, where Ian fumbled his keys out of his pocket.

"I was just as curious about it as you were," he admitted. "It's not every day I find a mysterious message hidden inside a wall, just like in an Agatha Christie novel."

"The message wasn't mysterious, just a loving letter from an aunt to her niece." She paused. "I only wonder why Esther didn't keep her diary in the box with her other treasures."

"Diary?" Dropping the keys, he scrabbled for them in the lawn. "There's a diary too?"

"Well, yes. Didn't I tell you?"

"Tell me what? You're so tight-lipped, you should work for the NSA." He glared at her.

"I was at the bank yesterday, and the teller gave me the key to Esther's safety deposit box. There was nothing in it, though, except a passport and an old diary, the kind little girls write in. I thought I'd read it one of these nights when I didn't have anything else to do."

He stared at her, and then, to her surprise, laughed. "For a treasure hunter, you must be the least curious person I've ever met."

"I thought we'd established that there probably wasn't any treasure, so there didn't seem to be any urgency."

"We still haven't established anything," he said, getting into the truck and slamming the door. "Happy reading, Paisley. See you tomorrow afternoon. Hopefully you'll feel like telling me what the diary says."

Chapter Nine

Ian's parting jab nettled Paisley. What right did he have to try to make her feel guilty? She was under no obligation to share any information, even if he had volunteered to do research, and gotten the letter from Auntie Adelajda translated.

Okay, he had been helpful. And trustworthy. And the truth was, she liked having him around.

Paisley tried to remember why she had welcomed Ian into her confidence in the first place. After all, he had started out as just some guy she had hired to fix up the house, based on a call out of an out-of-date phone book. What did her quest have to do with him?

And yet, at some point in time, their relationship had subtly changed into something more than mere employer/employee. He'd offered friendship generously, and his assistance had proved valuable. Best of all, Ian took her concerns seriously.

How different from Jonathan, who had hardly taken her seriously at all, who used to mock her weaknesses until she learned to toughen up and fight back. Paisley suspected that he'd married her not for love as much as for what she could do to enhance his career.

With effort, she forced her thoughts away from that dangerous topic. There was still too much unexplored pain. Even so, deep inside, she felt something was beginning to heal.

Paisley reached for her cell phone. Enough of Ian, Esther, and those blasted jewels. It had been a busy week, and she was going to spend the rest of the day doing what she had come to River Bend for. Relaxing.

"Hello, Shirley?" she asked into the receiver. "Want to go shopping?"

The shops along River Bend's main street were full of appealing merchandise oriented toward tourists, but Paisley's budget didn't stretch to much more than a hand-tied Guatemalan hammock she found in a gift shop next to Shirley's used bookstore. The hammock looked like it would fit perfectly between two of the big oak trees in the back yard. Paisley remembered her desire to spend long afternoons swinging in the shade of the large trees. Maybe she could fit a nap in tomorrow.

She bought some handmade costume jewelry, too. Nothing like Ruth Perleman's legendary rubies, Paisley thought, dangling a pair of cheap enameled earrings by her ears and turning her head this way and that in front of the shop's mirror to admire the effect. So what? They were pretty.

In turn, Shirley snapped up a "wearable art" skirt in patchwork squares of purple and royal blue velvet that made her look like a lumpy hausfrau gypsy, and then sighed longingly at an overpriced ostrich-feathered pink straw hat with an enormous brim. "What do you think?" she asked Paisley, tilting it over her forehead and fluttering her eyelashes.

"Pretty," Paisley said sincerely. "It looks like something a British royal would wear to a wedding."

"But I'm not a royal, so I guess I'd never have anywhere to wear it." Shirley gave the hat a longing glance before setting it back on the shelf. "Speaking of weddings, have you thought of seeing anyone now that you're free? You know, romantically?"

Paisley started as if someone had pricked her with a pin. Shirley was always blunt, but this was extreme even for her.

"Go ahead and kick me if I'm being too personal, honey, but we don't live in the old days, where a widow had to wear black for a year. Honestly, Paisley aren't you at least tempted to look around? You don't strike me as a mourning widow, so why act the part?"

Paisley was silent. She hadn't confided the truth about her marriage to Shirley but her friend must have read between the lines.

She continued leafing through a rack of vintage clothes while thinking of her answer. "I'm not interested in looking around," she said at last, "but I'm not locking myself in my room, either. I've agreed to have dinner with my neighbor, Steven Lopez, tomorrow. It's not a date, exactly. Just a chance to get to know each other better."

"Really?" Shirley looked surprised. "Well, why not? He's darned good looking, and a hard worker. Ever since his father died, that young man has been trying to make something of that winery." She studied Paisley from the corner of her eye. "Actually, I thought you might be interested in that Ian McMullin, whose truck seems to be parked outside your house every time I drive by."

"I'd forgotten you knew Ian," Paisley said, feeling uncomfortable.

"Small town, remember? Ian's one of my best customers. Comes into the book shop all the time. Real bright kid. He won all kinds of scholarships when he graduated from high school. His dad was so proud of him." Shirley tucked her arm through Paisley's. "Well, forgive Aunt Shirley for being so curious about your love life, Paisley. As the anointed town gossip, I've always figured the quickest way to find stuff out is to ask."

"Well, now you know there's nothing to know," Paisley said cheerfully. Inside she thought from now on she'd better be careful to keep anything important to herself unless she wanted it blasted through the town grapevine. She could handle intrusive reporters and paparazzi, but Shirley Zacarias was another matter altogether.

The afternoon of female bonding was capped with éclairs and cold lemonade at the café on Main Street. These past few weeks had been caught up in repairing the house, working on the community-theater play, and amateur sleuthing with Ian. Maybe it was time to resume a more normal life, Paisley thought, finishing her last gooey bite of eclair. One that involved friends and social events. As the external scars were growing less noticeable, perhaps her inner ones were too.

At home after shopping with Shirley, Paisley struggled to hang the hammock between two oaks in the back yard, a task more complicated than she'd contemplated, but when at last it was done, she took a long nap that lasted until the heat lessened. Revitalized, she went into the kitchen, dug out Esther's old cookbook and, on a whim, whipped up a fragrant batch of homemade gingersnaps. Biting into one of the soft, brown cookies, she found them a far cry from the hard, cardboard-like versions sold in grocery stores. The house smelled like Christmas in July.

Pouring herself a cold glass of milk, Paisley marveled at how different life in River Bend was from her old transatlantic life. Barry Foster had worried she'd be bored. Bored? With some surprise, Paisley reflected she could easily get used to this slow-paced life where neighbors soon became friends. When the time came to leave, it would be with a pang.

Reaching for another gingersnap, Paisley opened Esther's childhood diary. If she was going to read it, better do it now. On Monday, Ian and his crew would be back to fill the air with noise, dust, and commotion.

Between the worn green covers, young Esther's account showed she'd adapted quickly to life in America. Nowhere in the diary's pages did the girl describe the traumatic separation from her parents or the long journey to America. Instead Esther wrote of the trivial details of daily life in River Bend: going to the local elementary school, playing kickball with her best friend, Georgiana, and rejoicing in the gift of a kitten for her ninth birthday.

Paisley wondered again if that long-ago kitten might be an ancestor of the elusive gray cat that now left the food bowl empty each evening. Hadn't Ray said the Perlemans always had cats? Something else Esther had written made her wrinkle her brow as well. "Georgiana." Why did the name of Esther's childhood best friend sound familiar?

Surprisingly the pages contained few references to the members of Esther's extended American family. Aunt Henka was mentioned, of course, and Uncle Borys. Those had been Jonathan's grandparents. Esther had two cousins as well who lived under the family roof: the elder, David, had grown up to become Jonathan's grandfather. But what had happened to Henka and Borys's second child, Leah?

Paisley closed the diary, trying to remember what Jonathan had said about his relatives. His father's sister had moved away and married. What was her name? Paisley was pretty sure Jonathan had never mentioned it. The young woman had apparently lost touch with the rest of the family. Perhaps she had had children. If so, they would be Jonathan's cousins.

Giving up on Jonathan's family tree, Paisley re-opened the diary. Her eye fell almost at once on a troubling passage: *"Auntie Henka asked me again today. Then she slapped me and took my coat away. I hope she will give the coat back."*

The reference to the slap startled Paisley. Physical punishment was more common in the old days, she reminded herself. After that, the entries became more scattered as young Esther's interest in her journal apparently fizzled out. After listing her Hanukkah gifts, which included a storybook and a wristwatch, Esther left the last portion of the diary blank.

Paisley flipped through the empty pages, frowning. No clues. Except, perhaps, the reference to Aunt Henka's slap. Perhaps, Paisley thought, Esther suspected that her diary might be read and so had deliberately left out anything that might ruffle anyone's feathers. Except that one telling sentence that had seemingly burst out of her pen in spite of herself.

She slapped me and took my coat away.

Paisley wondered what question Aunt Henka could have asked her niece that would have resulted in such an outbreak of anger? Perhaps Esther had declined to do some chore, or been ill-mannered or defiant. But the reference to the coat made Paisley wonder.

What if Esther had brought the jewels to America in the hem of the coat which her grandmother had carefully constructed for her and then refused to hand the valuable heirlooms over to her American relatives? That would certainly explain Aunt Henka's anger.

Scanning the diary again, Paisley tried to read between the lines and grew more certain than ever that young Esther had been miserable living with her American relatives. Yet she had returned as an adult to the very house where these events had happened, and some of her childhood friendships had lasted a lifetime. River Bend must have held some good memories for the young Holocaust survivor. Paisley certainly hoped so.

She put the diary with the worn green cover in the top drawer of her dresser for safekeeping. When Ian got back from Berkeley, he might find the contents of the diary as interesting as she did.

While preparing dinner that evening Paisley saw a flash of gray outside the kitchen window and opened the side door, hoping to catch sight of Esther's elusive cat. It must be out there, hidden in the shadows.

"Here, kitty," she cooed. "Here, kitty, kitty, kitty."

A pair of pointed ears appeared from the greenery, followed by a flat, whiskered muzzle with a pink nose. It put out one graceful white paw, then another, until its entire form was exposed. For a moment the cat crouched, staring at her from slitted yellow eyes, then, with a flash of its tail, it disappeared back into the shrubbery.

Impulsively she followed. Moments later, she realized it was not only the cat who had been in the back yard. A crushed stalk of honeysuckle in the flower bed and, magnified by the shadows of early evening, the clear imprint of a shoe in a bare patch of earth showed there had been a recent human visitor as well. In the footprint were two clearly legible stylized letters: "VA." She recognized the logo for Vans sneakers.

Paisley stopped short, staring at the footprint. Not only was it far larger than her own size six, but she did not own a pair of Vans, a brand popular with teenagers.

Briefly she thought of calling the police, then decided against it. They probably wouldn't take her statement any more seriously than they had after the break-in, even with this footprint as evidence. Besides, she could deal with this alone. She had a good idea who owned the sneakers.

Later that night, when Paisley climbed into bed, it was not the upcoming dinner with her handsome, dark-haired neighbor that filled her mind. It was Ian's implied criticism of her behavior.

Was she being greedy and materialistic in seeking Esther's lost jewels? Was the search a fun, fanciful way to spend the summer? A justifiable act of financial desperation? Or was it something uglier? Was the spirit of Esther helping her to find them, or was it warning her away?

Exhausted and full of self-doubt, she punched the pillow, fighting down warring thoughts.

For the dinner with Steve the next day, Paisley smoothed the wrinkles out of her red jacket and dabbed extra cover-up on the scar on her throat. She was glad to see it had faded somewhat. All those walks had put color in her cheeks as well, and her newly tanned legs no longer looked like white sticks.

What would Jonathan think of her having dinner with his former school mate? Paisley knew the answer: her late husband would have been furious. A stab of anger went through her at his hypocrisy. What he had done was so much worse. How many of her friends had known the truth, but had been too tactful or too loyal to Jonathan to tell her?

Frowning, she reached for her purse, ready to walk next door. Enough looking back. The past was over. It was time to move ahead.

Steve's warm brown eyes scanned her, from the shining updo to her strappy sandals. She was vain enough to feel gratified. He looked sharp himself,in a spotless white button-up shirt and crisp gray gabardine slacks. The house was as neat as before, everything in its place. The long, oddly shaped object she had seen propped in a corner was missing.

As promised, he'd had prepared Mexican-style enchiladas with what appeared to be homemade corn tortillas, black beans and a fiery salsa that burned her tongue. Two goblets stood on the table next to a bottle of red wine, its attractive label matching the hand-painted road sign: a wreath of grapes encircling the name, Lopez Wines, sloped in graceful script..

The dining room was empty except for themselves and a dark-walnut dining table and leather chairs. The plates were made of deep-red stoneware that looked hand-made, beautifully setting off the Mexican fare.

"Where's Kevin?"

Steve shrugged. "You know how teenagers are. They only like to hang out with kids their own age."

Paisley had looked forward to seeing Kevin, and the boy's absence made the dinner feel too intimate, almost like a date. On the other hand, now she could discuss the troubled teenager with his stepfather, something she had been wanting to do.

"Kevin's new to River Bend, isn't he? He told me he'd moved here this summer, from New Jersey." She took another bite of the enchilada. Her mouth burned, and she reached for water to wash it down, leaving her wine glass untouched.

Steve nodded. "Kevin came after his mother died back east, about six months ago."

"No dad in the picture?"

"His father died when he was a baby. I was probably the closest to a father figure Kevin's ever had. His mother and I were married for a couple of years when Kevin was a toddler. As you can guess, it didn't work out. We didn't stay in touch much after that. That's why the situation is a bit awkward."

"Aren't there other relatives Kevin could have lived with?"

Steve hesitated. "There was a grandmother on the dad's side that he stayed with at first. But she was getting too old and infirm to care for a teenager, so she wrote and asked if I would give him a home."

"Oh," Paisley said. She imagined how the boy must have felt, watching both his parents die and then his grandmother deteriorate into illness. How awful to fall into the hands of a stepfather—not even a stepfather; a *former* stepfather!—who probably the boy only out of a sense of duty.

She took another bite, thinking. Kevin had arrived in River Bend only a few months after Esther had moved to the Sunny Acres Retirement Center. Most likely, the teenager had never met the old woman. So why had he looked at Paisley so strangely when hearing she was related to the Perleman family? Perhaps she had just imagined that furtive look from under those dark eyelashes. She was no expert at reading the expressions of troubled teenagers.

"It's got to be a difficult situation for you and Kevin," Paisley said, breaking the silence that had fallen. "It was kind to take him when you had no legal obligation to do so."

He smiled wanly. "In other words, no wonder Kevin is having trouble adjusting?"

"I didn't say that."

"But you were thinking it. Cut off from friends, yanked across the country against his will, living with a stepfather he barely remembers...."

"I've noticed Kevin seems to hang around by himself, a lot," she admitted. "You mentioned yourself that he spends a lot of time in his room alone."

"True." He poured more wine into his glass and gazed into its dark-red depths. "Actually, he was having a hard time even before his mom died. I heard there were some incidents in New Jersey...." Steve's voice faded, and he shrugged. "His grandmother hoped coming to California would give him a fresh start. The poor kid had nowhere else to go."

"But Kevin's not happy here, is he?"

Steve looked up. "River Bend's a small town. It can be hard to fit in when everyone else has known each other all their lives, a city kid coming to the country." He shrugged again. "Kevin and I are both doing the best we can."

She changed the subject. "If you grew up here, you must have known Jonathan."

He settled back in his seat, as if relieved to talk about something else. "Not well. Jonathan was five years older than me, and was always at music lessons or practicing the piano. I was just the annoying kid next door, a jock who never really succeeded in breaking away from his home town." He noticed her untouched goblet. "Hey, you haven't tried my wine. It's a small vineyard, I know, but it compares well with some of the better-known labels."

Paisley pushed away her glass. "Sorry. I should have warned you that I'm a teetotaler. My father was an alcoholic, and I swore I'd never touch the stuff." She didn't mention the memories it brought back of Jonathan's betrayal. She glanced up, wondering if she had offended her host. Wine was obviously a big part of his life, and it should not have been surprising that he wanted to show it off.

"Sure. Why play Russian Roulette with genetics? But you've come to the wrong part of California if you want to avoid wine." To her relief he was smiling. Nor did he press her again.

"I take it you're not interested in visiting the winery, then?" Steve said when they had finished their meal.

"Actually, I'd love to." She blotted her mouth with her napkin and and set it down. "I've heard it's a fascinating process. Go ahead, lead the way."

He escorted her to a metal-roofed, stucco-walled building behind the house, and she could see pride in his expression as he reached behind a stone in the planter outside the door and removed a key. "I started the business after my father died," he told her, as they stepped into the dimly lit interior. "This land used to be part of a rancho owned by my ancestors under the old Mexican land grant system. They were original 'Californios,' or Mexican residents of California before it became part of the United States. With the success of Napa Valley nearby, I decided to try my hand at growing grapes."

The room was larger than it appeared on the outside, with rows of wooden barrels stacked five-high up the sides and a wide aisle down the center. "Someday I'll strap those barrels in case we have another earthquake like the last one," Steve continued. "But I'm waiting until we bring in more income. So far the winery barely pays for itself. We only produce a few thousand bottles a year, and most of those are sold locally. But by adding acreage, maybe we'll be able to compete with the larger producers. If we bring in some tourists, build familiarity with the brand, who knows what might happen?"

Ian had said her neighbor's winery was losing money, and that Steve was in over his head. But Ian must have been exaggerating, Paisley thought. The winery looked clean and prosperous, and Steve seemed sure it was poised for success. Perhaps Ian was jealous.

Looking at Steve's face, glowing with ambition, Paisley remembered how she had felt at her first national opera competition when she had realized she actually had a chance to win. When Jonathan, who had been one of the judges, came up to her after her performance and invited her to lunch to discuss her career.

"I'd like to add landscaping out front, build a tasting room, and buy a few dozen more wine barrels," Steve was saying. "French oak, ideally. Those add that touch of flavor that sets apart the best wines. But imported barrels don't come cheap. Still, the improvements will be worth the investment if we can build up word-of-mouth, and get rated by some of the top connoisseur magazines." He laughed uncomfortably, and smoothed his black hair. "Like they say, it takes money to make money."

"You seem to be doing all right," she said, looking around at the polished cement floors, the floor-to-ceiling bottles of wine, the spotless, shining stainless-steel equipment.

He thrust his hands into his pockets, disregarding the lines of his neat slacks. "Yeah, well, you know. Appearances can be deceiving."

Yes they can, she thought. The life she and Jonathan had lived had been a good example of false appearances. The good clothes, the fast cars, the appearance of being opera's "golden couple," even meriting an occasional photograph in glossy magazines. And it had all turned out to be a sham. Once again painful memories flooded through her: Jonathan's rage when she had asked about the woman in the hotel room, his jerk of the steering wheel as he turned to glare at her at just the wrong moment.

"Ray Henderson said that's why you want to buy my land," she said, anxious to change the subject. "To expand your vineyard. But I only own a couple of acres. That hardly seems enough to make a difference."

He nodded. "Your house is the first thing drivers see when coming around that big curve from town. I'd like to move my sign in front to enhance our visibility. The structure itself would be perfect for a tasting room and gift shop. And yes, I would like to add more rows of vines; an acre or two would help us more than you might think."

"Us?'"

"Kevin and I." He paused. "I might as well tell you that I'm putting in paperwork to legally adopt him. Since I'm his guardian, it seems the right thing to do. He needs a real father."

"I see." She wondered what Kevin thought of the idea. From what she had seen, the teen didn't seem overly fond of his new "dad."

"Things are quiet right now," Steven said, "but after the grapes are picked in late September, they'll be dropped into the crusher outside—that's the large metal equipment you passed when we came in—then pumped into these stainless-steel tanks for a day or so, to give the juice and skins time to interact. That's for red wine only, of course. We don't use skins to make white wine."

"Uh huh."

He smiled at her unenthusiastic response but continued. "Then we press the mixture and store the wine in these oak barrels. Each one holds fifty-nine gallons. Within one to three years, the wine will be ready to bottle."

"How do you know when it's ready?"

"We taste it of course. That's the hardest part of the job."

Paisley suspected everyone in Northern California must have heard that joke hundreds of times, but she smiled anyway. "I'm sure it is," she said dryly.

When they walked back toward the house, she asked the question that had been bothering her since learning of her inheritance. "Do you know how Esther ended up with the old

Perleman house? It used to belong to Jonathan's parents and grandparents, didn't it?"

"Good question." He frowned, as if trying to remember. "Let's see. I believe the house originally belonged to the first Perlemans who immigrated from Poland. They were peddlers, from what I recall, making their way to California around the turn of the last century. They opened a general store in River Bend. Esther's branch of the family remained in Poland. She came here as a child, sometime in the 1930s, probably."

Paisley nodded. She was familiar with this part of the story. "Didn't Esther move to Sacramento later?" she prompted.

"That's right. She taught high school there until Jonathan's grandfather retired and moved to San Francisco." He looked over at her. "When his grandfather died, Esther bought it. Jonathan was at Julliard by then, and his parents moved to New York to be with him. Unfortunately, they both died young."

"Why did Esther come back to River Bend?"

He shrugged. "Sentimental reasons, maybe. I didn't pay too much attention to the Perleman place after Jonathan moved away. I was back east, trying to make a go of it with my ex-wife."

They were back in the living room now. He sank into the leather sofa after waving Paisley into an armchair. She was relieved that he seemed contented to leave things at being friendly neighbors.

"It's surprising that Esther lived away from the house for so long," Paisley mused. "Her presence is so strong there."

Steve looked at her strangely, and she realized she sounded as if she were a superstitious lunatic. She didn't believe in ghosts, and he didn't seem the type to believe in them either. Abruptly, she changed the subject. "What took you to the east coast? College?"

He shook his head. "I'm not the intellectual type. Just wanted a change of scenery. But after my divorce and my dad's death, I came back and turned the ranch into a vineyard. Like I said, it seemed like a good idea, being so close to the Napa Valley. Same climate, same soil conditions. Someday, I'm sure I'll make a go of it."

"Did you keep in touch with Jonathan over the years?" she asked. "You said you used to hang around him a lot when you were little."

"Not much, after we grew up. I did send him a congratulatory email when his picture was published in *Time* magazine. He always was a lucky guy. Everything always went his way." His expression changed. "Sorry. I guess that was thoughtless of me to say that."

"It's all right. I know what you meant." She paused, looking around the room. "And when during all this time did you take up painting?"

He looked at her, startled. "How did you know I paint?"

She gestured at the enormous abstract painting over the couch, all reds and golds. "That's your signature at the bottom, isn't it? It's really good. As good as some I've seen in galleries. Do you do representational art also?"

"It was just a hobby. Now I'm too busy with the vineyard. I still pick up a brush now and then, when I have time, but that's as far as it goes."

"I don't suppose I could talk you into helping with the sets for the play?" she asked hopefully. "We need someone to supervise painting the pirate ship and some of the backdrops."

Steve grinned at her. "You're just like her, aren't you? Give or take sixty years."

"Like who?"

"Esther, of course. She'd get everyone in town to donate either time or money to the community theater. It was a really big deal for her."

"Maybe she wanted to turn River Bend into another Ashland, Oregon, or Cedar City, Utah." When he looked blank, she explained, "You know, one of those small towns that are famous for their first-rate annual theater festivals."

"She might have succeeded. We're located halfway between Sacramento and San Francisco, close enough to pull in a decent crowd from both directions. That's why I'm hoping to get more tourists out to visit my vineyard."

"So will you help paint the backdrops?" Paisley was intrigued by the idea of a summer theater festival at River Bend, using local talent. Why not? Although they'd need a better theater and a lot more publicity. The high school theater wasn't adequate for anything so ambitious. But with more donations, some big fund-raisers, and enough support from the local residents...

"I'll think about it." Steve changed the subject without committing himself. That seemed to be something her neighbor was good at.

By the time Paisley stood to go, she thought again that her handsome neighbor reminded her a little of Jonathan, not just because of his physique and dark hair but because of self-confidence and poise that bordered on arrogance. When he surprised her by leaning over to kiss her good-night, she pulled away.

Steve straightened. "Too soon?"

"I didn't think this was a date. Wasn't it just a neighborly get-together?"

He smiled down at her. "Sorry. Can I drive you home, at least? All of one hundred yards away?"

"Thanks, but the doctors said walking would be good for my leg. And it's true," she added, surprised. "I already feel stronger since coming to River Bend. Good night, Steve."

Paisley sensed his eyes following her as she set off toward Esther's little house, visible under the towering oak tree as dusk settled. No, Paisley told herself, quickening her step. Not Esther's house. *Her* house. Maybe that's why it tugged at her.

Why hadn't she been moved by Steve's attempt to kiss her? It couldn't be just because of Jonathan's death. Those wounds were beginning to heal. Besides, Steve looked like one of the dark, brooding men on the covers of the paperbacks on the racks at airport bookstalls. Why didn't his good looks have more of an effect on her? Paisley had the impression that Steve was great to look at in the same way as an attractive hand-painted porcelain statue, which was hollow inside and might easily crack.

She reminded herself that she was not a particularly good judge of character. Why not give Steve a chance? The poor guy had his plate full, with a troubled stepson to care for and a winery he was struggling to save. And Paisley *had* felt some physical response. Maybe, with time....

Paisley was nearly home when she remembered that she hadn't brought up her suspicions about Kevin breaking into her house. Oh well. She had seen how strict Steve could be with Kevin. Since her neighbor's way of dealing with the troubled boy did not seem to be working, it might be better to handle the matter on her own.

The steady trill of the doorbell the next morning was as effective as an alarm clock. Paisley fumbled for her cell phone on the bedside table and glanced at the time: seven-thirty. She swung out of bed and threw on her bathrobe, muttering under her breath. She wasn't surprised to see Ian with his finger pressing the doorbell, looking wide awake, freshly showered, and wearing his usual outfit of a clean but rumpled plaid shirt and jeans. She wondered if he owned any other type of clothes.

Although she'd always liked men who dressed well, for some reason, Ian's habitual dishevelment didn't bother Paisley. If he dressed any other way, he wouldn't be ... well ... Ian.

Fighting back a yawn, Paisley wondered how she had gotten the mistaken impression that her employee was a late sleeper. He seemed to rise with the larks, even after a late night on the road. Maybe it was an admirable habit, but to someone less disciplined, like herself, it was annoying.

Nonetheless, Paisley's heart lifted a little at the sight of him. When he was around, it always felt like something good was about to happen. Ian smelled good, too, she thought, sniffing. Irish Spring soap and clean skin. No after-shave today.

"Well?" Paisley stepped back for him to come in. The gesture was starting to feel habitual. "What did you learn from the library in Berkeley?"

Instead of responding, he studied her face critically. "You look better today. No purple circles under your eyes. And that tousled hair gives you a sort of sexy, Penelope Cruz look. So the intruder didn't return?"

"Uh uh." No reason to mention those betraying Vans tread marks in the garden. She had decided to deal with Kevin in her own way. "What did you learn in Berkeley?" Paisley repeated.

"Unfortunately, not a word about the Nightingale of Warsaw," he said, falling onto the sofa and crossing his sneakers on the coffee table. They were black-and-white Converse high-tops, not Vans, she noted. "But if you want some juicy stuff on scandalous 19th century babes like Lola Montez or Helena Modjeska, I can fill you in. Did you know Lola Montez lived near here in Grass Valley after breaking up with the King of Bavaria, and that she carried a stash of jewels with her everywhere? Apparently Lola also kept a pet bear tied up in her front yard. That is, until it attacked her."

Paisley drooped with disappointment. "So the trip was a waste?"

"Not at all. I whooped it up with my college friends until two o'clock in the morning at a great vegan restaurant. Too bad you didn't come with me," Ian added. "All this moping around the house alone can't good for you. You would have enhanced my prestige with my buddies as well. They were quite impressed when I told them I was restoring a house for a hot young opera star. One of them actually read about you in Newsweek magazine.

He said you won some prestigious national competition a few years ago."

Paisley did not want to think about her brief-lived opera career, nor the competition where she had met Jonathan. "Here." She sat next to him and held out the diary, pleased to see his eyes light up with curiosity. "Take a look and tell me what you make of it."

Ian took the small book, handling its brittle pages carefully, his lean face glowing with curiosity. "So this is Esther's childhood journal? Anything helpful in it?" he asked, leafing through its pages.

"I'm not sure. I want to see what you think."

He was a fast reader. As the minutes passed, his face grew absorbed. The light from the reading lamp cast dark shadows under his heavy brow ridges and highlighted the prominence of his cheekbones. Finally Ian looked up, his eyes sober. "I feel a definite chill between young Esther and Auntie Henka. Interesting."

Paisley's gaze wandered out the parlor window. Then she gasped, forgetting Aunt Henka, Esther, and the diary. "Is that the car?"

He followed her regard. "Yup. Sorry, I haven't had time to wash it yet—"

She didn't hear the rest of his sentence, already rushing outside as fast as she could despite her limp. The Volkswagen beetle was faded yellow with black racing stripes, and bore a striking resemblance to Herbie from *The Love Bug*. Paisley could tell the stripes down the hood were hand-painted because they were slightly crooked. The cracked vinyl seats were held together with black electrical tape. She ran her hand gently over the warm hood.

A car. A car of her very own. Not Jonathan's Porsche, which he refused to let her drive. Not a taxi or an Uber or a subway. A real *car*. A month ago she would have turned up her nose at the homely thing, and Jonathan's reaction would have been either laughter or scorn. Now, all Paisley could think of was the freedom that it represented. No more limping home carrying heavy bags of groceries, or relying on Shirley for a lift. It had been years since she'd learned to drive in high school, but she'd kept her New York license valid. Suddenly she couldn't wait to get behind the steering wheel.

Ian watched Paisley like a mother gauging a stranger's reaction to a beloved but remarkably ugly baby. "Like I said, it's been in the garage for a long time. But it runs."

"It's perfect."

Ian visibly relaxed. "Now that you've got wheels, you can explore the area. There's a lot more to Northern California than this small town. How about a drive to test it out?"

"With you?"

He shrugged. "I can point out the sights."

Sights? Paisley hadn't noticed much more than farmland and a few bland subdivisions strung along the freeway on the drive from the Sacramento airport. Besides, he had just got back from a long trip to Berkeley.

Nevertheless, after writing a check to pay for the Volkswagen and wincing a little at the thought of her depleted account, Paisley got behind the wheel while Ian folded his long legs into the passenger side.

"How did you ever fit into this little car?" she asked.

Ian slouched in his seat, his head scraping the car's ceiling. "This car was fine in high school, but I had to swap it with my dad's truck when I grew four inches in college."

Laughing, Paisley pressed the gas pedal. They passed rolling fields of grape vines and lavender. The river, which someone had told her was a tributary of the Sacramento River, wound lazily toward the east, along the road. She felt herself relax. There was something therapeutic about watching the peaceful fields roll by outside the car window.

As she drove, Ian regaled her with stories about pranks he and his friends had played on professors, of trips he'd taken overseas, of fond memories of Esther Perleman. Paisley opened up as well, about what it was like bouncing around the country while her father tried to find a job he could keep. About the singing competition that launched her career, the one where Jonathan noticed her and took her under his wing. The increasingly prominent roles, in the United states and abroad. Winning the part of Mimi, the role that would have put her in the top flight of sopranos, if not for that fateful accident in Germany.

Paisley was surprised to find she could talk about Jonathan and her old career without that old, dull pain in her midsection. And Ian didn't ever mention her hoarse voice. She almost forgot it herself. Was it her imagination, or was it less noticeable than before?

Just then, a neatly lettered sign announcing the Sunny Acres Retirement Home caught her eye. White-painted gates framed a steep private road that wound up a lushly landscaped hill which must have a gorgeous view over the river. The name of the place sounded familiar. Hadn't one of the men she had watched playing chess at the senior center—Hugo, was it, or Walter?—mentioned that Esther spent her last days at a retirement home? This must have been the one.

As if of its own volition, the VW turned and started up the long driveway.

Chapter Ten

When they left the main road, Ian sent her a questioning look. "Do you know someone who lives here?"

"No, but Esther did." Paisley steered up the twisting road. "Someone told me she spent her last days at this retirement center. Maybe she told someone something about the jewels. It's a long shot, but it can't hurt to find out."

Ian settled back in his seat. "Sure, why not? I've got nothing better to do this afternoon."

Without mentioning the thesis he was supposed to be working on, Paisley pulled into a parking space at the top of the hill. The facility center was spotlessly clean, with sand-colored stucco walls, a Mediterranean-style tile roof, and pots overflowing with geraniums. The gardens provided a lovely view over the valley, with the river winding past the town below like a curl of silver ribbon. Several residents sat on benches outside the low building, basking in the sun. They smiled and nodded as Ian and she passed.

As pleasant as the facility appeared, Paisley wondered how Esther felt about leaving her cozy house to live among strangers. On the other hand, she had probably immediately set about making new friends, organizing book clubs, and participating in shuffleboard competitions.

Accompanying Ian toward the information desk, Paisley saw a dark-haired teenager wheeling an old woman across the lobby. The youth saw them at the same time and stopped in his tracks.

"Kevin! What are you doing here?" asked Paisley.

He shuffled his feet. "Hi, Mrs. Perleman."

Sensing the boy's discomfort, Ian nodded a greeting at Kevin and continued toward the information desk. Grateful for his tact,

Paisley stopped to speak to her young neighbor. "Please call me Paisley," she reminded him. "Do you volunteer here?"

Kevin hesitated, while the white-haired woman tapped the wheelchair armrest, looking impatient. "Um, not really This is my grandmother. I come up here every weekend to visit her."

"How nice!" Paisley turned to the woman and held out her hand with a big smile. "Hello, I'm Paisley Perleman. I'm your grandson's next-door neighbor."

The woman ignored the hand, glaring at Paisley. She looked like a child's image of a witch, with knobby fingers, a turned-down mouth, and whiskers sprouting from her chin. A sticker stuck to the front of her blouse stated in black Sharpie that her name was "Maude Avery." Some activity must have ended for the residents in the nearby recreation room. Others, wearing similar nametags, were filtering out of the glass double-doors.

Paisley tried not to feel hurt at the woman's unfriendliness. Perhaps she resented Paisley for delaying the next activity, a bingo game or a big-screen broadcast of "The People's Court."

"Sorry." Paisley's hand dropped to her side. "I didn't mean to interrupt you. Kevin. When you're finished visiting your grandmother, I've a question to ask you. I'll wait in the lobby."

Kevin glanced at his grandmother. "Um, okay. I'll see you in a few minutes." He pushed the wheelchair away.

Paisley watched him leave. Did he think she was going to confront him about the burglary? Ian was still talking to the receptionist, an attractive young blond. She wondered what he was saying.

Shortly after, Kevin returned alone.

"Let's go outside, where there's more privacy," Paisley told him.

He nodded, hands shoved into his jeans pockets. They walked out the door, and she glanced at his shoes. Vans sneakers. The soles left a distinct pattern in the dirt pathway.

Roses were in full bloom, drenching the air with heavy perfume. They sat on a wooden bench, and Kevin twisted his hands, fidgeting. Paisley wondered if he suspected she knew he'd burglarized her house. Was his conscience bothering him? If so, now was the perfect time to confront him.

But something held her back. The fact that he had done such an amateurish job of searching her house proved he was no experienced criminal, and after all, nothing had been missing. Her purse and iPhone had been left out in plain sight, and yet neither had been touched. If she gained his trust, Paisley thought, maybe she could find why he'd gone through the house.

In the meantime, the play desperately needed a Pirate King. That could be a start.

Her still-raspy voice sounded business-like. "I heard you perform at open-mic night. You're a good singer. I'm helping with a musical production here in River Bend, and I'd like to offer you one of the lead roles."

The tension drained out of him. It was as if he had been expecting a blow which had not materialized. "A musical production? You mean *The Pirates of Penzance*?"

"So you've heard about it?"

He didn't exactly roll his eyes, but his look was one that has crossed every teenager's face at one time or another. "There's a big banner hanging over Main Street and posters in all the shop windows."

"The director, Shirley Zacarias, unexpectedly lost one of her stars and needs someone to replace him."

He looked up from under his long black bangs. "Shirley Zacarias? Is that the lady who owns that bookshop across from the coffeeshop?"

"Why, yes. How did you know?"

"Her store has a great Manga collection. Three whole bookshelves full."

Lots of kids his age were interested in Japanese comics,
Paisley remembered. "That's right. Anyway, I'm helping Shirley
with music for the show, and we're short on talent. Someone told
me you can sing, and they were right."

His face turned beet red, and he looked down at his Vans.
"Yeah? Who told you that?"

"A girl in the cast. Blond, about this tall." Paisley held a hand
a couple of inches above her own head. "She told me about open-
mic night, so I went."

"Is her name Chloe?"

Paisley kept her smile to herself. "Yes, that's right."

Kevin's face broke into the wide grin she remembered from
when they'd first met. Paisley vowed to get him onstage if she had
to wrestle him there. Underneath the adolescent awkwardness lay
charisma that could outshine klieg lights.

She turned on her own charm, doing everything but bat her
eyelashes. "I'll tell you what. Why don't you come to rehearsal
tomorrow afternoon? If you decide you don't want to participate,
then I won't try to change your mind. Scout's honor." Paisley
crossed her fingers behind her back. "You'll have fun. It's a
friendly group of kids. Some were there at Starbucks the other
night; you probably know a lot of them."

Kevin turned and glanced at the retirement center, as if
searching for direction. Then he met her eyes straight-on. "Okay.
One rehearsal. But I won't promise anything beyond that."

"Good enough." She held out her hand. After a hesitation he
took it. His grasp was nice and firm. Nice eyes, too: warm brown
under dark eyebrows and that shock of black hair. The girls would
love him. "See you at rehearsal. Five o'clock sharp at the high
school."

"Yeah. Tomorrow at five o'clock." He glanced at the
retirement home windows again before walking away.

Inside, Ian was still chatting to the receptionist, who was
giggling and twirling a lock of bleached hair around her French-

manicured finger. Ian must have been practicing his own brand of charm, she thought with a pang that felt suspiciously like jealousy. Then she caught herself. Ian could flirt with anyone he wanted. Good luck to him.

He turned as Paisley approached, and his grin widened, revealing long dimples in both cheeks. He might not have Steven Lopez's good looks but it was clear why the receptionist was batting her eyelashes at him.

"Hi, Paisley. Francesca here says Mrs. Georgiana Rivers would love to have visitors." He gave meaningful emphasis to his words.

"Georgiana Rivers?" Paisley frowned . "Oh!, Georgiana!" That was the name of the little girl who had given Esther a kitten for her fifth birthday. Georgianna must be a resident of the same retirement home where Esther had ended her days.

"Francesca says Georgiana and Esther shared a room," Ian told her. "Best friends reunited after decades apart."

"I'll buzz Georgiana's room and let her know you're coming, Mr. McMullin." Francesca tossed flowing blond locks over her shoulder. "Room 3-A on the right."

Whistling under his breath, Ian guided Paisley down a hallway decorated with watercolor paintings and potted plants. The door opened into an airy room with a stunning view over the valley. It held a large dresser and a TV mounted to the wall. A walker stood in the corner, and a slight whiff of Listerine mixed with the scent of roses. Birthday cards and a vase of flowers covered the dresser, while a bouquet of multi-colored mylar balloons bobbed in a corner, one of them saying "Happy Birthday!"

Almost hidden in the bed, a petite woman sat propped up by pillows. Paisley thought she was the spitting image of Mrs. Claus, pink cheeks, fluffy white hair, and all. A quilted housecoat was draped over her shoulders, and a fluffy object lay on her lap, which, on second glance, turned out to be a white shih-tzu. It yapped at them as they entered.

"Now, now, Fuzzykins," the woman scolded, tickling it under its chin. "These are friends."

The dog settled down on the comforter, watching suspiciously from under wisps of white fur tied with a pink bow.

Georgiana Rivers' cheeks plumped up like two Pink Lady apples. "Guests! How wonderful!" She reached out a hand, and Paisley took soft fingers that closed around hers with unexpected strength. Steel under marshmallow fluff. Paisley thought of Kevin's grandmother, but this smiling, fluffy-haired woman was nothing like the glowering harridan in the wheelchair. "Well, well, you must be Esther's grand-niece! What a wonderful birthday present, to have such a nice-looking young couple visit me!"

"I'm Esther's great niece through marriage," Paisley corrected her. "We were not blood relatives."

"Even better." Georgiana's blunt response didn't match her "just-took-sugar-cookies-out-of-the-oven" appearance. "Esther couldn't abide most of her relatives. Please, sit down, sit down, both of you!"

She waved them to a pair of chairs and focused her baby-blue eyes on Paisley. "So you're Jonathan's widow? Esther followed your career closely. She kept a scrapbook with clippings of you and Jonathan. It's in that bookcase over there."

Ian interpreted the wave of the plump hand and trotted over to fetch it. The scrapbook opened to the *Time* magazine cover featuring Jonathan. Glued to the opposite page was a yellowed newspaper clipping that mentioned Paisley's name in a review of Aida, her first performance in a supporting role at the Met.

Paisley was touched. "Esther scarcely knew me. Why on earth would she keep this memorabilia?"

Georgiana shook her head. "Esther told me she felt a connection with you at your wedding. I believe the words she used were, 'It was as if I knew her before.'"

Paisley had felt the same. Picturing the dark-haired old woman with the sparkling black eyes, she wished she had done more for Esther. But everything had been so rushed, and her career had seemed more important than relationships.

"Esther said she felt sorry for you, my dear," Georgianna said. "Or shall I say ... protective. Esther couldn't understand how a nice girl like you could put up with an egomaniac like Jonathan. She said he was just like the rest of his family."

Conscious of Ian's eyes on her, Paisley struggled to keep her face composed. She hoped he didn't think she'd married Jonathan just to advance her career. It wasn't true. At least, she hoped not. At any rate, Jonathan had benefited from their marriage almost as much as she had. The wedding generated a flurry of publicity, with many articles focusing on the attractive young couple.

Seemingly unconscious of the effect her words had on Paisley, Georgianna turned to her other visitor. A girlish expression appeared on the rosy features. "How nice to see you, Ian! My, you're even taller than your handsome grandfather. Did you know we graduated from high school together?" She and Ian chatted a while longer about mutual acquaintances before Georgiana transferred her attention back to Paisley, her eyes bright and curious. "So why did you both come today? Surely it wasn't just to visit little old me!"

Paisley cleared her throat. "I wanted to learn more about Esther's past," she confessed. "Especially her childhood. I hoped we might find someone who knew her long ago."

"Are you a family history buff?"

Paisley looked at Ian for guidance, but he blandly returned her gaze. She forged on. "Not really. But ever since moving into the house, I can't help thinking about her. Then Ian found a box containing an old diary of hers. She wrote about you in it."

Georgiana leaned forward, eyes shining. "A diary! Tell me, is it green leather with gold letters stamped on the cover?"

"Yes, it is."

"I gave that diary to Esther on her ninth birthday." Geogiana's eyes misted reminiscently. "She was new at our school, you see, and terribly shy. Thin, too, with big, black eyes. Esther only spoke a few words of English at first, but she had such a vibrant personality that I liked her at once. I invited her home, and after that we were inseparable."

"In the diary, Esther mentions you often. I wonder if she ever ... if the subject ever came up about...." For some reason, Paisley could not get the words out.

Ian's hand covered hers comfortingly. "Paisley wants to know if Esther ever talked about her life before she came to the United States," he told Georgianna.

A tiny frown knit the old woman's brows. "Hardly at all. The subject must have been painful for her. Parted from her family at such a young age, knowing she might never see them again... The horrible things that happened during the war didn't fully come out until years later, but somehow I'm sure she knew, even then." Georgiana's mouth trembled. Ian handed her a box of tissues, and she tugged one out, pressing it to her eyes.

Paisley looked down at her hands. The jewels' importance paled in the light of human tragedies, of human relationships. She hadn't meant to cause the old woman pain. Then something inside her, like a silent whisper, reminded her that Esther herself was the one who had started this. Leaving Paisley the cameo had not been just a sentimental gesture: it had been a pointed reminder of the old legend about the lost jewels. As if Esther was urging her to find them.

And she had bequeathed the house to Paisley, not to Jonathan, who had comprehended the message, even if Paisley hadn't. Esther had dangled the treasure just beyond his fingertips, laughing, even beyond the grave.

Even the dreams were a part of all this. Somehow Paisley had the sensation that Esther was urging her along, that the old woman wanted her to follow the clues. She would be disappointed if Paisley stopped now.

She cleared her throat. "Mrs. Rivers—"

"Oh, call me Georgiana, please!" Under the soft wrinkles appeared a glimpse of the friendly, impulsive girl who took young Esther under her wing.

"Georgiana, did Esther ever talk about...." Paisley avoided Ian's mocking eyes. He was letting her do most of the work. Well, why not? It was her quest, not his. "Did Esther ever mention a set of valuable jewels that she brought with her from Poland?"

"The rubies!" Georgiana's face lit in a broad smile. "That old story? My goodness, no, Esther always laughed whenever someone mentioned it." She chuckled, and then, seeming to lose her train of thought, changed topics. For the next ten minutes, she chatted about her grandchildren and great-grandchildren while Paisley, disappointed, tried to think of a polite way to take her leave. Then an odd expression crossed the old woman's face, and her forehead creased. "But that's not why you came, is it?. No, you were asking about Esther. That's right. Well, there *is* one story that might interest you."

"I'd love to hear it." Paisley leaned forward in her eagerness to hear. She sensed Ian next to her, alert.

"I'd almost forgotten. It's been so long...."

"What?" She tried not to sound impatient.

Georgianna batted a hand in front of her face, as if flicking away a fly. "Oh, it's probably nothing. I just remembered that when we were little, Esther once asked me if I'd like to see some pretty things her Polish grandmother had given her to bring to America. I thought she was talking about dolls or a tea set or something like that. Then something interrupted us. I don't remember what. Maybe another friend came to play, or maybe her Aunt Henka told her to do chores. I forgot about it, and Esther didn't bring up the subject again." She paused. "Later I did wonder about it, but it seemed rude to ask. I have no idea if there's any connection to what you're asking about."

Pretty things? It wasn't much of a clue, but Paisley filed it with the small amount of inconclusive evidence she had acquired.

"Is there anything else you can tell me?" she asked, not very hopefully.

The line appeared again between Georgiana's eyebrows. "Hmmm. Like I said, it was all so long ago. I do recall that she said her family in Warsaw had been quite rich at one time. I believe one of her ancestors had been a famous singer in Europe." She stroked the dog, and her eyes looked far away. "Or did I imagine that? We used to play pretend so often. Maybe that's all it was: just two girls playing pretend. The Perlemans—that's who you asked about, isn't it?— the ones who lived here in River Bend, that she came to live with, they were far from wealthy or famous. Just hard-working, middle-class folks, like the rest of us." She stopped and coughed.

Paisley hid her disappointment. She handed the old woman a glass of water from the nightstand. "Was Esther…." She hesitated again. Somehow this question seemed the most important of all. "Was Esther happy living with the American branch of her family?"

Georgiana sipped and set the water glass on the bedside table. "Esther was always a happy person, no matter what. She made it a point to be happy. But that's not what you mean." She leaned back against her pillow, and the soft fingers ran slowly through the dog's white fur. Her voice grew sleepy and vague. "Esther never liked Auntie Henka. I doubt there was physical abuse, as people would call it now, but Henka was a harsh, cold woman. Esther avoided her, preferring to come to my house to play. That's all I remember, my dear." Her eyes focused on Paisley again. "I do wish you could have come to her funeral. Her friends and former students burst the synagogue at the seams. Unfortunately Jonathan and you were not here, and the niece from back east was in bad health and could not come. But the service was lovely."

"I wish I had been there." Paisley meant it. "Where is she buried?"

Georgiana scratched the dog's throat. It made a sound astonishingly like a purr. "At the town cemetery, under a large oak tree just like the one next to her house. She bought the grave site long ago because the setting was so beautiful and peaceful."

An orderly knocked at the door and came in, carrying a tray. Georgiana looked like Shirley Temple shaking her curls in an old movie from the 1930s. "Oh, pooh! Time for my pills." She clutched at Paisley's hand. "You remind me so much of Esther, you know. That small, trim build with thick, dark hair. I'm sorry I couldn't help you, my dear, but I do hope you find whatever it is you're looking for." The old woman looked at Ian. "Esther would be so happy for the two of you. Such a wonderful young couple!"

They said their farewells and left, avoiding looking at each other. Walking down the hall, they passed a kind-faced young woman carrying flowers and wrapped presents, escorted by a pair of pink-cheeked children whose blue eyes bore a distinct resemblance to Georgiana's.

"Where did she get the impression that we—" began Paisley when they reached the car.

"Never mind." Ian opened the door. She thought he was blushing.

On the drive back, Paisley stopped at a flower shop and purchased a large vase of sunflowers. When they found the cemetery, Ian helped her search through the gravestones until they found the one she was looking for. As Georgiana had told them, it was under a large oak tree, just like the one that shaded the little white house. The simple headstone was engraved only with Esther's name and two dates.

Paisley set the flowers on the tomb, thinking of her benefactress whose unexpected gift had been there when she needed it most. Who had helped Esther when she was a young child, alone and frightened? Yet the child had survived and become a productive adult, with a rich and fulfilling life, even though she had never married or had children.

A reassuring feeling passed through Paisley, like the breeze soughing through the trees. *Don't worry, my dear, I'm fine.*

Yes. Esther was fine.

Paisley and Ian stayed a while longer before turning back to the car together. They drove away in silence leaving the flowers, a splash of yellow against the polished granite headstone.

Driving Ian home, Paisley wondered why she didn't feel disappointed that the visit to Sunny Acres hadn't yielded more information. Now she likely would never know what had happened to the jewels.

Sorry, Esther. I tried. I really did.

Now Paisley could turn her attention to more immediate matters, like her mounting bills and finding a job. So what if it would not be as a diva, as she'd once dreamed of? Life without singing? She'd survive, just as Esther had. She must be strong, like Esther.

Following Ian's directions, she stopped the car on a street not far from the town center. It was lined with 1950s-era bungalows, all of them immaculately maintained with lush green yards, white picket fences, and neatly trimmed purple oleander bushes in full glorious bloom. Ian's house was painted a crisp gray with white trim. The painted front steps were neatly swept and the shining windows practically squeaked with cleanliness.

So this was where Ian had grown up. He must have had an ideal childhood, she thought, surveying the tidy house. Paisley could almost picture his study inside: the drafting table, the rolls of architectural plans, the neat array of Sharpies and sketchpads. Although these days, architectural students probably did everything on computer.

It occurred to her that she had not asked Ian much about his personal life. She had taken him for granted, like the gray cat who took for granted the bowl of cat food she put out each morning and evening. Paisley felt slightly guilty, so she smiled at him with new warmth when he got out.

"Thanks for everything, Ian. For the car, for making my house habitable, for … well, for everything.

He looked startled. "You're welcome. Would you like to come in for a little while? I could make a snack if you're hungry. I make pretty good grilled cheese sandwiches."

Paisley shook her head, although she was tempted. There were sides of Ian she hadn't seen yet, and she was curious to discover them. At the same time, she mustn't give him the wrong message. They were friends. Just friends. She was a recent widow, and he was her occasionally amusing employee. "Sounds delicious, but not today. Thanks for the Volkswagen and the good company."

"Thanks for the five hundred bucks." Ian winked. "It'll help buy one or two textbooks. And watch out for the driver's side window," he called as she drove off. "It sticks."

The next morning, Paisley poured milk on her Mueslix, feeling well rested and at peace with the world. She had slept well, with no disturbing dreams. No whines and bangs of drills and hammers filled the air. Baby clouds scudded across a bright blue sky in the crisp, clear morning air. She finally had a car. No more limping on the long, hot walk to town! Even her voice did not sound as raspy as before. Best of all, she had persuaded Kevin to visit rehearsal. With luck, the problem of finding a suitable lead for the Pirate King might be solved.

That left the Major General. Ray Henderson had not yet called to volunteer, but then, Paisley hadn't really expected it. In community theater, one worked with what one had. The audience, mostly relatives, wouldn't care. Still, the ruddy-faced real estate agent would have been perfect for the part. She sighed.

By afternoon rehearsal, Paisley's spirits began to flag. Kevin was nowhere to be seen. She dreaded having to beg Nathan Primhurst to take his original part back. The unreliable thirteen-year-old was insufferably arrogant as it was, and she didn't look forward to his sneer.

While she was issuing directions for the final number, the doors at the back of the auditorium banged open and Kevin stood framed in the opening. Clad in a leather jacket and tight black jeans, he looked as if he were showing up for a casting call for *Grease*.

Wrong production, Paisley wanted to call out. Thumbs hooked in his pockets, tall and lean, he sauntered down the center aisle, ignoring everyone swiveling to watch his progress. Paisley knew Kevin's manner covered deep shyness, but the effect was supreme, swaggering confidence.

"Hey, Mrs. Perleman," he said.

"You came!"

He shrugged. "My stepdad needed my help, so this is the earliest I could get here. Sorry I'm late."

"Not a problem." Paisley thrust a score into his hands. "I don't suppose you can read music?"

"Actually, yeah, I can." He flipped through the pages like a magician shuffling cards. "Music pretty much runs in my family. Mom made me take four years of piano. I only gave it up when I started playing guitar. That was just before moving here from New Jersey."

"Great. Go ahead and look over *I am a Pirate King* for a few minutes before we run through it with the piano. We'll change to a key that suits your voice better, if necessary."

He nodded, dark hair flopping over his forehead and into his eyes. Something about the serious young face and strongly marked eyebrows stirred a memory inside of her. Paisley frowned, trying to figure out why.

Wanda picked out the song's tune with one gnarled finger on the piano keys. "Okay, got the melody?" Paisley asked.

"Yeah."

"Good. Let's run through it again. Sing aloud this time."

Kevin cleared his throat. The opening piano notes rang out, and a surprisingly robust baritone burst out of his slim frame. When he sang, Kevin's chin went up and he seemed to transform into another person. Someone bold and mature.

His leather-clad back was turned toward the rest of the auditorium, so he wasn't aware of the growing cluster of actors, but when the notes died away and the cast applauded, he whirled around. His face turned beet red.

"Well done!" Shirley slapped him approvingly on the back, and shooed the other actors onstage. "Okay, kids. Go ahead and get in your positions, just like we blocked it earlier. Chloe, you take Kevin backstage and help him find his costume."

They shuffled away, and Shirley came up to Paisley, beaming. "Way to go. You sure pulled a rabbit out of the hat this time."

"I don't know yet," Paisley murmured. There were still so many things that could go wrong. "Kevin's got talent, that's obvious. But he's awfully shy."

"Shy? Did you see his entrance?" Shirley rubbed her hands. "Just wait until that kid gets up on stage. He'll steal every scene. Why don't you come over to the shop after practice, and we'll celebrate?"

"Maybe we should save the celebration for opening night."

"So we'll celebrate twice. Come on over anyway. I have something to show you."

As Shirley headed away, Paisley suspected her friend's excitement was not just because Kevin joined the cast. What could it be?

After rehearsal, girls surrounded Kevin like fans besieging a rock star, including Chloe, the pretty blond who had been at open-mic night. Kevin's shyness melted rapidly away, and Paisley congratulated herself. Bringing her young neighbor into the production would be good for him *and* the play. Win-win.

"So you'll do it?" she asked, pulling him aside.

"Yeah, I guess so. I mean, I'll be in the play if you want me to. But everyone else already knows their parts. I don't want to ruin everything by forgetting my lines, or hitting the wrong notes."

What a polite kid despite his rough edges, she thought. What a shame that Steve always seemed to be so hard on him.

"I've already got a few kids coming over to my house for extra singing lessons," Paisley told him. "Why don't you come too? You'll catch up in no time."

Kevin's eyes lit up, but he hesitated. "I dunno know. Finances are kind of tight right now, with Steve expanding the winery and all. He might not want to pay for my lessons."

Paisley thought of Steve's gleaming Audi and the custom oak barrels recently ordered from France. Her mouth tightened. "Don't worry, I won't charge you for the lessons. Just study the score tonight and come to my house tomorrow after rehearsal, okay?"

"Do you really mean it?" His dark eyes met hers with unaccustomed frankness, and again she was struck by a nagging sense of something familiar about him. "Why are you willing to do all that for me? I mean, free lessons, giving up your time, and all that?"

"Because the play needs you. And heck, I like you. "

He regarded her with an odd look on his face. "Um ... Mrs. Perleman, maybe I ought to tell you something."

"I told you to call me Paisley."

"Um...."

Sensing he was about to back out, she interrupted before he had a chance. "Tomorrow, seven o'clock sharp, my house. Bring the sheet music with you."

Paisley had not forgotten Shirley's invitation to come over after rehearsal. The plump bookseller met Paisley at the door of the shop and led her upstairs to a cramped apartment upstairs. The homey, overcrowded living room was stuffed with furniture not quite old enough to qualify as antique.

After installing Paisley in a midcentury wingback armchair upholstered in a tangerine-colored floral fabric, she settled herself on the facing sofa, slipcovered in forest green.

"A little bird told me your boyfriend went to the Berkeley historical library last weekend," Shirley said, with a shrewd look.

Was that was why Shirley invited her over? Was she hoping to h ear a new tidbit of gossip? "First of all, Ian's not my boyfriend. Second of all, who told you that he drove to Berkeley?"

"Like I told you, I know everything that goes on in this town." Shirley kicked off her shoes and curled up her legs like a preteen girl at a pajama party. "That's why I wanted to ask you if that old rumor is still going around."

"What old rumor?" Paisley said cautiously.

"*You* know. We talked about it before. Those jewels that Esther Perleman supposedly brought over from Warsaw, just before the second World War. You're looking for them, aren't you?"

Paisley struggled to sit up straighter in her seat. "How did you know?"

Shirley looked smug. "It wasn't hard to figure out. There isn't anyone in this town over thirty years old who hasn't heard that old story. Your late husband used to brag about his Great-Grandmother Ruth's hidden stash of rubies. The neighborhood kids spent Saturday mornings digging in the back yard for them with our shovels and plastic buckets. That is, until we got bored and went home. So when you moved to River Bend and started asking questions about the family's past, I knew there was only one thing you could be looking for."

"Was it really that obvious?" Paisley could have kicked herself.

"Well really, what else would have brought you here? You certainly had no reason to be sentimental about the old Perleman place, and you could have recuperated from your injuries anywhere." Shirley winked. "I have a whole collection of old history books in my back room, gathering dust. Better than what Ian found at the library at Berkeley, I'll bet."

Paisley stared at her. "Like I said, how did you know Ian went to the Berkeley library?"

"Come downstairs," Shirley interrupted. "I'll show you everything I've got. There's some boxes of books Jonathan's parents sold when they moved away."

Shirley led her back down to the dimly lit bookshop and flicked on a light switch, illuminating the rows of shelves. "There." She waved her hand toward a rack of old books in a cubby in the back. "To be frank, if I wasn't so grateful with you for helping with the play, I'd be insulted you didn't ask me sooner. I thought we were friends."

Grabbing an armful of books, she sat cross-legged on the painted cement floor. After a moment's hesitation, Paisley joined her. For an hour they went through the titles until finally Paisley held up a large leather-bound book with strange lettering.

"Hey, look at this one. It's written in Polish." Paisley remembered the aerogramme Ian had found. Just like that letter, the words in this book were also heavily sprinkled with Ws, Ys, and Zs.

Shirley plucked the volume from Paisley's hand, inspected it briefly, and nodded with satisfaction, handing it back. "Yup, this is the one I thought you might be interested in. Jonathan's father sold the family's old books just before he passed on, but no one wanted this collection of biographies because it wasn't in English. There might be some pictures in here you'd be interested in. The world has more famous Poles than you might think."

"Chopin, of course. And Pope John Paul II." Accepting the challenge, Paisley opened the pages and rifling through them. "And I think Madame Curie was originally from Poland too, wasn't she?"

"Mmhmm. And according to that book, so was the astronomer Copernicus."

"Really?" Paisley's tone was abstracted. Her eyes were focused on black-and white photographs of men with handlebar mustaches and high collars, and engravings of sturdy women in peasant costumes. She stopped turning pages when she recognized two words in bold type. A woman's name.

Paisley looked up and met Shirley's eyes. The bookstore owner nodded. Carefully, Paisley lifted the fragile piece of tissue covering the black-and-white photograph, almost not daring to look. They both stared at the picture.

"That's her," Paisley said quietly. "That's Ruth Klaczko."

"And those," said Shirley, "are the jewels."

Chapter Eleven

Paisley refused Shirley's offer of a drink, and, clutching the book with one hand, drove home. Shirley had insisted on giving the volume to her. "It's priced a lousy two bucks, for goodness sake. It's the least I can do, after all the time you've spent helping me with rehearsals. If the book leads to anything, you can buy me lunch."

Paisley had intended to savor the discovery alone, but once she got home her hand strayed toward her cell phone.

He arrived in less than five minutes. Paisley stood on the porch watching the familiar green pickup truck turn up the driveway. Once, Esther used to invite him in for blueberry muffins when he was walking home from school. Had the old woman stood on the porch like this, anticipating the approach of the smiling boy with sandy hair and long, gangly limbs? But the older woman's feelings would have been maternal. Her own were more ... complicated.

Ian strode toward up the walkway, his eyes brightening when he saw her. She wondered what Jonathan would have thought of her male visitor. Most likely he would have looked down his patrician nose at the younger man, although Ian stood at least three inches taller. And yet, she thought with an odd lurch in her stomach, Ian matched or exceeded her late husband in every way that truly mattered: intelligence, kindness, and strength of character.

The realization took her aback, and she took a step back, a hand going to her throat in the newly habitual gesture.

Ian stopped in front of her. The smile faded, and his light-gray eyes grew puzzled. "Are you all right, Paisley? Your call sounded urgent."

"What? Oh. No burglars tonight. I just wanted to see you. Are you hungry? I just made an omelet."

"Mmmm. Do you need to ask?" Sniffing the aroma emanating from the kitchen, he followed her to the table, set with Esther's best dishes. Earlier, Paisley had cut some yellow roses blooming in the back yard, and arranged them in a mason jar. She'd tell Ian of her discovery after dinner. It would heighten the suspense.

After his first query, Ian seemed to take it for granted the invitation had been purely social. "There's a question I've been meaning to ask you," he said, after polishing off a second helping. Pushing away the plate, he leaned his chin on his knuckles and regarded her closely. "Why opera?"

Caught off guard, she stared at him blankly.

"I looked you up online. You were definitely on your way up before the car crash. First local productions, then winning some prestigious national competitions, then the Met. I'm no expert, but everyone knows music is competitive. So I wondered, if you have such a great voice...." She blessed him for not saying "had." "...Why pick opera for a career?"

"I'm sorry, Ian. I don't understand your question."

"There are a lot of other things a singer can do. Rock, folk, pop. Isn't opera pretty much a dead art form?"

She dabbed her mouth with a paper napkin. This argument came up many times with relatives and friends, and this was the perfect opportunity to set him straight. "That's a misconception. There are hundreds of thousands of opera fans all over the world. Maybe the style isn't as popular as rap or pop music, but that doesn't mean it's irrelevant. After all, Romance novels are the best-selling literary genre, but people still read serious books, don't they? Opera will last forever, like Shakespeare, or Charles Dickens."

At the expression on his face, she smiled. "Wow, that sounds pretty pedantic, doesn't it? I admit, opera can seem over the top at times with people hurling themselves off cliffs for love, or dying of consumption while singing at the top of their lungs. But at least it admits the power of passion. Our times bend to the other extreme, don't they? We're embarrassed to admit the power of human emotions."

He considered this. "Hmmm. I've seen rock concerts where the emotions seem pretty intense."

"Screaming and waving cell phones around isn't the same thing. I'm not saying I don't like popular music. My play list is probably at least as diverse as yours. But when you get home, download *Carmen* and see if you don't agree with me."

"I know a little about the story. A sexy cigarette factory worker leads a young man astray, right?

She chuckled. "I know it sounds silly, but if you don't like it, you'd have to have no sense of romance, of passion."

"No sense of passion?" At his expression, her heart skipped a beat. He started to push himself out of his seat. Quickly, she said, "I saw them today, Ian. They existed. They're real."

He froze in an awkward half-standing position, then plopped back in his seat. His face wore a comical mix of disappointment and anticipation. "What do you mean? The jewels? How do you know?"

"Ruth did pose for a photograph wearing the jewels. The picture must have been taken just before she quit her singing career. I've got the proof." From the side table, Paisley fetched the book from Shirley's store and flipped open to the page.

Ian studied the black-and-white picture and whistled softly. His eyes lingered on the wide, multi-stranded pearl choker that lay across the singer's creamy throat with several large pendants flaunting enormous gems. Matching earbobs dangled against the woman's swanlike neck and a sparkling tiara crowned the thick, wavy hair. A matching bracelet encircled one slender wrist, and a large ring adorned her finger.

"Wow. So it's true." His voice was hushed.

"It's Ruth. Even if the book hadn't given her name, I'd have recognized her from the portrait. She looks different in the photo in the hallway, the one taken when she was middle aged. The photograph proves that at least the jewels weren't imaginary."

He couldn't take his eyes off the page. "Are those rubies, sapphires, or emeralds? It's hard to tell in black and white."

"The family legend says rubies. They're enormous, aren't they? They look like the crown jewels of England."

"More likely those of Russia. All right," he said, handing her back the book. "You win. They existed. Unfortunately, that doesn't change anything. We're no closer to answering the question of where they are now."

"At least we can narrow down the possibilities." She began to tick them off on her fingers. She'd had a long time to think about it, and the old excitement was back. "Ruth might have returned them to the count when he wouldn't marry her. I bet when he gave them to her, she thought it was a proposal of marriage. That's the kind of naïve girl she was, and how she would react when she found she was wrong. Don't ask me how I know that Ruth was emotional and naïve. I just *do*." She didn't tell Ian about her dreams, where somehow she had melded into the other woman, feeling her emotions and thinking her thoughts. Someday she might, but she was afraid he would mock her belief that somehow those experiences had been *real*. He was too logical to fully understand.

Something in the way Ian looked at her, waiting patiently without immediately jumping in to contradict her like she'd expected, made her think that somehow, perhaps, he *did* understand the psychic connection she had with that long-dead woman. She remembered that he was the one who had pointed out the resemblance between her and the photograph of Ruth hanging in the hallway by the kitchen.

She cleared her throat and continued. "In those days, returning the jewels to a man with dishonorable intentions might have seemed the honorable thing to do. I hope she kept them, though. He was a swine, he didn't deserve them."

"How do you know he was a swine?"

"Really, Ian! I just *told* you! The man refused to marry her although he purported to love her. Why? Not just because she was an opera singer and of lower caste, but because she was a Jewess, which was the term they used in those days. She was good enough to be his mistress, but not good enough to be his wife. Of course he was a swine!"

He thought about it and nodded. "All right. I'll concede the point. It does make sense."

"Options two, three, four, and five for what happened to the jewels," she went on, holding up her other fingers in turn: "Ruth kept them, but they were lost somehow. Or they were stolen. Or sold. Or hidden. One thing is certain: she never wore them again. Her husband wouldn't have approved of her flaunting a gift from a former lover, and besides, she wouldn't have had anywhere to wear them. She was the wife of a conservative, bourgeois factory owner. Raising seven children would have kept her too busy for fancy parties."

Ian pensively tapped his fingers on the table. She pictured him leaning over a light-table designing a skyscraper surrounded by rolls of trace paper and razor-point pens, considering some difficult problem. He would have the same expression on his intense, narrow face. "All right, since we're conjecturing anyway," he said at last, "I'll place my bet that the legend was correct, and the jewels did make their way to California. Why not? Oral traditions are often based on a germ of truth. Look at Herman Schliemann: he's that German guy who believed that the Odyssey and the Illiad had their roots in fact and ended up discovering Troy."

"Aha!" Her eyes glowed with triumph. "Then you believed the jewelry existed all along!"

"I always accepted the possibility," he reminded her dryly. "I just didn't think it was likely."

"Well, thanks to Shirley, now we know. How lucky that she saved this book! It used to belong to the Perlemans." She looked at the old black-and-white photograph again, noting again Ruth's thick dark hair and large, expressive eyes. The singer must have been at least a decade younger in this image than in the family portrait that hung in Esther's hallway. Ruth really *had* been a beauty, Paisley thought with a pang. Perhaps it was disappointment that had drained some of that eager, hopeful loveliness out of the singer's face.

Then Paisley's eyes dropped to the three-stranded pearl-and-ruby necklace around the Polish singer's throat. Up until now, the existence of the gems had seemed mostly an intriguing riddle. Now, the knowledge that they were real lit a fire inside her. For the first time, she could understand why men had sacrificed their families, their sanity, and even their lives to track down gold in the Sierra Mountains in the mid-1800s. She imagined the feel of those bracelets around her wrist, the pressure of the necklace against her throat.

"Now that I'm convinced the story wasn't made up of whole cloth," Ian's voice penetrated her awareness, "it seems reasonable to assume that the jewels did make it to California. Why not?"

"You've skipped a step. Just because the rubies existed doesn't prove that Esther had them." She was playing devil's advocate, though. Paisley was sure Esther had brought them with her. It was as if some unseen force was guiding them, step by step.

Ian shook his head. "And yet this photo strengthens two pieces of circumstantial evidence indicating that she did. One is the letter from Auntie Adelajda referring to Esther's homemade coat, which, like you pointed out, may well have had the jewels sewn in the lining. That was a common way to smuggle valuables back then. The other evidence is Esther's childhood diary, which cites Aunt Henka's endless badgering about mysterious missing objects." He paused for dramatic effect. "And there's one more thing."

"What?"

"The crowning evidence, which we haven't even talked about yet: Aunt Henka's firm belief that the jewels were on the premises. She wouldn't have spent the rest of her life looking for them if she hadn't been convinced her young niece had brought them."

"That sounds reasonable," Paisley admitted. "But if so, that means Esther must have hidden them soon after she arrived here, or Henka would have found them."

Ian seemed to be enjoying the game as much as she was. "Hid them or lost them. And kept it a secret her whole life." He stood up and started pacing the way he always did when he was deep in thought. Paisley was startled at the realization of how comfortably familiar his mannerisms had become to her. "But if the jewelry was in the house," he continued, "surely it would have turned up. Aunt Henka would have found it eventually, with all her endless searching."

"And yet it's pretty clear that she never found the box hidden in the wall in Esther's room," Paisley pointed out.

He awarded her the point with a nod. "It's a shame Esther's diary didn't tell us why she didn't hand over the jewels to her American relatives when she arrived, like a good little girl."

"Or why she spent the rest of her life denying their existence."

"I'm sure she wouldn't have denied it so heartily without a good reason," Ian said reminiscently. "I remember a sparkle of enjoyment in her eyes when the subject came up, as if she knew something no one else knew. At the time, I thought it was that the jewels didn't exist. Now, I suspect it's because they did."

"All right." Paisley was ready to move on to the next point. "Let's say that Esther had them. Where are they? We've been through every inch of this house. And I'm sure Auntie Henka searched it more thoroughly than we have. She had fifty years to look."

Ian poked his fists deep into his pockets. "If those jewels haven't turned up, it must be because Esther didn't want them to."

"Maybe she sold them," Paisley said doubtfully. She'd never seriously considered this possibility, perhaps because she didn't want to. That would mean they had been wasting their time all along.

"She didn't sell them," he said with certitude. "If there's one thing Esther never cared about, it was money. I can't see her selling Great-Aunt Ruth's heirloom jewels for extra cash."

Paisley thought he was probably right. Esther seemed like one of the least materialistic women she had known. She stretched her arms high above her head, kicked off her shoes, and wriggled into a more comfortable position on the couch. "I'm sick of going around in circles," she complained. "Let's accept for the sake of argument that Esther did hide them after arriving in River Bend. That brings us back to the old question: where? I want to grab a shovel and start digging."

Ian stopped pacing and slumped into the recliner nearby. "Wherever she put them, she hid them well," he agreed. "Think of the box inside the bedroom wall: if we hadn't torn down the plaster while remodeling, we'd never have found it."

"Are you saying we should tear down the entire house looking for another hiding place?"

He smiled at her wanly. "We could. But I don't think it would help."

"Why not?"

"Think about it," Ian said. "She already had a perfectly good hiding spot in her room. Why would she go to the trouble of creating another one?"

Paisley thought about this. "So you really think she kept the jewelry in that dusty old box?"

"The box was half empty; there would have been plenty of room. Maybe she took out the pieces to show her best friend some 'pretty things,' like she wrote in the diary."

Pretty things. Georgiana had used that very term. He was right.

Still, Paisley felt obligated to play devil's advocate. It was a role that came naturally to her. "If the jewels were what Esther was referring to. She could have been describing anything. Like flowers, or pictures."

"True, but we have to conjecture, since we have no hard evidence," Ian reminded her. "And if she did take the jewelry out of her box of treasures, why would she have gone to the trouble to hide the pieces somewhere else? The hiding place in her room was perfectly adequate."

"Why would she do anything?" Paisley was growing more and more frustrated.

Ian nodded. "I'm just saying the jewels are unlikely to be hidden behind a wall or under the floors of the house. I doubt we need to get out a crowbar or hammer and destroy all the work my crew and I just put in."

Paisley shook her head. "So you're suggesting she took the jewels from her hiding place, but something happened before she could put them away again? That maybe they were stolen?" If so, the search was over before it had begun.

"That's one possibility." Ian left the easy chair and plopped beside her, dropping his long arm across the top of the couch. She smelled Irish Spring soap and damp hair. He must have showered immediately before coming over. He was frowning intently, as he always did when he was thinking. "The robbery could have happened without her knowledge. Someone could have found the hiding place, removed the valuable contents, and replaced the container where we found it."

Paisley enjoyed his closeness with one part of her brain--the part that wasn't busy trying to figure out where the jewels might be. "Why would burglars bother to put the box back?"

"One reason is so Esther wouldn't know the jewels were gone immediately. If that scenario is correct, the thief was someone who lived in this house."

Paisley felt the conversation was getting farther and farther from reality. She was growing increasingly aware of Ian's warmth, centimeters away, his breath on the top of her head. She leaned her head back against the sofa cushions, her long hair brushing his shoulder.

Dragging her mind back to the point, she said, "We know it wasn't Aunt Henka. She would have worn those jewels triumphantly and openly, and we wouldn't be sitting here wondering what happened to them."

Ian scratched his chin. "It could have been one of Aunt Henka's children, but neither of them ever spoke of it or showed unusual wealth in later years. So we're back to Esther taking the jewels out of her treasure box herself."

"It probably wouldn't have been the first time," Paisley said, picturing a childish Esther decked in her Great-Aunt Ruth's glittering finery, playing dress-up. Withdrawing her bare feet from the coffee table, Paisley tucked them under her, and turned to Ian. Their faces were only inches apart. "Of course she wanted to play with the shiny trinkets. What little girl wouldn't?"

"But that day, she was interrupted before she could put them away," he said slowly. He seemed to be unaware of her nonverbal hint that she was tired of the endless conversation about something that could never be proved, that she was ready to move on to ... something else. "Esther had to find a place to hide them in a hurry. Buried them in leaves, or shoved them under a bush, or dumped them somewhere. It makes sense."

Paisley buried her head in her hands, her hair spilling over her fingers. "Does it? We're building so much on speculation. We have no way of knowing if any of this is true."

Remembering her presence, he patted her on the shoulder. "Remember, the scientific method begins with a hypothesis." His tone sounded very much like that of a Berkeley student debating a professor, or, she thought fleetingly, like the TV character Sheldon, on *Big Bang Theory*. "Then you test it to see if the hypothesis pans out. If not, you start over. That's what Sherlock Holmes did. And yes, I know he was a detective, not a scientist, but the point is the same."

She didn't say what she thought: that Ian was neither a scientist nor Sherlock Holmes. He was a fledgling architect. Architects created things, incredibly elaborate things, out of their imagination. They dreamed things into existence. Which was the opposite of what she was trying to do, which was to pin down what really happened. An impossible task.

Then she felt ashamed of her mental criticism of the person who had been her greatest ally in the hunt for the jewels. Laying a hand on his forearm, she said, "I don't mean to sound ungrateful, Ian. I know how much time you've taken out to help me, and I don't even know why." It was true. She realized that he did not stand to profit from any of this, whether Ruth Klaczko's rubies were found or not. So why was he spending so much time helping her try to find them?

"You don't know?" He looked at her and raised one sandy eyebrow. She caught her breath at the expression on his face, then laughed, a little hysterically. She remembered their earlier discussion of opera and passion. If there was one thing long, gangly, intellectual Ian didn't look capable of, it was passion. He certainly hadn't seemed like it a moment ago, when she had snuggled next to him, hoping almost unconsciously that he would pick up on the hint.

Apparently he was not entirely clueless after all. The next thing she knew, he caught his breath sharply. Then he reached out, pulling her close with unexpectedly strong arms. Working with a hammer these past few weeks had made him buff. Or maybe his body had always been this way, and she just hadn't known it.

Under his rumpled plaid shirt, she felt a hard chest and his heart, beating rapidly. Her laughter died away, and she looked up at him. The expression on his face was perfectly serious, endowing its earnest features with a sort of dignity. She felt a stronger flutter of that feeling she had not experienced in a long time, something which Steve, with all his good looks and charm, had failed to arouse.

He released her suddenly. "I'm sorry. I shouldn't have done that. I know it's too soon after ... after...."

She cleared her throat. "Never mind. It's late, we're both excited about the discovery, and we...we got carried away. So, um, you were talking about Esther when she was a little girl. That she might have been playing with the jewels when she heard something—"

Ian seemed grateful for the change of subject. "—Or saw something," he added.

Paisley nodded. "—That interrupted her, and she quickly hid them. It couldn't have been in her room, or Esther would just have put them back inside the box in the wall. Most likely, she didn't hide them in the house."

"You're right. If so, they would have turned up by now." It was as if Ian had forgotten their moment of closeness. His scholarly air was back. "As I said before, Aunt Henka was a notoriously meticulous housekeeper. She'd have known every inch of the house and would see anything amiss with her beady eyes."

Paisley could not let this go unchallenged, although she was having trouble getting her mind to stick to the point. "How do you know her eyes were beady?"

"Trust me, they were." He shuddered. "She was still alive when I was a little boy, remember? The woman would have looked at home in a pointed black hat and red-and-white striped socks."

"So, where are they? Buried somewhere? Or at a friend's home?" When she had believed the jewels might be in the house, the search had seemed daunting enough. It would be impossible to narrow down the entire outdoors. "She could have put them anywhere."

Ian shook his head. "Speculating will get us nowhere."

Somehow, her hand was in his, and she felt the warm feeling that had flooded throughout her veins when his arms had encircled her.

"I'm sorry, sweetheart," he said softly. "This meant so much to you, but I think the hunt is over."

When he was gone, the house seemed more silent than usual. Paisley sat on the couch trying to comprehend what had just happened. What was that he had called her? Sweetheart. What a corny, old-fashioned term, a meaningless expression like one used with a small child or a pet. After all, Nigel called her "darling" all the time, and he had no more interest in her *that* way than in the proverbial old shoe. So why did Ian's use of the word make her tingle all over?

To escape that line of thought, she went to look for the *Carmen* soundtrack, then remembered with a sound of exasperation that she had given the CD to Ian a few days ago. She put on *Aida* instead, and turned up the volume on the old stereo full blast. Esther's speakers were powerful: the house echoed with tragic melodies and powerful, swooping voices that fit her mood perfectly.

Without thinking, Paisley began to sing along, before the tightness in her throat reminded her that she didn't want to risk damaging her still-healing vocal chords. Still, the first few notes had come out of her full-bodied and strong, just like the old days. Maybe there was hope. A surge of elation went through her. She would call her oto-laryngologist tomorrow and see if he thought she was ready to try some vocal exercises to strengthen her voice. At least it would get her mind off of other things, things she wasn't ready to think about.

When the recording of the aria ended, Paisley heard a high-pitched, yowling coda through the open window. Maybe the cat was an opera lover too—or hater? Chuckling, she went to the kitchen and opened a can of tuna, thrilled that the ghost cat was finally making its presence known. It must be getting used to her. Maybe, with luck, it would someday stay around long enough to be petted. Carrying the ceramic bowl outside, she peered into the thick growth of bushes.

"Here, kitty, kitty, kitty."

The bushes bent and shook slightly near the ground, but nothing emerged. Setting the bowl on the back-door step, she straightened, searching through the trees that lined the small back yard for any sign of movement. She sensed the cat was still out there, somewhere, not far from the house.

On impulse, Paisley decided to try to track it down. It was high time that she built a relationship with Esther's pet, she thought. After all, they both shared the house and its grounds. It was silly for them to keep avoiding each other.

Quietly, to avoid scaring off the animal, she followed what she imagined was its path. Branches and leaves scratched her arms and tugged at her clothing, but she brushed them away, biting off an exclamation when an unseen twig lacerated her forearm.

Twenty yards away, the bushes opened into a small clearing, edged with ivy and small pockets of violets. The clearing was occupied by the cat, and someone else.

Chapter Twelve

Kevin appeared to be fast asleep. Leaning back against an oak tree almost as old as the one in front of her house, he appeared for once utterly at peace. A cloud of gray fur rested on his lap like a purring pillow.

Not wanting to invade the youth's privacy, she stepped backward, but apparently sensing her presence, he opened his eyes. A moment later, Kevin was on his feet. The cat swarmed down his leg with a loud, angry meow, and several red stripes appeared on his forearm.

Paisley's words burst out without thought: "So it was you!"

"What are you talking about?" His face grew pale.

"The one who fed the cat after Esther died. I figured someone must have taken care of the poor thing, but I didn't know who it was."

The startled expression cleared. "I found the cat prowling by Steve's house after I moved in. She looked hungry. I guess she wasn't used to fending for herself."

"Why didn't you just adopt it? Keep it at your house?"

He tensed again, and his face grew shuttered. "Steve wouldn't let me have a pet. Besides, it wasn't much trouble bringing the food over here." He paused. "I used to have my own cat, once. Back in New Jersey."

She didn't know what to say. The words had given away more than Kevin intended. Then Paisley got a closer look at his forearm and caught her breath. Kevin was unconsciously rubbing his arm, smearing the blood.

"Stop doing that, you're making a mess." She found a clean tissue in the front pocket of her jeans and dabbed at the scratches. "Come on, I have Band-Aids at home."

"No thanks, I'm fine." He pulled his arm away, his jaw setting stubbornly.

The edges of her mouth tugged upward. "Aren't those the same words I used after the cow attacked me in the pasture?"

After a moment, the jaw relaxed and a tentative smile appeared. "Yeah. I remember."

"Then please let me return the favor. Come on." She guided his reluctant steps in the direction of the house.

"This time, you're the one who was trespassing," she said a short while later, swabbing the scratches with cotton balls and hydrogen peroxide and ignoring Kevin's wince. "That clearing is on my property, you know."

"I guess so. But I didn't think of it that way. The place was just somewhere to hang out with the cat where no one would bother me, that's all. The only time I went inside the house was when—" He stopped as if he'd walked into a wall.

Gently, she said, "I already knew."

His startled gaze flew to her face. "How?"

"You left a footprint in the flowerbed after it rained." She nodded at his sneakers. "Size tens, right? Same size my late husband wore. If you're going to turn to a life of crime, Kevin, you'll have to cover your tracks better. Literally."

"But if you knew, why didn't you...?" Despite his height, he suddenly looked very young.

"Turn you in?" She paused to consider, holding the bottle of hydrogen peroxide. "I just didn't feel you were out to harm me, somehow. Call it intuition, or just plain stupidity."

During a long silence, he fidgeted while she put the Band-Aids back in the drawer and slipped into the chair across the kitchen table from him. "Why did you do it, Kevin? I don't understand why you would hate me enough to do that."

"You're wrong!" he burst out. "I don't hate you."

"Then why did you break into my house?

He didn't answer. She sighed. Getting an adolescent boy to talk was harder than cracking open a walnut with one's bare fingers.

Then he cleared his throat and peered up at her from under his spiky bangs. "Um, Mrs. Perleman, does this change anything about, ah, you know, the play?"

"Of course not. I might feel differently if you'd taken anything or done significant damage but...." She paused. "The fact is, we need you, Kevin. With you playing the Pirate King, I think the show could be really good. The Sacramento Bee said they'd send out a reporter to review it. The publicity would be great, for the production and for you."

His fingers played with the Band-Aid, unconsciously rubbing across its surface. "I don't get it. Why do you care?"

"I don't know," she said, shrugging. "Now that I'm involved, I want the production to be the best it can be, that's all."

"That's not what I meant." He hesitated. "Why do you care whether the publicity would be good for *me*? What do *I* have to do with it?"

She rested her elbows on the table and leaned forward, choosing her words with care. "Don't let this go to your head, but you have great natural talent, Kevin. With a couple of years of acting classes, you could go on to a career as a performer, maybe even on Broadway or in the movies. You have the stage presence for it. And the voice."

He was listening, intently, his eyes fastened on hers. "You really think so?"

She straightened in her chair. "Of course I can't promise anything. An entertainment career depends a great deal on luck. But I believe those with real talent usually make it to the top, especially if they have the right connections. I know a few people in the business, and I'd be happy to put in a word for you. So yes, Kevin, you do have a chance, if that's the path you choose."

He sat silently, perhaps envisioning the future she had painted. She remembered hearing him practicing guitar in his room, his performance at open mic night. Of course he had dreamed of being successful. What kid his age hadn't? But until now, he had probably not seen a career in music a real possibility. Then he pushed back his chair and stood. "Thanks for the Band-Aid, Mrs... I mean, Paisley. I'll think about what you said."

"Great." She stood up with him. "I'll pick you up for practice tomorrow. We can car pool, being neighbors."

"Okay. Sure."

Not long after Kevin left, she began to second-guess herself. She'd just let him off the hook for burglarizing her house, and even promised to help him start a career in show business, a fairly hefty commitment. Why? Just because she felt sorry for the kid? Because she was impressed by his undeniable talent?

Kevin's stepfather had called him "troubled," which hinted the boy may have done such things before. Perhaps she was not really doing the boy any favors by helping him evade the consequences of his actions.

Tidying up the kitchen, she realized she never pressed Kevin on why he had broken into her house. He didn't seem the type who did such things for a thrill. In fact, she suspected the youth had been about to tell her the reason, but something had stopped him.

At least, Paisley thought, she believed her young neighbor's claim that he had not invaded her home out of malice, and that he had no intention of harming her. Perhaps because she was a soft-hearted fool, she believed him. But that left the question dangling: why, then, had Kevin done it?

By rights, she should have had trouble going to sleep. Instead, she slept soundly, dreaming once again of the dark-haired opera singer from the past. After a longer-than-usual bubble bath, she started for the stairs to prepare breakfast, humming her favorite aria from Carmen, which still lingered in her head.

As she made her way down each step of the staircase, a strong sense of déjà vu swept over her, almost as if she were in the dream again, making a grand entrance onto the baroque stage of the Paris Opera. Her surroundings melted away. In her imagination, she wore a ruffled scarlet satin gown, tightly fitted in the bodice and sweeping around her ankles like a hollyhock's petals. She sensed the hush of the people staring up at her; the satin sashes across men's chests, the feathers and sparkling jewels in the upswept curls of the women ... all of them staring up at her, waiting, *longing*, to hear her sing.

Her mouth opened and the words of the song poured out, bold and powerful, as if she were singing to the last row of that imagined audience. *"L'amour est enfant de bohème, qui n'a jamais, jamais connu de loi...."* "Love is a gypsy child, that has never, ever known a law." Richly, effortlessly, the notes swelled to the aria's magnificent crescendo: *"Si tu ne m'aimes pas, je t'aime, et si je t'aime, prends garde à toi!"* If you do not love me, I love you, and if I love you, beware!

The old house's high ceilings created excellent acoustics. The notes glided higher and higher, the beautiful gypsy's sensuous challenge reaching to the final row of the upper balcony. The air was still vibrating like the strings of a violin when at the bottom of the stairs she bumped into a tall figure and was jolted out of her trance.

"You!" she blurted. "What are you doing in here?"

"Wow." Ian's eyes were wide and his mouth hung open. He stared at her as if he had never seen her before. "What was *that*?"

Embarrassed at having been watched when she thought she was alone, she spoke angrily. "How long have you been standing there?"

"Long enough."

Neither of them moved; they were inches apart. His face still looked dazed.

"You didn't answer my knock, so I let myself in." He paused. "I thought you had the stereo on. Playing one of those old albums of Esther's."

"Why are you here?" she asked again, ignoring his comment. "It's Saturday. You don't work weekends."

"Never mind." He kept staring down at her, his expression still stunned. "Let me process this for a moment. I didn't know you had a voice like that. You sounded like a ... like a freight train."

"A freight train?" She tried to back away, but he reached out and pulled her close, so close that she could feel the warmth of his body.

"In volume only," he amended in a low voice. His breath stirred the hair at her temple. "A beautiful and extremely musical freight train. I thought you couldn't sing anymore."

"I thought so too." A feeling of joy pumped through her, but she tried to keep her feelings rational. Singing a verse of one song didn't mean her voice was back permanently. In fact, for all she knew, she might have damaged it by using it too soon. Also, she was very aware of Ian's hands on her upper arms, of how close he was standing. Adrenaline and butterflies were coursing through her body, veins, and heart.

"I probably shouldn't have sung like that just now," she admitted, lowering her gaze to his chest. He was wearing one of his usual plaid shirts with rolled-up sleeves, but this one was less rumpled than usual. He seemed to be taking more care of his appearance these days. "The doctor warned me to take it easy." She pulled her hand free and touched her throat, unable to hold back a smile. "It does seems to be coming back, though, doesn't it? I'll call my doctor and ask if it's safe to start singing again. He may want me to fly back to New York so he can check it."

"I'd say the prognosis is encouraging." He was looking down at her, and she noticed he was still gripping her arms. "I listened to that CD you lent me of *Carmen* last night, by the way. Just now, you sounded like the recording, only better. Much better. I didn't understand what the character was saying, though. The opera is in French, isn't it? That's strange, considering it's set in Spain."

She nodded. "Bizet was French. Naturally he would write the opera in his own language. The song is simple: Carmen compares love to a gypsy child, wild and untamed, and warns that if she loves a man, he'd better beware."

"That Carmen must have been one dangerous chick." He was smiling down at her, but there was a new expression in his light-gray eyes. She did nothing to stop the increasing pressure of his hands as they slid down her back, or the slow descent of his head, or ....

Love *was* like a gypsy child, wild, passionate, joyous, and untamed. When Ian raised his head after a long, sizzling kiss, they were both breathless, and her heart was beating like a tambourine in a tarantella dance. She tried to remember the question she had asked. It took a few seconds for her head to clear. "Uh ... so, why *are* you here, Ian?"

"Haven't you noticed? I come over every morning."

By now his arms were wrapped around her waist, and she felt absolutely no desire to move. She was enjoying how secure it felt to be held her like that. As a result, it took a few moments for his words to sink in.

"Of course you're here every morning," she said. "But today I don't hear any construction going on. Where's your crew?"

"I came to let you know that the work on the house is complete. We're done. Finished. *Caputo*. I'd have announced it yesterday, but we both got carried away speculating about the jewelry case, and I forgot."

"Finished? Already?" With effort she pulled away from his embrace and looked around the. With all the distractions of late, such as buying the Volkswagen, giving music lessons, and working on the play, she hadn't noticed how all the gradual improvements had added up. The construction equipment had vanished. Dust and broken wall plaster had been swept up. The newly stained walnut floors shone, and the repaired living room window sparkled in its freshly painted frame. Except for the worn furniture, the house looked like a page from an interior design magazine, with its view into the front garden and buttercup-yellow paint that replaced the torn wallpaper. How could she not have noticed that there was nothing more that needed to be done?

"It looks very nice," she acknowledged, surprised to feel a hint of regret.

"How about a celebration?" Ian suggested, looking pleased at her positive reaction. "We could drive to San Francisco, or Old Town Sacramento, or up to the giant sequoias, or maybe go visit the lavender fields. There's a lot to see around here, and we only scratched the surface the other day." He reached for her again, smiling down at her. "You haven't seen any of the tourist stuff."

"I'd love to." Her regret was real as she wriggled out of his arms once more. "But I've got a couple of students coming over later for singing lessons, and tomorrow is the beginning of Hell Week. I'll be too busy."

"Hell Week?"

She laughed at his startled expression. "That's what theater people call the last week before opening night," she explained. "We'll be practicing all day, every day. No breaks, no distractions, and catered food only. Sometimes we won't get home until after midnight."

Reluctantly, Ian dropped his arms. "Okay," he said grudgingly. "I've got to work on that thesis, anyway. Been putting it off all summer." He sounded as glum as a boy who had just unwrapped a Christmas gift and found a pair of gym socks instead of a new iPad.

"Another time," she said, feeling the same regret. She already missed the feel of his face against hers, the slightly scratchy feel of his jaw despite the fact that he had recently shaved, and the bony ridges of his nose and cheekbones. At the same time, something inside her felt fearful. Things were moving too fast. In spite of the new, raw feelings mixed up inside her, she was not yet ready to promise Ian anything. The painful past was too recent, her future too uncertain.

"Another time? Okay. I'll hold you to that." He looked down at her and an odd expression crossed his face. "Paisley, we have a lot to talk about. Maybe it's too soon, but...."

Her eyes dropped.

As if sensing her confusion, he kissed her soundly once more and was gone. Hearing the rusty pickup pull away, she realized she had forgotten to tell him of her discovery last night that Kevin had been the burglar. Maybe it was for the best, she thought, walking into the kitchen to make breakfast, which she ate without appetite. The fewer people who knew of Kevin's lapse the better. She suspected Ian might be understanding, but the fact was, the burglary really wasn't his business. This was between Kevin and her.

Chloe arrived precisely at 10 o'clock for her private singing lesson, and Paisley taught her techniques for reaching the difficult top notes of her character's signature aria, "Poor Wand'ring One."

"Wow," Chloe said when the lesson was over. "Thanks. I could never have got through that tricky part without your help."

"You have more natural ability than you realize," Paisley told her. "It's a matter of learning how to use what's already there."

Chloe nodded, blushing. "You're the best, Mrs. Perleman. I wish my pre-calculus teacher could make things look so easy. See you at rehearsal."

Paisley stood at the window watching the girl heading toward her mother's waiting car when Kevin appeared from the direction of Steve's house. Through the sheer curtains, Paisley watched the adolescents stop in the center of the path, presumably to speak. She could only see Chloe's back, but after a few moments the girl tossed her long, silver-blond hair and Kevin's face lit up like a

Christmas tree. Chloe stepped lightly past him and he turned to watch her get into the car, as if mesmerized.

Paisley felt a pang of jealousy. Had Jonathan ever looked at her that way?

The car pulled away and Kevin bounded up the steps, all teenage angst seemingly evaporated. Despite of the black T-shirt and silver lip-ring, he looked as sunny and wholesome as a young actor in a Disney Channel TV show. "Hi there, Mrs. Perleman!"

"It's Paisley," she repeated, stepping back to let him in while trying not to show her surprise. Where was the tormented boy she had talked to over the kitchen table yesterday? "Have you been practicing the sheet music I gave you?"

Head bobbing in assent, he followed her toward to the black Yamaha piano, which she had tuned and polished until it looked new. While he performed his Pirate King solo, she was again impressed by the power and range of Kevin's voice. Chloe had a pretty voice, pleasant to listen to, but Kevin had something more. Although Paisley's reassuring words to Chloe had been true, either you had the talent to make it professionally or you didn't. Kevin definitely had it.

The car pulled away and moments later Kevin bounded up the steps, all teenage angst seemingly evaporated. In spite of his black T-shirt and silver lip-ring, he looked as sunny and wholesome as a young actor in a Disney Channel TV show. "Hi there, Mrs. Perleman!"

"It's Paisley," she said automatically, stepping back to let him in while trying not to show her surprise. Where was the tormented boy she had talked to over the kitchen table yesterday? "Have you been practicing the music I gave you?"

His head bobbed and he followed her to the black Yamaha piano, which Paisley had tuned and polished until it nearly looked new again. While he performed his Pirate King solo, she was again impressed by the power and range of Kevin's voice. When he sang, he appeared far more self-confident than in real life. In

Paisley's experience, despite the importance of training, either you had it or you didn't. Kevin definitely had it.

Funny, she thought with surprise, to find so much talent in this small rural town in Northern California. Even the formerly rag-tag chorus of pirates and the Major General's daughters were shaping up nicely.

As Kevin ran through his lines in *Away, Away! My Heart's on Fire*, she couldn't help thinking about his future. Several regional singing competitions existed for kids his age. If he did well in those, there were the national ones, prestigious events that would get him noticed. That was how she'd started: teachers who had taken an interest in her, mentored her in her early years, leading to Nigel, the conservatory in Omaha, and ultimately Jonathan and the Metropolitan Opera. She could do the same for Kevin, she thought: coach him, introduce him to the right people, steer him toward the events that could launch his career. The things Nigel had done for her.

She made a mental note to discuss her ideas with Steve. Kevin didn't seem to think his foster parent cared, but the boy must be wrong. Once she'd explained, Steve would surely support the boy's activities. This might even be all that was needed to bring the two feuding males closer together.

And while she was at it, Paisley would remind Steve that the backdrop for the play still needed to be painted. Only a week remained before opening night, and time had a way of slipping away.

When the lesson was over, she handed the sheet music back to Kevin. "Good job, kiddo! Keep that up and you'll be the star of the show."

"Thanks, Mrs. P ... Paisley." He was already beginning to withdraw again. His spiky bangs hid his face as he flipped through the stack of music, but he did not move. She had the impression he was gathering his courage to tell her something. She waited patiently.

Finally, he raised his head. His dark-brown eyes met hers. "Um ... I was thinking about, you know, about what I did the other week. You know, coming into your house when you weren't home and going through your stuff. I want you to know it wasn't my idea." He spoke rapidly, perhaps trying to get the words out before changing his mind.

"Oh," she said, trying to keep her tone neutral, although his confession surprised her. If not his, then whose idea had it been? And why? Paisley sensed he would clam up if she asked.

Her intuition to stay quiet proved correct. The silence lengthened, then suddenly broke. It was as if he couldn't keep back a torrent of words that had been held back too long. "I'm not saying I'm not to blame: I know it was wrong, and I'm sorry. But it was *her* idea. She's the one who told me that you.... That I ...." He stopped again, as if running into a wall.

"Who, Kevin?" Paisley kept her voice soft, as if talking to the skittish gray cat who'd run away and disappear into the bracken outside when startled. "Who hates me?"

"It's not *hate*. She didn't think you had right to them, being an outsider."

"I felt that way at first myself." Paisley spoke soothingly, although she was dying with curiosity. Whom was he talking about? "Why does this ... this person think she has a claim to them?"

"Them" meaning the jewels, of course. What else could have been the object of his search?

"Not her. Me." He grimaced and rolled his eyes, like any embarrassed seventeen-year-old. "She said they were my rightful inheritance. Claimed Esther had no right to leave the family heritage to someone else." He snorted. "As if I wanted a bunch of dumb jewels. But she kept insisting, so I did it. And I told her you didn't have them."

It took a moment for what he had said to sink in. *Kevin?* Staring at his features, she remembered the flashes of recognition, the unexpected familiarity of the handsome face with its heavy dark eyebrows. You!" she exclaimed. "You're one of Jonathan's relatives from back east!"

Chapter Thirteen

Facts began clicking into place. Jonathan had told Paisley that he had relatives in New Jersey, and Georgiana had mentioned that Esther had a cousin who had left California years ago: the east-coast relatives who had not come to the wedding. A name popped into her head. *Leah.* Henka and Borys' Perleman's younger daughter, whom Esther had mentioned in her girlhood diary. Leah Perleman must have been Kevin's grandmother.

Bemused, Paisley took in the boy's black hair, dark eyebrows. She was still processing the fact that her talented young neighbor was Jonathan's ... just what *was* the word for their relationship, anyway? Jonathan's second cousin once removed?

On the heels of her astonishment came another disturbing thought. Steve Lopez had been married at one point to Kevin's mother, who was Jonathan's second cousin. Why had Steve never mentioned the connection?

On the other hand, she told herself, why *should* Steve have mentioned it? Maybe he wasn't the type who offered up personal information easily. Or, maybe Steve assumed Paisley already knew. Certainly everyone else in town must be aware of his former relationship by marriage to the Perlemans. Even Shirley. Even Ian. Why hadn't *they* said anything? In the one instance that mattered most, the famous grapevine had broken down.

Kevin shifted uncomfortably, and she realized he had been waiting for her to speak.

"I still don't get it," Paisley said, wrinkling her forehead. She pictured the hostile-looking old woman in the wheelchair Kevin had been pushing at Sunny Acres Retirement Center, wearing the hand-printed name tag, "Maude Avery." "If your grandmother knew about the jewels and thought they should be your inheritance, why not come forward and state your claim? Why all this cloak and daggers stuff?"

"How would it help?" Kevin shrugged. "No one knew where the jewels were. No one even really believed they existed. It wouldn't have done any good to tell anyone."

"But your grandmother, Maude Avery, did believe in the jewels, and she went to great lengths to find them, even up to inducing you to burglarize my house. Why did she feel justified doing that?"

Pain darkened Kevin's eyes. He hesitated. Finally, looking down at his feet, he mumbled, "Grandma Maude thought it was the only way. When Mom got sick…" His voice faltered and he struggled to gather his emotions. Then his jaw firmed, and he lifted his head, meeting Paisley's eyes straight-on. "…Well, Mom told Grandma Maude her family might have valuable jewels hidden on this property. Grandma Maude thought that was Mom's way to provide for me after she was gone, since Dad … my real dad … was dead. If there was any treasure, she figured it by rights belonged to me. So after the funeral, Grandma Maude sold her New Jersey house and arranged for me to live with Steve. That way I could search the property without raising suspicions. That was the plan, anyway."

Things were starting to come together. Sort of. "Seems awfully convenient, that Steve lives right next door to this house," Paisley said dryly.

He shook his head. "That's how Mom met Steve. She was visiting her California relatives not long after my Dad died." Kevin shrugged. "I was just two or three years old, and Mom had left me behind in New Jersey with Grandma Maude during the trip, so I don't remember much about it.

By then, Jonathan would have been living away from River Bend, Paisley thought. Intent on his career, he probably never thought about his long-lost second cousin or her young son.

Meanwhile Esther, living in Sacramento and alienated from the family, had probably never met her cousin Leah's granddaughter, or young Kevin either.

"Why didn't you and your grandmother live together while you searched for the jewels?" Paisley wondered. "Wouldn't that have made more sense?"

The shadow crossed Kevin's face again. "Grandma Maude was getting older and was planning to go to a retirement home anyway, so she picked one out here. The other old lady, the one who lived in this house—Esther, I mean—died not long before that, so it was easy to break in. I looked all over the place for the jewels, but I didn't find anything. We gave up. Then a few months later you showed up...." His voice trailed away.

Paisley felt a gut-wrenching wave of regret. Esther Perleman, Kevin's only remaining relative on his mother's side, might have taken him under her wing and even befriended Grandma Maude if not for troubled family dynamics.

Kevin ducked his head and his fingers crumpled the edges of the sheet music. "I never felt right about doing it. Breaking into the house, I mean. But Grandma Maude told me no one would be hurt. She said, 'They should be yours anyway.'" His voice subtly took on the tone of an older female, and Paisley thought with admiration, *Holy Moley! The boy really is a born actor.*

"And therefore the broken window and disarranged shelves." Paisley nodded. "But again, why didn't you just come forward, Kevin? After all, you *are* the last blood descendent of the Perlemans."

He looked up at her from under his dark eyebrows. "Grandma Maude said we couldn't expect anyone to hand them over when we showed up. She said we had to find the jewels before anyone else. If we had to fight for them in court, the lawyers would end up with everything.

Grandma Maude might well be right.

"Have a seat, Kevin." She waved at the couch. "We have a lot to talk about."

Going into the kitchen to heat some cocoa, she threw a handful of miniature marshmallows on top, thinking wryly that she needed the sugar kick more than he.

Returning, she took the chair across from him and handed him a mug. "Why did you go through the house again? You'd already searched it."

He swirled the mug, watching the marshmallows melt at the edges. There was a smudge of chocolate on his upper lip, like a pirate's mustache. "When nothing turned up, I thought my grandmother was wrong or that the jewels were hidden some place we'd never find them. Buried in a field somewhere, maybe."

Paisley remembered Shirley's stories of neighborhood kids digging around the yard with spades until giving up and going home.

Kevin continued, "But Grandma Maude said your coming to River Bend *proved* they must be here. Why else would a famous opera star like you come to a small town like this?"

"I'm not famous," Paisley muttered under her breath. Funny, how many people assumed that her coming to River Bend was associated with the jewels: Ray, Steven, Ian, Shirley. And being called "famous" caused a pang. She had never reached the top, not really, in spite of winning the National Opera competition, of being hired by the Met, of being Jonathan Perleman's wife. All that had been a promising prelude to a career that had barely begun.

Despite that thrilling moment when her voice had briefly come back while singing *Carmen* while descending the stairs, Paisley knew there was a good chance she would never sing professionally again. Then what? She could not imagine a life without music.

Kevin was still talking. "Grandma Maude figured you must know something we didn't, and she told me to keep an eye on you, in case you led us to it. So I went through the house again to see if you might have left some clues. It was harder to get in this time, though. There were always workmen around. Finally one day I lucked out and found the house empty." He hunched his shoulders. "Back then, I didn't know you."

"Let me guess." Paisley visualized the hawk-faced old woman in the wheelchair. "Your grandmother called me a greedy stranger who'd come to steal your inheritance."

He smiled faintly, both hands wrapped around the steaming mug. "Something like that. Grandma Maude can be kind of ... ah ... um...."

"Strong-willed?" suggested Paisley. "A bully?"

His smile curved crookedly, making him seem even younger than seventeen. "Not exactly. Just the kind of person it's hard to say no to. Especially when she's sure she's right."

Once again Paisley thought of the old woman in her wheelchair, glowering like Norman Bates' mummified mother. "Just like Aunt Henka," she muttered under her breath. At least Maude Avery was just trying to preserve her grandson's rights.

Kevin looked down at his cocoa again, and his mouth twisted. "The day you asked me to be in the play, I told her I wouldn't help her anymore. We had a big fight. That's why I was late to rehearsal that afternoon." He looked up again. "Grandma Maude is the only family I have left."

"You're not entirely alone, Kevin. There's always Steve—"

"Steve doesn't count." Kevin's voice turned harsh. "All he cares about is his stupid vineyard and his fancy car."

Paisley fell silent. She thought she understood Kevin's divided loyalty. Besides, hadn't she forgotten about the house until Barry had reminded her? If Kevin's grandmother had written a letter explaining the situation, Paisley might have signed the whole thing over to him without thinking about it twice. Now, she was attached to the place. That strong feeling of homecoming, the sense of invisible arms pulling her in still surrounded her.

"Your grandmother is wrong, Kevin. I have no proof that the jewels are in River Bend. There's nothing of value." Reluctantly, she added, "Except this house, of course. It's not worth much, but at least it's something."

"This house?" He blinked. "I don't know if Grandma even thought of that. She only talked about the jewels."

"Well, it's something we need to discuss." Paisley set her empty cup on the coffee table. "The jewelry is likely missing forever, but if Esther had known about your mother's situation, she might have left the house to her rather than to me." She stood up, brushing her palms on the thighs of her jeans. "I'll go talk to Maude."

His face drained of color. "Now?"

"Why not? We have a couple of hours until rehearsal." It wasn't a conversation she looked forward to, but there was no point delaying the inevitable. At the expression on his face, she added, "Don't worry, you don't have to come along." She patted his shoulder. "Your grandmother and I can come to some sort of agreement. For heaven's sake, Kevin, she's just an old lady. I'm not scared of her."

He muttered something that might have been, "Maybe you should be." With an air of resignation, Kevin added, "She can't talk much since her stroke. But if you want to see her, go ahead. Good luck."

Paisley thought she'd probably need it.

Chapter Fourteen

The attendant at Sunny Acres Retirement Home led Paisley to an empty waiting room furnished with a scuffed, white baby grand piano and a pair of wingback chairs, apparently a place for residents to meet with visitors. She leafed, bored, through an issue of AARP magazine, reading about pensions and annuities until the man returned, pushing Kevin's grandmother, Maude Avery, in her wheelchair.

Paisley was unprepared for the malevolence in the woman's glare. It appeared Kevin was right: Maude considered Paisley to be out to steal his inheritance, and she would stop at nothing to gain her grandson's due.

"Hello, Mrs. Avery," Paisley said, standing and proffering her hand with what she hoped was a conciliatory air. "How nice to meet you."

After a hesitation, the talon-like fingers closed around hers. Paisley found herself transfixed by their unexpected strength, and by the steady, alert, intense gaze of those ice-blue eyes.

"Could we have a word alone?" Paisley asked, glancing at the attendant.

"Sure. You two ladies let me know when you're finished." The glass-paneled door swung closed behind him, cutting off the muted sounds from the lobby.

Stay positive. Stay positive, Paisley repeated to herself, although the old woman's gaze was unnerving. "Your grandson, Kevin, is a special young man," she said, wincing inwardly at the triteness of the words. "He's an amazingly talented singer, you know."

The other woman was silent, although the light-blue eyes widened a little in their crepey folds.

Taking a deep breath, Paisley went on. "He obviously cares for you very much, Mrs. Avery. He'd do anything for you." *Even burglarize a neighbor's house.*

When the woman remained silent, Paisley plunged into what she had come to say. "I'm very sorry Kevin was left out of Esther's will, Mrs. Avery, but I suspect she never knew he existed. I just learned myself that Kevin is the last of the Perlemans, and my late husband's only blood kin. This may surprise you, but that fact means a great deal to me. "

Maude's sparse eyebrows lifted slightly. She was listening after all. The dry, whispery words were difficult to hear. "I told my grandson you were taking what was rightfully his. Should sue you."

"I could have Kevin arrested for burglary. But I won't. And you're the one who made him do it." Paisley stopped. She wasn't here to stir things up, but to resolve them. "I know nothing about the jewels at all, Mrs. Avery. Less, probably, than you do. I'm afraid your efforts to recover them were a waste of time. But I like Kevin, and I want to make things right."

Maude's faded cheeks grew pink, whether with anger or embarrassment, Paisley didn't know. Impulsively, she took the old woman's hand. To her relief, Maude did not yank it away.

"I'd like to be friends," Paisley said. "In return, I pledge to help Kevin in any way I can. I've been thinking about things, and it seems that by rights he should own at least half the house. And part of the jewels, whatever they're worth—if they still exist and if they ever turn up. They are his morally, if not legally. When I'm on my feet again, I'll sit down with my lawyer and we'll discuss things. Somehow, we'll find a way to make sure he gets what is rightfully his. There's no need for anyone to feel taken advantage of, and certainly no reason to break into Esther's house."

The woman remained silent, but her eyes seemed to be sizing Paisley up, as if deciding whether to believe her. Paisley hoped that would suffice. At least, she was fairly certain Maude Avery was no longer an enemy.

Feeling that she had given her best effort, she nodded to Maude and to the returning attendant, and took her leave.

Perhaps the interview had not been totally successful, but neither had it been a complete waste of time. She sensed she'd forged a fragile truce. At least, Paisley thought, driving down the hill, she wouldn't be facing any more burglaries. Not from that quarter, at any rate.

*   *   *

Home again, Paisley put out a new dish of food for the cat on the porch step, made herself an egg-salad sandwich with sweet pickles and lettuce on whole-wheat bread, and ate at the kitchen table while perusing the latest *People* magazine.

She stayed up late watching an old black-and-white movie on TV, and then, yawning, looked at the clock, and saw that it was past midnight. Despite her exhaustion, she did not think she'd be able to fall asleep. Too many images were running through her head: Maude Avery's ravaged, hate-filled features, Kevin's guilty expression after making his confession, and last but not least, the super-charged encounter with Ian at the bottom of the stairs.

Going upstairs and switching off the lamp, she tossed and turned until she got out of bed and went downstairs again to look for a sleeping pill. It had been a long time since she had felt the need to take one. Standing in the parlor room, she stared at them for a while before shaking one into her palm and dry gulping it.

Too tired to clamber up the stairs again, she stretched out on the sofa and pulled the crocheted afghan over her. The pill seemed to take effect faster than before, and she drifted off into a vivid dream.

This time the flowing gown was blood-red satin. Her dark hair was piled atop her head again, a few long curls draped over her naked white shoulders. Rubies gleamed at her ears and throat, the ones she had seen in the photograph in Shirley's book. The gas lights at the front of the stage threw the audience into shadow, but she was keenly aware of hundreds of unseen faces out there, staring at her. A *frisson* of new fear crept up her spine and she felt vulnerable, self-conscious, as if it were the first time she had been on a stage.

Then the orchestra began to play. Paisley took a deep breath and opened her mouth to sing, but a series of choking gasps emerged instead. Coughing, she took a staggering step or two toward the front of the stage, reaching out for help. The unseen audience began to mutter and shift in their seats. Their voices rose in a muted roar, until their sound drowned out the music, deafened her. She grabbed her throat, trying to breathe, unable to scream for help.

With difficulty Paisley pried her eyes open. They felt glued shut. Although she was certain she was awake, she still couldn't breathe. Then her eyes began to sting and water, and she coughed.

In the distance, a hammering sound grew louder and louder. A voice was shouting. "Paisley! Are you in there? Paisley! Open up!"

In a daze, she rolled off the couch and crawled toward the door. At least, she hoped so. It was impossible to see which direction she was heading, the air was so thick with smoke; she could only follow her instincts. She heard a crash like a door being kicked in, followed by rapid footsteps and a familiar male voice.

"Paisley! Where are you?"

She tried to call out, but a new bout of coughing cut off the words. A pair of strong arms wrapped around her, and the next thing she knew, she was being dragged across the floor and outside, and laid on a cool, springy surface, where she gathered in whooping lungsful of air like a thirsty woman guzzling water.

"Paisley! Paisley, are you all right?"

Her eyes fluttered open to see Steve crouching over her, the smoke-blackened planes of his cheeks and jaw reflected in flickering light. He looked nothing like the usual remote, neatly dressed neighbor she knew. Awareness filtered into her brain that he was cradling her face in his hands, while the whites of his eyes stood out dramatically against the soot, making him look like an actor in blackface.

"The house!" she exclaimed, suddenly realizing what had happened. Her voice croaked worse than it had in weeks, and she fell into a spell of coughing. Her voice! Was it gone again, just as it had been recovering? She twisted her head to see flames shooting inside the living room window and her heart sank again. The house.... She had grown such an attachment to it. It was like a physical blow to see the smoke pouring from the windows.

The roar of an engine penetrated her mental fog. Men in yellow slickers jumped out of the big red firetruck, and before she knew it, they streamed over the lawn, aiming hoses at the freshly painted siding. Powerful streams of water poured over the structure that Ian had so beautifully restored, quickly putting out the flames and resulting in a thick cloud of curling white smoke.

"I saw flames coming from the direction of your house and telephoned for help," Steve explained, clutching her tight against his chest until she could hardly breathe. She felt his heart pounding against hers. His soot-streaked T-shirt molded his muscles over a pair of gray sweatpants, and dimly she wondered how he had happened to notice the flames. Wouldn't he have been asleep this late at night? Maybe he was an insomniac, or he had just returned from a night on the town and was preparing for bed when he saw the flames through the trees. "The firemen hadn't come yet," he muttered against her hair. "But knowing you were in there, I couldn't wait for them."

She wrenched herself out of his arms and, still coughing, started back toward the house, ignoring his concerned yelp. A few yards from the door, a stocky fireman blocked her. "Not yet, lady. You can go in later."

"But my things!"

"Other than some water damage, most of your stuff should be okay. The fire started in the kitchen, and thanks to your neighbor here, we got the call before it spread too far." The fireman threw a glance at the house. "Pretty little place. Looks like you'd been fixing it up."

"He's right, it could have been a lot worse," said Steven from behind her, putting a strong hand on her shoulder to pull her back. "But I know how much that house meant to you, Paisley."

She didn't respond. Her heart was beating too fast, and her thoughts were running wild. "What do you think caused it?" she asked the fireman, trying to sound calmer than she felt.

"Could be almost anything, ma'am. You a smoker? No? How about a pot left on the stove?"

She tried to remember. "No. I just made a sandwich."

The fireman shrugged when she shook her head. "Might be bad wiring. Happens a lot with these old houses. We'll let you know after the investigation."

"Investigation?" Steve's grip tightened on her shoulder, and she winced. "Why should that be necessary? It's obvious that the contractor messed up the electrical wires. Crossed them or something. Paisley, you should consider suing McMullin for faulty work. I bet he's not even licensed."

"Maybe it was the wiring, and maybe it was something else," said the fireman. "We'll find out soon enough." His eyes ran over Paisley's face sympathetically. "Want us to place a call to an ambulance, ma'am? You should get checked for smoke inhalation."

The fireman's words reminded her of that moment of blind panic on the couch when she could not breathe, and she put a hand to her throat in the old, habitual gesture. The fit of choking was over, though, and now that she had fresh air in her lungs, she no longer felt dizzy. "I think I'm fine. Thank goodness Steve got me out so quickly."

"I'll take you over to the E.R.," Steve said, frowning. "That guy's right, Paisley, you should be looked at by a doctor."

Paisley stepped out from his embrace, puzzled but grateful. Before tonight, he had always seemed polite, friendly, but somewhat remote. The fire seemed to have changed him. Although she didn't like other people making decisions for her, she was smart enough to know they were right."

"Thank you, Steve."

The sun was rising by the time they returned to River Bend from the ER. Paisley was too exhausted to think, but relieved that the doctor had given her a clean bill of health. "The smoke must have just started to penetrate the living room when you were rescued," he'd said, after examining her lungs and throat. "You were lucky your neighbor noticed the fire in time."

Now, after stepping out of the car, Paisley turned to Steve. "I haven't adequately thanked you for saving my life," she began.

"I don't know if I can take full credit for that." He followed her, slamming the driver's door behind him and coming around to her side. His teeth shone white against his soot-darkened skin in the dim light. "The fire department was pretty prompt. They got here moments after I did."

"No, I mean it. Just think, if you hadn't seen the flames...." The full import of what had happened struck her, and her knees gave way. Steve caught her, and she was grateful for the support. She was more shaken than she had realized.

"Look," he said against her cheek. "You're exhausted, probably in shock. You can't stay in your house tonight. It's going to smell pretty smoky for a few days. You're welcome to stay at my place while you figure out what to do next. I have a comfortable guest bedroom. After that, if you decide that you've had enough of River Bend, we'll all understand. This summer has hardly provided the peaceful convalescence you must have been expecting."

He was right, she thought. It would be demoralizing to have to start fixing up the house again. The fireman had minimized the losses, but there would surely be water damage and smoke damage. She couldn't remember if her lawyer had said the place was insured. Why hadn't she paid closer attention? And although the income from music lessons was helping, the fire would be another blow to her limited resources. The logical thing was to cut her losses and move on. Except she was now emotionally involved with the town and the people already.

She considered all this while Steve waited patiently. But the old sense of belonging she'd felt emanating from the house reached out its arms and pulled her back. Paisley shook her head.

"I'll wait and see before deciding anything. Maybe I can air the place out, wash the curtains and the bedding, and repaint. That won't cost much. And the fireman said it could have been a lot worse."

Steve shrugged. "Your call. What about staying at my place? My offer still stands. You must be exhausted."

She shook her head. The cool night air had reinvigorated her. "He said the upstairs wasn't touched by the fire. I'll open the windows and let the breeze freshen it out. But thank you."

His face still showed lines of strain under the layer of soot. "You are a stubborn minx, aren't you? At least come over and have breakfast with Kevin and me later, when you've rested a bit. One thing is certain: you won't be able to cook in your kitchen for a while."

She felt some of her tension drain away. At least she was not alone anymore: with the support of helpful neighbors and friends like Steve, Ian, and Shirley, she could get through anything.

"Thank you," Paisley said, smiling at him warmly.

Paisley held a hand towel over her nose to block the smell of smoke and walked through the house to determine what was salvageable. Somewhat surprisingly, when she experimentally flicked the living room wall switch, the overhead light turned on. Apparently the wiring was all right in this part of the house. Not in the kitchen, though. That would certainly be a gut job.

After checking the main floor, she decided that despite the blackened walls and water-drenched furniture, the remainder of the house seemed intact. She'd ask Ian to look around later.

Miraculously, Esther's extensive record collection, which was stacked against the wall of the living room farthest from the kitchen, appeared to have escaped damage. The kitchen, was another story. Black tongues of soot licked up the walls, all the way to the ceiling, and the range was melted into deformity.

Had she accidentally left something on the stove after all? The pills had made her groggy last night; maybe she had forgotten. Paisley checked the melted dials on the range but couldn't tell. The damage was too complete.

Finally the odor of smoke drove her back to the living room, where she threw open the windows to let cool, sweet air rush in. She was already mentally adding up the cost of repairs.

The ancient stove needed to be replaced anyway. The orange and brown striped Herculon couch, a relic of the 1970s, stank of smoke, but then, she had never liked it much. Maybe this was an opportunity to do what that old cliché advised, Paisley told herself: take life's lemons and turn them into lemonade. Or lemon meringue pie. Or lemon *something*. She could finally get rid of the ugly old pieces she'd inherited and decorate the house the way she liked.

The vintage furniture store next to Shirley's bookshop had some interesting stuff. A newer couch, coffee-table, and appliances should be affordable. The recent income from her music lessons might stretch enough to do it. After all, the more expensive work of fixing the plumbing and roof had already been done. And Ian was sure to charge her a good rate for redoing the kitchen.

In spite of the fresh air pouring through the open window, the smoke overcame her again, and she went outside. The morning light showed that the fire trucks had left the front yard a gashed, muddy wreck.

She was leaning against the porch railing, inhaling clean air and fighting off exhaustion, when a familiar green pickup pulled up. A tall figure rushed up the walkway toward her.

"Ian!" Relief coursed through her when he caught her up and crushed her in his arms. Her ribs were still sore from when Steve had dragged her out of the burning house, but she didn't care. It was nice that everyone seemed to be so concerned about her these days, she thought, burying her face in his leanly muscled chest. Lucky, popular Paisley. Lucky, alive Paisley.

"You're okay! Thank God you're okay!" His hard chin dug painfully into the top of her head while he clutched her furiously against him. Something was different about his embrace than Steve's, something she could not identify. She didn't bother to try. She was tired of thinking. There would be plenty of time for that later.

"How did you know?" she asked, the words muffled against his shirt.

His grip did not slacken. "A friend saw fire trucks heading away from your house. When you didn't answer my call, I threw on my clothes and came right over."

By now everyone in town must know about the fire, she thought, closing her eyes, enjoying the secure feeling of his arms. The grapevine worked perfectly, even at five-thirty in the morning.

Then he moved back, his face growing accusing. "Why didn't you call me right away?"

"In all the commotion, it didn't occur to me. I'm so sorry, Ian! All your beautiful work on the house, gone up in smoke." She started to giggle. Of all the clichés she had thought of so far, this one was the most literal.

"It's not funny," he said grimly, looking down at her.

She stopped laughing. "No, it's not. Please let me go, Ian. You're hurting me."

Instantly, he released her. She rubbed her upper arms, bruised from when Steve had hauled her out of the living room. Her grape-growing neighbor had been, perhaps, overly dramatic. Why hadn't he just woken her up? She could have walked out on her own two feet. Still, that didn't change the fact that Steve *had* been a hero. He'd saved her life, and she shouldn't quibble about how he had done it.

"Everybody in town must know about the fire by now," Paisley said. "I'll probably be getting a call from Shirley soon, too. Is the damage as bad as it looks, Ian? The firemen said the fire was limited to the area near the stove."

He didn't turn to look. "The heck with the house. What about *you*? Are you sure you're all right?"

Self-consciously, she ran a hand across her cheek and stared at her blackened palm. She could only imagine what she looked like. Even the oversized T-shirt she slept in was grimy, as were the bare legs poking out from under it. She shivered. If Steve hadn't arrived when he had…. If the firemen had pulled up only a few minutes later….

"I didn't swallow much smoke, thank goodness. I got checked out at the ER and I'm fine." She looked down at her hands. They were shaking, and she thought to herself, *Well, maybe not so fine.* "I'm going over to Steve's for breakfast. He invited me, since I won't be able to use my kitchen for a while."

"Neighborly of him," Ian said, scowling.

"Don't be mean. Steve saw the fire and dragged me out in time. He saved my life." Ian was jealous, she realized. He wished he had been the one to be heroic. Suddenly exhaustion and shock caught up with her, and, just before her legs gave way, she plopped into the swing hanging from one side of the porch. The striped yellow fabric cushion was soft under her thighs, the slats firm against her back. In front of her, the morning light grew brighter along the boards of the rest of the porch, sunbeams slanting through the leaves of the towering oak tree.

Ian sat down next to her, putting his arm companionably around her shoulder. The freshly white-painted porch appeared unscathed except for smudges of soot rimming the window sills like borders of black lace.

As Ian's arm tightened around her shoulder, she thought vaguely that they were starting to act like a couple, and yet they'd never really talked about their changing relationship. At some point, she'd have to tell him that, although his attentions were not unwelcome—a phrase Esther herself might have used in her courting days—they would not lead anywhere. She was just passing through River Bend for the summer, and soon, she would be leaving.

Because of these ruminations, she only caught the last of Ian's words: "And we'll find out who did it and make sure they're arrested."

Her head came up abruptly. "Find out who did it? You mean you think the fire was set on purpose?"

"Of course. This was no accident. "

She shook her head vigorously. "You're being just as melodramatic as Steve Lopez."

His intense expression did not alter. "I checked every inch of wiring myself. There was nothing wrong with it. I wouldn't be surprised if the firemen discover it was arson."

"But that's ridiculous. Why would anyone—?" She broke off, remembering her conversation with Kevin yesterday. The burglary. Maude Avery's hostility. But of course, Kevin had nothing to do with this. The teenager had vowed he would never do anything to hurt her, and she believed him. And Maude could do nothing without his help.

After a long pause, Paisley said slowly, "Are you telling me you believe this fire has something to do with Ruth's missing jewels?"

"What other motive could there be?"

"And yet yesterday you said...."

"That was before the fire."

She was silent for a moment longer. "This isn't exactly evidence. It's an old house."

"I told you, the wiring was fine. I brought everything up to code and did a thorough inspection when we were through. There was nothing wrong with the electricity."

"But we agreed that no one knows if the jewels are around here, so what motivation could there possibly be? We've gone over this ad nauseum, Ian!"

"We don't know that they're *not* here," he pointed out grimly. "And it seems clear that someone else believes you have them, and they're willing to kill to get them."

"K-kill?" She stumbled over the word. She remembered that terrifying moment when she realized the house was on fire, and a cold feeling ran down her spine like an ice cube. Not Kevin. It couldn't be Kevin. Maude Avery would never have put him up to that, especially not after her peace mission yesterday. But if not, who?

Fear burned in her stomach like spilled acid, and she barely prevented herself from clutching Ian's arm. She'd been leaning on others too much for support these past few hours. She did not want to appear completely spineless, and besides, she did not want to buy into his paranoia. The fire was an accident, pure and simple. She'd left a burner on and forgot about it. It wouldn't be the first time she had done something foolish like that.

She shook her head again. "We've done plenty of crazy speculating before, but that was different. You can't speculate about something like murder."

"It's not crazy if it's true." His face had taken on its customary brooding look, as if he were figuring out a complicated algorithm for erecting a skyscraper, but his eyes were colder than she had ever seen them before. "That burglary was no accident. If it turns out this fire was deliberately set, it proves that someone is willing to see you dead. If Steve hadn't seen the smoke in time, as you said, it could easily have spiraled into something tragic."

She passed over his comment about the burglary, not wanting to bring Kevin into the discussion. "But why would anyone want to see me dead?"

He gave her a long look. After a moment, her eyes dropped. "I know, I know," she mumbled. "The jewels. It always comes back to that, doesn't it? But it doesn't make sense. For the thousandth time, I don't have the jewels that belonged to Jonathan's ancestor, Ian. Or anything else of value, for that matter, except the house. Either way, how would burning down my home help them, whoever these imaginary persons might be?"

"I have no idea. Maybe they thought that you'd panic and grab the jewels, revealing their location. Or malice. In any case, it's clear that they've upped the ante. If this started as a game, it isn't anymore."

She pulled away from his warmth. She needed to process this new idea, now that the shock from the fire was draining away. "Who would do such a thing?" she protested.

Without answering, Ian stood and paced across the gray-painted boards of the porch, thick with wet ashes and puddled water, rubbing his stubbled jaw. Waiting for him to finish his rumination, she pulled up her legs onto the swing and wrapped her arms around her bare knees. Should she tell him that Kevin had been behind the burglary a couple of weeks ago? No. She was convinced the teenager had nothing to do with this latest incident, and the news would just prejudice Ian against him. Besides, Ian seemed so impressed with his own powers of deduction, she wanted to see what he came up with.

Finally Ian stopped and ran his hand through his sandy hair, leaving it standing on end like one of his crew's paintbrushes. "I was thinking about that list of suspects we made the other day. To make it unbiased, maybe you should put me on it too."

She rolled her eyes. "Next to me, you're the only person I'm sure had nothing to do with it." And Kevin, despite everything.

"Not necessarily. After all, I've had plenty of opportunity to lay the groundwork for an 'accidental' fire. I could even have been the one to burglarize your house. I wouldn't even have had to break in, since I've been working here practically every day since you moved in."

She played along. "Okay. What would your motive be?"

He shrugged. "The same as for anyone else, of course. The jewels. Maybe I've been pretending to be on your side, using my charm to wheedle out any information you might have." He looked sideways at her, trying to look mysterious, and she laughed aloud. Ian could not look mysterious if his life depended on it. He wore his emotions on his sleeve. Another cliché. She seemed to be full of them these days.

"I have no information, which you know perfectly well," she said when she stopped laughing. "Besides, you didn't even look in the box that was hidden in Esther's room, when, for all you knew, it might have contained Ruth's rubies. Sorry, Ian, you're off the list. Any other suspects?"

"Don't you have any ideas? You're the heroine in this mystery, after all; I'm just the sidekick."

She considered. He was right. If there was some plot, she appeared to be at the center of it. "If Hercule Poirot was on the case, he'd probably include everyone in town," she said at last. "You hinted that the story about Esther and the jewels is better known than I'd believed. Doesn't that mean everybody might have a motive?"

Ian rubbed his chin again as if trying to conjure a genie from a magic lamp. "Maybe there's something to that theory. Closeted town meetings, furtive spying on the new woman in town. In *Murder on the Orient Express*, they were all guilty, remember?" He perked up. "Maybe this house is bugged, and they're all over at the town hall, listening in on us right now." He gave up pacing and plopped back onto the porch swing, next to her.

She elbowed him in the ribs. "I was kidding, silly."

He grunted and rubbed his side. "So was I. At any rate, you need to file another police report. There was nothing funny about the fire."

She sobered. "You're right. It could have been serious. But I'm not going to file a police report. Not unless they prove it's an arson, which, I feel obliged to remind you, we have no reason to believe at this point."

"If it is, the time for amateur sleuthing is over, Paisley. We'd better let the experts take over at that point." He hesitated, looking into her eyes seriously. "Don't take this wrong, but maybe you should consider staying somewhere else for a while. You can always stay with me."

She remembered that Steve had said the same thing. "Thanks. It's over now. I want to stay here."

Paisley wasn't sure why she was rejecting the well-meaning invitations. It had something to do with the house. She had felt pulled to it ever since she'd first seen the photograph on her lawyer's desk, and the attachment had only increased since she'd moved in. The prospect of leaving, even when the summer was over and her injuries completely recovered, made her mind wince away.

He didn't like that. He started to say something and bit it back. Eventually, he left, frustrated.

When he was gone, she was glad she had not told him that Kevin had been the "burglar." Ian would immediately assume her young neighbor was the most likely suspect for the arson. If Kevin was tainted with suspicion for an act he did not commit, his young, promising life might be ruined. No, she had better keep that information to herself.

Chapter Fifteen

"Sure, it looks a bit odd this happened so soon after a burglary," Officer Elliott said, standing on the porch with his notepad and an unconcerned look on his blunt-featured face. He wasn't the policeman who had shown up when she had called before, but the two could have been brothers, down to the silver-framed sunglasses, slightly pudgy waist, and bushy tan mustache. "But there's no evidence to show this was a crime. My advice is to be more careful when cooking, ma'am."

"Please." She remembered what Ian had said. "Is it possible to have someone come out and at least look?"

He hesitated. "I'll see what I can do, ma'am. But I wouldn't worry too much if I were you."

She watched the officer drive away. It was a relief to be told some mysterious malefactor was not likely to be targeting her, she told herself. Still, the incident had shaken her. River Bend no longer seemed as safe and peaceful as it once had. Once opening night was over, she really should consider what to do with her future. In the light of recent events, Nigel's offer was growing more attractive. Now that she knew that she liked teaching young people, the prospect of working at the conservatory no longer seemed such a dire prospect.

Better still, her voice was definitely coming back. Perhaps it was not silky smooth or powerful like before, but the improvement was encouraging. Even her limp was much better. All that walking lately had been helpful, before Ian sold her the car. Soon, she thought hopefully, she might be able to take up the reins of her old career. It was time to update her website, send out emails to various opera companies, respond to the many concerned queries from her old peers and let everyone know she was still in the game. Soon, she would have no reason to stay in River Bend.

The thought did not bring her the joy she had thought it would. She pictured her new friends: Shirley, Ian, her students.... Maybe the decision would not be so easy after all.

Somewhat to her surprise, Officer Elliott followed through on her request. An arson team arrived and poked through the house. When they left, Paisley stuffed smoke-damaged curtains from the living room into large black plastic trash bags and pulled them down the porch steps to the side of the road. She had just gone inside for another load when the doorbell rang. Paisley opened the screen door, and Shirley rushed in, dropping a bulging canvas tote bag on the floor and sweeping her into a hug.

"I heard about what happened," Shirley said breathlessly. "I was out of town at a book fair, or I would have been over yesterday. Are you all right? Let me take a look at you."

"Not a singed eyebrow." Paisley struggled out of the hug.

Shirley looked around at the soot-blackened walls, the muddy footprints across the once attractive rug, her eyes horrified, mouth agape. "Oh, my dear. You had this house looking so lovely. Now look at it!"

Paisley felt the same sick feeling, but there was no point dwelling on it. "Sit down, Shirley. I'm afraid you'll have to come out on the porch and use the steps. The city truck came by this morning and took away most of the furniture so there's nothing to sit on inside. Besides it smells better outside. Can I get you something to drink?"

"No thanks, I brought *you* something." Shirley sat on the top porch step, which Paisley had hosed off earlier, when trying to clean up the worst of the damage. She pulled a quart of Ben and Jerry's Chunky Monkey ice cream out of the shopping bag and plunked it on the step next to her. "I thought this might settle your nerves. It always works for me." She glanced at Paisley sideways. "Unless you never indulge before noon? I've heard about your abstemious habits."

Paisley laughed. "I'll make an exception for Ben and Jerry's." She went to get two spoons from the smoke-blackened kitchen. She sighed as she looked around, fighting off discouragement. That morning she'd washed all the cutlery and dishes, relieved to find the faucets still worked and that most of the crockery was salvageable.

"My nerves are pretty much settled by now," she said, sitting on the top step of the porch and reaching for the container. "But I'll eat ice cream any time. How did you know about the fire?"

Shirley gave her one of her shrewd looks.

Paisley sighed. "All right, so you hear about everything that goes on in town. What, did the firemen communicate with you by smoke signal?" She took a huge bite of ice cream and felt better immediately.

Shirley ignored Paisley's quip. "There are rumors about other things that have been going on in this house as well," she said darkly. "I thought we were friends, Paisley. Why didn't you tell me anything about the burglary?"

Paisley looked guilty. "How on earth did you know about that? Never mind, don't tell me. The reason I didn't tell you is because nothing happened. Nothing was taken, nothing was damaged except for a gouge in one wall. It was just someone rummaging around the house. And I have reasons to believe it was unrelated to the fire." She dug her spoon into the carton of ice cream.

Shirley looked at her sharply. After a moment, the bookseller shook her copper curls and dug into the ice cream as well. "I think you know more than you're letting on," she said, licking her spoon. "I know it's none of my business, but I just don't want to see you get hurt."

"Me neither," Paisley said emphatically.

Shirley set aside her spoon. Reaching into the canvas bag like Mary Poppins, she pulled out a slim glossy paperback and plunked it onto the porch step, next to the carton of ice cream. "I brought you something else you might be interested in. After we found that book with Ruth's picture in it, back when she was the Nightingale of Warsaw, I thought I'd do a little further research of my own. The Internet may be a sexier source of information, but nothing beats some of these old books for finding out-of-the-way facts. You'd be surprised how much stuff *hasn't* been posted online."

When Paisley craned her neck to see, Shirley laughed and handed her the volume. "Don't get too excited. There's nothing specific to what you've been looking for. I just thought you'd find the subject matter intriguing."

"What is it?" Paisley flipped the book open. It was full of color photographs that immediately captured her interest.

"A catalogue of famous jewels. I found it at the book auction near Fresno. Cost me all of a buck fifty." Shirley stabbed a stubby finger at one of the pages. "After reading it this morning, I now consider myself a semi-expert on the topic. Look at that picture: the DeLong Star Ruby; isn't that one a beauty? That one's called the Patricia Emerald. And do you recognize this pretty blue one?"

"The Hope Diamond," Paisley said, her tone awed.

"I thought you'd know it. There's a passing reference in here to some high-ranking Russian prince whose family was rumored to have a nice collection, and who was supposed to have had an affair with a Polish singer, but nothing directly related to Ruth Klaczko."

"That's to be expected, isn't it? Ruth lived a quiet life after retiring, and she wouldn't have worn her jewelry after her brief years on the stage. The gems in the book exchanged hands multiple times, and would have been more frequently displayed in public."

Shirley took back the book and flipped its pages, face rapt, her glasses sliding down her short nose. "I guess you're right. Here, this is the one I wanted you to see. Remind you of anything?"

"That choker being worn by Queen Alexandra?" Paisley said slowly, looking at the page Shirley held up, with its large color photograph. "It looks a lot like the one Ruth was wearing, with those multiple strands of pearls and large pendants. But the ones on Ruth's necklace would have been rubies, not sapphires."

"Mmmhmmm." Shirley flipped to another page, and held the book up. "And look at this one. Ruth's brooch is an almost exact replica of this brooch belonging to Catherine the Great. That can't be accidental; the two pieces are too similar. Ruth's Russian lover must have had the famous pieces copied to impress her." She looked down at the picture, her face contemplative. "How big do you think that emerald is? Forty-five carats? Fifty?"

Paisley swallowed, feeling a new tingle of excitement while gazing at the photograph. The treasure hunt was becoming less academic, and more visceral. She wasn't sure that was a healthy development. "I wonder how much Ruth's brooch was worth," she said, trying to sound casual. "Her stone looked nearly as big as that one."

Shirley grinned at her. "I know. It's not just theoretical anymore, is it?"

Paisley shook her head, feeling slightly dizzy. She'd forgotten all about the ice cream. The truth was she didn't know anything about jewelry, had done virtually no research on value because...well, because it had never seemed real enough to bother. But she was beginning to realize that the family treasure trove might be worth vastly more than she had previously imagined. If it still existed.

"Based on the legend, and on Ruth's photograph, I knew the pieces would be valuable," she admitted, "but to be honest, I really didn't think about their actual dollar value. I hoped for enough to pay my debts, that's all. A few thousand dollars, at most. And even that was a fantasy."

Shirley's plump face took on an air of concentration. "A long time ago, I saw a TV special on Elizabeth Taylor's jewelry. At the time she died, her collection was valued at $150 million. A single necklace with 100 carats of sapphires and diamonds sold for $380,000, and that was twenty years ago. Of course, Ruth probably didn't own nearly as many pieces, but if you put together just what she was wearing in that photograph, I wouldn't be surprised if it added up to a couple of million dollars."

Paisley was glad she was sitting down, because her legs suddenly felt weak. Shirley had just provided plenty of motive for murder. But that only made sense if one had the jewels, and she didn't. Unless, like a character in an old Alfred Hitchcock film, she knew something she didn't know she knew. If so, what could it be?

Shirley set down the book she was holding, hazel eyes growing serious behind her glasses. Her words confirmed Paisley's thoughts. "I can't help wondering.... Do you think someone has targeted you? I mean, it seems odd that your house would suddenly go up in flames like that."

"That's overstating it. It was just a small kitchen fire."

"And you're understating it. I saw the arson team leave. It could have been a lot more serious, Paisley. Think about it. If it turns out that fire was set, who knows what will be next?"

Paisley shrugged, and tried to make her tone light. "Well, if that's the case, they're wasting their time trying to steal something I don't have. And why would they do anything that would potentially damage what they're searching for?" Remembering the ice cream, she grabbed the spoon, took a huge bite, and experienced instant brain freeze.

"So nothing has turned up?" Shirley sounded disappointed. "No more information, no clues, nothing?"

Paisley swallowed the last of the ice cream. "Nothing that anyone who's interested couldn't dig up for themselves. I'm not sure I care about them anymore, Shirley. Not even after seeing how much they might have been worth." She stopped and thought, gazing at her spoon. "The treasure hunt was a silly idea, and I'm not going to knock myself out looking anymore."

"The worst thing you can do is give up," Shirley said earnestly. "You can bet *they're* not going to, whoever 'they' are. And if they find it first, there won't be any quibbles about rights of ownership."

Paisley's hair stood up on her arms. She could almost hear Kevin's matter-of-fact young voice: "If you found them first, it would have been too late." What if someone else was trying to find the jewels before she did? It would be a lot easier with her out of the way. It was the first time the idea had crossed her mind that she might be a target.

When she fell silent, Shirley licked her spoon clean and sat with her back against the porch railing, still leafing slowly through the book. "What a tragedy if those gorgeous jewels were cut up or taken out of their settings," she commented.

"Do you really think anyone would do that?"

"I'm a bookseller, and I read a lot about crime." Shirley wiggled, making her ample bottom more comfortable. "The problem when stealing a well-known work of art is finding someone to buy it. If it would be recognized, like, say, the Mona Lisa ... which was once stolen from the Louvre, you know ... the police would come down on the seller immediately. The only way to make any money is to find a private buyer who would never display them. Apparently, that isn't as easy as it might sound."

"But we're not talking about a famous work of art. And Ruth's rubies might be valuable, but they are not well known."

Shirley shrugged. "The point is the same. We're talking about historically unknown jewels which, once found, would likely be extensively covered in the media. Just think of the news stories! A beautiful Jewish opera singer, a smitten Russian count, a small child fleeing the Nazis.... Then, mix in your own personal tragedy.

The press would pounce on the story like dogs on fresh meat. Photos of the jewels would be plastered online and in the newspapers. No thief could hope to fence them intact. His or her only hope would be to cut the gems down so no one would recognize them."

Shirley was right. The publicity wouldn't be bad for her own career, either, Paisley couldn't help thinking. She didn't like the thought of the reporters dragging up the tragedy of the accident, but it was a truism that having one's name in the media was not a bad thing for someone trying to launch a career like hers. Jonathan had been a master at it.

"You keep talking as if it's inevitable that Ruth's jewelry will be found." Paisley stood up and paced the porch to release her tension, forgetting that Ian had done the same only a few hours earlier. "For three generations, people have been looking for them, and we have no more to go by than Aunt Henka did."

Shirley watched her. "Have you gone to the police?"

"Twice." Paisley made a face, remembering her experiences. "Both times, they made me feel like an imaginative idiot. I'm still waiting to hear the arson team's results."

"Huh." Shirley's mouth drooped. "But it can't be a coincidence. I've lived in this town my whole life, and the worst thing that's happened to me was a parking ticket. And that was for blocking Main Street on the Fourth of July when I ran into Abe's Soda Shoppe for a bottle of water and held up the parade. Why didn't you call me after the fire? We're friends, right? Friends care about each other."

Ian had said something similar. Paisley hung her head. Shirley was right; she had failed as a friend. "I didn't want to worry you," she muttered. "Besides, the whole jewelry connection seemed so childlike. I've been chasing my tail over something that until recently I wasn't sure ever existed. It's like something out of Robert Louis Stevenson: the next thing you know, we'll have some pirates show up looking for treasure, and I don't mean soft-hearted pirates, like in *The Pirates of Penzance*. I mean ugly, murderous ones armed with real cutlasses."

"Well, you've known for a while now that Ruth's jewelry wasn't a fantasy," Shirley said matter-of-factly. "I'm the one who showed you that picture of her wearing the rubies, remember? And if someone thought you had them ... the wrong kind of person...."

Well, if the fire turns out to be arson, you'll know someone is willing to kill for them."

The dramatic words hung in the silence, reverberating like a drum. Ian had said the same thing. And Paisley had come to that realization herself, moments ago. But she still had trouble believing it.

Shirley's round eyes were serious. "You know what I think? Your best bet is to find the jewels before the bad guys do, lock them up in a bank vault, and let the press know about them, as soon as possible. Call the Sacramento Bee, the San Francisco Chronicle, the TV news stations. Get the jewelry photographed and be interviewed on the nightly news flashing them proudly. Then the jewelry won't be any use to a thief. It would be hard to find anyone who'd risk fencing them."

Paisley swallowed. "That's assuming the jewelry exists, and that I can find it. What happens if I can't?"

"Be careful, that's all." Shirley leveraged herself to her feet, rubbing her hips. "My, your porch is hard. And even out here, your house smells like a thousand campfires put together. Maybe you should stay with me for a few days till things get cleaned up."

"That's funny. Steve invited me to stay at his house, and so did Ian. I'm popular all of a sudden."

Shirley chuckled. "On a lighter note, I went over to Ray's real estate office yesterday, to see if he'd considered your invitation to perform in the play."

Paisley was glad for the change of subject. Any topic was better than jewels, arson, or death. "What did he tell you?"

"He said he'd been thinking about it. Like the saying goes, you could have knocked me over with a feather. At least he didn't laugh at me, or chase me out the door beating me over the head with a stack of "for sale" signs. In fact, if I didn't know better, I'd think he felt ... flattered."

Paisley laughed. "Actually, he already told me he'd take the part. His accepting isn't as odd as you think, either. Ray likes to be the center of attention. I bet he'll love having an audience."

"Well, I think you're magic. When this is over, I don't suppose I could talk you into living here permanently, could I?" Shirley said hopefully. "Into becoming the new director of the community theater? It would be a volunteer job, but you could build up a nice clientele through word-of-mouth. This town sure could use a music teacher." Shirley cleared her throat and got to her feet, shouldering the bag. "Aw, who am I kidding? It's obvious your voice is coming back and soon you'll be leaving us for Paris or Milan. Yes, I heard about that too. Ian's one of my bookstore's regulars. Well, maybe we'll get lucky and you'll come visit us in the sticks from time to time." She headed toward the steps. "Finish up that ice cream, would you? I've eaten most of it myself. See you at practice, Paisley."

Paisley stared after her, stunned by Shirley's off-handed invitation. The thought of staying in River Bend permanently had never crossed her mind. It was ironic, she thought, absent-mindedly picking up the plastic trash bag: in one breath, Shirley warned her that her life was in danger here, and in the next she had asked her to stay.

Paisley stuffed some smoke-damaged cushions in the trash bag and dragged them to the curb, piling them with the rest. Unlike Shirley, she wasn't certain that her voice was coming back to stay. If it didn't, should she remain in River Bend? And would she in fact be risking her life to do so? Her future was as hazy as it had been when she had arrived.

The investigator's report came back: there was no evidence of arson. The fire, it stated, had likely started with a range burner that had been left on. Torn between relief and embarrassment, Paisley mocked herself for her melodramatic theorizing. No one was targeting her; the danger had all been in her mind. Never mind that Ian and Shirley had been equally melodramatic. That's what happened when people let their imaginations carry them away, she told herself.

At least, she was now free to turn her attention to pulling the play together, while Ian's crew returned to fix up the kitchen and living room, and repaint the walls and ceiling. Thank goodness her lawyer, Barry Foster, had paid the insurance premiums. Even with her income from giving singing lessons, Paisley would have had trouble paying for the additional repairs on her own, even though Ian's quote was so low that she suspected it only covered the cost of materials again. She felt a rush of warmth for him as she drove her yellow Volkswagen toward the high school that afternoon.

Hell Week was living up to its name: long days of grueling rehearsal, broken only by breaks during which the cast devoured stacks of greasy pizza and sandwiches. The production was finally taking form together, although there were plenty of glitches to keep her and Shirley busy. Would the red-headed policeman ever remember his lines? Would the costumes be finished on time? Could the carpenter fix the ship's listing mast? Were the backdrops ready?

The backdrops! While the cast sang "Pour, oh Pour the Pirate Sherry," Paisley sat up straighter in her usual front-row seat, belatedly realizing that the snowy-white canvas backdrops remained unpainted. How could they have been overlooked? Paisley punched Steve's number into her cell phone, thinking he must have forgotten his promise.

While it rang, she cursed herself for not following up sooner. True, the fire had been distracting, and her last brief conversation with Steve had focused on the additional repairs to the house and how much longer she planned to stay in River Bend. She'd told him the truth: she'd likely move on when the play was over. An odd expression had crossed his face. Impossible to tell if he had been relieved or disappointed.

Steve picked up, and she got right to the point. "You forget about the backdrops!"

"What backdrops?" he said blankly.

"Don't you remember? For the play! You promised you'd paint them."

"Oh. That's right. I did." He spoke slowly, stupidly, as if from a distance. For a moment, she wondered if Steve was a secret pot smoker. He didn't strike her like the type to get high, but if there was one thing she had learned since marrying Jonathan, it was that you never really knew about people. "You said a seascape with a beach, and a Victorian graveyard, right?"

"Opening night is coming up fast" she reminded him. "I'll paint them myself if I have to, but they'll turn out better if done by someone with your talent."

There was a pause. "Okay," he said at last. "I'll try to get over there tonight."

"Great. The building's open until ten. You'll find the paint and brushes in the supply room behind the stage."

Paisley felt relieved. Another task checked off her list. She slipped the cell phone back in her purse and looked around with satisfaction. The chaos had taken on a sense of purpose, and everyone knew what needed to be done. Nor was it a room full of strangers: she now knew the names of all the young actors and those of most of their parents. She knew which kids had crushes on whom, which formerly best friends were on the outs, and who had mended their relationships.

In the center of them all was Kevin, singing his big solo onstage. He had lost his initial reserve, and now he was lunging about in his loose-sleeved, open-throated pirate shirt with a red sash around his slim waist, plying his cutlass as if born to it. His unexpectedly rich baritone brought out the irony in the lyrics, and when he finished his solo, the other actors burst into spontaneous applause. Grinning, he strode to the front of the stage and swept a theatrical bow. With the kerchief tied around his black locks and the beginning of a mustache darkening his upper lip, he looked suave and sexy. At least the girls in the cast seemed to think so.

"Go, Kevin!" one of them screamed. Someone in the rear of the auditorium gave an ear-splitting whistle. He bowed again, and a cluster of actresses rushed toward him. Chloe managed to maneuver so she was standing closest to him. Kevin looked down at the pretty blond and returned her broad smile. They looked like a couple. Paisley wondered when that development had transpired.

Paisley smiled, remembering a similar interplay of relationships between cast members backstage at the Met. Then her smile wavered. At this moment, someone else was performing Mimi at the Met, no doubt to thunderous applause, the part that was supposed to have launched Paisley's career into the stratosphere. And here she was, working an amateur production in the middle of nowhere. *La Bohème* and the professional world of opera had moved on without her.

With an effort, she shoved aside her self-pity. There was no point denying that she had enjoyed this summer, far more than she had expected. It had been surprisingly satisfying to work with young actors, using her skills to give what could have been just another amateur production the polish of, well, perhaps not a *Broadway* show, but an off-off-Broadway show. All modesty aside, Paisley knew if the show was successful, as she had no doubt it would be, it would be largely due to her help.

And, the truth was, the experience had been good for her, too. It had been healing to feel the others' respect, to have them seek her advice and implement her suggestions. After the extreme competitiveness of the professional opera world, and the devastating losses she had undergone, her self-confidence had gained a much-needed boost.

But it was time to move on. On the day Ian had caught her singing on the stairs, she'd suspected she could start practicing again without injuring her voice. Tomorrow, Paisley determined, she'd call her oto-laryngologist to schedule an appointment. If things went the way she hoped, she'd call Nigel immediately afterward and turn down that position at the conservatory. Then there would be other phone calls to make, professional relationships to renew, auditions to schedule. She may have missed out on the role of Mimi this season, but so what? There were always others. She wouldn't be totally forgotten by the opera world, not yet, and there would be other productions to try out for. Paisley's heart started beating faster while she directed her attention back to the stage.

Shirley's thick-rimmed glasses slipped down to the tip of her snub nose as she ran back and forth in the auditorium during rehearsal making sure everything was taken care of, but she took time to joke briefly with the members of the cast when she passed by. Finally she flopped into the seat next to Paisley.

"Okay, everyone! Break!" Shirley took a bottle of Evian from her oversized patchwork handbag and took a long slug. "Best thing I ever did, bringing you aboard," she muttered to Paisley, grabbing a second bottle of water and passing it to her. "I never could have pulled this thing together without you. Have a drink. You must be thirsty."

Paisley gratefully unscrewed the cap and took a long swallow. "You're doing fine," she told Shirley, recapping the bottle. "And I haven't done anything any decent vocal coach wouldn't do."

"Don't give me that false modesty, honey, you're fantastic with these kids. If you had told me a month ago this group would sound that good, I wouldn't have believed it. Now all we need is to get those backdrops painted. Dress rehearsal is in two days, and they're still not finished."

Paisley hid a start of guilt. "I just called Steve. He said he'd come paint them tonight."

"You *are* a miracle worker!" Shirley turned to her, amazed. "How on earth did you get Steve Lopez to agree? He's a fabulous artist, but he's always turned me down when I asked him before."

"You knew Steve painted?" Paisley's eyes opened wide in surprise.

"Well of course! After high school he went back east to try to become an artist. That's when he met up with Kevin's mother again and married her. Both former neighbors from River Bend, it was natural that they would seek each other out. But the marriage only lasted a couple of years. When his art career didn't take off, he came back home, and he's been trying to make a go of that vineyard ever since."

"Then you must have known about—" Paisley stopped. She had never asked why Shirley hadn't mentioned that Steve's wife was related to Jonathan. But then, Shirley must have assumed Paisley already knew. It would have been natural for Jonathan to tell Paisley all about his family. But he hadn't.

Shirley raised her voice and addressed the room in general. "Five more minutes, then we'll do the graveyard scene!" She turned back to Paisley. "Have you given any thought to what I asked the other day?"

Paisley scanned her memory. "You mean about my staying in River Bend?"

Shirley nodded emphatically. "I was thinking about it some more, and I thought I gave up too easily last time. This community needs you, Paisley. And to be honest, I think you need us. We have a lot more to offer than you might think."

"Spoken like a true manager of the chamber of commerce," Paisley muttered under her breath, but she smiled.

Shirley leaned forward, her hazel eyes serious behind their frames. "No I mean it. Take your time and think about it, Paisley. Don't rush into a decision." Then she chuckled. "No pressure, of course."

Paisley hadn't planned to tell Shirley that she had already made up her mind to leave – and soon. She had found what she had come for—not the jewelry, but healing and peace of mind. Of course, leaving River Bend wouldn't be easy. Ian's face popped into her mind, and she tried to thrust the image away. But it seemed fate had spoken, and it was time to go back to her old life.

Looking at Shirley's hopeful face, she found it hard to find the right words while haltingly explaining. "But don't tell anyone," she finished. "I don't want the kids to feel bad."

Shirley's expression reflected the disappointment Paisley had expected, but she nodded. "I understand. Of course. It's what we all expected. I just hoped...." Shirley sniffed and blinked twice. She pulled out a tissue and blew her nose. Then she opened her mouth and bellowed, "All right, everyone! Break's over! Take your places!"

The day of dress rehearsal, Shirley gave the cast a much-needed break after lunch, and ordered Paisley home to rest. "And don't forget to eat dinner before you come back," she said sternly. "You're looking pale again.

Paisley nodded obediently. Half an hour later, she found herself sitting on the swing of the newly repainted front porch, eyelids drooping with fatigue. The smell of smoke had been replaced by the sharp scent of newly applied paint and varnish, mixing with the fragrance of the yellow roses.

She knew it was silly to spend yet more of her meager funds on furnishing a house she would leave soon, but the house had looked so bare, so desolate, *so reproachful*, once all the water-damaged furniture removed. Now the place looked cozier than ever under its fresh coat of buttercup paint and with its comfortable new furnishings. It was impossible to regret the expense. Besides, she told herself, leasing the place furnished would likely bring in more rent, if she chose not to sell it after all.

Either choice brought a pang. It was hard to believe she would be leaving in a few more days. What choice was there? She had to leave, had to see if she could make a go of her career again.

In the meantime, there was a certain sense of peace that came from knowing she had done all she could this summer, both with the house *and* the play. From now on, the success or failure of *The Pirates of Penzance* depended on the cast and the crew, not on her. She wasn't a participant any more, but a spectator. *It's no longer up to you. Your task here is finished.*

There *was* a certain restfulness in knowing there was nothing else to do. Lulled like a baby in a cradle by the swing's slow, rhythmic motion, she fell half-asleep before realizing she was not alone.

The gray cat had appeared out of nowhere, like smoke from the fire, and hovered by the bushes, watching her from unblinking, golden eyes. Paisley met its stare, knowing from experience that any effort to coax it closer would merely spook it away. Nevertheless, when the cat remained motionless, staring at her, she couldn't resist trying again.

"Here, kitty, kitty, kitty." She leaned forward and offered her hand, pretending to hold out a treat. Maybe she could trick it into coming over to the porch.

It stared at her for several long moments from round yellow eyes, motionless like a child's stuffed toy. Then, gathering itself together, it launched itself upward and swarmed up the oak tree, as swiftly as a squirrel.

Paisley stood and moved to the edge of the step. She angled her head back, watching for the cat to come down again. The animal seemed to be gradually losing its fear of her. It would be nice to make friends with it before she departed and left it in Kevin's care again. Maybe the cat would even let her pet it if she were patient enough.

Several minutes passed, and it did not reappear. She began to grow concerned. Might it be stuck up there in the upper branches? Jonathan had once said sardonically that it was a waste of time rescuing cats from trees, adding, "Have you ever seen a cat skeleton in one?" *Fine, then, cat.* She shrugged and returned to the porch seat, where she reached for her lemonade with its melting ice cubes. *Stay up there.*

She lazily continued to swing, pushing with one foot, and waited for the cat to descend the giant oak, when she noticed something on the edges of her vision, so subtle that she was not sure if she had imagined it or not. A strange feeling grew in the pit of her stomach, like being on an elevator that dropped too swiftly. She had the impression of seeing a double exposure in an old photograph, a ghostly image superimposed over the actual scene before her. In the shade of the towering oak tree, she saw a young black-haired girl wearing a shimmering white dress, while a small, gray kitten romped nearby. Another girl ran toward her from the direction of the road, golden sausage curls bouncing. The friends waved at each other and sat down to play under the tree.

Just then, a taller, dark figure moved from the door of the house, just a few feet from where Paisley was standing. Paisley caught her breath while the shadow brushed by her. *Through* her? She felt a chill and shivered.

Frozen, she watched the girls' smiles vanish. The blond girl leaped to her feet and ran away. The other girl—Esther, who else could it be?—quickly hid something in the folds of her skirt.

Paisley's heart quickened. Somehow, she knew the dark shadow was not aware of the girls' presence, had not yet turned in their direction.

The dark-haired girl seemed to be wondering the same thing. She stood with the hidden objects still bundled in her full skirt, and looked around desperately. The gray kitten had disappeared.

The images faded.

Paisley blinked. As if still in a dream, she rose from the porch swing and moved toward the spot under the tree where the girls had been playing, the same spot where the cat had launched itself upward. Her head tilted, and she squinted into the overhanging tree branches.

"I wonder," she said softly.

Esther had been searching for a perfect hiding spot, one accessible to a child but not to an adult, especially one of Aunt Henka's age and dignity.

It had been years since Paisley had climbed a tree. It was more difficult than she remembered: gravity pulled harder on her adult body, and some of the smaller branches threatened to give way under her weight, but steadily she pulled herself higher. She tried not to look down. Finally, from above, she heard a surprised meow.

"I'm coming," she said grimly, and adjusted her grip on the branch. She winced as a twig dug into her thigh. No doubt she'd have plenty of cuts and abrasions when she got down, but she didn't want to think about the process of descending. *Just think about going up.*

The cat sat directly above her, staring impassively down. Cats were always expressionless, not like dogs, who always showed what they were thinking. Was the cat urging her onward? Or was it silently mocking her clumsy progress?

"I made it," she said, drawing level to the cat. She half-expected it to reach out a paw and swipe her face with its claws. Instead, the cat presented its furry gray hindquarters to her and levitated to the next branch.

At that point, she hardly paid attention to what the cat was doing. She was too busy staring at what had been hidden behind it.

Chapter Sixteen

Perhaps the tree had been hit by lightning long ago, causing a branch to fall off. Since then, the scar in the trunk must have been attacked by fungi and pests, leaving a hole whose opening was slightly wider than Paisley's fist. Without allowing herself to think what might be in that hole—bats? spiders?—she closed her eyes and reached in. Her groping fingers touched something solid but yielding, like an object wrapped in thick cloth. Her heart pumping harder, she pulled it out.

Afterward, she never remembered climbing down the tree. She might have floated down like a leaf in autumn. Safely back in her bedroom, she placed on the quilt the heavy pouch of soft leather, gray with dust, twigs, and less savory debris, and contemplated it.

Her hand approached the drawstring of the bag like an iron filing to a magnet. Then, with difficulty, she stopped. Once before, she had made the mistake of not including Ian in her discoveries. Things had been different, then. Now, she knew he had a right to be here.

Punching his number into her cell phone, she tapped her foot, phone pressed to her ear. After an interminable series of rings, his voice invited her to leave a message. She looked at the phone in frustration. Then, belatedly, she remembered he'd planned to spend all day working on his thesis. No doubt, he had turned his telephone off to avoid interruptions.

She left a brief message and turned back to the grimy chamois bag. She'd have to be less than human to resist any longer; surely Ian would understand, she told herself. After all, Esther had *meant* for her to find this. By now, Paisley was convinced the old woman had left the house to Paisley, left clues, and even, hard as it was for her rational mind to believe, created paranormal manifestations to prod her along.

Why Esther had done all this for her, Paisley doubted she'd
ever fully understand. She remembered that instant feeling of
liking when her eyes had met the old woman's at the wedding.
Perhaps the old woman somehow sensed that Paisley would need
the jewels some day; more likely, they may have been a symbol of
the connection between her, Esther, and that other opera singer
who married into the Perleman family more than a hundred years
before.

Flinging aside any lingering feelings of guilt, she struggled
with trembling fingers to unloose the wrappings. And there, right
before her eyes, the elusive treasure lay.

The rubies had been gorgeous in the black-and-white
photograph. In full, splendid, glittering Technicolor, they took her
breath away. The chamois bag had protected them well: not a
speck of dust diminished the gems' brilliance or the luster of their
settings.

Holding her breath, she ran fingers over their hard, cool
surfaces, trying to believe that they were real. Then, carefully, she
sorted through the jumble. There on her bedspread lay the three-
strand pearl collar, with its dangling ruby pendants. Each blood-
red gem must weigh at least thirty carats, she guessed,
remembering the book on jewelry that Shirley had showed her.
Next to it lay the matching ear-bobs, and the ring, which she
couldn't help trying on at once. The style of the round-cut ruby
surrounded with diamonds reminded her of the famous sapphire
which graced the fingers of the Princess Diana and, later, Kate
Middleton. Somehow, she wasn't surprised when the heavy band
slid easily over her third finger, fitting perfectly.

The tiara from the photograph was missing, of course. That
piece of jewelry was too large to fit in the hem of Esther's coat,
and so it must have stayed behind in Poland. Paisley wondered if
Aunt Adeladja had hidden it or sold it to finance Esther's escape to
America. Another mystery, one that might never be solved.

Feeling as if she were moving in one of her dreams, she
fastened the clasp of the necklace behind her neck. The tiers of
pearls warmed quickly, conforming to the contours of her neck.
While dangling the ruby earrings in front of her earlobes to picture
how they would look when inserted, she glimpsed the clock in the
mirror and gasped. She had forgotten the time!

She had promised Shirley to arrive early and make sure everything was ready for dress rehearsal. Instead, she was playing dress up, like the little dark-haired girl in the dream. It *must* have been a dream, mustn't it? Yet it seemed even more real than the others she had experienced.

At first Paisley was tempted to skip practice. But she couldn't let Shirley and the others down. Dress rehearsal was too important. So many things could go wrong at the last minute, and the cast had come to rely on her. Reluctantly she unclasped the pearl-and-ruby necklace and gently replaced it in the chamois bag with the bracelet and earbobs. The ruby ring, which had slid on so easily, now contrarily stuck behind her knuckle and refused to slide off. Yanking it and even rubbing soap on her finger failed.

Chewing her lip, she considered her options. She didn't dare leave the jewels unguarded in the house, which had already been burglarized twice. Perhaps she could return the jewels to the hollow in the tree, which had proved a secure hiding place. But the climb was slow and difficult, and welts and scratches were appearing on her arms and legs. She'd have to change into a long-sleeved top and slacks to avoid provoking unwelcome questions.

Giving up on prying off the ring, she turned it around on her finger, ruby-side inward, so only the plain gold band showed. It looked like an ordinary wedding ring. Tomorrow she would announce the discovery after the jewels were stored in a bank vault, but that left the question of how to keep them safe tonight.

Then the perfect solution occurred to her.

Using the key Shirley had lent her, Paisley let herself into the high school to make last-minute preparations for the dress rehearsal. Her heels echoed down the vacant halls, which reminded her of the old Steven King movie, *The Shining*. Fortunately the auditorium felt more welcoming, especially after she flipped on the lights. The backdrop gleamed with wet paint and the props were all laid out on the prop table, ready to go.

The finished set looked even better than Paisley had imagined, and she surveyed it with pleasure. In front of a painted ocean and sunny sky, a plywood pirate ship took up a third of the stage, the mast and reefed sails reaching upward, almost to the catwalk. Someone had hauled in sand to create a real-looking beach, on which a massive treasure chest spilled its glittering trove of dime store beads and foil-wrapped chocolate coins. Behind the beach rose painted cliffs down which Chloe would descend later, twirling her parasol while singing the showy aria on which she had worked so long with Paisley: "Poor Wandering One." Paisley felt confident that after all their practice together, the waitress would hit all the notes.

She turned to study Steve's enormous backdrop, which smelled of wet tempera paint. Skillful brushstrokes made the water shimmer; the azure sky with its puffy white clouds heralded a perfect day in the coastside village of Penzance. Behind the back curtain waited the backdrop for Act Two, with its elaborate tombstones, ghostly shadows, and a bust of Queen Victoria.

She made a mental note to send Steve a bouquet to thank him for his efforts. Or, rather, a gift certificate to that steakhouse he'd once mentioned. He wasn't the type for flowers.

Moving over to the prop table, she checked that everything was there: parasols, swords, the head policeman's whistle. The stage was neatly swept and everything appeared to be in its proper place. Everything, that is, except for a coil of rope someone had carelessly left in the center of the stage. Tut-tutting, she bent and picked it up.

A loud creaking sound startled her. She jumped aside, just as a gush of wind swept over her. The next thing she knew, something struck her violently on the shoulder and sent her sprawling. Too stunned to move, she lay on the wooden floorboards for several moments, trapped under by yards of billowing canvas and trying to comprehend what had happened. Finally she shoved the heavy weight aside and crawled out from underneath, gasping in pain and clutching her shoulder. Cautiously, she angled her head upward.

The pirate ship's mainsail had been fastened to the catwalk until it was to be lowered just before the performance began. Somehow it had come loose and fallen.

Pushing herself to her feet, Paisley stared down at the length of rope clenched in her hand. The cable had been fastened to the mast, she thought distantly. Odd, that the mere act of picking it up had triggered the fall. The mast must have been carelessly fastened, making an accident inevitable. But perhaps it wasn't an accident at all. Was it possible that someone had left the rope there as a trap, knowing someone was bound to pick it up, and that it would bring down the entire rigging?

Her legs turned to sand and she sat down again abruptly, crosslegged in the center of the stage, thoughts rushing through her head. If she had stood another inch to the right ... had not felt that warning gush of air ... her head would have been smashed in. Her shoulder was throbbing painfully. She really should get home and put some ice on it, she thought dully.

Instead, she remained sitting on the stage, staring at the broken mast and mainsail that lay in the center of the stage like a dead bird. A burglary and two near-deadly accidents should pierce the complacency of even Officer Elliot. Could she really be that accident prone? Or was this done deliberately?

If so, the rope must have been rigged sometime after last night's practice to bring the mast crashing down like that. Although the school should have been secured, someone could have left a door unlocked, or the perpetrator could have broken a window and crawled in. Was it possible he was there even now?

Running footsteps broke the stillness, causing her to jump in fright, and the doors to the auditorium banged open. "What was that?" demanded a familiar voice. "What was that noise? Is anyone in there?"

The stage lights switched on, blinding her. Instinctively Paisley scrambled to her feet, poised for flight, although in the recesses of her slow-working brain, she knew a murderer was hardly likely to be charging noisily down the center aisle. As her eyes adjusted to the sudden brightness, Kevin jumped onto the stage and skidded to a stop in front of her. "What happened?" His eyes went from her face to the mainsail.

"I saw a piece of rope, and I didn't want anyone to trip on it." Paisley slowly got to her feet again—they felt steadier now—and held it for them to see. "When I picked this up, *bang!* The whole set piece came down." She wondered who the intended victim was. Then she blinked. "What are you doing here so early, Kevin? Dress rehearsal doesn't start until another half an hour."

The teenager ignored her question. "Are you sure you're okay? Wow, that must have been a close call." He crouched to inspect the crumpled mainsail. "Lucky we came early, huh? Steve gave me a lift because I wanted to run through my solo before rehearsal. You had a great idea for staging that I wanted to practice. Something about me swinging onstage from...."

Kevin broke off. His head swiveled toward the broken rope, and the color drained from his face, leaving it an ugly gray color.

Paisley didn't see Steve until he bounded onto the stage like Kevin, although with considerably more grace. He seized her in his arms with the surprising strength she remembered from the fire. His heart beat wildly under his tailored, pin-striped button-up shirt which was freshly pressed and smelled of starch and Arm & Hammer detergent.

"Paisley! Thank heaven you're all right!"

When she winced, he said quickly, "I'm sorry." He stepped back but kept his grip on her upper arms, while he stared down into her face from worried brown eyes. "I'd just gone up to the light booth to turn on the stage lights when I heard the crash. For a moment, I thought...."

With her good arm, Paisley pushed him away. "I'm all right," she repeated, although her legs still felt wobbly and she wanted to sit down.

Once again, the auditorium doors banged open, and once again Paisley jumped. This time, Shirley appeared, her legs encased in bright-orange sweat-pants making her look like a moving bag of Fritos as they moved with unexpected speed down the center aisle and up the steps. Panting, she elbowed Steve out of the way.

"Shut up and let me have a look at her. What happened, Paisley? How did the mast come down? Did it hit you? Where? Let me see."

"No!" Paisley jumped back before Shirley could prod her wound with fingernails tipped with peeling green polish. "If someone can find me an ice pack, I'll be fine. If anything was broken, I wouldn't be able to move my arm. See?" She turned to Steve. "Pull the mast backstage and find someone to fix it. And," she added, looking at all three of their concerned faces in turn, "please don't tell the others. We can't conceal that it fell, but don't say I was here when it happened. It'll upset the cast unnecessarily."

"But...."

"I don't want anyone distracted," she said, raising her voice over Shirley's instant objection. "The kids are stressed enough, with tonight being the last rehearsal. It's over, and no one got hurt." A nasty bruise didn't count, she told herself.

After a quick conference, the others reluctantly agreed, but Paisley saw Shirley sneak concerned looks at her while the other cast members trickled in. Paisley smiled back reassuringly. She was safe, and that was all that mattered. No one would try anything with witnesses around.

Then her smile flagged. What if the accident wasn't rigged for her? Kevin could have been the one standing under the mainsail when it dropped. If she hadn't arrived early, he would have been the first one on the stage. And no one knew she was going to be here an hour before rehearsal; she had told no one. But who would want to kill Kevin?

Ray Henderson was the last of the cast members to arrive. Although he was running late, he was already in full makeup. His beard was glued on, and he was wearing the Major General's military costume with its double breasted buttons and bicorn hat with an enormous, flowing ostrich feather. His big face seemed flushed and his eyes sparkled as if excited for dress rehearsal. *I always knew he was a ham*, Paisley thought, smiling to herself.

He winked at Paisley while passing her on his way to the refreshment table. "Here," he said, returning and handing her an open can of cold Pepsi. "I noticed you're always sipping water or something. Must be working. Your voice doesn't sound like you used to smoke four-packs a day."

That was an improvement, Paisley thought wryly, considering she'd never had a cigarette in her life. It was good that others noticed her voice was getting better after the car accident that had landed her in the hospital and threatened to end her career.

He was studying her. "You look a little pale. You really ought to get out in the sun more. I thought you were here for rest and relaxation."

"Thanks," she said wryly. So she didn't sound like a four-pack-a-day smoker anymore?

She took a pain pill and a refreshing gulp of Pepsi before plopping into her usual seat in the center of the front row, where she could watch the actors up close. Ray grabbed a few M&Ms from the refreshment table and tossed them in his mouth on the way backstage, whistling to himself. She was glad he was in a good mood. Maybe he'd sold a house that day.

Steve came over next. "Everything's cleaned up backstage," he told her, searching her face anxiously. "Are you sure you're okay?"

"I'm fine," she said a bit too sharply. "There's nothing more you can do. I'll make sure Kevin gets a ride home after rehearsal."

He left, looking crestfallen, and she kicked herself for not being nicer to him. Really, why was she always so hard on Steve? There had been a time when she had actually thought that something might happen between them, someday in the distant future. When she was ready for a relationship. He was trying so hard to be a good stepfather and to get his struggling winery off the ground. She mentally thanked Steve for taking care of everything so quickly. His quick action had averted a lot of distracting questions. She only wished she had shown more gratitude. And he really *was* very good looking, with that shiny black hair and those slim hips. She'd always been attracted to dark men.

A chorus of high-pitched giggles distracted her. The Major General's daughters were lining up in front the curtain, corkscrew curls bobbing, pastel-colored crinolines swaying, and ruffled parasols twirling. On the other side of the stage, the young pirates joked and jostled each other, brandishing their plastic cutlasses and checking their glued-on beards and mustaches. The broken mast had been cleared away before the actors arrived, and no one knew of the accident.

As the first sprightly notes of the overture began, Paisley's mind returned to what had happened earlier. There was no way to brush this one off, she thought. It was very possible that Ian was right: someone was trying to injure or kill her. The culprit was doing it in a slapdash, amateurish way, but that didn't make it any less serious. Apparently they didn't care who else got hurt, either. Her hands curled into fists at the thought of how easily the mast could have fallen on Kevin, or any other crew member who arrived early. Or was Kevin the intended victim?

She mentally kicked herself for not insisting someone call the police right away to report the sabotaged set-piece. Everyone had assumed it an accident, and she had not contradicted them, not wanting to disrupt the rehearsal. Although, her previous experiences had prejudiced her against the local law enforcement, but that was no excuse. She'd better call them now, and make the report herself.

She'd just borrow someone else's phone after rehearsal. There was no hurry, since all the police could do was take another report. Certainly they'd find no clues. By now the crime scene had been swept clean by an over-enthusiastic stage crew and compromised by dozens of bustling actors. Nor could they do anything to protect her against future incidents.

In her mind, it all boiled down to one fact: someone wanted her to leave River Bend. Too bad, she thought humorlessly, that the unknown enemy didn't know she had already decided to do just that, much as the desire to stay tugged at her. If the falling mast was a message, it had been a wasted one.

Then her mouth tightened. She'd leave, all right. Tomorrow, *after* the play's first performance in front of an audience. No way would she'd leave River Bend before seeing the payoff for all her hard work. After the cast's final bow, she'd recover the jewels from their newest hiding place, drive the VW to San Francisco, and fly out on the first plane. Her former mentor, Nigel, would be thrilled to see her. After receiving her message, he had hinted that he might set up some auditions, which would possibly allow her to segue back into her old life.

As soon as she got home, she would make a plane reservation. That was it. It was final. She was leaving River Bend, going back to her old life. Back to trying out for parts, maybe having to start at the bottom and fight her way back to the top again. It was the life Paisley had always dreamed of, fought for. She had done it once, she could do it again.

Instead of feeling satisfied, she sensed a strange emotion wash over her, unrelated to either her headache or her still-throbbing injured shoulder. In front of her imagination swam a picture of the cozy little white house Ian and his friends had labored to fix up; Shirley's kind eyes and sympathetic air, the friendly tête-a-têtes over bowls of Ben & Jerry's ice cream and aromatic, out-of-print books. Ian's tousled hair and whipcord-strong arms, and.... She didn't want to think about Ian.

At least, Ruth's rubies were safe. Although Paisley had read some famous jewels were thought to bring bad luck, like the Koh-i-noor and Hope diamonds, these gems were different. They reminded Paisley of strong women who had showed courage and perseverance in the face of difficulty. The jewels had survived for nearly a hundred years. In a crazy way, she felt a responsibility to continue to guard them.

The house lights came up. Ray towered over her with an odd expression on his face. "Are sure you're all right?" She looked up, blinking in surprise, to find the actors fanning toward the exits. She had missed the whole last act. The pain pill had made her sleepy and she must have dozed off.

Ray removed his plumed hat and false beard and wiped sweat off his broad forehead. Shirley was nowhere to be seen; no doubt she was backstage taking care of something that needed to be taken care of.

"I'm fine," Paisley mumbled, pushing herself to her feet. Her head swam and she staggered. Ray caught her by the arm with his free hand, and frowned when she winced and pulled away.

"Hey, you're hurt."

"It's nothing serious. I had a ... a little accident before the show."

With unexpected sensitivity, he didn't press her about it. Perhaps her face told him she did not want to talk about it. He drained his ceramic coffee mug and said firmly, "Well you certainly can't drive in this state. Let me take you home."

The thought was tempting, but she remembered, "I can't leave my car here overnight. I need to use it tomorrow." To drive to the airport, but she didn't tell him that.

"That's no problem. Kevin lives next door to you, doesn't he? Why not ask him to drive you home? I'm sure he has a driver's license."

She turned her head. Kevin had changed back into street clothes. His lower face was still pink from where the spirit gum had adhered to his false mustache and sideburns. Ray's florid jaw was even pinker, where he had stripped away his beard. He must have had trouble doing so, for one side of his face looked raw and discolored. She really should give him tips on applying artificial facial hair correctly, she thought.

Kevin had overheard Ray's words. "Sure, Paisley," he said, turning toward her. "I'll drive you home."

Paisley saw a look of disappointment on Chloe's face. Earlier, she had heard the two teenagers agree to walk with a group of friends after rehearsal to a nearby eating spot for a snack. She didn't want to interfere with the couple's plans.

"Why don't you take Chloe out to eat, and drop the car off at my place afterward," she suggested. "Maybe Ray can give me a lift home." She looked over at Ray. "Is that all right?"

He looked startled, but recovered quickly. "Sure. That's a great idea."

She took her car key off the key ring and handed it to Kevin. "Just leave the VW in front of the house. And, please," she added, remembering that she was talking to a teenager, "drive carefully."

"Sure." To give Kevin credit, he didn't roll his eyes at her warning. He and Chloe left together, surrounded by a large group of cast members.

"Thanks," Paisley told Ray. "I should have warned you, though, it might be a while before I can leave. There's lots of last-minute things that need to be taken care of before opening night tomorrow."

"No problem. I can wait."

She checked that all the props were in their proper places, the costumes were hung up neatly, and the stage was swept clean. And that this time the building was locked up securely. She tested and double-tested the doors, to make sure. It took even longer than she'd expected to arrange all the little details, especially because her shoulder hurt and her mind was sluggish, but Ray was surprisingly patient. When she was finally ready, he offered his bulky arm with old-fashioned courtesy, and she took it, grateful for the support.

There was another reason Paisley lingered in the auditorium as long as possible, although she would not have admitted it to Ray or anyone else: she was not looking forward to spending the night alone. Recognition of her vulnerability had finally sunk in. All Paisley's claims that she could handle things just fine by herself felt particularly hollow tonight.

Maybe she could ask Ian to stay over tonight, she thought while following Ray to his big Tahoe, parked behind the high school. She could tell Ian to sleep on the couch downstairs or in the spare bedroom. It was worth risking the gossip of the neighbors. Or, better yet, maybe he'd invite her to spend the night at his house, where she wouldn't jump at every strange noise that disturbed her sleep. As soon as she informed the police about tonight's accident, she'd dial Ian's number. Too bad she hadn't thought of it sooner.

"Ready?" Ray sat in the driver's seat with the door open, drained his big, heavy coffee mug and put it in its cup-holder. She realized they were the last to leave the parking lot.

"Sorry for holding you up," she said again, and got in. "You've been very patient."

"My pleasure."

Once they were on the road, they spoke little. The moon was full, and a panoply of stars tossed across the sky like white sprinkles on a chocolate donut made the scene unusually bright. Perhaps the real estate agent was reviewing his lines for the play, she thought drowsily, resting her head against the leather seat. The rapid patter of "I am the Very Model of a Modern Major General" was notoriously difficult, and Ray had stumbled over more of the words than usual in the dress rehearsal tonight. This was his last night to polish the routine before the curtain went up tomorrow.

Then Paisley's thoughts turned to Ian again. She pictured him buried deep in his master's thesis, ignoring the urgent call of his cell phone. Or maybe he had turned it off, to reduce distractions. That would be like him. He liked to give tasks his full attention.

As they approached the curve in the river, Paisley came out of her reverie. She gasped and put a hand on Ray's arm. "Look, there! What's that?"

The Tahoe's headlights revealed a glint of buttercup yellow paint, down at the bottom of the embankment. For a moment, she thought she had imagined it.

Ray started, and the car swerved slightly. "What?" he asked. "I don't see anything."

"No, stop, Ray. I mean it. Down there, in the river. It's the VW!"

Chapter Seventeen

At the sight of the Volkswagen beetle in the river, Ray clamped his hand around her upper arm so tightly that later she found bruises matching the one left by the falling mast. "Stay in the car," he ordered. "I'll go take a look."

"But—"

"Stay here," he repeated more firmly. "I'll see if the kid's all right. River's running fast this time of year. No sense both of us putting ourselves in danger."

He carefully climbed down the steep sides of the ravine toward the half-submerged VW. The powerful headlights of the parked SUV lit his progress, like a spotlight following an actor across a stage. The little car must have come down the hill too fast and failed to negotiate the curve, Paisley thought, slipping out of the Tahoe and following Ray. She had no intention of obeying Ray's order.

If not so worried about Kevin's safety, she'd have resented the man's high-handed manner in assuming he was in charge of the situation. But then he was ex-military, no doubt accustomed to barking orders; perhaps it wasn't entirely his fault. Still, it rubbed her the wrong way.

Her sandals slid in the gooey mud down the slope. If only she hadn't allowed Kevin to drive! He was young and inexperienced, and the old car might have been hard to control, although she hadn't noticed any problems with it since she'd had it, just as Ian promised.

A few clouds drifted across the full moon, making the light unreliable. After a few yards one of her sandals came off, and she sat on a nearby boulder to put it back on. Something off to the side caught her eye: a long, dark form on the ground that almost blended into the brushes. Heartbeat quickening, she clambered in its direction, searching carefully in the shadows. The veil of clouds parted and a cold beam of moonlight shone down, revealing a fallen log where she had thought she'd seen a body. Paisley let her breath out in a gush of relief.

Ahead of her, she heard a stream of curses. Ray had reached the half-sunken Volkswagen and was on the bank, peering inside the open window.

"What? What is it?" In spite of her best effort, her voice shook.

He looked at her, and it seemed a wave of annoyance passed over his craggy features. Or perhaps it was just the uncertain light of the moon from behind shifting clouds. "I thought I told you to stay in the car. Looks like he's missing."

"That's good, right?" Her hopes rose. "Kevin must have gotten out!"

"He might have been swept downstream." Ray's words fell like a blow. "And if he's still in the river, it's likely too late. The water is deeper and swifter than it looks. And there's always the danger of hypothermia."

She swallowed. "Maybe he made it to shore."

Ray looked at her. She had the impression that he was trying to break the news gently, like a doctor confronting a terminally ill patient. "Sure, there's a chance. But with a moon this bright, you'd think we'd see footprints in the mud on the bank."

Paisley wrung her hands. "We've been wasting time! We need to call for help right away." Her fingers scrabbled in her purse, sifting through lipstick, comb, pens and notepad, and came out empty. Then she remembered she'd left it at home.

"You make the call," she told him. "The sooner rescuers get here, the better chance they can find him."

Ray was already pulling out his cell. He waited for a moment, pressing the electronic device to his ear. "Hello? Yes, ma'am, I'm calling to report a yellow Volkswagon beetle went into the river at the bottom of the hill, just east of the town of River Bend. No, ma'am. The car was empty when we found it. Mmmhmmm. Yes, ma'am, that's right. A teenage driver, about seventeen years old. Name's Kevin. No, no passengers. Uh huh. Thank you. Please hurry."

He pocketed the phone and turned toward Paisley as a cloud passed over the moon, casting his face in shadow. "She said a search crew is on its way." He breathed heavily through his nostrils. "If anything happens to Kevin, it's going to kill Steve. He worries a lot about that kid, even if the brat drives him crazy."

Her brows rose in surprise before she remembered that Ray and Steve had grown up together and must know each other well. And Ray was her neighbor's real estate agent as well as hers. Would she ever get used to the ins and outs of small town life?

Her teeth chattered despite the warm night, and she hugged her arms around herself. "Shouldn't we keep looking, Ray, until the rescue team gets here? Every minute could make a difference."

He flung her a look that had a hint of contempt mixed with sympathy. "It's clear you don't know the first thing about search and rescue, ma'am. Amateur bystanders often drown when trying to help. At best, they get in the way of the professionals. Best thing we can do is clear outta the way." He started climbing back up the ravine, toward his SUV, and motioned for her to follow. "They'll be arriving any minute."

She stared in disbelief at his retreating form. "But we could still—"

He stopped and cocked his head toward the road. "Listen. That must be them."

All she could hear was the song of a night bird and the rushing of water. Or was that a car engine she heard in the distance? Ray came back to her, put his big hand on the flat of her back, and guided her up the hill. "I told you, we'll just be underfoot. Let me take you to an emergency room, so they can look at that shoulder, and then I'll call Steve about what happened. He'd rather hear the news from me. Hopefully by then, they'll have found Kevin."

Paisley stumbled on a loose rock and pain shot through her injured shoulder. Ray was right, she thought dully. She was so accident prone that she probably *would* get in the way, and end up needing rescuing herself. Certainly she did not want to divert attention from the urgent crisis of finding Kevin.

Nevertheless, half-way up the ravine she turned back to scan the half-submerged Volkswagen. Its curved hood glimmered in the moonlight like the hump of some fabled sea creature. Wasn't it wrong to leave the scene of an accident? she wondered. Or did that rule apply only if you caused it? Her brain didn't seem to be thinking coherently; perhaps she was still in mild shock from the earlier mishap with the falling mast. And the strong painkiller wasn't helping.

Ray helped her into the cab of the SUV, more gently than she would have expected from a man of his bulk, and she remembered to close her fist around the large ruby, which dug into the palm of her hand. Only the gold band showed, and he didn't seem to notice it. Even if he did, she was sure he'd assume it was her wedding ring.

"Here, put this around you," he said. He pulled out a fuzzy brown-and-green afghan that smelled like wet dog and settled it around her shoulders. Knitted by his ex-wife, perhaps, and relegated to the car for emergencies? she wondered vaguely. He revved the engine and pulled away. "You don't look too good. It's been a pretty rough night, hasn't it?"

"It's awful," she said, her teeth chattering. "I can't help thinking about that poor boy. What if he's still in the water, clinging to a branch, waiting for someone to rescue him? Or worse, what if...." Her hands clenched convulsively at the edge of the blanket while she pictured Kevin's pale face, eyes closed, the river closing over his head. Overlying the image was the memory of that other accident, months earlier, that other still body with black hair falling over a high forehead.

"I told you, search and rescue is almost here." He looked in the rear view mirror. "The van's pulling up already. They found the spot right away. Nothing more we can do to help." He glanced over at her. "What happened to you at the auditorium earlier tonight, anyway, Paisley? That must have been more than just a 'little accident."

There was no reason not to tell him. "One of the props fell on me before rehearsal. The mainsail of the pirate ship."

He whistled. "That was a hella big beam! No wonder your shoulder's sore. That explains why the piece of scenery was missing from the stage." Ray paused. "Why didn't you tell the rest of the cast members what happened?"

She felt foolish. "I didn't want to disrupt the dress rehearsal. It's the most important night, next to opening night. The kids needed to focus on their lines, not be distracted by what happened to me. 'The show must go on,' you know." Paisley paused, rousing herself a little. "But maybe I should have spoken up. If someone else got hurt, I'd never forgive myself.

What if Kevin did get hurt...or worse? If the car accident is connected with what happened earlier this evening, it's my fault for not warning him.

Ray glanced at her as the Tahoe accelerated, its powerful engine a restrained roar parting the darkness. "Yes, you should have spoken up. Might have dislocated your shoulder, maybe even broken a bone. Could get worse if it's not treated."

"It's not so bad," Paisley mumbled, touching her shoulder and wincing again. "Just a bad bruise." But Ray was right, she admitted to herself. Everything she had done that night was pretty dumb, up to and including allowing him to talk her into leaving the scene of the accident before the search party arrived. How could she have done that? No matter what Ray had told her, they *should* have stayed. Not only was it their moral duty, but the rescue workers might want to question them further.

She sat up straighter. "Turn around, Ray. I mean it. I'm not thinking clearly because of that pain pill I took, or else I'd have insisted sooner."

"It's more important to get you to the hospital. You're hurt worse than you think, Paisley."

"I'm fine. An ice pack when I get home is all I need." She was about to remonstrate further when she heard a thump from behind. Despite the pain, Paisley tried her best to crane her neck around. "What was that?"

Ray flung an impatient look over his shoulder and pressed harder on the gas. The car leapt forward. "Some tools rolling around in the back." He reached for the radio, cranking the volume up. A country tune filled the cabin, Billy Ray Cyrus singing about his Achy Breaky Heart. "I guess this kind of music probably isn't your kind of thing," he said, glancing at her. "Sorry I don't got anything more high-brow, like what you probably listen to."

"It's fine. I enjoy all types of music." But she wasn't thinking about the song. That thump didn't sound like it had been caused by loose tools. A cold feeling passed through her, like a shiver up the spine. She cast a sideways look at Ray's profile, trying to read his expression in the shadows. It occurred to her he had never offered her a ride home before, had never lingered after rehearsal. He was being friendlier than usual, very generous with his time, in fact.

She looked out the window just in time to see the little white Queen Anne house flash by, a blur in the shadows. "You passed my house."

He did not look away from the road. "I told you, your shoulder needs to be checked out. The closest emergency room is thirty minutes away, in Davis."

"But I don't want to go to —." Paisley bit off the words. They were heading deeper into the countryside every second. Was he really planning to take her to a hospital in Davis? She didn't know this area enough to tell where they were going, and she was starting to realize that she didn't really know Ray very well, either. What she did know was that someone had tried to harm her tonight and, very likely, several times before tonight. And suddenly she wanted to be somewhere else, anywhere except in this car.

As Billy Ray Cyrus's repetitive chorus hammered into the side of her head, she suddenly felt a strong counterbeat from the seat directly behind her, thumping between her shoulder blades. With the music blaring, Ray did not appear to notice it this time. His thick fingers tapped on the wheel in time with the radio while he whistled along, and she sensed a subdued excitement in him, as palpable as his Old Spice aftershave. Seconds later, the cell phone in Ray's pocket rang and Paisley almost jumped of her seat.

Ray reached into his shirt pocket, glanced at the caller ID, and swore under his breath. He switched off the radio. Silence settled over the car's interior like a blanket, making his voice seem all the louder by contrast. "Hello there, I was going to call and tell you, but...." He paused and listened for a moment, then grunted. "No, no, don't worry, I'm sure everything will be okay." He fell silent, listening to a faint, squawk emitting from the receiver. "Uh huh. Uh huh. Seriously, it'll be fine. Trust me."

He snapped off the phone and put it in his pocket and stared again into the darkness ahead of them. In the weird light of the dashboard his face appeared to struggle with different conflicting emotions, and for a moment she thought he had forgotten her. She pondered the fact that he had just contradicted what he had told her earlier about Kevin's chances. What else could he have been talking about?

"Was that Steve?" she asked.

His voice was gruff. "I knew I should have called Steve right away. The rescuers called him first. Poor guy, I knew he'd be cut up when he heard the news."

She felt the sharp raps between her shoulder-blades again. Three quick, three slow, three quick. She didn't need to know Morse Code to understand what the signal meant.

Outside, it was pitch dark again. Now she was convinced they were not heading for a hospital. Fear crawled inside her like a worm. Not just fear for herself, but for whomever it was tapping the seat behind her. "Ray." She made her voice as firm as she could. "Please take me home. Really, I insist. I feel fine."

"Sorry. Can't do that." Without warning, Ray twitched the wheel and the SUV lurched off the main road and bumped down a dirt path barely wide enough for the wheels. He must have known where the dirt road was, because outside the windows, she could see nothing but blackness; the cloud cover had completely hidden the moon. Even the stars had disappeared.

"I don't think this is the way to the hospital." She tried to sound calm although a sinkhole seemed to have formed where her stomach used to be.

He didn't bother to respond. Instead he pulled the car to a stop near a large prairie oak tree, turned and faced her. The shadows had the eerie effect of creating hollows beneath his eyes and cheekbones, making his broad face look like a skull. He rubbed his forehead. "Look, Paisley, we've got to talk."

She edged closer to the side of the door. "Oh?" she said, fumbling covertly for the latch. How she wished she had paid attention to its location earlier. Why did every car have to be built differently? "Let's go back to my house, and I'll make you come hot chocolate. We can chat there."

He ignored her question as irrelevant. "Where did you put them, Paisley?"

"Put what?"

A rumble in his chest sounded like an angry pit bull. "No more pretending, okay? We're past that now. I was one of the group of neighborhood kids who used to poke around the yard with shovels when Jonathan's grandmother wasn't looking. Finally Jonathan decided the jewels were just a myth, like Jackalopes, or Sasquatch, or one of those other stories they tell around a campfire. So did the others. But not me. I sensed those rubies were around somewhere, waiting for the one guy who didn't give up. The one who *deserved* to find the treasure."

Paisley listened with half an ear, wondering how far away the main road was. Somewhere she had read that one should never allow a kidnapper to take one into a quiet deserted area, yet she had stupidly done just that. She tried to think what her options were. She'd noticed that the door latch was electronically locked from the driver's side. Even if she somehow managed to get out of the car, she could hardly hope to outrun Ray. Besides there was the problem of that unknown person behind her. How could she escape and leave whomever it was at Ray's mercy? Maybe, if she could keep him talking long enough, she could think of a plan.

Fortunately Ray needed no urging to talk. As she had noticed before, he was a natural-born ham in search of an audience. "When Jonathan's old aunt died last year," he was saying, "I thought, well, why not try looking again? Maybe this time I'd have more luck. By now, I really needed the money. Things didn't go too well for me after I got kicked out of the Army. Anytime anything went wrong on base, I was blamed for it. Pilfering, unnecessary violence, and other things."

His voice trailed off in self-pity, and his beefy hand clenched on the wheel. When he resumed his narrative, his voice had an edge to it. "I got the dishonorable discharge, and ended up back in this two-horse town, selling tumble-down shacks and trying to pay off gambling debts. Then my wife left and took half of everything that was left." He looked at her as if seeking sympathy. "Life just isn't fair, sometimes. That's when I remembered those jewels were buried somewhere nearby. A fortune, just waiting to be found. No one else cared enough to look for them, so that made them mine by rights, didn't it?" His voice grew plaintive, an odd-sounding mix of menace and self-pity.

"Uh huh." Her automatic sound of agreement meant nothing. She was busy thinking, her mind growing more alert with every passing moment. Either the pill was wearing off, or fear was countering it effects. Ray must have spent all summer hoping she would lead him to the jewels, but he couldn't possibly have watched her by himself. His office was all the way across town, and she would have noticed his big black Tahoe lingering about.

Then she remembered the strange-looking metal object in Steve's Lopez house, like a walking stick with a circular projection at the bottom, that had caught her attention the day she had fallen crossing the cow pasture. Now she knew what it was. A metal detector.

Paisley cleared her throat, forcing her hands to stay calm in her lap. "So how is Steve involved in this? Is he your, ah, henchman?"

"Steve?" Ray's heavy brows came together in the dim light cast by the dashboard, and his expression looked displeased. "We've been buddies since we played football together in high school. I got his back, he's got mine. He was supposed to keep an eye on you, let me know if anything unusual happened. Truth was, he didn't turn out to be much help. I've had to do almost everything myself."

She flinched at the stab of betrayal, startled into speaking her thoughts. "I ... I thought Steve and I were, well, friends."

"That was the problem." Ray glanced at her, scowling. "Pretty-boy Steve started falling for you, which made him unreliable. We'd agreed at the beginning to force you to leave so we could tear the old Perleman place down wall by wall, looking for the treasure. I knew it had to be there somewhere when I caught you showing that dusty box to that McMullin fellow."

"You were wrong. They weren't in the box."

"I figured that out eventually. But it meant you were getting close. The fire was meant to scare you away, give me a chance to take over the search on my own, but Steve was right: that was a mistake."

She thought of her neighbor's stricken face after the fire, the look of fear in his eyes. Steve Lopez had been right to worry. He had signed on for a spot of larceny, not murder.

Murder. She darted a look at the heavy-built man behind the wheel and dug her nails painfully into her palms. If ever she needed to think clearly, it was now. "I don't understand," she said, still trying to control her voice. "Why would Steve agree to spy on me? He had everything: nice cars, an attractive home, a business that he was building into a success...."

"Steve did it for the usual reason: money. He needed money to expand the vineyard and to pay for those nice clothes and expensive cars. I'd promised to split the booty with him. A pirate term, get it? Booty." Ray gave a belly chuckle. "In this version, the Major General turns out to be the pirate." His smile disappeared.

"Unfortunately, our partnership wasn't as helpful as I hoped. It was just luck that I happened to be leaving his house when you were climbing down that tree tonight. It only took me a moment to realize what was in that bundle you were holding so carefully."

So that was how he had known. While Ray rambled on about how clever he'd been to figure out that she had finally found the jewels, Paisley discreetly fumbled around for something, anything, that might help her escape. She was no athlete; there was no way to outrun Ray, even if she did manage to get the car door open.

"So what did you do after you saw me climb down the tree?" she prompted, reaching under the seat with her fingers and feeling around. Nothing but carpet, and some food crumbs.

"Well, I waited until you drove away, then searched the place real good. I figured you didn't have much time to hide the jewels again, so there was a good chance they'd be easy to find. Then Ian came hammering on your door, hollering your name. He was mighty surprised to find me instead."

Ray slowly turned his massive head and met her eyes straight-on. She felt as if she were in a dream again, this time a real, old-fashioned, scream-at-the-top-of-your-lungs nightmare. She hadn't fully understood the danger she was in until now. Now she knew who her mysterious enemy had been all along. He was sitting right next to her.

Desperately she tried to remember her telephone message to Ian. She'd revealed nothing directly about the jewels, she was pretty sure. Then the memory popped into her head. She'd typed a single word, *Eureka.* The state motto of Califorrnia: "I have found it." It had seemed clever at the time, a private code between her and Ian. Ian must have known immediately what the message meant.

She could picture what happened next: he'd left his thesis half-written and rushed over to her house, intending to share the great discovery. Instead, he'd arrived just in time to find Ray searching the house. There'd been a confrontation, and Ray, bigger and heavier and trained as a soldier, had overpowered the younger and less experienced Ian, tying him up and throwing him in the back of the van. It was all her fault. Her stupid fault.

At least, based on the vigor of the kicks she had felt through the seat behind her, Paisley thought Ian must not have been hurt too badly. For now.

Ray's voice roughened. "I still wasn't completely sure, though, until you showed at rehearsal wearing *that.*" His eyes flickered to her hands, now folded in her lap. As if on cue, the clouds parted, allowing moonlight to glint off the ring on her finger, the one she had been unable to remove earlier. At some point the wide gold band had turned around, and now the huge ruby glinted in the dim light—all thirty carats. She instinctively slapped her other hand over it, but it was too late.

"I figured you'd lead me to the jewelry eventually," Ray said, and his eyes turned into the cold, hard eyes of a stranger.

She could easily imagine him wearing Army fatigues, standing at the other side of a M-16, ready to pull the trigger on an enemy. But everything was topsy turvy. Somehow, *she* was the enemy.

"Where's the rest of 'em?"

She didn't answer immediately. If she told him where the jewels were, then what? He'd hardly let her walk to the closest police station to report that she and Ian had been assaulted and kidnapped, and Kevin possibly murdered for having the misfortune to have borrowed her car. It could be no accident he'd driven her all the way out here, to this deserted spot far from the nearest town.

It was too bad Ray hadn't found the jewels himself, she thought wearily. Finder's keepers. Possession was nine tenths of the law. What you didn't know couldn't hurt you. There a dozen aphorisms that fit the situation.

But instead, she'd unexpectedly shown up in River Bend and interfered with what Ray had figured was a sure deal. His treasure hunt had turned into something deadlier.

"Okay," she said. "I'll tell you. You're right. You were here first, you've been looking for them longest. Why shouldn't you have them? Here, take this."

With a painful yank that removed several layers of skin, she managed to pull off the heavy ring and tossed it to him. Instinctively, he reached to catch it, and while he was distracted, she grabbed the wheel and jerked it hard to the right.

"Hey! What are you doing?"

It was too late. The Tahoe lurched off the road and into a ditch. It didn't turn over, like she'd hoped, but before Ray could turn his attention back to her, she grabbed the heavy ceramic coffee mug from the holder and smashed it across his temple. It was as hard as a rock, and the effect equally effective.

Ray slumped against the steering wheel. The Tahoe continued rolling until it stopped, stuck in one of the ditches between the lines of grapevines, canted at an angle.

Feeling slightly sick, Paisley didn't look too closely at the man in the seat next to her. She'd never hurt anyone in her life, certainly not intentionally. She was afraid of what she would see. She dropped the mug, somewhat surprised it hadn't broken. The ring had landed in the console between them, and she grabbed it and jammed it on again, as if it were a good-luck talisman. For some reason, she was reluctant to leave it behind.

Next, she poked desperately at the electronic buttons on the armrest to release the door locks. Hearing a reassuring *click*, Paisley snatched the keys from the ignition and jumped out, leaving Ray sprawled across the steering wheel.

Within seconds she was at the back of the Tahoe, fumbling with shaking hands to open the hatch. "Ian? Ian! Are you in there?" Paisley was peering and clawing around in the darkness when a heavy hand grabbed her bad shoulder from behind. She shrieked and whirled. The moon chose that moment to come out again, and she saw Ray's big face looming over her, his eye sockets two dark hollows, a smear of blood streaking down his temple.

He called her several terms she had never heard before. Then he struck her cheek hard enough that she saw stars. "Where did you put the rest of them, you little...?"

Paisley wished with all her heart that she had struck harder with the mug. She opened her mouth to tell him what he wanted to know. Why not? It made no difference now. Ray would dispose of her and Ian here, in the middle of nowhere, and most likely no one would find their remains for days or months. Maybe not for years.

Just then a man-sized object lunged from the open hatch of the Tahoe, knocking Ray over. It was awkward, clumsy, and heavy, and tied up with rope. Ray shouted and tried to dodge to the side, an instant too late, then fell heavily in a heap at her feet, with the object on top of him. It wriggled and made muffled noises that sounded vaguely like her name interspersed with curses.

Paisley fell to her knees and ran her hands over the bony form. Legs, torso, shoulders. All intact. The figure grunted again, louder, as her hands passed over a thatch of short hair that must be his head. She yanked off the gunny sack and, fumbling, managed to maneuver a wet, nasty gag out of his mouth. "Ian! Are you all right?"

Instead of praising her actions, or burbling about how happy he was to see her, Ian croaked, "Ray's pocket. Knife. Grab it."

Ray was stirring; Ian had stunned him but failed to make him fully unconscious. Hollywood movies made it look so easy to knock someone out, she thought with disgust, yet between them she and Ian had barely managed to put Ray out of commission for more than a few moments. The real estate agent was big and sturdily built, and both of them were too well-bred to do real damage. Desperately she patted around her opponent's rocklike waistline in the dark, felt the hilt of what must be the knife, and swiftly slid it from its sheath.

"Hurry. Hands first, then my feet." Ian thrust his forearms toward her. Paisley tried to saw through something that felt as tough as wire, while on the ground Ray mumbled and tried to sit up. When the bonds around Ian's wrists fell loose, she desperately started on his feet.

"Here, give me the knife. You take care of Ray." Ian grabbed the knife and continued working at the bonds while she looked around for something else to hit Ray with. Her hands closed around a fist-sized rock. Feeling queasy, she hesitated, then dropped it onto Ray's temple. He fell again, prone onto the dirt. The sound of breaking glass told her his cell phone must have shattered also.

"Now check his pockets for a gun," Ian said grimly. "Ray pulled one on me, earlier. That's how he forced me into the back of the car."

A gun. Of course there would be a gun.

But there was nothing in the unconscious man's pockets, no holster. She scrabbled around again in the damp dirt, feeling for the cold touch of metal. If Ray had a pistol, it may have fallen near his body, but clouds covered the moon again, and she could not see a thing. Her fingers did close around the smashed cell phone, though. Paisley tossed it away, regretting that she could not use it to call for help, and dusted her hands.

"Got my feet free," Ian said. "Find the gun?"

"He could be lying on it, but I can't budge him. He's too heavy."

Just then, Ray moaned and moved.

Paisley's heart froze. "I think he's waking up. What should we do?"

"*Run.*" He grabbed her hand and pulled her with him into the darkness, like two squirrels diving into a hole. Weeds and brambles snatched at Paisley's clothes and stabbed her arms. Next to her, she heard Ian's gasps for breath and sensed his lurching stride. Soon, despite the titanium rod in her leg, she was setting the pace and he was barely keeping up. Had he been wounded in the fight with Ray? Something tightened in her gut.

"Gotta be ... farmhouse ... this way," he gasped. "Saw a light from the road."

"You okay?"

"My ribs.... That jerk ... punched me." Ian saved the rest of his breath for running, and she didn't blame him.

She was starting to pant, too. Her leg, which hadn't bothered her much the past couple of weeks, was beginning to ache. She wondered how much longer it would hold out. The furrows were littered with roots and hard clods of dirt, and she stumbled. One of her sandals came off. Conscious of Ray's presence behind them, she didn't stop to find it.

She wasn't sure which direction they were going -- the moon had gone behind a cloud again, eliminating any visual cues -- but she thought they were running away from the main road. Surely there must be a farmhouse somewhere around here, in the middle of the country. The night was silent enough that, far behind, she thought she heard faint sounds of swearing and a heavy body treading loudly over broken stalks.

Just then the moon broke through the clouds, and she heard Ray's voice faintly behind them: "Stop, or I'll shoot!" Neither she nor Ian slowed their pace, and they heard a cracking sound, like a firework going off.

The moon chose that moment to disappear again. She hoped the cloud cover would hold this time. It was their only chance, for the field was flat, with no hills or trees to hide them.

She lost track of how much distance they had covered, but their pace inevitably slowed, and she began to think again. Her big mistake—all right, one of many—was that she had never taken seriously the possibility that she was in danger. Another mistake was keeping her search for the jewels secret. She should have told everyone about their existence, flaunted the photograph of Ruth bedecked in them, made it clear that if the valuable artifacts surfaced, *she* was their owner. That would have ended Ray's hope of selling them without attracting notice. But she'd held back, afraid that others would mock her for being a fanciful treasure-seeker. But why should she care? Pride, foolish pride, had led to all this.

Her breath came in stinging gasps and her bad leg wobbled painfully, ready to give out. The field stretched out ahead. What if they were running away from help rather than toward it? Ian's breath was becoming more ragged. He had said nothing for a long time. If he fell, there was nothing she could do about it.

She held onto Ian's arm, to support him as well as to support herself and wondered how close Ray would be by now. She could no longer hear him. Was he catching up or falling behind? He could be right behind them, or he might have stopped chasing them altogether. She did not dare turn around to find out.

The uneven field gave way to a cultivated field of grapevines, whose loose, hilly soil was even harder to navigate. They limped down an endless ditch until Paisley could not take another step. She bent over, gasping, pain cutting through her leg. "Sorry. Can't ... go ... any farther."

Ian did not reply. Under her horrified gaze, he slowly crumpled to the ground.

She dropped to her knees next to him. "Ian! Are you all right?"

His eyes opened and he looked at her dully. "Ray got the best of me when we fought. Broken rib ... maybe some internal bleeding, even. We need to get to a phone. Get help."

She probed his chest, feeling for a broken bone. His sharp intake of breath told her she'd found it. "I think you're right," she said grimly. "Maybe if I use your shirt to wrap around your torso, like a bandage, it would help."

He shook his head. "Slow you down. That farmhouse over there ... they'll have a phone. I'll stay here, catch my breath. Join you later."

"But if what if Ray finds you?"

"Dark. Hundreds of rows ... grape vines. Best chance."

Farmhouse? She looked ahead. Silhouetted against the night sky stood an old-fashioned structure, no doubt belonging to the owner of these grapevines. The moon glinted off a large, round, metal apparatus behind it: a wine crusher, like the one Steve had once shown her. The house's windows were dark. The farmer and his wife must have gone /to bed.

"All right, I'll look for help." Paisley planted a quick kiss on Ian's mouth, then a second one, not so quick. When she raised her head, warmth ran through her veins. So he wasn't entirely out of commission.

Reluctant to leave him but knowing Ian's advice was their best chance, she hobbled toward the house. Until now she had hardly noticed the pain of running with one bare foot across twigs and small rocks, but it was bleeding now. Her bad leg was throbbing. She was stumbling now, having difficulty putting one foot in front of the other.

Nearing the house, she stopped in her tracks. All the local farms looked similar, especially by night, but something about this place seemed unsettlingly familiar. Paisley tried to make out the architectural details. Moonlight glinted off peaked gables and the boards of the wide front porch and revealed the curved lines of the outbuilding behind the house. The place could have been the twin of Steve's home, she thought with a sinking feeling in the pit of her stomach. Those double chimneys, and the large juniper bush that grew by the steps....

Behind her, she heard the low purr of a car engine and the crunch of gravel. A double swath of white headlights swept the long drive behind her, and she jumped back into the shadows just before it raked across her form. Her luck had run out. Had he seen her?

Step by step, Paisley backed up, holding her breath. She needed somewhere to hide, fast. The only place she could think of was the building that housed the winery. She groped behind the decorative stone near the threshold of the door and her fingers closed comfortingly around the key. Thank goodness Steve had not found a new hiding place for it since their dinner together.

Quietly, she inched the winery door open and squeezed inside. Her eyes, adjusted to the dark, saw a narrow central aisle lined by enormous stacked oak barrels on both sides. The shadowy niches between the barrels were large enough, barely, for a small woman to squeeze into.

She hoped Steve would go into the house after parking the car, leaving her free to leave her hiding place and run the hundred yards to her own house. Then she could call for the police to help Ian. But moments later slow footsteps in the gravel crunched toward the winery, and her heart sank. She tried to wriggle farther back in her shadowy niche. Had her neighbor seen her heading this direction? Heard something? What had given her away? She thought of Ian, lying in a ditch in the vineyard, dependent on her help, and muttered a brief prayer under her breath.

The hinges of the door were well oiled: she did not hear it open, yet somehow she grew aware that another living presence now shared the darkness with her. Holding her breath, she listened. The intruder was gulping air loudly, laboriously, while the light, halting footsteps drew closer to her hiding space. She heard a sharp catch of breath, as if from pain. Her heart leapt. Could it be Ian? No, Ian's footsteps would be heavier. He would have called out to reassure her, had he followed her here.

Then an epithet, low but clearly audible. Filled with relief, she inched out of her hiding place.

"Who is it? Who's there?" The low-pitched voice was sharp with alarm.

"Don't be afraid, Kevin," she whispered. "It's me, Paisley."

A small light pushed back the darkness. It was a small penlight, attached to a keyring. In the resulting circle of visibility Kevin's pale face appeared, eyes wide. His forehead was shiny with sweat.

"Hey, Mrs. Perl ... Paisley! It's you!" He hobbled a few paces toward her, holding the small light slanted downward, no doubt so it wouldn't flash in her eyes. "What are *you* doing here?"

"Same as you, I bet." She tried to fight down a burst of hysterical laughter, stemming from relief that he was alive and from the absurdity of their situation. "The car brakes went out going down that hill, didn't they? It was no accident. Ray Henderson cut them. You know him, don't you? He's the guy who plays—"

"—The Major General. The big guy."

Of course Kevin would know. The cast was close-knit, spending hours together every day, including those who had joined the production late. "It turns out he's after the jewels, Kevin. He's in league with your stepdad, Steve. They're trying to get rid of us, so no one stands between them and the treasure."

She reached out and patted Kevin's shoulder to reassure herself that he was alive. What she really wanted to do was hug the boy until his eyes bulged. It was almost enough to make her forget that Ian was still out there in the night, with a killer searching for him. Almost.

Kevin extinguished the penlight, and as darkness swallowed them she heard him collapse onto the floor. "It feels good to sit down," his voice floated upward. "I think I broke my ankle getting out of the car. Or maybe it's just sprained. It took me forever to limp here from the river."

"What about the rescue workers? Didn't they find you?"

"What rescue workers? I waited for an hour or so for help, but no one came. That's why I decided I'd better try to make it here myself."

With a mental head slap, she realized Ray must have only pretended to call 911. Steve's panicked call to Ray must have expressed worry that his stepson had survived the accident.

That was what this night's business had been about, wasn't it? Eliminating witnesses. She thought of Ian again, and her fingernails dug into the soft flesh of her palms.

Paisley slid down next to the teenager. "Why didn't you flag down a ride?"

"I didn't dare," he said simply. "I didn't want him to see me."

Him. The flat tone spoke volumes. And she had assumed his dislike for his guardian stemmed from conflict between a headstrong teenager and a well-meaning adult!

She reminded herself that neither Steve nor Ray had set out to kill anyone. The "accidents" had been meant to scare her away. Something had changed tonight, something that had brought things to a head. What could it be but the discovery of the jewelry?

Kevin seemed uncharacteristically talkative, despite his injuries. "You walked right by me, you know, Mrs. Perleman ... I mean Paisley. I was hiding in the bushes when Mr. Henderson pretended to call the search and rescue workers. You sat down on a log a few feet away."

She revived. "Why didn't you call out to me?"

"I couldn't. That guy—Ray—he would have heard."

She pictured the teenager hiding in the damp bushes by the river, shivering, a few yards from the man who was trying to kill him.

Kevin continued, his voice matter-of-fact. "I already suspected those guys were up to something. Steve was always kicking me out of the house, or going outside with that metal detector he sent away for. And that telescope wasn't set up for stargazing. Steve couldn't care less about astronomy. When I tried to use it to look at a comet one night, he shooed me away." Kevin's tone dripped with contempt. "I decided they must be up to some business thing, maybe something to do with the winery. It wasn't until tonight that I connected them with the jewels. I knew my grandma wanted those stupid rubies, but I had no idea *they* were after them too."

She felt an urge to reassure the boy. "Ray and Steve were searching for the jewelry long before you came to River Bend, Kevin. My arrival just kicked everything into high gear. They were convinced I knew where to look for them. And I did. I found them tonight."

"You did? Really?" His voice perked up. "So Grandma was right." A pause. "But I still don't get it. Why the mast falling, and the brakes being cut? Ray and Steve were behind both of those, right?"

At the memory of the mast falling on top of her, Paisley shuddered. But she had foiled him by hiding the jewels again. He had expected to find them still in the house. When he searched unsuccessfully, he'd naturally assumed they were with her.

She shuddered again. A big mistake on his part. If the mast had crushed her, or the car accident drowned her, he'd have been back where he started.

"They were after me, Kevin, not you. It was just bad luck, you borrowing my car tonight." She reached for his hand. "Remember, too, Ray was behind all this." She said the words gently, as if that would somehow make it better. "Steve didn't cut the brakes thinking you would be driving the car. He'd already left the theater when you asked to drive my car home."

There was a silence while Kevin pondered this. "My cell phone got wet in the river. Then, when I got to your house, the lights were out and no one answered the doorbell. My ankle was hurting pretty bad. I couldn't walk all the way back to town, so I decided to sneak into my own house to call for help." He cleared his throat. "Then I saw Steve's Audi parked in the driveway."

Her path and his had brought them both to the same place, Paisley thought.

Kevin yawned. The adventure was taking its toll on his young body. While he fell into a fitful doze, she pondered their fix. Ian was lying among the grape vines in need of medical attention with Ray scrambling about, wielding a pistol. The only glimmer of hope was that she knew where the jewels were, which gave them motivation to keep her alive. But even that thought wasn't very reassuring. Ray knew he could get that information out of her easily. All he had to do was threaten Ian, or Kevin. Then he would probably kill them all anyway.

She remembered that Aunt Esther had called the jewels "a few bits of colored rock." It was hard to believe anyone would annihilate a fellow human being over something so small, but then, Ray had killed before. Perhaps he was one of those rare sick-souled men who couldn't distinguish between killing an enemy combatant in the heat of battle and killing for personal gain. Hadn't he admitted to being released from the military for ... what was it? unnecessary violence against civilians?

Distracted, this time she failed to hear the footsteps in the gravel. By the time the door began to swing open, Kevin had wriggled into an opening between the barrels like an eel into a crevice in a coral reef. Slower to react, Paisley jumped to her feet when the overhead lights turned on, blinding her.

Steve stood looking down at her, breathing heavily. His soaking-wet cotton shirt clung to his chest like plastic wrap. Black hair fell in wet strands across his forehead, and his brown eyes were flat and muddy, like coffee dregs. The fresh mud on his formerly polished Bruno Magli boots showed evidence of a long tramp along the river banks.

"You're here," he said, sounding surprised. "Ray said you got away."

She raised her chin, trying to sound self-confident. "How did you know I was in the winery?"

He shook his head like a dog after a bath, as if trying to clear his thoughts. "I saw muddy footprints on the porch steps. They didn't track into the house, so I figured I'd check here instead.

She looked down at her feet. One was shod, one was bare. Both were covered with dirt, grass stains and blood. Thank goodness Steve had only seen one set of footprints. At least he didn't know Kevin was here.

With as much dignity as she could, Paisley stood. Better to meet her executioner standing. Hopefully the fact that Steve had said nothing about Ian meant they had not found him yet.

"Fine, you win," she said, tossing her hair carelessly. "Take the jewels, they're yours and Ray's. Sell them for whatever you can get for them." She fumbled to pull off the ruby ring. This time, perversely, it came off with a single tug. She held it out on her palm, where it glittered with dark-red luster, the jewel the size of a cherry. "I'll tell you where the rest of them are if you'll let me go." Paisley prevented herself, barely, from saying "us." It was imperative that they believe she was alone. "I'll leave on the next plane and you'll never hear from me again."

Steve didn't move. He was staring at her like a statue, while his chest heaved up and down. It was, she noted, a smoothly muscled chest, under the clinging shirt. "I don't want any of it," he said after a moment.

"What?" Her voice unintentionally rose to a soprano register. "You don't want the jewels?"

"I never intended it to go this far. He told me that if we found them first, you'd never even know, no one would be hurt." He took a deep breath, like a ragged sob, and stumbled toward her, sweeping her into a clumsy embrace. "He lied." His breath was warm against her hair. "He lied about everything. Paisley, I couldn't find Kevin. I've been looking everywhere for the past two hours. I'm so afraid...."

"Dammit, Steven, what are you doing?" The deep voice, dripping with contempt, came from behind them, causing them both to jump. They turned, still in each other's arms, and stared at the husky figure that aimed an unwavering pistol at each of them in turn. Paisley cursed herself. Ray kept turning up, like the character in *Halloween*. If only she had time to search more carefully, had found the weapon! But both she and Ian had been anxious to put as much distance between themselves and Ray as possible before their assailant regained consciousness.

"Get back from the girl, Steve, you fool, you're in my way," Ray growled.

Steve released Paisley but did not move. His face flushed dark red under the tan and streaks of dirt. "You never said you were going to kill anyone, Ray. You said the fire would give off some smoke, that's all, just enough to scare her off. But none of it was true. That mast could have crushed her, too. Or Kevin. And you never told me you planned to cut the brakes. You had no right!"

"You weakling." Ray's voice dripped contempt. "What was that saying we learned in Mrs. Olsen's French class? You can't make an omelet without cracking *les oeufs*."

Steve took an angry step toward Ray. "I don't care about the jewels anymore. I looked all over for Kevin, and there's not a trace of him. If not for you, I'd have called for helicopters, for a search team, had the whole town out there, searching. But no. Because if they found out the brakes were cut...."

"They'd start investigating and eventually find out that you were involved in all the accidents surrounding Paisley this summer?" Ray sneered. "You *are* a coward. The accident involved a teenager, inexperienced driver, late at night, taking that curve a little too fast. Most likely, the cops wouldn't even have checked the brakes. Not the idiots around here, anyway."

Ray grabbed the ring from Paisley's palm and shoved it into his pants pocket with less care than she would have expected from someone who had gone to so much trouble to get it. His eyes glittered, and his lips were drawn back in a grimace of excitement as he turned back to her. "Where are the rest of the jewels? You didn't climb back up that oak tree, and I've searched your house. So you must have hidden them again."

"Brilliant deduction." She could not hide her sarcasm despite the fact her life was in imminent danger. "Come with me, I'll show you where they are." She moved toward the winery door. Anything to get him—both of them—away before Kevin made a sound, a movement, that gave away the boy's hiding place. And before daylight revealed Ian still lying helpless among the vines, assuming he had not gathered the strength to escape.

"They're not around here," she continued. "We'll have to drive to get there." She couldn't help adding, "You really don't think you can get away with this, do you? By now there are too many witnesses. You can't kill all of us."

Ray fell back to allow her to precede him, the cold muzzle of the gun pressing between her shoulder blades. "By tomorrow I'll be out of the country." He sounded relaxed. "Plenty of places in the world a guy can live comfortably on a couple of million dollars. Belize or Costa Rica, for example. All right, then, where are they?"

A squeaking sound came from behind them. Paisley's heart sank while her head swiveled along with Ray's and Steve's. Kevin tottered behind Ray on his bad ankle, a bottle of Merlot raised high in both hands, looking like he were about to christen a ship. His face was white. "They're not yours," he said grimly. "They belong by rights to my family. Now let Paisley go."

Ray's mouth curled with contempt, and he took a step toward Kevin, but Steve moved to block his burly partner.

"No, Ray, this has already gone too far. If—"

He never completed his sentence. With a snarl, Ray shouted, "Get out of my way!" At the same instant a deafening explosion erupted from the pistol in his hand. A look of shock appeared on Steve's face, an instant before he slid to the floor like a bag of cement. Something about the angle of Steve's head, the stillness of his graceless form on the cement ground, told her he was not merely unconscious.

No.

Paisley heard herself scream at the top of her lungs. Without thinking, she leaped forward and knocked Ray's arm with all her remaining strength, causing him to drop the still smoking pistol. It went spinning into a shadowy corner of the room. Ray turned toward her, scowling, and struck her in the jaw. It was like a bear swatting a fly. She lost her balance and fell backward. Her head hit the cement wall with a painful *thunk*, and the room spun.

At least she had succeeded in causing Ray to turn his back on Kevin. The teenager took advantage of the older man's distraction by leaping forward and bringing down the bottle of Merlot over his head. Ray seemed to sense the coming gesture, because he turned his head at the last moment and received only a glancing blow.

Swearing, the older man turned on Kevin. Paisley saw fear on the boy's features, but he faced his rival gamely. For several moments they grappled, an almost farcically uneven pairing. Ray slid his hands upward and they closed around Kevin's throat. His big fingers tightened.

Kevin's face grew dark red, his arms flailed. Paisley pushed herself to her feet. But before she could launch herself onto Ray's back, the big man's foot slipped on the bottle of broken wine, mingling with blood on the floor. Swearing, he lost his balance and released his grip on the boy. As he fell backward, he landed heavily against one of the wooden barrels, knocking it out of alignment.

Time seemed to slow. The barrel creaked as the pressure on it built from the others above. Gradually it slipped. Ray seemed unaware of the building weight above him, as he tried to regather his balance. But Paisley watched in horrified fascination as the other barrels became unbalanced as well. With a low rumble, like falling dominoes, the heavy containers tipped and rolled into the aisle, some of them crashing and breaking open, spilling their liquid contents. One hit Paisley's bad shoulder as it fell, and she let loose another full-throated scream, this one of pain.

"Shut up!" Ray took a step back and put his hands over his ears, glaring at her. "Shut up!" A barrel knocked him back, and at the same time she dove for the relative safety of the corner.

It was too late. It seemed like the entire world was caving in with deafening cacophony, a waterfall of enormous barrels bouncing and breaking, spouts of wine gushing and splashing them up to the knees. Paisley watched in disbelief until the last few barrels finally bounced and rolled to a stop. The din ended, leaving an eerie silence.

She saw Kevin cowering in one of the corners opposite her, his eyes big and round. Ray's body lay crushed under one of the heavy barrels, not far from where Steven lay. Wine poured from broken staves, mixing with blood and flooding the floor.

"Will someone tell me what's going on in here?"

She and Kevin turned toward the open doorway. "Officer Smith!" Paisley recognized the stocky figure, whose mouth was open in astonishment.

Behind the policeman figure crowded more uniforms, guns drawn. The red and blue beams of a police car's light bar pulsed in the background. In the center of it all stood Ian, jaw battered and hair tousled, eyes wide as he took in the scene.

Chapter Eighteen

"It was the scream that did it," said Officer Smith, slamming the back door of the police cruiser and getting behind the wheel after they left the hospital. "My Irish grandma woulda sworn it was a banshee. Sent chills up my spine. Never heard anything like it in my life. Carried clear across the fields. Then, when we got closer, there was a whole lot of clattering and banging in the winery, like an earthquake. Thought the whole place was falling down."

"The scream? That was nothing," Ian said from the back seat, putting an arm around Paisley's shoulder and ignoring her bush. "In terms of volume, there's nothing like hearing this woman sing *Carmen* after getting out of the shower."

On the drive home, Ian explained to Paisley what had happened after she'd left him. He'd managed to drag himself back to the Chevy Tahoe while Ray was still blundering around looking for them. Remembering that the keys were left in the trunk lock, Ian drove straight to the police station.

"Everything will be fine now," Ian told Paisley, tightening his grip around her shoulder. She tried not to wince. It was worth it to feel his warm, protective arm around her. "Nothing's wrong with Kevin except a few bruises, and a sprained ankle."

Ian's own ribs were taped up, and an x-ray had shown that Paisley's shoulder was bruised but not broken. Kevin was dozing in the front passenger seat, next to Officer Smith, who listened to the soft crackle of the police scanner while humming a Queen song under his breath.

"The doctor said if Kevin is careful, he'll be able to perform in the play tomorrow," Ian continued. He glanced at his watch. "I mean, tonight. But—" he gave a rueful smile—"I think you're going to have to find someone else to play the Major General."

She nodded, thinking of all the things she hadn't had time to tell Ian yet: about discovering the jewels and hiding them again, and being hit by the falling mainsail.

As if reading her mind, he looked down at her. "So, it's true, then? You found them?"

The police car purred through the night toward River Bend. Sighing, she nodded and leaned her head back onto his chest. "They were in that big oak tree in front of my house. When Esther was a little girl, she hid them in a hole in the trunk and never retrieved them."

He chuckled, a low, comforting vibration. "I wonder if she decided to leave them there as a joke on everyone else. She didn't need the jewels, and no one else deserved them. Sounds like Auntie Esther." He nuzzled the top of her head, his voice sleepy and distracted. "Are they in a safe place now?"

"Yes, I hid them again." Her tone changed. "And it's a good thing, because Ray saw me coming down the tree. They'd be in his hands by now, if I hadn't."

"Where did you put them? That is if, if you trust me enough to tell." His voice held gentle amusement. "It would be a pity if they were lost for another eighty years."

The police officer still hummed, and Kevin slumbered peacefully in the front passenger seat. Still, she instinctively lowered her voice. "Have you read Edgar Allan Poe's *The Purloined Letter*?"

His brow furrowed slightly. "Yes. In the story, the missing letter was hidden in plain sight, because no one thought to look there."

"Well, that's exactly what I did. I put the rubies in the most public spot imaginable, visible to everyone." She couldn't help smiling, in spite of the long, eventful night.

"Public? What do you mean?"

"The jewels are in the pirate's treasure chest at center stage, mixed in with all those faux trinkets Shirley bought from the dollar store." She giggled as Ian's jaw dropped.

The remainder of the night, Kevin slept in Esther's childhood bedroom upstairs at Paisley's house, while Ian stretched out on the couch downstairs. While the males slept in, Paisley cooked breakfast and then made a phone call to the boy who had originally been cast as the Major General. "Um, yeah, okay," he said after a pause. "I still remember the lines and stuff."

Paisley thanked him and hung up. With everything else going on, somehow having a perfect cast for the play didn't seem as important as it once had. All that mattered was the show would go on.

Next, she telephoned Barry to ask the lawyer how she could apply for guardianship of the boy until he turned eighteen. She'd tell Kevin about her request later. Somehow, she thought he'd be okay with it.

Someday, Paisley thought, she'd even talk to him about how wrong they'd been about Steve, that he had in fact tried to be the best guardian he knew how to be, even if he had failed.

That night, while watching the play, Paisley marveled at teenagers' resilience. Kevin, leg in a cast, hid whatever emotional trauma he had experienced the previous night so well that it might never have happened. "Long John Silver only had one leg, right?" he quipped to the other actors before the curtain went up. Using a crutch to hop about the stage with bombastic arrogance, he made a charismatic Pirate King. When it was over, the packed auditorium gave him a standing ovation, refusing to stop until he came out and bowed several times.

Paisley listened with satisfaction to the waves of applause. For three hours, the boy had been able to shut out the nightmare of the previous night, although when the curtain dropped the final time Paisley saw a new maturity around the teen's mouth and in his dark-brown eyes.

Hosting the cast party at her house afterward, Paisley looked around at the people crowding into the living room and overflowing onto the porch. Soda pop flowed as freely as the conversation, and hip hop music thumped from the stereo's ancient speakers. The tall redheaded kid who had played the lead policeman set himself up as DJ, and the kids drifted outside to dance on the front lawn. Kevin and Chloe sat and watched from the porch swing, his cast stretched out on a hassock.

Paisley made a circuit from kitchen to refreshment table, making sure everyone's glasses were filled, fielding congratulations, and pausing for brief conversations with friends.

Guests crowded on the porch, including Ian, who talked animatedly with Shirley.

Paisley watched them with a peculiar pain in her heart. Friends. That's what they were, these cherished, familiar faces who crowded her house. And she would likely never see them again. She thought of the airline ticket she had purchased this morning.

Ian looked up from his conversation and saw her. "Oh, there you are!" he said, beckoning her to join them. "Time to stop working and join the celebration." He bent over to kiss her, and when he raised his head, he was smiling. "We make lousy detectives. If not for that cat, we never would have found the jewels."

She shuddered. The memories of the previous night were too fresh. "I don't want to think about it. Oh, Ian … I was wrong about Steve. He wasn't an evil guy, just a weak one, doing the best he could. He didn't deserve to die."

"Don't think about it. Whatever happened to Steve, he brought it on himself." Ian allowed her another moment to grieve, then gave her a gentle squeeze. "So, my lovely heiress, what do you plan do with your loot? Keep it or sell it?"

"Neither." Paisley had spent all night awake, thinking about her course of action. "I think Esther would have wanted me to split the jewels with Kevin. It's only fair." Paisley held up her hand, letting the ruby flash under the porch light. "He'll probably want to sell the rest of it, but I'd like to keep this ring."

Ian took her hand and brought it to his lips, like the Russian courtier from her dream, although with his jeans, rumpled shirt, sticking-up hair and outsized ears, Ian did not look nearly as suave. She would not have wanted him any other way.

"Very honorable of you, my dear," he said. "But what do you think your newly discovered nephew will do with his portion of the jewelry? He surely won't wear it."

"I'll advise him to auction them off to finance his education. We can easily find a museum to buy the collection, considering the jewels' unique history. And with the money that's left over…." Her eyes brightened. "You know, the other day Kevin was telling me this town needs a decent theater. With the inheritance and some community fund-raisers, we can build something here that could rival that place in Ashland, Oregon, where they put on a

Shakespeare festival every year. Maybe you could design the building, Ian. People would drive from Sacramento or San Francisco to see our productions, right here in the heart of wine country. I can see an enlarged copy of that antique photograph of Ruth wearing the rubies, hanging in a big, golden frame in the lobby. We could name it the Ruth Klaczko Center."

Ian's hands tightened on her wrist. "'We?'"

Paisley took a deep breath and looked into his hopeful eyes. "Yes, we." And at that moment she knew there would be an empty seat on the plane to New York in the morning.

ABOUT THE AUTHOR

Catherine McGreevy is a former newspaper reporter, an avid reader and historical enthusiast with particular interest in Gold Rush history. She lives in Northern California. Look for upcoming books in her favorite genres, including suspense and historical.

Visit the author's web site at cathymcgreevy.wordpress.com or follow her on Twitter at: https://twitter.com/cathy_mcgreevy.